HUNTSMAN

HUNTSMAN

Naima Simone

BRAMBLE
Tor Publishing Group
New York

This is a work of fiction. All of the characters, organizations, and events portrayed in this novel are either products of the author's imagination or are used fictitiously.

HUNTSMAN

Copyright © 2025 by Naima Simone

All rights reserved.

A Bramble Book
Published by Tom Doherty Associates / Tor Publishing Group
120 Broadway
New York, NY 10271

www.torpublishinggroup.com

Bramble™ is a trademark of Macmillan Publishing Group, LLC.

EU Representative: Macmillan Publishers Ireland Ltd, 1st Floor, The Liffey Trust Centre, 117–126 Sheriff Street Upper, Dublin 1, D01 YC43

The Library of Congress Cataloging-in-Publication Data is available upon request.

ISBN 978-1-250-35294-1 (trade paperback)
ISBN 978-1-250-35295-8 (ebook)

The publisher of this book does not authorize the use or reproduction of any part of this book in any manner for the purpose of training artificial intelligence technologies or systems. The publisher of this book expressly reserves this book from the Text and Data Mining exception in accordance with Article 4(3) of the European Union Digital Single Market Directive 2019/790.

Our books may be purchased in bulk for specialty retail/wholesale, literacy, corporate/premium, educational, and subscription box use. Please contact MacmillanSpecialMarkets@macmillan.com.

First Edition: 2025

Printed in the United States of America

10 9 8 7 6 5 4 3 2 1

To Gary.
1432.

To Connie Butts.
I'll miss you forever and love you longer than that.

To Rev. Wayne L. Alston.
You said my fight scenes read like a Batman comic strip, and you loved me enough to fix them.
Love you, Daddy!

Author's Note

From the pen of Eshe Diallo:

Welcome to the world of *Huntsman*, bishes, where the patriarchy gets fucked and so do we! We love it over here! Listen, I'm ready for you to flip this page so you can get to know lil' ol' me and my boo the Huntsman better—touch him and die, by the way—but we got some housekeeping to do first. Being the sensitive soul that I am, I fully recognize that *Huntsman* is a dark romance, and it contains scenes that may be disturbing to some readers, so please proceed with caution and care. Your mental health matters! Mine, on the other hand . . .

So here's what you need to know!

Huntsman includes: Blood play (no worries! He likes it!), stalking (I fall first), murder (of mostly baddies), torture, violence, explicit sex (real filthy with all the bad words), choking during sex (no worries! *We* like it!), violence / mutual combat between FMC and MMC (we both got hands), and a skosh of mass murder.

HUNTSMAN

Eshe

BEFORE...

"Eshe, wake up. C'mon, baby. Get up."

I slowly blink, sleep clinging to me, for a moment refusing to release me. But then my mother's voice penetrates the thick gray fog blanketing my mind, and just as she grips my shoulder and shakes me, I'm already rolling over and sitting up.

"Ma, what's wrong?" Throwing back the bedcovers, I swing my legs over the side of the mattress. The last wisps of sleep vanish, and I'm alert, ready, as she's taught me to be over the past five years since I turned eleven. Fighting age. Killing age. "Where're you going?"

She doesn't answer. Instead, she straightens and moves across my bedroom, the beams of moonlight streaming through the bulletproof windows snagging on her long, tightly coiled curls, the tight, black long-sleeved shirt, pants, and boots. Seeing as how the last time I saw her, she'd been in a royal-blue lounge set, I know her clothes for what they are—armor. She's headed to battle.

And somebody's about to die.

As the queen, or the oba, of the Mwuaji family, she's not above getting her hands dirty. But she also has plenty of people under her to handle that. So, if Aisha Diallo is making a personal appearance, best believe somebody's going to bleed. A lot.

Excitement churns in my gut, but so does anxiety. So does fear. And I hate the nasty taste of that. Hate that I can't get rid of it no matter how hard I've convinced myself I'm better than that,

I'm stronger than that. Fear doesn't give a fuck about my damn-near-hourly mantras. It's been sticking to my ass like a fucking penicillin-resistant STD. The shame crawling behind that knowledge has me launching from the bed, almost running across the room to my closet for my own clothes.

I don't want to leave my mother's side, to be left behind.

Part of me bitterly acknowledges it's because I'm scared of what will happen—again—if I am. If I'm out of her sight once more. Staring into the closet full of clothes, I'm suddenly a little girl clinging to her mother's shirttails instead of a nearly grown, scarred young woman who's been through hell and back.

"What're you doing?" she asks, just as my hand closes around the neck of a shirt that's identical to hers. "Where do you think you're going?"

"With you." I jerk the shirt off the hanger and quickly tug it on, shoving my arms into the sleeves and yanking it down over my tank top.

I'm reaching for a pair of pants when her flat but firm "no, not this time" halts me.

The fuck?

Frowning, I lower my arm and turn around to face her. Immediately, an insecurity I'd never experienced prior to three weeks ago floods into my chest, threatening to drown me in doubt and uncertainty. My fingers curl and straighten in a reflexive motion, and I welcome the flash of pain in my barely healed hand. The stitches around the place where my right pinkie finger used to be were removed a week ago, but the physical and mental ache haven't gone anywhere.

I'm betting they won't for a while. Especially the mental.

Giving my head a small shake to try and rid myself of useless and agonizing thoughts, I look back at my ma standing at the foot of my bed, arms crossed over her chest, her long, slim legs spread slightly apart.

"You think I'm weak now," I whisper.

Fuck, I wish that hadn't come out sounding so . . . soft. So scared.

"Weaker, yes."

My belly bottoms out, then seizes in a cramp. Her thick eyebrows furrow over narrowed hazel eyes, both of which she passed down to me along with her wide, full mouth. But my thicker, shorter frame, dark auburn hair, and strong, almost-too-sharp features come from the father I barely remember since he died nearly a decade ago.

I can't help but compare us. Maybe if I were taller, leaner, fucking stronger, I wouldn't have been taken.

Tortured.

Broken.

Maybe she wouldn't believe the same thing.

"I'm not," I object on a telling rasp.

"Don't be silly or prideful. Both will get you fucked up, Eshe." Her harsh words aren't softened by a tender or gentle tone. There's nothing tender or gentle about the reigning queen of the Mwuaji. And yet I've never doubted her love for me. Not even in this moment when she's emotionally eviscerating my confidence. "You were kidnapped, held hostage, beaten, and mutilated. That would fuck up anyone's mental even if their body were fully healed. And you're not healed. Not in any way. So, yeah, you're weaker than you were before."

I swallow hard, dipping my head so I don't have to see the disappointment in her eyes. Disappointment where there used to be only pride.

"Look at me, baby girl." The order comes just a second before two fingers grip my chin and tilt my head up. "It also means you'll get stronger, faster, sharper, wiser. You're going to be a gotdamn force to be reckoned with and a better oba than me and your grandmother. Any good leader and ruler must know weakness in order to burn it from her body. She must experience brokenness in order to be pieced back together and forged into something unbreakable. Leaders who haven't been through hell won't have the strength or cunning to not only avoid going through it again but to do anything in their power to save their people from it. So don't despise being weak, Eshe. Embrace it. Sit in it. Learn from it. Then do what it takes—steal whoever's life it takes—to eradicate it."

Her gaze burns into mine for several seconds as if she can brand her words into my brain; then she releases me and, pivoting on her heel, stalks toward my bedroom door. The sharp, hurried movements snap me from my temporary paralysis, and I turn back to the closet to snatch down the pants. Swiftly, I drag them over my sleep shorts.

You're going to be a gotdamn force to be reckoned with and a better oba than me and your grandmother.

Her words rev and race in my head like the engine of her favorite Dodge Challenger. I can't believe or accept that promise in this moment. Mainly because it would mean losing my mother. For me to be oba, she would have to die.

I want no parts of that shit.

"No, Eshe. I meant what I said. You're not coming with me. Not this time," Ma snaps.

"Okay," I say, my voice even while I zip my pants and fasten the button.

I'm not arguing. Since I was fourteen, I've been right by her side as she ran our family. She hasn't excluded me from anything—not a meeting with the family kapteni or a negotiation with an arms dealer, not a killing of a betrayer to the Mwuaji.

Blood before belief.

The Mwuaji creed.

Meaning family before everything, including faith.

I've been spoon-fed that creed since before I was old enough to understand its power. And though I love this family, I'd slit every one of their throats and watch them slowly bleed out while eating a bag of Funyuns before turning my back on Aisha Diallo. She's not just my queen; she's my mom—my everything.

Which is why if she thinks I'm letting her leave without me, she's been hitting that good shit we sell. Broken or not, I'm going to be by her side.

Yeah, and you need to prove that you're not a liability. That you're still worthy to be by her side.

"Eshe, I'm not telling you this as your mother but as your oba: Stay. Here."

I freeze again.

Dammit. *Gotdammit.*

"That's not fair," I breathe.

My mother, I could disobey. But my queen? I can't. And she knows that.

Damn her.

She gives a soft snort. "Pretty much nothing in life is fair, baby girl. You'll find that out on your own. And, as the future oba of this family, it's your place, *your duty*, to make that shit balance out as much as possible. Remember that, Eshe."

Future oba. There she goes again. What the fuck? Does she know something I don't? Fear whistles through me. Is she . . . is she sick and hasn't told me?

"What's with this teachable moment, Ma? Where you going?"

"Business meeting."

"Then why can't I go?" I demand, frowning. "I've been able to before. What's so different with this one?"

"Because I said so, Eshe. I'm not doing this with you. Now wait here until either I get back or Zuri comes for you. Me or Zuri, baby girl. No one else. And do not go back to the obodo. You understand me?"

She doesn't want me to go home, to the Mwuaji compound? Why? And why wouldn't *she* return for me? Yeah, Zuri is her right hand, the person she trusts most besides me. But why . . . ?

An ugly, grimy feeling winds its way up from my churning stomach to coil around my ribs. What the fuck is going on?

"Eshe? Do you understand me?"

"Yes, Ma," I murmur, my mind whirling.

"Good." She nods and reaches for the door handle, but she hesitates, her hand hovering above it. For a second, her head bows, her shoulders drop. Shock ripples through me like a tidal wave. I've never seen my mother look . . . tired.

Defeated.

But just as I move toward her, that head lifts, her chin raised in the proud, stubborn tilt I'm used to. Her shoulders rise, pulling back as if drawn by a bow. When she looks at me, a fierce light seems to glow in those eyes, all golden brown and green.

"Remember who you are, Eshe. Remember *whose* you are. Never forget that."

Before I can loose the questions piling up in the back of my throat, she gives me a firm nod and exits the room, not once looking back.

I remain standing there, frozen, for long moments, possibly minutes. Long enough to hear the muffled purring of her engine start and fade. It isn't until the deafening silence crowds in on me that I snap into motion.

"Nah, fuck this."

I whip around to the closet and grab my boots, then drop to the bed. Quickly, I stuff my feet into them and jerk the laces tight. After shooting to my feet, I stride across my bedroom and out the door. Instead of heading for the front door, I cut a left for the kitchen and the rear door.

Since we're at our cottage—the place we retreat to every summer for a couple of weeks—I don't have to worry about avoiding a security detail. Ma doesn't ever bring one with us. And as I open the rear door and step out in the crisp autumn night, I'm reminded why we came here in mid-October instead of July. Like I'm a damaged animal, I was brought here to lick my wounds.

Grinding my jaw, I make my way toward the separate covered garage, the crunch of leaves under my boots sounding like piles of crumpled, old paper. No one can hear it, but I still wince at the noise. Reaching the outer building, I grab the doorknob and yank the door open. As I step inside the dim interior, I settle my gaze on the matte black-and-red Suzuki Hayabusa, my sixteenth birthday gift. Most parents wouldn't give an extremely powerful and fast sports bike other motorcyclists call *Roadkill* to their teens. But most parents aren't Aisha Diallo.

Still, if she'd known I would use it to disobey a direct order, she would've snatched the shit away faster than I could fucking blink.

In seconds, I slip on the black leather motorcycle jacket and gloves lying across the handlebars, hit the button on the wall to lift the garage door, and mount my bike. Nudging up the kickstand, I wait until the wide door rises, and as soon as there is enough room, I pin the throttle and surge forward. My ass hits the seat, and the wind slaps at me. If not for the circumstances, I'd laugh at the adrenaline pumping through my veins, at the steady increase of speed. At the heady spread of power. Before I hit the end of the winding drive, I hit the button on the bar, lowering the garage door, and I bend, intent on eating up the New Hampshire road toward Boston.

An hour and a half later, I roll onto dark, rain-splattered streets. I was born and raised on these streets, and they're more familiar to me than my face. But in this instant, trailing past blackened windows of empty warehouses along the waterfront, I feel like a foreigner.

I glance down at the custom display and glimpse the blinking green dot that shows Ma's location. We've never hidden our locations from each other. Maybe she forgot that . . . or maybe she trusted I'd remain at the cottage. Doesn't matter now. I see she's only feet ahead of me, and it looks like she's headed for the Thirty-Third, the club just ahead that fronts as a popular after-hours spot but doubles as a business to wash money. In the back is a designated pickup place for all that cash.

Yeah, it's one of the family's most profitable rackets, but what's going on tonight that's so important, it had to drag Ma all the way here from New Hampshire? Why couldn't Abena deal with it? She isn't just Ma's sister but also the olori. As second-in-command, or what other families would call an underboss, it's in her damn job description to handle issues that come up. So why . . . ?

Ma's black Bugatti Veyron glides into view, drawing to a stop outside the Thirty-Third, and I lower my feet to the street, letting the bike idle. Staying out here all night isn't an option. For one, security is too tight around the club—sooner or later, someone's going to see me and rat me out. And second, it's cold as hell even with my jacket and gloves. Adrenaline kept me warm all the way here, but as I sit still and watch Ma step out of her car, regret for acting foolishly is already setting in.

Shit. She's going to kill my ass—

Gunshots ring out.

I don't scream.

I can't.

Not even when my mother's body jerks over and over and then hits the pavement, showered by shattered glass.

My own body spasms, shock and pain radiating through me in suffocating, paralyzing waves.

Shrieks from partygoers waiting to get into the club pierce the air, along with shouted orders from black-dressed employees pouring from inside the club.

But it's too late.

It's way too late.

Our oba—my mother—is sprawled on the street, her blood pooled around her torso and outstretched arms like a thick, sickening, ever-growing puddle. The crimson, appearing obsidian under the streetlamp, saturates her beautiful curls, leaks from the corner of her mouth and streams down her chin.

In the chaos of the surging crowd, my aunt pushes out of the club door, her hand flying to her mouth as she stares down at her sister.

An icy, bony hand reaches into my chest, scraping its nails along my ribs before reaching my heart and squeezing tight. Tighter.

Wheezing out a breath, I tear my gaze from Aunt Abena,

desperate to find my mother again. Mwuaji soldiers surround her, their legs and feet almost blocking my view. Almost.

I find her.

Oh God, I find her. And I stare because my numb mind knows this will be the last time I'll see her alive.

No. *Nononono.*

Given the distance separating us, it's not possible that she hears me. Especially since the sharp cry is only in my head. It's also not possible that she sees me. But I swear . . . I swear our gazes connect and she looks straight at me.

And her lips move to mouth, *Go.*

Doesn't matter if I imagined it or not.

I go.

No one notices me racing off on my 'Busa in the chaos.

And no one's there to hear when my throat finally unlocks and my screams are ripped away by the wind.

CHAPTER ONE

The Huntsman

NOW . . .

"Bring me her heart."

I swallow a grunt.

Bring me her heart.

How cliché and . . . expected. Then again, there's nothing particularly fucking original or inspiring about Abena Diallo. Yeah, as "queen" of the Mwuaji for the last nine years, she's ruthless, with a moral compass that's permanently pointing somewhere south and no conscience to speak of. And those are her better qualities. Still, in our world—a world where crime and murder are just appetizers to the main course of power and corruption—that's standard operating procedure. Hell, that shit's required.

Still . . .

No imagination.

"I want it done as soon as possible." Abena spins around before striding toward the high-backed ebony chair rimmed in silver and glittering black diamonds, the top fashioned into a crown of wickedly sharp, deadly blades.

Like a throne.

She's really leaning into the "queen" thing. The ornate chair. The black raised dais. The huge oval mirror with the ornate, gold-encrusted frame behind the "throne." The velvet drapes pulled back to reveal a view of the Boston skyline and the gleaming waters of the harbor as moonlight hits it. The cavernous room with a cathedral ceiling of glass that invites the night sky inside.

The array of weapons—swords with jeweled hilts; short daggers with gems decorating the actual blades; shields with the Mwuaji "coat of arms" mounted on the walls.

It's overkill, if you ask me.

And hints at compensating for the lack of something. Curiosity about exactly what that deficiency could be flickers in my mind like a candle's flame before sputtering to darkness.

Yeah, I don't give a fuck.

As an assassin, I don't usually question the motivation behind a kill order. I have allegiance only to myself, and if it doesn't affect this party of one, I don't care about the who or why someone finds themselves at the end of my gun or knife. Or whatever weapon I choose to dispatch a target.

My lone rule is no children.

But Abena isn't commissioning the death of a child.

Just her niece. Because the woman is a threat to her crown.

See? No imagination.

She sinks down on the chair, settling her fingers on the arms, her back ramrod straight. Her gaze, as black as the chair underneath her, meets mine. If she expects me to flinch or shrink from her dark scrutiny, she'll be disappointed. Even that flicker of lust that's simmering just beneath the calculation doesn't move me. Someone would need to feel curiosity, interest, or fear to do that.

Someone would need to *feel*, period.

That someone isn't me.

"This is time sensitive, and I need her dead before the week is out. How much?" she presses, crossing long legs encased in white leather.

"Five million."

They're the first words I've spoken. She's given me the target and a time limit; I don't need anything else. I can get to work.

She glances to her left at the only person in the "throne room" besides us. The man stands nearly as tall as my own six-foot, six-inch height, with shoulders damn near as wide as the huge window behind him, and his pure white locs brush against his elbows as he bends his head over a device in his hands. Moments later, his blue eyes—even more brilliant against his umber skin—meet mine before he turns to Abena and gives her a small nod.

"The money should be in your account now. Remember, Huntsman. By the end of the week. And no failure."

I don't bother responding to that.

One, she might have just dumped five million in my untraceable account, but I don't work for her. She doesn't employ or own me. No one does.

And second, failure is never an option. And it hasn't ever been an issue. What I set out to kill ceases to exist.

After turning, I stride across the room and leave without glancing back at the woman who issued a death warrant for her niece. From personal experience, I already knew this, but . . .

Family is a muthafucka.

I don't stop as I leave the office building constructed of steel, glass, and bad intentions and shove out into the humanity teeming in the downtown streets, regardless of the late hour. It's nearing one in the morning, but people crowd into the business sector as if it were the North End or the Theater District. This is Mwuaji territory though. Business never stops. Not while there are guns to run and stolen goods to import and export. The family, known for supplying most of the Eastern Seaboard with weapons and illegal goods from art to drugs, controls Boston Harbor and several other piers and docks in Massachusetts and western New York. Business and crime never sleep.

"We good?"

I don't jerk at the sudden appearance of the tall, wiry, hooded figure next to me. I sensed Jamari several minutes ago when I exited the Mwuaji headquarters and he fell behind me, tailing me. Covering me. Even though I've ordered him to beat it several times.

But he's stubborn. And sixteen.

He's also lucky I don't kill kids. But if he keeps fucking with me, as soon as he turns eighteen, he might be fair game.

"Yeah," I say, my answer abrupt with a whole lot of *get the fuck on*.

But as usual, Jamari ignores my tone and keeps pace with me. Even though he's still a teen, he's nearly as tall as me and his long legs easily eat up the ground.

"What'd she say?" He doesn't wait for my reply . . . probably because he knows by now there won't be one. "She wants you to off her niece, doesn't she? Bet. I know she does," he prattles on, at least keeping his voice down as we reach a corner and turn into the alley where I parked my restored, modified raven-black 1969 Pontiac GTO.

Slipping several bills to each of the kids I asked to look out for my car, I open the driver's door and slide inside. A second later, Jamari drops on the passenger seat and slams his door shut, then lowers his hood, revealing his shoulder-length dark brown locs and damn-near-too-pretty profile.

"I've heard things, and it's the worst-kept secret in Boston that she wants Eshe offed," he continues, his fingers drumming a beat on the door panel and his leg jumping in an impatient rhythm. The kid is like a downed wire after a storm: Restless. Popping. Never still. "Shit, some of her own people even think she's the one behind Aisha's death. I know the Mwuaji are fucking killers, but taking out your own sister just so you can be queen and leaving your niece motherless? That's some nasty work."

Just shows how young and naïve he still is, even for someone who's seen some of the worst shit humanity can do to one another and themselves. Nothing surprises me at this point. Greed and power are some of the tamest reasons for murder. Some of the sanest.

"Most people don't pay attention to a kid," Jamari says. I snort. Only the dumbest fucks don't consider any- and everyone a potential threat to their lives. Age, sex, size . . . None of that measures up against desperation. "They say things," he continues, fingers drumming faster, knee bouncing quicker, "and more than a few in that family would rather see Eshe as their queen. Feel it's her rightful place. And if someone hadn't gunned down her mother, she would be. If I overheard that talk, I'm pretty fucking sure Abena has."

He's not telling me anything I don't already know. People kill not only to grab power but to keep it. And Eshe Diallo, whether she covets the role of queen or not, is a threat. Simply because others would like to see her there. Too many.

So she has to go.

And unluckily for her, it's become my job to see that she's no longer a threat . . . or competition.

It isn't personal. It never is.

A faint pinch of *something* echoes behind my rib cage.

An image of Eshe Diallo flickers in my mind like a projector's beam hitting a screen, and though I met the Mwuaji's olori only one time, that visual is crystal clear, branded on my brain, my memory.

A stunning face that isn't pretty—at least not in the classical sense. It's too bold, the bone structure too severe, too strong for something as simpering and weak as *pretty*. She's *arresting*. Those stark cheekbones, stubborn jawline, flared wide nose, piercing, oval-shaped hazel eyes, and fucking prurient offense of a mouth are like jigsaw pieces gathered from different puzzles but ones that somehow fit together to form a fierce, striking image. And then there's that petite body with its deceptively soft-looking curves. The firm handful of her breasts. The flare of her hips, perfect for a bruising grip. The thickness of her gorgeous thighs.

Pretty? No.

Lethal and fuckable? Hell yeah.

I would say it's a crime that she has to die when her only sin was being born to a queen. But that would be a lie. Eshe Diallo has committed plenty of sins in her short life. All anyone has to do is look into those multicolored eyes and see that soul is as clean as a Boston gutter.

And for a man like me, that's as beautiful as her face.

"H-Man," Jamari murmurs, his leg and fingers suddenly stopping their twitching. My own shoulders twitch at that ridiculous nickname he insists on calling me. "Are you really going to . . . ? I mean . . ."

"Don't go there, kid," I say, my growl rolling through the car's interior in an ominous warning.

I don't discuss business with anyone. Period.

And once I accept a job, I don't fail. Ever.

Jamari falls silent, and his fidgeting resumes as he turns his head toward the passenger-side window.

That pinch pulses in my chest again, but this time I ignore it.

Eshe Diallo will be dead by the end of the week.

And there's no room in this world for regret or second-guessing.

That, too, is part of the job.

I stare at the cottage nestled in the middle of a New Hampshire forest like it's a dog that took a big shit on my boot.

What the fuck is this?

It took me the better part of three days to track down Eshe's location, and a cottage straight out of a goddamn fairy tale didn't even register on the list of places I'd find her. Built to almost disappear into its surroundings, the dark brown, pitched, and deeply sloped roof and dark green walls blend into the trees so well, the light seeping out from the wooden shutters almost appears like sunlight filtering through leaves. Whoever constructed this building either had a flair for the whimsical or was defensively strategic. Maybe both.

Still, this . . . bit of playful fancy doesn't fit the cold, reserved olori I've come to kill. A sterile, spartan apartment with blackout curtains, well-planned exits, and maybe even some deadly booby traps, sure, but not this . . . thing that belongs to dwarves hi-hoing it to work in the mines.

What—and I repeat—*the fuck*?

For some reason, Eshe disappeared to this place, and as much as I resent the curiosity poking a dagger-sharp fingernail at me, squashing the questions, the *interest* is undeniable. Why the hell is she out here in the middle of nowhere, in southern New Hampshire? Out of protected Mwuaji territory by herself? No backup, none of her family? Who does this property belong to? Why does it even fucking exist?

Just as the last inquiry parades across my mind, I deliberately shut the shit down.

Not my fucking business. And neither is Eshe Diallo.

Only how to infiltrate her current location without tipping her off before my knife meets her neck concerns me. Not the woman herself or her life choices.

My eyes narrow on the two shuttered windows bracketing the wide, green-painted wooden door as I slip on my "hood." I never hunt without the black leather balaclava, and though it's only me and the olori in these godforsaken woods, this time's no different.

There's been minimal movement in the cottage, a shadow breaking the golden light trickling from inside just three times since I've been standing here, hidden behind a huge tree trunk and its thick, heavy canopy of leaves. Either she's getting ready to turn in for the night or—

The tingles stabbing at the nape of my neck are my only warning.

I whip around, my hand flying to the middle of my lower back and the knife tucked there.

But it's too late.

A hot pain flares in my neck, followed quickly by a sensation of burning lava pouring through my veins.

Reflex has me slapping at my throat, and I snatch a needle out of my skin.

Rage explodes inside me, and a growl rolls out as I meet a pair of gleaming eyes surrounded by thick dark curls.

"You," I snarl.

Then everything crashes to black.

CHAPTER TWO

Eshe

God, he's beautiful.

It's unfair, really.

I drag the tip of my blade across the broad plane of his brow. Down the proud, arrogant bridge of his nose and across each narrow patrician nostril.

Slumber doesn't soften the hard, wide curves of his mouth. As lush as those lips appear, my knife doesn't even dent the dense flesh. The sharpness of his cheekbones rivals the blade's edge I currently trace over that almost-savage bone structure.

The thick fringe of his lashes grazes his golden skin, but I don't need to see his eyes to perfectly envision the color that resembles a sky heavy with clouds on the verge of a destructive thunderstorm.

How am I in the know?

Some might call it stalking.

I call it reconnaissance. Preparation.

Because from the moment I laid eyes on this man two years ago, he was mine. He just didn't know it.

Fucking shame I have to kill him.

Scowling, I lift the knife from his face and start skinning the apple I grabbed for a snack right after chaining him to the bed. Pisses me off that he's put us in this position.

His fault though.

He came here to kill me first, after all.

Several things I can't let slide:

Dumbass mu'fuckas. Nothing will unalive you faster than a mu'fucka whose titty or dick size is bigger than their IQ.

Messy mu'fuckas. If someone is messy and mouthy as fuck with their shit, they have no problem being the same with mine.

And disloyal mu'fuckas. Loyalty is like blood in our world—we need it to breathe, to survive. Fear doesn't last long. Not when there's always someone else out there who's bigger, harder, more ruthless. More willing to slit the throat of their own mother to gain power, to get richer, to rule. Money can buy power.

But it can't purchase loyalty, faithfulness.

That's why it's more precious. Why it's rarer.

Then there's the final thing I can't let slide:

Someone trying to kill me.

It would fall under *dumbass mu'fuckas*, but there's nothing foolish about the Huntsman. He's everything careful, exacting, and lethal. He's the bogeyman whispered about in fearful, trembling undertones even as eyes slide from side to side, nervous, as if a shadow, darker than the others, will creep from among its brethren.

Yet here he is. Chained to my bed for committing the ultimate sin against me.

And I have to kill him.

He's lucky he doesn't have any parents, sisters or brothers, nieces or nephews for me to hunt after I'm done with him. Never leave family alive after you put a person down; I've learned that lesson the hard way. They're like roaches—they never die and always come back, hiding in nooks and crannies, just under your feet, waiting to jump out when you least expect it.

But I don't need to worry about that with him.

The Huntsman is a bastard, and not just in personality but by birth. No parents. He had one sister. Miriam. He lost her when she was four and he was just nine, in one of Boston's not-so-finest foster homes. And at the age of ten, he murdered the man responsible for his little sister's death . . . beat the back of his skull in with a baseball bat. His first kill.

Like I said, I know everything about him.

He's my calling. My ministry.

My obsession.

And because he's my obsession, I make it a habit of tracking his movements.

No, literally. I placed a tracker on his car.

Nothing says caring like not respecting boundaries.

Still . . .

Anger flashes inside me, and I swallow a hiss from the quick but searing burn. A part of me hates him for this relentless, hungry fixation. The only thing I've obsessed over as much as him is revenge for my mother. Yet that same part wishes I were a fervent atheist instead of a devout disciple to the religion of *him*.

The Huntsman may be my would-be assassin, but Malachi Bowden is my weakness.

And anyone who wishes to not just survive but fucking thrive in our world knows that when a weakness is discovered, you cut that bitch out and cauterize the site so nothing grows in its place.

A small, nearly imperceptible sound snags my attention.

My gaze narrows on his face, which remains at rest. Nothing about it has changed. But I know what I heard.

A soft hitch in breath. A switch in rhythm. A nearly infinitesimal higher rise of his chest.

The Huntsman is awake.

Despite his imminent murder, a delight blooms deep within me, spreading until its warmth radiates through my chest and belly and pulses between my thighs.

Oh yeah.

I don't even try and pretend that the anticipation of him—of all that visceral power and strength and fucking *malice*—doesn't make me wet. That I'm straddling it, controlling it, has me downright soaked.

"Wakey, wakey," I softly taunt, skinning the apple until one long, seamless rind plops to his abdomen. "I know you're not asleep." I cleanly slice a piece of apple off and bite into the crisp fruit. The sweet and tart flavor fills my mouth, and I hum. Then set the juice-dampened tip of the blade just under his chin. "Or maybe the great Huntsman prefers to die with his eyes closed. Can't face death head-on? Blood makes you squea—oh. There you are," I purr, as the dense fringe of his lashes lifts and his gray-blue gaze crashes into mine. "What's that saying about pride? I'd say you're headed for a fall, but you're already kind of ass planted on my bed. Lucky me."

No one in their right mind would goad this man, even with him chained to their bed.

But then again, I've been accused of many things in my twenty-five years—blackmail, armed robbery, bribery, assault, murder—but no one's ever leveled *sane* at me.

"That's much better. You have such pretty eyes," I murmur, tracing the knife's point up over his chin, the corner of that lewdly carnal mouth, the blunt thrust of his cheekbone, to settle just under the rim of his lashes. And press hard enough to dent the tender, softer skin.

He doesn't even flinch.

And that steely, crystallized stare doesn't waver from my face.

But it promises all kinds of things. Mostly pain. And screams. Mine.

A shiver ripples down my spine. Not one of fear though.

Pleasure. Delicious, dirty pleasure.

"Mmm," I hum, shifting low on his stomach and nearly hissing at the frisson of lust that pops and spider-webs over and through me like the cracks across a shattered windshield. "I'd love to let you try it," I whisper. No, he didn't vocalize a thing, but we both know what he relayed, nonetheless. And it thrills me. "I know I'd enjoy it. I think you would, too."

I lean back, straightening, and resume eating my apple. After cutting off another slice, I pop it into my mouth and chew, contemplating him. His gaze flicks to the fruit, then back up to stare into my eyes.

"But back to the matter at hand. Which is my assassination attempt." I tsk-tsk. Cut another slice. Chew. "I don't need to ask who sent you. Although there's a plethora of people who'd love to kill me"—why, yes, that might be a hint of pride that slides through my voice—"only one person would be foolish enough to try it. Or . . ." I cock my head. "Solicit it. Abena."

He doesn't react. Not one muscle twitches. He just continues to stare at me, unblinking.

I smile.

"Still not talking?" I shrug. Cut. Chew. "Like I said, I don't need confirmation. Abena is a coldhearted bitch and a sociopath, and those are her good qualities. It's that nasty penchant for murdering her family members that pisses me off."

Do I have proof my aunt was behind my mother's murder nine years ago? No. Do I need it to kill her for it? Again, nah. This isn't a courtroom, and fuck preponderance of evidence. All I need is to hold on to the image of my mother bleeding out on that street. Or of her body laid out in that glass coffin, looking asleep instead of dead as we filed pass her, saying our last goodbyes.

That's my fucking evidence.

I'ma molly whop that bitch before I put a hot one right between her eyes. Unlike how she did with my mother, she's going to see it coming from me.

A wave of anger ripples through me as I deliberately slice off the meat of the apple and crunch it between my teeth, letting a drop of the juice dribble down my chin. And I do nothing to stop it from dripping to my chest, framed by my black tank top. The Huntsman's gaze dips to that drop, briefly lingering before rising back to my eyes. Anyone else would've missed that quick glance.

But not me. Nothing about the Huntsman escapes me.

"It's not the who, Huntsman. It's the what I need from you. What did she pay you? What were her instructions? Did she want you to assassinate me or bring me back to her? What were her plans, if she had any? And what proof did she request? Abena is nothing if not dramatic." I sigh. "An ear here. A finger there.

Even an eye once. What memorabilia did she demand you bring back to her?"

Cold silence.

Irritation should snap through me like fire. I even wait for it. Pause for that initial crackle of emotion and the hot spread of it.

But no. There's no annoyance.

Just delight. Pure, unadulterated delight.

And anticipation.

Without breaking eye contact, I sink my teeth into the apple, biting out a huge chunk. Chewing, I toss the rest of the half-eaten fruit aside and ignore the soft thud of it hitting the floor.

"I can't lie," I murmur, leaning forward and flattening a hand on his wide shoulder. I release another hum, this one of pleasure, as heat from his massive body seeps through his long-sleeved black shirt to warm my palm. Twirling my knife between my fingers, I balance myself on my hand, rising a little on my knees. My pussy rails against me, practically weeping over the loss of his hard frame pressing between my legs. Not that I can blame her. "I was kind of hoping you'd stay quiet. I haven't had a chance to practice my skills since I came out here. You'll do." I lower the blade to his throat, at the last second curving upward to caress his jaw with the sharp edge. "Wonder how many cuts it'll take to get you talking. Please don't disappoint me, Huntsman. Hold out for a while," I softly say.

Call it twisted, perverse, dark—I really don't give a fuck—but a part of me wants to cut him. Aside from the obvious reasons; a bitch hasn't forgotten about him coming here to off me.

No, I'm talking about the vengeful, hungry part that desires to punish him for making me crave him to the point where he's a liability. My liability.

I know it.

Abena knows it.

After all, that's why he's here in my sanctuary, the hideaway my mother left for me.

By accepting this job, he provided my enemy with not just a way to kill me, but to hurt me.

Honestly, I don't know which is the bigger sin.

"Let's start again," I say, pushing off his shoulder and rising higher on my knees. Stroking a finger down the handle in a loving caress, I lower the knife to the base of his throat, just above his collarbone. I catch his gaze drop to my missing finger, and it's almost like a physical touch over the now smooth, nerveless skin. That stare is calculating, judging, assessing. "Oh, don't worry, that doesn't bother my balance or skill in the least. It's a bitch doing pinkie swears though." I scrunch my nose.

His flat gaze flicks back to my face, and once more pleasure hums beneath my skin, spilling its honeyed warmth through me. His life is literally in my hands, and the power of that—of knowing with one well-placed slice, I could end his existence, bleed him out—is an addictive aphrodisiac. "What were her instructions? Kill me or bring me back?"

That frigid stare bores into me, and I smile.

And slice his skin.

Enough to sting. Enough to bleed. But just a little. I want this to last.

The barest flare of his nostrils. That's all the reaction I receive. And honestly, I'm surprised he even gave me that. But then again, if every one of my senses weren't attuned to him, to his special frequency, I would've missed it. He's that good.

I'm better.

Tilting my head, I probe again.

"Instructions, Huntsman. What did she have planned for me?" I pause. "Nothing? Oh goody," I breathe.

With a flick of my fingers, I cut him again, same spot, going deeper, widening the wound. Yeah, that had to hurt. It bleeds harder, crimson fluid sullenly seeping from between the clean edges. Dragging my attention from his sliced flesh to his face, I find that arctic stare still on me. It's damn near physical, and . . .

and not so cold. Heavy, deadly, promising retribution, but there are twin flames in those gray-blue eyes. For some reason, the deadened nerves where my finger used to be throb in a phantom ache. As if just one look from him ignites my pain, reconnects the memories of blood and torture like tissue and veins.

The breath evaporates in my lungs. The never-dormant ravenous need inside me stirs. He fuels dual cravings. Violence and lust. Torture and intimacy.

"What proof did she require you return to her?" I ask.

No answer, and the *fuck you* in his blazing glare doesn't count.

I strike again, lacerating the taut skin under his chin. Blood bubbles up, slipping down the front of his neck. The hiss that releases from him is so low, so muted, I almost miss it. Almost.

My heart thumps against my sternum at his first overt reaction, and excitement howls a vicious war song through my veins. I jerk my gaze up to his and am *incinerated*.

By hate. Oh yes. He wants my throat under his own blade. Or his hands covered in my blood.

But there's something else. Something more complicated than rage or hatred. Something hotter. Something dirtier . . .

No.

Confusion snakes its nebulous arms in and around my rib cage, sticky and clinging. And underneath, winding like a graceful yet devious vine, lurks suspicion.

And glee.

Hmm.

Those patrician nostrils flare, and the audible breath he draws in is the sweetest melody that has ever graced my ears. Fuck my ears—it strums over my entire body. Skimming over my skin like calloused fingertips, eliciting shivers and electrical shocks of pleasure. My pussy hums in approval, spasming around an emptiness she finds inexcusable.

Dipping my head, I lap at the base of his throat where the trail of blood has already pooled. The metallic, salty flavor flirts with my tongue, filling my mouth, my nose. A growl, feral and low, rumbles against my lips, and it only stirs my hunger for more of his essence.

His chest heaves beneath me, and continuous growls emanate from him. His hips punch upward, showcasing that beautiful, long, and hard dick pressing against his pants. Oh, and it's lovely. I almost purr in satisfaction at the sight of it. I'm more aware than ever that a great predator lies chained beneath me. Not that I ever truly forgot. These manacles in no way diminish the power he exudes like pheromones or that scent of leather, gun oil, and sun-warmed skin. He's Prometheus, bound to a rock. Captured but not lessened, not cowed. Still a dangerous, seductive threat.

Sitting up, I stare down at him, wiping the back of my hand across my mouth.

"You taste amazing," I murmur.

"More."

The order is so rough, so gravel torn that it's nearly indecipherable.

I arch an eyebrow, running the blade over the pad of my thumb. "Oh, so you can speak. I was beginning to wonder."

"Give me more."

He doesn't beg. No one with a single working brain cell could interpret that as a plea. Yes, I straddle him, but he's issuing demands. And though I don't bow to any living person, I want to surrender to him.

Because I want it, too.

So I give it to him.

"Lick it."

Slowly, I obey, lowering my head and sucking on the lacerated flesh, groaning at the rich, briny taste.

"Fuck," he snaps, and the chains at the head of the bed rattle. The sturdy black iron bedposts creak, but they hold. "Again. A-fucking-gain," he snarls.

An instinctive *who the fuck you talking to?* surges to my tongue. And only years of icy control hold me back from plunging the knife somewhere painful but not life endangering in his body. But even that wouldn't save him, just as the same restraint didn't save the other mu'fuckas who'd dismissed my size and sex, then fucked around and found out.

No, only one thing is keeping him from becoming my personal pincushion.

Liquid heat doused in gasoline pours through me, swirling over my breasts and beading the nipples into tight, aching points, twisting in my belly, stroking my pussy... The rigid steel in his tone should have me homicidal, not hovering on the edge of orgasm—but it does. I'm teetering, and all it would take is a firm, lingering glide of my fingers through my wet, swollen folds... a glance over my pulsing clit... and I'd tip over that edge.

Tip, hell—plummet. I'd plummet into an orgasm that I suspect would be better than half the sex I've had. And he hasn't even touched me.

Somehow it seems fitting that I'm betraying my hardcore values—betraying myself—for this man. From the moment I first laid eyes on him two years ago, I've broken rules for him.

Lucifer's fall from grace, if you believe in that kind of thing, has nothing on mine.

My tumble started a long time before finding him in the woods surrounding my cabin.

So why stop the plunge now? Especially when there's only the two of us here and one won't see morning.

"What do I get out of it?" I ask, letting my voice harden as I slowly lower and shift backward until my pussy glides over the obscenely large length and width of his cock.

Fire races up and down my spine, and I don't try and contain my groan. He feels too good. Too necessary.

That groan slides into a gasp when he rolls his hips, thrusting against me. For a moment, I'm riding all that power, that strength, that... pure sex. It's empowering, intoxicating.

And in that instant, with his dick grinding against my pussy, I'm drunk.

"Fuck," I breathe, my knife nearly sliding from my grasp.

Blinking, I refocus on his too-angular, bold face and find that hooded gaze on me.

And for the first time in years, I battle the urge to fidget, to avoid, to . . . hide. Which doesn't make sense. People see what I intend, what I project. Only one person could peer beneath the mask, and she's been gone nine years. Yet I haven't forgotten the feeling of being seen.

And I don't like it.

"Is that your final answer?" I ask, harsher than I meant. "You'd rather give me a good, hard fuck than information about Abena?" My lip curls in disgust, but honestly, I'm kind of impressed by his loyalty.

Isn't going to stop me from trying to break him though.

Who are you kidding? This isn't about interrogation anymore.

I want to cuss my bitchy inner voice out. But I can't. Not when it's right.

At some point, this stopped being about grilling him and punishment and more about pleasure. His. Mine.

Ours.

I inch up his shirt, reveal a gorgeous, tightly muscled body riddled with scars. Given our time together, I'm eyeing them through a new gaze now.

"Tell me, Huntsman." I continue to poke the predator, staring into his eyes even though it's like peering into the deadly radiance of the sun. "You'd rather be my whore than hers?"

If he could rip free of those chains, I'd be a dead woman.

It's in the subzero blast from his gaze. The damn-near-savage pull of his lips back from his teeth. The strain of his arms and body underneath me. He wants at me, and not to fuck.

To annihilate.

He could try.

And like others before him, he'd fail.

But, fuck, it would be fun.

Smiling, I whip out my hand and slice a thin cut above his pierced nipple. A second later, I bow over his chest and suck hard on the wound and the small, taut light brown crest. His animalistic growl rumbles against my mouth, my breasts, my belly. Giving him my own hum in return, I draw harder on his flesh, clamping my teeth over the silver barbell and rubbing my wet, swollen sex over the steely length shoving against the front of his pants.

Exquisite pleasure rolls through me like a thunderstorm, and I grind harder, writhe wilder.

The jangle of the manacles breaches the haze fogging my head, and after giving his nipple and cut one last long, indulgent lick, I lift my head, slide my tongue over my lips.

Well, now.

He no longer looks like he wants to murder me.

"Since you're not feeling chatty," I murmur, scraping my blunt nails down the corrugated ladder of his abdomen, "I'll do all the talking. On your dick."

CHAPTER THREE

Eshe

My . . . threat—warning? promise?—echoes in the room. The Huntsman doesn't make a sound, but that gaze dares me to follow through. Demands it.

Instead of unbuckling his leather belt, I carve through it, then slide the button through its hole and jerk the zipper down. I could drag this out, taunt him . . . taunt myself. But I'm only patient when I have to be. And for two years, I've waited for him. Now that I have him where I've needed him for so long, I'm too eager, too excited, too fucking *starved* for this.

For him.

For the brutal strength of the Huntsman.

For the hidden layers of Malachi Bowden.

I want to peel them away until he lies exposed and vulnerable beneath me, as weak as he's rendered me.

Payback is one fucked-up bitch.

Like an affectionate kitten, I rub my cheek against the long, thick length tenting his black boxer briefs. Which is fair. I mean, he has become my new scratching post, my favorite chew toy.

His cock flexes beneath me, a not-so-silent command to get on with it, but I don't. My conscience's smaller than a gnat's asshole, and my boundary list is even tinier. But there *is* a list. And sexual assault and rape are on it.

"Is this what you want?" Setting the knife beside my hip so it's not a distraction, I then stack my hands on his stomach, propping my chin on them and meeting his eyes. "And I get talking isn't your thing, Huntsman, but you're going to have to give me the words. You're chained to my bed, and I'm going to kill you. You don't have a choice in that. But whether I touch you right now? Whether I put my mouth on your dick? That's completely your choice. So yes or no, Malachi?"

He stiffens; his whole body goes rigid, and for a second, those gray-blue eyes flare wide and blank with shock. I'm not certain if it's because I'm offering him the chance to make his own decision or because I've said his real name. Maybe both.

Shadows cloud his gaze, concealing any emotion as if it never existed, and I'm staring into the crystallized, soulless eyes of an assassin again.

I tilt my head, frowning.

Huh. Maybe not so soulless.

Absently, I inch my bottom hand free and crawl my fingers up his still-bared torso until I reach his pierced nipple. Without breaking our visual showdown, I tug on the barbell and then press a fingertip against the cut above it, studying his savagely beautiful face for a reaction.

A struggle wars across his expression. But lust wins out. It's in the firming of that generous but cruel mouth. In the flash of heat in his eyes. In the tautening of skin over his cheekbones. In the reflexive grinding of his jaw.

No. Someone devoid of a soul wouldn't be capable of this much passion. Whether it be hatred or lust. Or a gorgeous, toxic mixture of both.

"Yes or no, Malachi?" I push, once more deliberately using his name.

"Do it," he grits out from between clenched teeth.

Short, to the point. But I need more.

"Do what?" I press, goading him. Needing him to fully give me the permission I crave.

"Use that pretty, filthy mouth for something else other than talking my goddamn ear off and suck my dick."

In seconds, I scoot farther down his body, hooking fingers into the top of his boxer briefs and tugging down.

"Goddamn," I breathe.

I've rubbed my pussy all over him, so I surmised how big he was, but . . .

"I'm going to damn near dislocate my jaw taking this dick." I close my eyes, brushing my lips back and forth along the wide base of his length, the coarse nest of dark blond hair tickling my chin. "And I'm going to enjoy every second of it."

Rising on my knees, I fist that beautiful, intimidating dick with its broad, plum-shaped head and veiny, heavy shaft, and pump it with both hands piled one on top of the other. By no means is this my first dick, but my fascination with him belies that fact. I inhale his heady musk, and that leather, minty, storm-filled scent is thicker here, more intoxicating. Lowering my head, I nuzzle the hair-roughened balls that hang low beneath his sex, darting my tongue out and dragging it over each one.

Another of those rough, menacing sounds rumbles out of him as his powerful thighs tense on either side of me and his belly goes concave. With a sample of his unique flavor slamming into my taste buds, I swallow him down.

Goddamn.

He's a fucking experience.

On a greedy moan, I draw back, releasing him with an indulgent *pop*. Losing myself in him, in the pleasure of him, I lick him like a lollipop, tracing the highway of veins interconnecting over his skin. His body bucks, rocking the bed as his hips jack toward the ceiling in an unspoken but deafening demand to stop teasing him. To put his dick back inside me.

Look at him trying to top from the bottom. As if those chains and cuffs aren't enough clues that I'm in control.

Wrapping my hands around his dick again, I stroke, tightening my hold, instinctively knowing he wants a hard, damn-near-punishing grip. And as he releases a harsh hiss from between flattened lips, his hips rocking into my touch, I see I'm right.

It's almost . . . freeing.

I can be as nasty, as ugly, as cruel as I want—as I need to be with him.

Not only will Malachi not condemn me for it, he welcomes it. He craves it as much as I do.

Besides . . . dead men can't judge.

"Tell me to stop, Huntsman," I murmur. "If this is all you want, we can quit now. What do you need from me?"

He raises his head, and a snarl lifts the corner of his mouth. "If you stop, I'll find a way out of these chains and choke you with them. Put your mouth back on me."

"Alrighty, then."

I smirk, then gather spit in my mouth and release it onto the tip of his dick, watching it slide down over the flared rim. Catching the drops with my fingers, I use them as natural lubricant, pumping him faster, firmer. On the next downstroke, I part my lips over him, taking his brutish flesh inside, hollowing my cheeks and sucking him deeper. Bobbing my head over him, I work to take more and more of this beautiful cock. Even with my considerable talents, I can't deep throat all of him, but fuck that, I can enjoy conquering as much as possible.

A deep grunt and full-body shudder are my rewards. I moan, slowly easing back, stroking my tongue along the underside of his flesh. *More of that, please.*

With one hand still working his dick, I dip my head, returning to his balls, and suck one inside my mouth, rolling my tongue over it. That musky flavor explodes over my senses, and I not only savor it, I *breathe* it. Switching to the other testicle, I hum in anticipation and swallow him, teasing, savoring. There's no part of him I want to leave untouched. I need to claim him *everywhere*.

A faint tremor shakes his thighs, and I place a gentle kiss high on the inside before sliding back down his length like a firefighter on a pole headed out on a call. The bulbous head bumps my throat, but instead of retreating, I hold still, allowing him to slip inside. A primitive growl echoes from above me, like the warning timbre of a predator. The hairs on the back of my perspiration-dampened neck and arms stand up at the sound. Not out of alarm or fear. Never that.

Out of excitement.

Anticipation.

It's almost enough to make me free him of the shackles to find out exactly how he would follow through on that rumbling, menacing threat.

Almost.

Craving that sound again, I relax my throat more, push air through my nose, and he slips deeper.

Moisture stings my eyes, and I don't care. I'm not moving. Because there went that rumble again. My reward.

I set a punishing pace, going hard, pushing him farther and farther into the channel of my throat with each thrust over my tongue. His big body shakes beneath me, his hips jerking, straining toward me. Demanding I let him fuck my mouth. But this is my show. My punishment. My torture.

Giving him a growl of my own, I pull him back inside me, hunger leading the way and throwing skill out of the window. I release him, fumbling, searching for the knife on the mattress. As my fingers close around it, I press him into my throat, farther than he's been so far, gagging myself. Tears burn my eyes, and my nose stings, runs, but I don't back down.

I cut a careful, shallow slice just below my lips.

A thunderous roar echoes in the room. His back tightly arches off the bed as violent tremors ripple through his body.

I cut him again, at the base of his dick.

Cum strikes the back of my throat, hot and thick and as salty as his blood. I pull back only slightly, to drag in a breath, but don't miss a drop of his seed. Fuck, he's delicious. And still hard as I drink him down, then lap at the sluggishly seeping slit at the crown of his dick. I continue to pump his flesh, and when I finally release him, crimson smears my palm. Meeting his gaze over his rapidly rising and falling chest, I lick my skin free of his blood.

"You're welcome, Huntsman. I usually don't dole out happy endings to my would-be assassins. But I'm glad I made an exception in your case."

Bending over, I smack a kiss on the tip of his dick . . . then dash up his torso, snatching my Glock from under the pillow. In the next second, both my hands are wrapped around the grip and the muzzle hovers centimeters above his forehead.

Lust disappears from his blue gaze, and it freezes over, biting my skin. That gaze. It doesn't beg, doesn't plead for mercy.

Good. I have zero to offer him.

I pull the trigger.

CHAPTER FOUR

The Huntsman

The blast from the Glock roars in my ears. The heat of the bullet expelling from the muzzle sears the side of my face.

The side of my face.

I braced myself for the impact of the bullet piercing me, but only splinters from the headboard fly and embed into my forehead, cheek, and neck. And fuck yeah, they hurt. But not as much as being dead would've.

Why didn't this bitch kill me?

She sucked my fucking soul through my dick, damn near introducing me to my dead parents with that mouth, and then she pulls a gun on me?

She's going to regret that shit.

There's not head good enough in this fucking world for me to forgive that.

The trails of blood trickling down my skin tickle, but the chains wrapped around my arms keep me from wiping them away. *That* reminder—along with the pleasure humming through my veins like flame-lit gasoline and a still-hard, wet dick—has me mad as all fuck.

Killing mad.

This is about more than the contract.

This is personal now.

She called me *Malachi*.

"Bitch, kill me."

She blinks. Then a smile—a diabolical, fucking beautiful

smile—slowly spreads across her face, and I'm momentarily stuck. Just as I was when those lush, pink lips were wrapped around my shit.

Just as I was when she called me by the name no one knows. The name I haven't heard since my baby sister whispered it on the grubby carpet of our foster father's house as she bled out from a beating.

She leans down over me, but she's no fool. There's just enough distance that I can't rear up and bite something off. "Be careful what you ask me for, Huntsman. Unlike you, I don't charge for dropping bodies. And I love free shit."

With a pat to my shoulder, she hums what sounds a lot like Tupac's "How Do U Want It" and climbs off me. I watch her as she shrugs into a shoulder holster and tucks the Glock into it, then stretches across my restrained body and picks up her knife, wipes off the blade on my pant leg, and slides it into an ankle sheath. That shit is insulting as fuck, and I curl my lip up at her, but she doesn't notice, because she isn't looking at me, her attention focused on the phone in her hand. And that's another offense I'm keeping track of like a running tab. Chained up or not, I'm the apex predator in this bitch. When I get out, Eshe Diallo's gon' have to see me.

"Well, Huntsman, it's been fun, but I gotta get out of here. People to see. Parricide to commit." She flashes me another of those slightly off smiles that both irritate and *fucking fascinate* me as she slips her phone in the back pocket of her cargo pants. "I'm sure we'll be seeing each other. And while I should be regretting leaving you alive, I think I'm looking forward to it."

She lifts her thumb to the corner of her mouth and wipes it as if cleaning up any remnants my seed she might've missed, and just like that, lust pumps through me fast and furious like a gotdamn hurricane set on destruction. And I'm set on taking her little crazy ass down with me. Fuck her. Kill her. I'm good with both.

"You'll be seeing me," I warn on a low growl.

"Promise?" She winks, and on anyone else, it would be an asshole gesture.

On her? Well, she's still an asshole, but it's somehow . . . cute. Another point against her. It's like a damn rap sheet now. Like the bitch doesn't already have one.

My anger, which hasn't dialed down one fucking notch, ratchets higher when she practically skips out of the room. Seconds later, a door slams, and an engine too loud to be a car revs and gradually disappears. And I'm left alone in this freakish fairy-tale cottage, the scent of my cum in the air and the rattle of chains marking my every movement.

"Fuck." I jerk against the cuff circling my wrist, and just like every time before it, the metal remains tightly locked. *"Fuck."*

Dropping back against the pillow she so fucking *graciously* placed behind my head, I stare up at the ceiling, my mind whirling. *Think, gotdammit,* think. *You've been in worse situations than this. Much worse.* None come to mind at the moment, but shit, I'm still alive so . . .

Why didn't she kill me? I came here to assassinate her, and I would have if she hadn't gotten the drop on me. And Eshe knew that, so when she had the chance, why didn't she . . . ? It can only mean one thing. Eshe wants something from me. As long as I'm useful, I'll remain alive, and not for one second longer. But that won't stop me from completing the job I was sent for. Especially not now.

Kill the Mwuaji olori and bring Eshe's heart to her aunt.

I close my eyes, and that's a mistake. Because immediately, I feel the red-hot edge of her knife on my skin, splitting me open. Feel dark pain, delicious pain. Feel the wet, hungry suck of her mouth on the seeping wounds.

Feel that same mouth swallowing down my dick as she cut me, smearing blood and cum on her and my skin.

Shit.

She is a dream and a nightmare.

Heaving a sigh, I open my eyes and turn my head—and my gaze lands on the bedside dresser.

And the key sitting on top of it.

Son of a bitch.

So fucking close, but it might as well be a damn state away. Her petty ass knew what she was doing. Another gotdamn torture tactic—letting the literal key to my freedom be within my reach but not accessible.

When I get out of here, I'm definitely gutting her ass. Up close and personal. Heavy on the *personal*. Shit, I might take this job pro bono.

Eshe Diallo fucked up; she's become my motivation.

Gritting my teeth, I inhale a deep breath, brace myself—then pop my shoulder out of socket. Pain shoots through me, and I clench my jaw harder, exhaling hard past the initial agony. I inch closer to the edge of the bed, going as far as the chains will allow. When my hip brushes against the end of the mattress, I block out the radiating pain and focus on moving my arm, though with the dislocated shoulder, there's a very limited range of motion.

By the time my fingers fold around the key, sweat pours off my forehead. In seconds, I transfer the key to my other hand and release my injured arm from the handcuff and then my ankles. Turning to the heavy wooden headboard, I lean against it, suck in a deep breath, draw back, then slam my shoulder against it, popping it back in place.

My chest rises and falls on harsh, grinding breaths filled with a deep, grim satisfaction. Quickly, I free my other hand and, rising from the bed, tuck my dick in my pants. Bitch couldn't even fix my shit. Just got me hanging out in the gotdamn wind.

Another thing she's got to answer for.

They just keep adding up.

And that ass is gonna pay.

Three hours later, I pull my GTO into the underground garage of the warehouse that houses my loft. As I whip into the parking spot between my dusty Land Rover and my white Chevy cargo van, my shoulder complains. It isn't the first time I've dislocated it—purposefully or by accident—and it won't be the last, so I ignore it. Besides, compared to the other shit I've suffered, it's not even worth mentioning. Pushing open the car door, I slide out, and though it's in my secure garage, I still hit the fob, locking it. When you come from where I have, which is Ain't Had Shit, you don't take anything for granted. You protect what you have at all costs.

Heading for the elevator, I stride past my custom black-and-green Kawasaki Ninja H2R, and like a switch, my mind flips right back to Eshe. Shit, not like it's been far from her. Not with my shoulder throbbing, the cuts on my body stinging until I can get some ointment on them, and my cock still half-hard.

I bet she rode away from the cottage on a bike. Though my feelings for her lean toward the homicidal, seeing her with a powerful motorcycle—because the kind of woman she is, she wouldn't have been on top of no pussy touring bike—between her legs would've been hot as fuck.

Shaking my head, I aggressively stab the button for the elevator, and a second later, the doors soundlessly slide open, and I step into the ruthlessly clean box. After I twist the key in the lock, the doors close, and I swiftly rise to the only floor accessible by elevator. When it stops and I step out directly into my loft, legs as skinny and soft as a spider's creep across the back of my neck. My pulse throbs in my head for several moments, then quiets, and every one of my senses go on high alert.

Something's wrong. Off.

This is my home, and I know every inch of it.

The light left on over the oven isn't an accident; the razor-thin string stretching from the counter over the island and to the bar has been disturbed.

I don't use air fresheners, don't use colognes. They cling to your skin and can give witnesses something to identify—that is, if I left witnesses. Still . . . there's a hint of jasmine on the air. Faint. But it's there.

And I've smelled it before.

I reach behind me for the . . . *Fuck*. My knife and my gun are gone. Eshe removed them both from me before she chained me to that fucking bed.

She fucked me. And not with her mouth this time.

"I have to admit, I'm disappointed. Having heard so much about *the* Huntsman, I expected, I don't know, more excellence and care with your work." Abena strolls out of the darkness of my living area, the cream of her long fur coat and pantsuit stark against the shadows enshrouding my place. Strolling around the nearly bare room, she trails her long, elegant brown fingers over the back of my black leather couch, strokes a hand over a shelf of the full bookcase. Stares at the blank exposed-brick walls.

She lifts her hand and curls her fingers, rings blinding in the light.

"Come here, Ekon."

From behind her, her right-hand man steps forward, his long white locs covering his chest and those unblinking blue eyes fixed on me.

"I didn't formerly introduce you last time, but this is my counselor Mirror."

Mirror? If that shit is on his birth certificate, his mother must've hated him.

Abena glances at the still-silent man and says, "Tell him the news you brought me not too long ago."

"Eshe hasn't been killed. She's alive."

Since that ain't news to me, I don't say shit.

First, I don't owe her an explanation. She gave me a week to kill her niece, and it's been three days. Second, rage wraps around my voice like barbwire, tearing into it, shredding it.

She's violated me. Her and her man. They've violated my space.

Doesn't matter that this room is nearly empty and reveals nothing about me. Doesn't matter that the few precious things I own are locked away behind a steel-enforced door in my closet that's only accessible by retina scan.

This world hasn't given me shit. Everything I have, I've fought, stolen, and killed for. I've bled and have been broken for. And for her to touch it, to walk up in it like she owns it, like she has rights to it? This woman who has never known what it is to sleep in a gutter with only a stolen magazine for cover? Never known what it is to paw through a restaurant's trash and fight rats for dinner? Never had to wear shoes until her toes pushed through the soles and were scrubbed raw by the pavement?

Yeah, she's violated me tonight by being here. This is my shit. And I don't know how she found the place I lay my head, and I'll figure that out later. Right now, though, the only heart she needs to be worried about beating outside its chest is hers.

"You want to explain to me why I received word less than an hour ago that my niece was spotted riding through downtown Boston? I paid you to get a job done. To carve her fucking heart from her chest and give it to me in a box. This shouldn't have been too hard a job for the gotdamn bogeyman of the underworld. She's one woman. You mean to tell me the Huntsman can't kill one fucking woman?"

The question ends on a shrill scream, and my fingers ache to wrap around her skinny-ass neck and snap it like a fucking chicken's. She knows as well as I do that Eshe isn't just any woman. If she were, Abena would've sent one of her bitch-ass boys after her niece. But Eshe would've sent them hos back to her in pieces. Probably with smiley faces carved in them. After officially meeting her, I don't put it past the crazy bitch.

"That whole selective mutism shit might work when you don't have five million of my dollars with nothing to show for it." She tilts her head, a sneer riding her face. "I guess underneath the reputation and all-black clothes, you're just like any other man. Get right up to the edge but, when it comes down to it, can't get a woman off. I'm sorry—I mean, can't off her."

She smiles, but there's no warmth there. Whoever gets fucked by Abena deserves whatever they get. When you get in bed with a cobra, you're knowingly taking your life in your hands.

"Did you even find her?" she presses.

I continue to stare at her, mentally counting the seconds it would take me to cross the space separating us, snap her neck, disarm her underboss of the Heckler & Koch P30L under his suit jacket, and blow his jaw off with it. Four point seven, max.

Abena chuckles, slightly shaking her head.

"What? Are you too good to speak to me? To acknowledge me when I'm talking to you? You're a fucking killer. An assassin with no loyalty, no family, no goddamn name, and you stand there and disrespect me? I'm a fucking *queen*, Huntsman. I wouldn't even have bothered to come to this hole you call a home if not because I wanted to see for myself the look on your face when you're humbled because you failed. The great Huntsman who never misses his mark, never quits until the job is done is a *failure*."

Better people than her have insulted me, hell, tried to kill me. But . . .

An assassin with no loyalty, no family, no goddamn name.

That, for some reason, strikes me dead center in the chest, right over an atrophied heart that stopped beating years ago in a filthy, reeking rowhouse. Because I once had all three. And all three were stolen from me in blood and screams.

Whether I put my mouth on your dick? That's completely your choice. So yes or no, Malachi?

That voice of whiskey and vice whispers in my ear as if she's standing right next to me. Reminding me that I do have a name. And she knows it. Reminding me that she calls me by it. Reminding me that she knows who I am.

"And just think," Abena continues, dragging her gaze down my body, "I was going to offer you this pussy as a congratulations for a job well done." Her lips curve in a grin, her eyes narrowing, taking on a cold, calculating gleam. "I still might get the dick. But as I fuck your cold, dying body instead. The only good man is a dead one, after all."

My blood freezes in my veins.

And though I fight it, flashes of images bombard me, one

after the other. Only I'm not thirty-three but nine, scratched up and bleeding with a whimpering Miriam behind me as I jab a sharpened broomstick at foster father number three. The powerlessness and fear of the kid transforms into the icy rage of the man.

The demon I invited inside me as a child that refused to be exorcised raises its head, sniffs the air, and stretches in glee.

"Try it," I flatly invite.

For a moment, uncertainty and fear flicker in her dark eyes. Her second shifts forward, his steady stare finding me. But his blue gaze doesn't shake me. Don't no man put fear in me. Not anymore.

"Run me my money back, Huntsman," Abena snaps.

"Four days left on the contract, Abena."

"I don't think so. One thing I've learned well in life is if you want a man to do the job right, give it to a woman to handle. So consider that contract dead. And you right along with it." She addresses her counselor: "Mirror."

She doesn't pull her gaze away from me, doesn't say anything else to the man. But like they share some kind of weird-ass telepathy, he pulls a cell from the inside pocket of his suit jacket, dials a number, and puts the phone to his ear.

"Come here. Now. Same way."

It doesn't take a muthafucka from MENSA to figure out he's calling in hittas to take me out. The irony that Abena just hated on men as incapable yet surrounds herself with them to do her dirty work isn't lost on me.

Fucking hypocrite.

We stare at each other, the silence thickening, deepening with her intent and my rage. Nah, that's not entirely correct. Yeah, I'm hot that she plans to have me murdered. But after being drugged, chained, and threatened, I *need* this. Already, excitement sings its sweet melody in my head. Hunger creeps through my blood, whispering its craving to rip, to hurt, to *kill*.

A calm settles over me as the only door to my loft opens and two men dressed in black enter. Only one person should know where I lay my head. While I don't trust anyone and wouldn't put anything past a living person—shit, wouldn't put anything past a dead one either—I 100 percent believe Jamari wouldn't breathe a word about this location. So how did Abena discover my address? Yeah, as soon as I leave here, I'm going to make it my mission to find out. And when I do, they gon' see me. And I'm gonna be the last person they ever see.

Nobody betrays me and lives to tell about that muthafucka.

"This is where I leave you, Huntsman. I would say it's been a pleasure, but unfortunately, it hasn't," Abena says, edging backward.

See? Still so fucking unoriginal. No wonder Aisha was the better queen.

"I'll be seeing you soon, Abena."

She freezes, and again she's not fast enough to hide that flash of fear. It feeds the hunger. I almost smile. Almost.

Scoffing, she covers the betrayal of nerves with a flick of her fingers and turns her back on me as if she isn't afraid.

"Goodbye, Huntsman. Have a happy, painful death."

Her scary ass hightails it out of there, because that bravado is going to last for only so long.

When the door closes behind her and her second, I shift my attention to the remaining men in the room.

Young. Midtwenties at most.

Corded muscle. Wide, defined chests. Powerful thighs. Strong.

A three-point black crown with a red blood drop above and black praying hands beneath on their necks. Blooded-in Mwuaji soldiers. Killers.

These aren't innocents. Not that it makes a difference. When they came up in my place, they made their choice between living and dying.

Slowly, I back up toward my kitchen, a map of the room spreading across my mind. Island. Refrigerator. Oven hood.

Deliberately, I inhale, quieting the exhilaration, the joy, the need. The quiet pours in. I stop, my focus sharpening on the hitta to the right as he pulls his SIG P365 while the other doesn't move for his Glock yet. Cocky. That in itself will get him killed.

The two look at each other, and in the time it takes them to glance back at me, I move in a blur of motion. Leaping across the space separating us, I reach out, grabbing the Glock 26 attached underneath the edge of the island. I hop onto the shooter to the right, wrapping my legs around him. Arm outstretched, I shoot the other hitta in the eye before dropping, rolling, and popping his boy in the temple as my back hits the floor. Warm blood splatters across my face and neck.

It takes seconds.

Not even enough to get me winded.

Gotdammit.

Irritated, I fling his body off me and shove to my feet, wiping my forearm over my eyes. I don't trust Abena not to send anyone else up here to make sure the job was done. But, shit, the way I'm feeling, I hope she does. Then again, she's so arrogant, she wouldn't believe her two men couldn't take me. It's why she left instead of waiting to make sure I was really dead. Frowning, I stride to the door accessing the front of the warehouse, close and lock it, then set the alarm by setting my hand on the wall keypad.

Cleaning up bodies isn't new to me; I don't trust cleaners to come behind me like some of the families do. That's more people who know my business. But I'm not used to doing it in my own home. And while I drag the bodies of the two men over my kitchen floor into the utility room, my annoyance grows. Quickly but meticulously, I strip them of their clothes and stuff them into a separate duffel bag to burn. Then each body goes into its bag for transportation to a pig farm outside the city. After returning to the kitchen, I mop and then scrub the floor and island and walls, ensuring no blood or brain matter or evidence of the two men—or even Abena and her second—can be located in my apartment.

Once that's taken care of, I head to the bathroom to shower and take care of the cuts on my body. Staring in the fogged-up mirror at the various bandaged or superglued wounds, my mind flies to the woman who is at the root of all this shit. No, she didn't put the wheels in motion, but it comes back to her. We have unfinished business.

I brush a fingertip over the slice directly above my pierced nipple, and a heated knot twists tight and deep in my stomach. For a moment, the pain of the knife and the pleasurable pulls of her mouth on my flesh sear my memory, my body.

My gaze drops to the red bruising on my wrist, and the lust hardens into something darker, something that I creep closer to like a naked, starved creature inching toward a nurturing fire. Something sticking, smothering that I want to backpedal away from on scraped palms and feet.

Chaining me to that bed tonight . . . Eshe took me back to a place I promised myself I'd never return to. Transformed me into a person I vowed never to be again.

A victim.

She'll pay for that.

Her and her aunt.

Starting tonight.

CHAPTER FIVE

Eshe

"Bitch. What part of 'you're supposed to be dead because Abena put a hit out on you' didn't you understand?" Tera growls in my ear through the mic in my helmet. I grin, steering my 'Busa down Atlantic Avenue.

She's one of the kapteni under me—one of my Seven. It's not her rank that allows her to talk to me like that though. Someone else could try it and find their tongue stapled to their chest like money on their birthday. It's sacrifice, commitment, blood, loyalty, love—that's the shit that binds us tighter than soldier and kapten. Closer than kapten and olori.

We're sisters.

Tera, Penn, Tyeesha, Nef, Kenya, Maura, Sienna, and I have been friends since we were in the third grade, stalking and fucking up Marcus Brown for shoving Sienna's younger sister at recess and then flipping her uniform skirt so his little pervert-in-training friends could get a look at her drawers. I saw the shit, and apparently so had my girls—who weren't my girls at the time. Sienna, slender and tiny even for a nine-year-old, had picked up a stick damn near bigger than her and slammed it into the back of Marcus's head. When his boys tried to jump in—even more reason they were pieces of shit—they fucked around and found out when the rest of us left them bleeding and leaking on that playground. We've all been besties since.

And fuck yeah, I said *besties*. Even killers need homegirls.

"Umm, the 'you're supposed to be dead' part?" I snicker.

Abena and I are similar like that. Both of us are ruthless and merciless as fuck. It's the why where we differ. And the where and the why sum up the reasons I won't sleep one night in the compound where my mother raised me. Yeah, I love my Mwuaji family, but I don't put shit past a muthafucka. My mama raised a sociopath, not a fool. If Abena ordered them and the money was right, they'd come for my neck.

We *are* criminals, after all.

"So what in the fuck made you think it was a good idea to prance your li'l ass down State Street like you're on a fucking float in the Juneteenth parade? I swear, Eshe, sometimes I think we should just go 'head and get a check for you. At least then the trouble you cause would literally be worth it."

"Listen, I know you don't get it, but there's a method to my madness," I assure her, weaving in and out of traffic as I near the Boston Waterfront. Not much beats the rush of flying down a road, my motorcycle humming between my legs and nothing but wind caging me. It's pure freedom.

"'Madness' being the key word here," Tera mutters. "But please, enlighten me."

"By hiring the Huntsman and putting a hit out on me, she fucked up and violated the cardinal law we have as a family. Even she isn't above it, and even God couldn't save her bitch ass if anyone found out. We both know there's only one punishment for that crime—death. So, in a way, I got that ho's life in my hands since me, her, the Huntsman, and probably Ekon's follow-the-leader ass are the only ones who know about the dirty shit she up to."

There ain't shit she does that Ekon—or Mirror, as everyone calls him—doesn't know about or doesn't have a hand in carrying out. *Mirror* because he reflects every thought, idea, or action of Abena's.

"Uh-huh. I already know all this shit since I'm the one who passed along the info about her meeting with the Huntsman to you." In another era or lifetime, Tera would've made a stellar spymaster. She possesses a network of spies in the compound that makes the CIA look like pussy amateurs playing at G.I. Joe. Her information never fails, is never wrong. Next to her love of guns—and using them—it's her most lethal quality. "I still don't see what that's got to do with you Meghan Markle–ing your ass down the center of Boston."

"Because I want her shaking in her fucking red bottoms with the knowledge that, at any moment, I can fuck all her shit up. That everything she's lied, bribed, betrayed, and killed to get can blow up in her face if I open up my mouth. I want her to know fear. Every time she looks at me, I want that bitch to choke on it."

Silence beats down the phone line.

"You know she's not going to admit to shit, Eshe, right?" Tera roughly asks.

On anyone else, it would be an attempt at tenderness, but this is Tera, sooo . . .

"Of course she's not. And because she's who she is, no doubt Abena believes she's covered her ass so no one can prove she's behind the attempted hit."

"Attempted." Tera snorts. "He's the fucking Huntsman, Eshe. We've heard so many stories about him, they're like urban legends by now. And the main one? He's like the gotdamn Terminator; he doesn't stop until he gets the job done. Shiiiid, I'm not a hundred percent convinced the mu'fucka ain't been sent by Skynet. Eshe, I love you like the half sister from my daddy's side chick, so no offense, but I'm kinda shocked you're still breathing. How did you walk away from him?"

"I have my ways." I smirk.

She grunts. "I don't even want to know what that means." The sounds of a horn and traffic hit my ears. "How far out are you? I'm pulling up behind the club now."

"I'm about five minutes out. You parking in the alley, right?"

"Yeah. See you in five."

The line disconnects, and I gun the engine, about to turn those five minutes into three. I turn my mind from thoughts of Abena and the Huntsman to more immediate and pressing matters.

And as I veer off Atlantic and steer my 'Busa down a narrow street, I focus on the meeting—or ambush—I'm about to walk into. The odds are pretty much fifty-fifty.

I can't even lie. A large part of me hopes for the ambush. It's been a few days since I've killed someone and had the fun of watching their eyes glaze over as their spirit left their body. I'm having mad withdrawals.

Rounding the corner into an alley a couple of streets over from the warehouse where the meet is supposed to happen, I spot Tera leaning against her Kawasaki Ninja. The hood of the black sweatshirt under her motorcycle jacket is pulled over her head, but I catch a glimpse of her face as she turns toward the mouth of the alley. I slow down, easing to a stop in back of her bike. We don't speak until we both roll our rides behind a large dumpster and cover them with a large tarp I keep in my saddlebag. Hey, I'm always prepared. You never know when you'll need to hide something. Or wrap a body.

"Ready for this?" Tera asks, her expression darkened by a deep frown. "I'll say it again: I don't trust this."

"You don't ever trust shit. Or anybody." I pull my own hood up and head toward the end of the alley, my boots splashing in small puddles left by an earlier rain.

"Shit, neither do you," she points out.

"Not true. I trust you and the rest of the Seven. I also trust that at least one Kardashian gon' fuck a Black man. Not much else though."

She snorts. "Big facts." She pauses as we turn onto one of the cross streets adjacent to the warehouse. We scouted out the area last night so we were familiar with it and had every exit or potential trap scoped out. "So, if you believe this meeting is suspect, why're we doing this?"

"Because it could be legit. And we need every edge over Abena that we can get. But we're not going into this blindly or stupidly. I don't know this bitch. I don't care that Dakari vouched for her," I say, referring to one of the Mwuaji soldiers loyal to me. "I don't put nothing pass nobody. Which is why we chose the location and have precautions in place."

Tera shrugs, her long-legged stride carrying her swiftly down a back street. "You rocking, I'm rolling. But fair warning: This bitch even twitch wrong, I'm putting a bullet in her head before God gets the news."

See? This is why she's my girl. All that protectiveness and those homicidal tendencies just warm my heart.

"Understood."

We near the warehouse and draw to a stop at the corner of the empty and pockmarked parking lot. The huge brick building looms against the gray sky like a silent, dormant giant. The windows not cracked or broken are dark and grimy. The wide steel doors and loading dock stretch across the bottom half like a big smile with dirty teeth. It's a lonely, abandoned place. The best thing about it is the scaffolding that rims the upper level. Perfect for a person to hide and lie in wait with a sniper rifle.

"I'll see you in there," Tera says, before taking off across the parking lot and disappearing around the building. From our reconnaissance yesterday, I can picture her accessing the metal fire escape and slithering through a window we left cracked.

Inhaling a deep breath, I tug the hood a little tighter around my face. Then, sweeping a glance over the area once more, I approach the warehouse, pull open one of the doors, and slip through. I pause just inside, allowing my eyes to adjust to the shadowed interior. Reaching behind me, I wrap my fingers around the butt of my Glock, slowly stalking forward.

A tall, slender hooded figure steps out of the gloom on the other side of the dusty, dark space, and I pull my gun free and point it at her.

"That's close enough," I order, holding the gun steady and aimed at center mass. I can't see Tera, but I can sense her. Know she has her scope trained right on the other woman. "Drop that bag and spread your arms out."

Carefully, she lifts the strap of a black tote over her head and lets it fall to the floor. Then she follows my instructions and stretches her arms out on either side of her. Tucking my gun behind my back, I cross the space between us and quickly but efficiently pat her down. Satisfied she's not carrying, I step back and nod.

"You good." I cock my head and watch as she lowers her arms back to her sides. "Now, you told Dakari you had some valuable info for me. I don't like my time wasted. Especially when I can be home streaming the new season of *P-Valley*. So whatever you tell me better be worth me missing Uncle Clifford swinging around a pole, or I'm going to be very angry. You wouldn't like me when I'm angry." I deepen my voice, Bruce Banner–ing her.

"I understand." A low, melodic voice caresses my ears a second before she lowers her hood, revealing herself to me for the first time.

I study the older woman standing in front of me. Even though she's a stranger and I'm certain I've never met her before, she seems oddly familiar. Gray hair brushes her shoulders in a sleek bob. Fine wrinkles fan out from the corners of her dark eyes and small mouth as well as crease her rounded cheeks. With her slim body clothed in a flowing black top, leather pants, and boots, she could be anywhere between fifty and seventy. She is the epitome of *Black don't crack*. Even her voice is a husky rasp that's both sensual and weighted with age.

"Thank you for meeting with me."

"Don't thank me yet. What am I doing here?"

She releases a soft sigh, but her dark gaze doesn't waver.

"I apologize for all of the dramatic subterfuge, but I couldn't risk my identity or my meeting with you to get to the wrong ears."

I cross my arms over my chest, impatience crawling through me. "And who are the wrong ears?"

"Your aunt. Abena."

Although I knew the information had to do with Abena, I still stiffen at this woman's revelation. Suspicion joins impatience for the ride, and I narrow my eyes on her.

"What's your name?"

A brief hesitation on her behalf and then, "Laura."

I snort. "Don't shit about you say 'Laura.' But fine. We'll go with that." I shrug, although my suspicion burrows deeper at her lie. "So, *Laura*, what about my aunt? And how do you know her?"

"I don't know her personally. I'm a bartender at the Thirty-Third."

The name of *that* club, the one my mother took her last breath in front of, sends a bolt of rage racing through me. I inhale a deep breath, hold it. Ten seconds later, I slowly release it.

Nope.

That did shit all to douse the murderous fury lighting me up.

"Go on," I grind out.

She bows her head, staring at the floor for several moments before returning her attention to me.

"A couple of nights ago, I delivered drinks to the back room where Abena often meets with members of your family. That night, they were joined by a man I hadn't seen in the club before. Usually, when I enter the room, they stop talking, but not this time." She pauses, swallows, and I glimpse the fear in her eyes. "I wish they would've stopped."

"Why?" I press when she hesitates. Urgency pours through me, pounding in my veins. Urgency and hot anticipation. "What did you overhear?"

"They were talking about a shipment arriving at the port. I wasn't paying much attention until I heard 'girls.' The man said 'a new crop of girls.' I knew then they were talking about—"

"Sex trafficking," I finish.

She nods. "Yes."

My throat squeezes closed, and my breath rushes inside my head like waves crashing against jagged rocks. The rage that swept through me seconds earlier was a spring rain compared to the tempest beating inside me now. I lower my arms to my sides, my fingers curling into tight fists. Fists aching to crash into Abena's face and body until she resembles a sack of flesh and pulverized bone.

Sex trafficking.

The Mwuaji has its hands in a lot of shit. Guns, loan-sharking, theft, drugs. There aren't too many things we draw the line at criminally. But selling women and children into sexual servitude and slavery is one of those bold red lines. As a matriarchal family where women rule, we would never involve ourselves in profiting off the sale of our own. And we have no affiliation with organizations or other families who do. Violating that code is punishable by death.

So, to find out Abena, the oba, is betraying her own family in one of the worst ways imaginable . . .

"Why are you telling me this?" I ask, my voice even, calm, belying the vicious storm of disgust and anger roiling within me. "Why come to me with this?"

I really want to know because part of me feels like it's too convenient that this information is falling so easily into my lap.

The older woman lifts her slender, surprisingly unlined hand to her neck, the long fingers circling the base of her throat. A diamond ring and wedding band wink at me in the dim light.

"My niece disappeared two years ago after answering an ad for a new job. She was beautiful. Kind. So innocent at nineteen in a way that made me and my sister—her mother—worried for her." Laura's eyes briefly close, and a spasm of emotion passes over her face. When she meets my gaze again, pain swamps the dark depths. "She wasn't so beautiful or innocent when her body was found in a dumpster eighteen months after she went missing. Her body showed visible track marks on her arms and bruises on her wrists and ankles—evidence she'd been tied down or cuffed for long periods of time. The medical examiner also discovered she'd . . . she'd been . . ."

"You don't have to finish. I get it," I murmur.

She clears her throat. "Anyway, that night, I reached out to Dakari. He's friends with my oldest nephew, and I knew he was involved with your family. I spoke with him, and he made me contact you and share what I overheard."

I nod, digesting everything she said. Everything sounded plausible. Even if I doubted her story a little, there's no way I can take the chance of letting those women slip away into a trade that destroys. And I'm not even talking about death.

"What're the details of the shipment?"

"It's arriving at eleven o'clock two nights from now, at the East Boston DPA," she informs me.

I study her for several long moments. "How do I know you're telling me the truth?" I ask, not caring if I offend her. Shit, I don't know her like that.

"I figured you'd want proof." She bends down and scoops up her tote bag to pull out a palm-sized golden apple. "Cameras aren't allowed in the Thirty-Third, but Abena has the back room wired, and it records everything that happens there. Security goes on break every night at nine thirty. I managed to get in the control room and download the conversation and sneak it out in this." She extends the golden apple toward us. "They check us when we arrive and leave, but no one scans the apple. Every employee and person entering the club must show theirs like a membership card. I carved out a hole in the bottom to slip the flash drive inside."

I take the apple and turn it upside down. Sure 'nuff, there's a circle scored into the base.

"What do you want for this information?"

"Nothing."

I scoff. "Boo, no one lives rent-free. So I repeat, what do you want?"

Laura stares at me, and then her gaze dips. *Got her.*

"I can't go back to work. Sooner or later, they'll figure out it was me who snitched. I need for me and my family to be moved out of Boston to somewhere safe."

"You got that," I immediately say. "When are you scheduled to work next at the club?"

"I'm off today and tomorrow."

"Good." I nod. "Good. Give Dakari all the details of who we're moving. I'll have you out and set up, at the latest, two days from now."

She exhales, and her shoulders drop. "Thank you," she whispers. "Thank you so much."

"Yeah."

I turn around and walk out the same way I came in, confident that Tera is covering me. I start walking in the direction of our bikes, and minutes later, Tera appears beside me, her stride matching mine.

"What do you think?" I ask after several moments of heavy silence.

She stuffs her hands in the pockets of her jacket.

"I don't know, Eshe. On one hand, she sounds credible. And Dakari vouched for her. But on the other . . ." She frowns, shaking her head. "This seems a little too . . . neat."

"Bitch, right?" I buck my eyes at her. "I was thinking the same thing. Someone serving Abena up on a silver platter to us? My word was 'convenient.'"

"Still, we have to check it out. We can't afford not to. For those women and to speed up our timeline of taking out Abena."

"Yeah." I lightly squeeze the golden apple, looking down at it. "Meeting tomorrow at my house. Call everyone and let them know. We can't go into this without a plan."

"Got it." We near the dumpster, and I snatch the tarp off the motorcycles. Tera grabs her helmet and looks at me, eyebrow arched. "Where're you headed now? You know, since you're supposed to be dead 'n' all. Don't think I forgot about that."

I laugh, grabbing the handlebars and rolling my 'Busa out into the alley.

"I'm taking my *Walking Dead* ass home."

"Good. Call me when you get there."

I jerk my chin up at her and grin.

"Aw, fuck." She groans, then puts on her helmet.

Snickering, I mount my bike. A half hour later, I'm parking the 'Busa in my garage and pressing the button on my key fob to bring the door down. I have several homes, and none of them are on or near the Mwuaji compound. Once I was old enough, living there wasn't an option anymore. It becomes exhausting constantly having to be on guard. Exhausting but necessary.

Fuck survival of the fittest. It's survival of the cruelest. The fucking craziest. Survival of the one most willing to burn all this shit to the ground if it means getting what you want.

Pulling out my phone, I lean against my Charger. Humming, I navigate to a folder on my phone and find the app I'm searching for. One tap, and several squares fill the screen. It's a video feed of the obodo. Nef and Maura secretly installed several cameras around the compound, and so far, no one has discovered them. Thanks to those tiny devices, I am able to monitor the foyer, throne room, kitchen, Abena's study, and the hallway right outside her bedroom. The video feeds haven't provided anything earth-shattering. Yet we have been able to ferret information regarding shipments, meetings, alliances. And we've taken advantage of that info, disrupting deliveries, sabotaging meets, planting rumors—well, lies—to damage any possible alliances. Calling in a bomb threat or two. I study my screen, and after several minutes, I close it out since nothing of import is going on.

I tap the screen and open up a new video feed.

Malachi's apartment. He doesn't appear to be there. Huh. I wonder if he's made it home yet. Another tap, and six squares pop up. One for his living room. Another for his kitchen. His bedroom. Guest bedroom. Utility room and back door. And the last for his front door.

I've had these hidden cameras installed in his place for about a year, and one of my favorite pastimes is checking them to make sure he's good. Or to see what movie we're watching for the night. Or to check out what book he's reading. Those Chronicles of Narnia seem to be a standard fave.

Some people have physical touch or words of affirmation as their way of expressing love.

Mine is stalking.

I close out of the app for good and dial Tera. She's serious about all of us calling and checking in when we get to wherever we're going. I wouldn't call her a mama bear because, well, the bitch too crazy for that. But I'll say she's mama bear adjacent. Protective as fuck.

"Hey, you're there?" Tera answers before the first ring even finishes.

"Just got in."

I put her on speaker and set my phone on one of the attached shelves. After snatching off my motorcycle gloves, I pull out a drawer and carefully store them next to the other sets. I shrug out of my leather jacket and fix it just so over a hanger before storing it in a locker with the other four of various colors. Nef has accused me of being anal, while Kenya has thrown straight-up OCD at my head, but neither of the labels fazes me. I like my shit in order so I know exactly where I can find it. No surprises. Surprises aren't fun; they're chaos. And chaos gets people killed.

I sigh, bending down and unlacing my boots, then toeing them off.

My chest rises and falls on my harsh, burning breaths, my fingers curling into tight fists at my thighs. Rage rolls through me, and I don't try to stifle it. Nah, I inhale it, drink it down, let it spread through me, engraft itself on me. Rage and I have become more than lovers in the nine years since Ma's murder. We have soul ties.

I punch in the code to the garage entrance, then lean forward for the retinal scan. Once the subtle pop of the lock disengaging echoes in the silent room, I snatch up the phone and press down on the handle before pulling the door open.

"A'ight. I'm going back to the compound. See if I can get up with Dakari."

"Sounds good. I—" I glide to a stop in the doorway, going still. "Let me hit you back."

"What? What's wrong?" Tera sharply asks.

"Nothing. Just let me hit you back."

"Fuck that. I'm on my way over there."

The calls ends, and I shake my head. No respect, I tell you. I'm her olori, but does she listen to me? Oh nooo. Still, she's on the other side of town, so that gives me a good twenty-five minutes before she gets here. If she calls one of the other Seven to beat her here, I don't have long, since Kenya lives the closest to me.

It's still more than enough time.

And yet not nearly enough.

The corners of my mouth slowly curl upward even as the nerves across the back of my neck dance across my skin in flame-tipped boots.

He's found me.

Sooner than I expected. But then again, if there's one thing I've come to discover about him in the time I've . . . researched the Huntsman, it's never to underestimate him.

Shit. Where's the fun in that?

"I would ask how you got in past my security system, but I'd hate to ruin the mystery in our relationship."

I close my eyes, shivering as all that delicious and gorgeous hate damn near rolls off him in waves and singes my skin through the layers of my clothes. It's our thing, I think. Our form of fore-play. Well, one of them. I smile wider as I lower my hand and caress the black handle of my karambit knife.

Slowly, I turn around, unerringly finding him in the darkness of the den. This man might be able to meld into the shadows and become one with them with everyone else. But not with me. I could peep those wide shoulders with the divots next to his neck as if my fingers notched them there themselves. Could detect his particular scent of leather, gun oil, and scarred golden skin from a room permeated with others. Could pick up on that deafening void of sound in a space packed full of inane, useless chatter and laughter. His silence is more important, says more than a fucking State of the Union speech.

I know Malachi Bowden better than anyone alive.

And yet I am excruciatingly greedy to fill my well with my knowledge of everything *him*.

I move toward him, and like the devil rising from the gates of hell, he emerges from the deeper shadows beneath the stairs. And fuck if my breath doesn't catch in my throat at how all that visceral, lethal strength and beautiful grace work together in a macabre ballet. The sharp angles and lines of his face appear even more brutal and stark with his fixed gaze and hard, wide mouth. His expression is flat, undecipherable, and yet I can read it clearly as if I alone possess the code. He's death—my death—walking, and the insane part of me wants to drop on all fours and crawl toward it.

"I hope I haven't kept you waiting long. One thing my mother taught me—well, besides how to properly torture a person and keep them alive for at least forty-eight hours—is promptness. Tardiness is such a sign of disrespect."

When he doesn't reply—shocker—I shrug. But then I blink when he moves backward a step, reaching behind him. Reflex has me reaching behind me, too, for my Glock, but when he just removes his and sets it on the small desk behind him, I relax my grip but not my stare. Only when he continues to strip himself of the rest of his weapons—a deadlock dagger, a full-tang knife, another Glock 26, and a garrote—do I get his intention.

Excitement that's almost lust races through me.

I mimic him, and it's like stripping out of my clothes for sex.

I pull my Glock free as well, stepping close to the wall and placing it on the shelf. My SIG P320 follows, then come my karambit, Combat Troodon, and Colonial throwing knives. I stand before him naked, in a sense, and the vulnerability is startling, unfamiliar.

The last time I was this bare, I was strapped to a chair in a freezing room, my blood staining the cement floor beneath me, my severed finger a gruesome party favor several inches in front of me.

I blink, and the image dissipates like the morning mist burned away by a steadily rising sun. Only, it's Malachi's gleaming, hooded eyes causing the memory to fade away.

I resent the relief that trickles through me.

Hate more the phantom ache of my pinkie finger that has been gone for years.

Rolling my shoulders back, I bounce on my feet, then bring each one up to peel off my socks and toss them over my shoulder. "All right, let's get to it. I mean, fighting is my second favorite thing that starts with 'f.'" His eyes flash like dry lightning, and I still, tilt my head. I frown at him, practically frostbitten by the blast of ice emanating from his body. "Funnel cake, Huntsman. What did you think I meant?"

He stares at me, a wrinkle appearing between his eyebrows. Besides the lust that stamped his face when I swallowed his dick, this is the most I've seen him emote. "What the fuck is wrong with you?"

Shaking my head, I tsk-tsk. "Glass houses and throwing stones and all that. All of us are fucked up in some way. Isn't that true . . . Malachi?"

Yes, I'm deliberately goading him by using his name. And it gives me such a rush glimpsing the flex along his jaw. Tiny enough that most people wouldn't have noticed. But most people aren't Ph.D.-level students in everything *him*.

"Enough talk." I grip the bottom of my shirt and drag it up and over my head before dropping it to the floor, leaving me in my racer-back sports bra. Kicking the top to the side and out of my way, I deliberately loosen every muscle in my body. But I can't do a damn thing about the anticipation running rampant through me like I'm an overhyped kid in a candy store.

Anticipation and excitement. My body count as far as fights

is too high to remember, but one thing for certain, two things for sure . . . I've never gone up against anyone as skilled or deadly as this man. This beast.

Because I'm a self-admitted asshole and a lover of old Bruce Lee movies, I curl my fingers in a *let's get it* gesture.

He suddenly straightens, his shoulders rolling back. His eyebrows arrow down, and his stare is downright frightening. And sexy AF.

"What?" I drop my arms, slapping my thighs. "We fightin' or what?"

"Is that my shit?" he growls, and it's so delicious as it rolls over my bare skin that I almost forget what he's talking about. "Is that my chain around your neck?"

"Oh." I grin, brushing my fingers across the thick rope chain with the axe-shaped pendant that I happened to pilfer from his apartment the last time I visited. When he wasn't home. "Yeah. It's so nice. And I feel so much closer to you when I wear it."

Fury darkens his face, and I read my painful death in those eyes. If he only knew how that makes my pussy weep, he'd probably go around smiling like Pennywise the Clown when near me.

Flashing one last smile, I don't wait for him to make the first move. For two years, I've watched and waited. Finally touching and tasting him earlier was like breaking the seal on a dam already plagued with cracks and fissures. Now there's no shutting off this thirst, this unquenchable hunger for more. There's no locking it away again now that I've had his hard, disfigured flesh under my fingers and his blood on my tongue. While I have a reputation for being cold and interminably patient, with him, not so much.

With a flurry of jabs, cross punches, and side kicks, I attack, not holding back. He blocks me with a blur of motion, using my momentum against me by grabbing my wrist and flinging me against the wall. Wind whistles past my ear as his fist crashes into the space where my face was, crushing the drywall.

Oh goodie. He's not holding back.

That's so fucking hot.

Slipping to his side, I deliver a backfist to his temple, slightly turning his head away from me long enough to knee him in the gut twice. I'm not fast enough to dodge the elbow he sends flying back toward me, and it slams into my mouth, gouging my teeth into the soft flesh of my inner lip. Blood floods my tongue, and I grin at him, catching the narrowing of his eyes seconds before he whirls around and we face off against each other. With not a little bit of satisfaction, I notice the line of crimson trickle down from his cheekbone where my ring must've cut him.

This time we charge at each other, and when we clash, it's like a clap of thunder in the room. I rain down blows center mass and at his throat. Again, he blocks them, returning punch for punch. Bobbing and dodging each one, I latch on to his arm and, sharply twisting, flip him over my shoulder. His huge body slams onto the floor, and I swear the whole damn house shudders.

Before I can drop on top of him, my arm crossed over my chest to crash into his windpipe, he pulls his hips up, flattening his hands by his ears, then uncoils that big body and lands on his toes.

Well. Damn.

My momentary distraction costs me.

His boot lands in the center of my chest, piledriving the air from my lungs and flipping me over my couch. Pain radiates through me as my back and tailbone slam into the floor. For a second, I'm stunned. But just for a second. Because he's leaping over the couch, and at the last moment, I roll, just missing his feet landing on top of me.

Gritting my teeth against the pain, I dart to the side and grip the outer edges of the coffee table. Picking it up, I swing it like a Louisville Slugger. The wood doesn't crack when it strikes his back, but it stuns him enough that he lists to the side. Dropping the table, I run a couple of steps, kick my rear foot, and land a flying punch to his jaw. The power of the impact sings up my arm like a discordant melody, but my gratification at his head snapping back is extremely short-lived as he cuffs my wrist and tosses me across the room.

He stares at me, those cold, narrowed eyes promising me death.

And I stare right back.

I flick my gaze to my Glock on the shelf in back of him.

His goes to the gun behind me.

For a long moment, we don't move.

And then we're in motion at the same time, in a race to see who can grab their weapon first and fastest.

"Do it," I invite with a bloodstained smile. And I even lean into the barrel pointed at my forehead. The gun in my hand doesn't waver, trained at his head. "Go ahead. We can go together on the count of three. Or . . ." I slowly draw my Glock back and raise my other hand, palm out in a temporary white flag. "You can hear me out and then try to kill me later?"

He hikes a dark eyebrow.

I frown. "Yeah, mu'fucka, I said '*try*.'" Shaking my head, I tsk-tsk. "I swear, the shit is true. Give you an inch, you try to take a mile. I still got your dick on my breath, but don't think I'ma let you punk me. I got another coffee table and bullet with your name on it."

He mugs me, but after a long, tense moment, he eventually lowers his arm, taking the gun with him. I notice he doesn't put the safety back on. Smart man. Neither do I.

"Just a heads-up," I say, poking the corner of my mouth and wincing at the soreness. Peeping the blood dotting my fingertip, I wipe it across my hip. "Abena knows you didn't get the job done. I'd watch your back for the next little while. She's a vindictive li'l bitch when she doesn't get her way."

He doesn't utter a word, but something quick and cold flashes in those silver eyes. And I'm reminded of a rabid wolf in the wild with its prey caught in its sights. There's death there. Death and pain.

I cock my head. "Oooh. You already figured that out. What happened?" I pop up a finger. "Lemme guess. She had somebody waiting on you when you got home."

"How do you know that?" he growls, his voice like a rusty old engine.

It sends shivers racing down my spine on feet of pure fire. Just remembering how that serrated voice demanded I lick his blood and do it a-fucking-gain has my pussy leaking into the seat of my underwear.

"Know what?"

"That she was waiting for me." Menace rolls off him as he steps toward me, and I swear, a part of me does fucking snow angels in all that beautiful hate. "Do you know the location of my house?"

Of course I do. Like I said, the better question would be what *don't* I know about him. But common sense and a strong sense of self-preservation urge me to keep that question to myself. Still . . . where's the fun in that?

"Sure do."

"And did you tell your aunt where I stayed?" he asks, that voice somehow becoming deeper, rougher . . . deadlier.

I ball my face up, offended. "Hell nah. You might want to weed out the rat in your circle for whoever delivered that info to her. But it wasn't me. I wouldn't give that ho a cold, much less intel."

I squint at him as anger crawls through me. Not so much at his accusation as the thought of someone betraying him. I mean, yeah, we still got beef—he did try to kill me as recently as two minutes ago—but he's mine. Doesn't matter if he or anyone else knows it. And whoever gave him up to Abena now got more than the Huntsman on their ass. They got me, and they might want to start going to altar call now to pray that he finds them before I do. Because he has a reputation for quick, emotionless kills.

Me? Not so much. I'm all about taking my time and emoting.

"Now, how did I know she was waiting on you? I didn't. Well, not for sure. It was a guess because that's what she does. Ambushes people where they're most comfortable to catch them with their guard down. Mainly because she's a fucking bum bitch and coward. But . . ." I tilt my head. "I *am* shocked that she actually showed up to handle the deed herself."

He grunts, and in that monosyllabic note, I read, *As the fuck if*.

"*Oh*, of course." I nod. "She just showed up to gloat. Abena did the same shit with my mother, y'know. Couldn't resist wallowing in her handiwork even though she didn't have enough pussy to pull the trigger herself."

My tone is light, but inside . . . inside, the rage and hatred for my aunt coil and rattle like a venomous snake. They've seeped into my veins, my blood, for so long that my organs pump them throughout my body, giving me breath, giving me life.

"She had my mother—her sister—murdered. I'm sure you've heard the rumors. It's like the worst-kept secret that no one will admit out loud even though we all know it's true. She had my mother gunned down in the street like a sick dog in Mwuaji territory, where she should've been safest. And then, moments later, Abena happened to show up, standing over her body."

That night is branded into my head; there's no escaping it. I still wake up with the pop of those shots ringing in my head. The harsh scent of cordite in my nose even though I know it's impossible for me to have smelled it with the distance separating me from my mother. Can still feel the rain dampened air on my face.

Can still see Abena's slim hand tremble as it covered her mouth that was wide in horror and disbelief . . . But her eyes . . . her eyes told a different story. There wasn't terror or shock darkening that wide gaze. Then, I was too numb myself to dissect the emotion. Only days later, while standing across from her over Ma's elegant and majestically adorned body in her glass casket, did I decipher what I'd glimpsed in her dark eyes:

Triumph.

That's when I knew two things beyond a shadow of a doubt.

One, she'd had my mother—her sister, our queen—murdered so she could supplant her as ruler of the Mwuaji.

And two, I would one day kill her.

"That doesn't have shit to do with me," he says, his dispassionate words and tone tearing me from the past. Part of me wants to go for his throat for it. "All I care about is that she tried that shit with me. And for that she's going to die. Both of you are."

"Seriously?" I arch an eyebrow. "You're that much a stickler for the rules that you're going to honor a contract after she came for your ass?" I snort. "I bet they just loved you down at the playground."

"I wouldn't fucking know."

Silence congregates between us like gossipy bitches, and I just manage to lock down my wince. Shit. If anyone's aware of his background, it's me. Hell, I might be the only one. And that shit I just said was callous as a muthafucka. Not that I did it on purpose, but still . . .

"Malachi . . ."

"Don't call me by that fucking name," he growls, taking another step toward me.

Then another. And another. Until he's so close that his leather-and-skin scent wraps its gunmetal cold hand around my throat. His size dwarfs me, but I'm sure if he suspected what he meant as an intimidation tactic only has my nipples beading tight under my bra and my pussy contracting like it's in the middle of a coronary, he'd back up until his spine hit the opposite wall. "That's my last time warning you."

"Or what?"

No, really, I'm curious.

He edges closer, and that wide, rock-hard chest brushes my breasts. There's no way he can't feel the effect he has on me, but kudos to him, he doesn't even glance down to get himself a look. That kinda discipline is hot as fuck. How would he use that if we fucked? Would he be as focused, as controlled? Or with me, would he allow himself to lose it?

I can't decide which thought entices me more.

"Or I use that knife behind you to cut that little tongue from your mouth and tuck it in my pocket like loose change so you don't have a choice."

I close my eyes, and even if I wanted to, I can't restrain the hum that rumbles from my chest or the shiver that rolls through my body. "I love it when you talk dirty to me," I whisper, lifting my lashes. "If you want me to drop to my knees and get out my knife again, just say that."

His jaw does that little flex-and-jump thing again, as if he's literally chewing on another threat to my life.

"Where's your aunt?"

He bites off the words as if he would be rather biting off my head.

I chuckle and shift backward. Is it so I can inhale a breath that isn't infused with his scent and can concentrate on something other than how he sounds when he comes?

Maaaaybe.

"Why? I should let you beat me to the prize? Nah, yo. If anyone's going to take that bitch's life, it's me. Tell you what, though: I'll mail you a body part. Give you a li'l souvenir since you're obviously into that." I wrinkle my nose and contemplate him like getting him here wasn't part of my plan in the first place. Well . . . after the blow job and not shooting him in the face. The plan that came to me on the way home from the cottage. "Unless . . ."

I lick my lips because I'm about to play a very dangerous game. Up until now I've been toying with the Huntsman—because I can. But what I'm about to do now . . . It isn't the Huntsman I'll be dealing with but Malachi Bowden. And it's him who may decide to kill me.

It's him I may have to kill.

A tingle tickles an empty space behind my rib cage, and I almost lift the hand still holding my Glock to rub it.

"What's the saying, Huntsman?" I ask. "Enemy of my enemy

and all that?" He doesn't reply but continues to stare at me, his body unmoving. "You might not care about my mother being killed by Abena, but do you care about yours?"

Almost every reaction of his up until this moment has been cold, calculated, nearly imperceptible. But not this one. At the mention of his dead mother, it's damn near volcanic.

In a burst of movement, he lunges at me, his beautiful features twisted in a terrifying mask of fury, skin pulled tight over those sharp cheekbones until they appear to be slashing through his golden flesh.

I jerk up my arm, and only the press of my barrel against his forehead prevents him from colliding into me. From crushing me to the floor or into the wall.

Doesn't prevent him from wrapping his huge hand around my throat and squeezing. Or jamming his own gun under my chin.

No woman, man, or god puts fear in me. But I'm looking into the nearly black eyes of a demon. Of the monster they call him. So a tiny trickle of alarm worms its way through my belly. But that's not the dominating emotion.

No.

Pain.

For him.

For me.

For motherless children.

Yet I don't drop my weapon.

Because Aisha Diallo didn't raise no fool.

"You pull that trigger, you don't find out what I know," I lowly remind him.

"Talk. Now."

Neither one of us lowers our Glocks, but I have great arm strength, and it won't be the first time I've held a conversation at gunpoint.

"Twenty-four years ago, Abena hired a mercenary by the name of Ghoul for a job. I don't know if you've heard of him;

only reason I have is because my mother told me about him when I was thirteen," I say, not waiting for him to answer. "Apparently, he was legendary in her and my grandmother's time, but by the time I was a teen, he wasn't talked about anymore. For good reason. He'd become a cautionary tale. And that's the only reason Ma told me the story."

"Eshe," he snaps.

"Ghoul worked for a shadow organization of assassins. They didn't have allegiance to any one family, only to money."

"You mean the organization Creed."

I nod. Well, as much as I can with a gun jammed under my chin.

"Yeah." I've always wondered if the Huntsman worked for them. It's the one thing I could never discover about him. "Abena contacted Creed for the job, and they assigned the hit to Ghoul. Even among mercenaries, he was revered. He never failed, never missed. But it's said when he discovered what the job entailed, he refused to do it. See, Abena wanted the son of a rival family murdered. But not just him—his pregnant wife, too. They used to be lovers, but he dumped her when he fell in love with another woman and married her. Finding out they were having a baby was the last straw for her, and she wanted both of them dead. Didn't fucking matter that she could've started a gotdamn war over that shit; she wanted revenge over not being chosen. And she wonders why my grandmother appointed Ma to be her successor."

I shake my head, disgusted.

"I thought Abena was the oldest. That could be why she believed she would be queen," he says, his tone begrudging, as if he hates even voicing it. Hates being invested in my story.

Again, I shake my head.

"We don't work like that. We are matriarchal, but the Mwuaji isn't a hereditary monarchy. The reigning queen chooses her successor from the strongest, most capable leader. The majority of the time, that's from her daughters, but not necessarily. Abena was the oldest daughter, and yeah, she felt entitled to the crown and hated my mother for receiving it. But when she did something like put a hit on the heir to a family for some petty bullshit, it was crystal clear why to everybody but her."

"So your aunt's a petulant bitch. I still don't see what this has to do with my mother."

"Don't you?" I pause, but when he doesn't say anything, I sigh. "Ghoul was your father. And—"

"You're a fucking lie." The words are barely a murmur, but from the shove of tendons in his neck against his skin, they might as well have been roared.

He drops his arm, the Glock disappearing from under my chin and his hand from around my throat. Though no sound emanates from him, he stalks across the room like a wild animal let loose from its cage after years of confinement. His long, powerful legs eat up the space of the room, and when he reaches the opposite wall, he rears back an arm and rams a fist through it. Drywall and dust coat the air. The blow doesn't seem to release the storm of rage and pain inside him. No, if anything, he goes harder.

The gun falls to the floor, and he drives his other hand through the wall. Blow by blow, he punishes my den wall until plaster litters the floor at his feet.

I'm already itching to clean that up.

I would almost rather he yelled, howled his agony at the ceiling. Not that I give a flying fuck about my wall. It's just . . . hearing it would've been less painful than that violent yet utterly silent display.

Finally, he stops, and his shoulders heave up and down, his heavy, labored breaths the only sound in the room. When he whips around, pinning me with his arctic glare, I don't move, somehow suspecting that one unwise motion would set him off, and neither one of us would survive it.

"You're a fucking lie," he repeats on a growl so low, so guttural, it's nearly indecipherable.

Instead of contradicting him, I tilt my head.

"The Ghoul, also known as Mordechai Bowden, born March

24, 1970, to Denis and Maria Bowden, first-generation Russian immigrants who changed their name from Lebedev to escape persecution. Mordechai married Sharon Bowden, formerly Williams, an Afro-Latina woman from Rosedale, New York. They moved to Boston in the late nineties. Had two children, a son, Malachi, and a daughter, Miriam, born five years apart."

Nothing in his face softens, but . . . something glints in his eyes. Something that seems almost vulnerable.

Damaged.

"He became known as Ghoul in 1990 and joined Creed in 1995, but by then he'd racked up forty-six kills to his name." I cock my head. "Look at you. Following in your father's footsteps. You don't kill children either, do you, Huntsman?"

"But you're not a kid."

That almost makes me smile. Almost.

"You didn't know your father was a killer like you." It's not a question but a statement. I suspected it, but his reaction affirms that for me. "And like you, Abena had a bounty put on your father's head when he refused to carry out a hit."

He shakes his head. "That wouldn't've been her. Creed handles any failure on behalf of their assassins in only one way—death. *If* my father was this Ghoul, Creed would've killed him, Abena wouldn't have."

"True." I pause. "If only your father died when they first came for him," I say, ignoring his stubbornness in refusing to accept that Ghoul and Mordechai Bowden were one and the same. I don't know why it's so difficult for him to believe. Hell, look how he turned out. "But Abena doubled the price, requesting a hit not just on him but on his family—his wife, his son, and his daughter."

It's faint, but I catch the snag in his breath. The stiffening of his already-stone-hard body.

"From the story, he didn't make it home in time to hide his wife. Creed took him with a bomb to his car, but your mother had already left your home by the time they came for her, you, and your sister. She drove to Connecticut, hid you in plain sight in the foster care system under assumed names, then disappeared. But they eventually caught up with her, too. She was killed as she tried to cross over into New York a week later. And the rest you know. Miriam died—"

"Stop. Shut the fuck up. Shut the. Fuck. Up."

I do as he says. His baby sister is as sore of a subject for him as my mother is for me. Maybe more. Because Ma lived—she left behind a legacy. His sister died a baby without a chance to do, to fucking *be*. And, like me, he witnessed her death.

His chest rises and falls on silent but heavy breaths, and my fingers tingle and itch with the need to touch his chin, lift his head, and stare into those mercury-colored eyes. To bathe in that pain, that rage, that confusion. Where the Huntsman is known for betraying absolutely nothing, I want to gorge on his emotion. Consume it until I'm fat and sick on it.

"Do you believe me now?" I finally ask into the silence after several moments.

He raises his head, and a lesser person would recoil under that flinty stare. But that ain't me, and never has been. I was forged in the same fire as him.

"How do you know all this? Where did you get all this info about my family?" he asks.

I shrug, not about to admit that he became my obsession long ago. It was my mission to learn everything about him—from his favorite meal to his favorite way to kill to how he became the Huntsman. Who created him. Little did I know the seeds of this obsession had been created long ago, when my mother relayed that cautionary story about the Ghoul. She'd told me it so I would heed the unstable bomb that was my aunt.

No way she could predict she'd germinate a fixation on the son of that tragic figure.

"I have my ways and sources. Does it matter, though? I'm a thief, murderer, criminal, and a whole list of other things, but I'm not a liar." I snicker, waving a hand. "Nah, I'm lying. I'm a liar, too. But this time, I happen to be telling the truth. And you have reasons to hate Abena—more than you thought. She stole everything from you. Just like she did me."

I move forward, taking a calculated risk and closing the distance between us, even though his expression warns me off. Advises me against it. Still, I keep going until the tips of my boots nearly bump up against his.

"I get you want to kill me, but shit, Huntsman, you came for me, so what did you expect me to do? And honestly? I spared your gotdamn life, so actually, you owe me. I'm the one who should be offended in this situation, not you." I mug him, and the more I talk, the hotter I get. The mu'fucka got some damn nerve. "But I'm willing to let bygones be bygones and work together to get what we both want. Which is Abena dead. If we do this, though, it's my way. I know her better than you. Know her routines, the way she thinks, her habits. So you follow my lead."

His mouth twists in a snarl before I even finish talking, and I sigh and mentally roll my eyes.

"The fuck you think this is? A partnership?" He chuckles, and it sounds like a rusty nail driven into dented metal. "Just because you relayed a bedtime story about some assassin that's supposed to be my father? In order for me to work with you, Eshe Diallo of the Mwuaji, I'd have to trust you, and I don't trust your li'l ass as far as that third fucking blind mouse could see you." He leans down so his nose pushes against mine and his breath pulses against my lips. "Fuck a bygone. And fuck you. We gon' have beef forever, mu'fucka. You chained me to a bed. You pulled a gun on me. You should've killed me when you had the chance, because the next time you're in my sight, I'm damn sure not gon' miss. You and your bitch-ass aunt. I haven't failed a mission yet, and I don't intend on breaking that record."

He straightens, then pinches my chin in a painful grip where his thumb presses my bottom lip against the ridge of my teeth. The faint tinge of blood taints my tongue.

"My jobs are never personal. But for you and your aunt? I'm making an exception."

Releasing me, he stalks past, ripping his Glock 26 from my hand. He collects all his weapons from the desk where he placed them before our fight and heads for the door that opens to the garage.

I frown.

"Ay. Where you going? You think you just gon' leave me? Nope. That's not how this works. I cut yo' dick. We go together. Real bad." I whip around, grab my dagger, and hurl it across the room. It flies over his shoulder and embeds in the wall. He stills. "I almost nicked you but decided against it. This is about punishment, not reward."

His shoulders damn near hover below his ears. Then he turns and faces me. Gotdamn. The *nothingness* of his expression only emphasizes the gray blue of his eyes. And in those eyes? Hatred. A promise of agonizing pain. Of death.

Yeah, I might've pushed him too far with that one. But ask me if I give a fuck. He's mine. He just don't know it yet.

"Go ahead and walk out that door, and do it knowing I'm not worried about you coming for me. It's 'if I don't see you first' in this bitch. See you soon, Huntsman." I wiggle my fingers at him in a little wave goodbye.

He stares at me for a long moment, and maybe I'm projecting, but he's probably imagining all the different ways he can take me out. A shiver runs through me, and part of me wants to ask him to run the list down like a bedtime story. Or pillow talk.

Finally, he silently turns, shoves the door open, and moves out into the garage, quietly shutting the door behind him. Leaving me alone in my den with my damaged wall and the scent of leather, gun oil, and sun-kissed skin behind him.

Slowly, a smile curves my lips.

The man threatened me. By rights I should be headed to the safe behind my closet wall and arming myself to the teeth and calling in all manner of reinforcements.

Instead of calling Tera and letting her know I'm good and she can turn around, I'm standing here, grinning. Anticipating the next time we see each other. The next time I'm in his sights.

He promised to kill me.

I can't wait.

CHAPTER SIX

Eshe

The wind rushes past me as I bend low over my 'Busa, the motorcycle hugging the curve in the road bordered by the towering trees, their leaves changing colors with the advent of fall. Though the family's main headquarters for business is downtown Boston, the obodo—or the Mwuaji compound—is located in the quiet, picturesque suburb of Needham. Close enough to Boston where the city is easily accessible, but far enough away where the sprawled, mansion-like multipurpose complex is secluded and secure and surrounded by acres of land.

In minutes, I pull up to the tall iron gates with the elegant *M* embossed in the middle of each wide door. Leaning forward, I punch in a code and then place my palm on the scanner. Seconds later, the gates slowly open, and once they're just wide enough for me to fit through, I pull in, traveling up the long drive at a speed that's probably too fast and unwise. But I don't care. Every time I arrive here, ephemeral yet adamantium-strong shackles wrap around me, chaining me to this place. Stripping me of my freedom, of my choice. Of my voice. More and more I lose memory of when I was happy here, when I was carefree and . . . safe here.

In too short a time, the elaborate, expansive building that's the real heart of the Mwuaji family comes into view. In spite of my antipathy toward it, there's no denying its beauty. Marble white, it glistens like a huge jewel under the late-afternoon sun. Tall, proud columns line the front of the structure, black diamonds embedded like tears. The family coat of arms decorates each mammoth arched door—four squares with a panther, an ichthys, the baobab tree, and an apple. Ferocity, feminine power, family, and wisdom. The tenets we hold as sacred. Diamond-encrusted black shutters bracket the many windows adorning the front and sides of the walls. It's a testimony to the wealth of our family, the pride of it.

I park my motorcycle in front of the short marble flight of steps, even though Abena forbids vehicles barring the front of the building. She, of all people, don't get to tell me what to do. And I dare anyone to touch my shit. They not crazy.

Unlike me.

Just as I slip my phone from the pocket of my motorcycle jacket to send off a quick message to the Seven to let them know I'm here, the doors open, and they file out. I don't wonder how they knew I arrived. Given Nef's affinity for all things tech, she no doubt hit them up as soon as I drove through the gate. Ol' girl's been hacking into the obodo's security system since she was fifteen.

Tera, Penn, Tyeesha, Kenya, Maura, Nef, and Sienna descend the steps and form a circle around my bike. Without me having to say a word, they show up for me. It isn't about them being my personal guard. At least not all about that. It's about love, sisterhood, loyalty. The kind of loyalty Abena has never experienced and will never know from the people she surrounds herself with.

"You about to go up in here and start some shit. I can see it all over your face," Tera mutters. Yeah, she might sound like she's complaining, but that gleam in her eyes tells a different story. My girl would welcome some shit popping off.

I grin, neither confirming nor denying her accusation. C'mon though. I definitely plan to go in there and cut the fuck up.

I tilt my head, squinting at them. Stepping forward, I reach out and touch the necklace hanging around Penn's neck. A gold and diamond-encrusted pendant in the shape of an apple rests just between her breasts. All of them wear identical pieces.

"This is new."

Penn sucks her teeth. "Yeah, it is. A few days ago, Abena gifted all the kapteni these necklaces. We're supposed to wear them at all times."

"Seriously?" I raise my eyebrows.

"Seriously," all seven say like a chorus.

That's some shit. Abena isn't known for her generosity. Knowing her, the necklaces probably have bombs embedded in them.

"Hey, Tera told us about your run-in with the Huntsman at the cabin," Nef says in that even, damn-near-flat tone that gives nothing away. And unlike Tera, her eyes don't either. If we were going on a moonlit bike ride through the countryside or about to commit mass murder, she wouldn't show emotion one way or the other about either activity.

We're all sociopaths here should be our motto. Ooh. Maybe I could get us matching T-shirts and Glocks with that printed and engraved on them for Christmas.

Before answering Nef, I arch an eyebrow, and she flips her hand over down by her hip, revealing the tiny scrambler. Talking here isn't safe. Abena has cameras everywhere, and I wouldn't discuss what I wanted for dinner in these walls or on these grounds without some kind of protection.

"Yeah." I smile. "It was . . . memorable."

Tyeesha snorts. "Only you would call an attempted hit 'memorable.'"

"And hot." Kenya holds up a church finger. "Let's not pretend it ain't incredibly hot, too."

Tera sighs, while Maura and Penn cosign Kenya. Sienna gives her a high five.

"Something's wrong with you bitches." Tera shakes her head, lip curled. "Anyway, what's the plan with us walking up in here? Anything we should be aware of other than having your back and front?"

"Yeah. This is a game of chess with Abena. She knows as well as I do that the Huntsman isn't dead. But admitting that means she sent him after me in the first place. So I'm going in here to fuck with her and let her know that shit didn't work out the way she wanted it to. Since her focus will be on me and mine on her, I need all of you to keep an eye on everyone in that room. Study the faces. Take note of the expressions, the body language. Of who they're standing with. Our number of defectors is steadily growing, but we need more. And knowing who to watch and follow to see if we should approach is key. Step to the wrong person and all our asses are fucked."

"No doubt." Penn nods. "We got that."

"When we leave, Nef, stay behind."

I don't say any more than that, but I don't need to; she understands. When she wants to, Nef can be a ghost. She can move through a room and disappear, not be seen. The bitch makes Mata Hari look like an amateur. Any whispers, conversations, or possible plots, Nef would catch it all.

"A'ight." I crack my neck. "Let's get it."

After climbing the steps two at a time, I gain the porch and pull the doors open, walking through like my boy Aragorn popping up in Helm's Deep after being ridden hard and put away wet by some orcs. As soon as I step into the vast entryway with its crystal chandelier, black-and-white jeweled floor, and array of framed weapons mounted on the walls, I school my features into a blank mask and nod at the soldiers flanking the doors and standing at the entrance to the throne room. Large AR-15s and the triple-pointed crown branded into the side of their necks set them apart as the oba's special guard, and though I'm their olori, my fingers still itch with the need to reach for my gun.

Wait here until either I get back or Zuri comes for you. Me or Zuri, baby girl. No one else. And do not go back to the obodo. You understand me?

One of my mother's last orders whispers through my head as I scan the opulence of the place that should be the safest for me. That should feel like home. Instead that tingle in my hand gets stronger, and by sheer will do I not shift my hand behind me.

I never did find out why she didn't want me to return to the compound. And Zuri never did return for me. Matter of fact, Zuri didn't return, period. She disappeared. Which meant someone—Abena—had her taken out before Ma, or she had a hand in taking out my mother and went ghost afterward. Either way, I never saw Ma's right hand again, and my question will always go unanswered. Leaving me distrustful of this place, of the people I call family, because there had to be a reason Ma warned me not to go back . . .

Shaking my head to clear it of the memories, of the useless thoughts, I focus. Going into this den of snakes without a laser-sharp mind, even with my Seven at my back, would be like playing thumb wars with a fucking black widow. Dumb as fuck and deadly.

The sad part? Not sad as in *boo-the-fuck-hoo* but sad as in *bitch-ass pathetic*. Most of the people here in Abena's "court" aren't bad people. Damn sure not lazy or dumb as a bag of wet hair. Nah, most are earners or worked their way up to where they are now—kapteni over their own thriving crews, bringing in millions for the family. Most are charming, funny, and smart as hell. Or they're like me and have no choice but to be here, caged until they find some way to fight free.

No, it's the sycophants I despise. Those who all turned a blind eye to Abena assassinating my mother, pledging their loyalty to her and looking me dead in my fucking face as they offered me condolences for my mother's death even as they profited from it.

That kind of weakness, that kind of snake shit, is unforgivable.

And unforgettable.

And I got a memory like a gotdamn elephant.

The familiar rage and bitterness embed themselves in my chest like wire spikes, and giving the soldiers on guard a nod, I cross the foyer, my boots thudding on the marble. As I approach the throne room, the atmosphere shifts. It's small, the subtlest of ripples, like a tiny pebble thrown into a smooth, shallow pond, but I feel it. Tension invades my body, but years of discipline and

Bitch-I'm–Viola Davis–level acting prevent me from betraying it to the rubberneckers crowded in the room.

Fixing a smirk on my face, I slowly saunter past Abena's guard, meeting the gazes fixed on me, arching an eyebrow until some of those slide away, unable to hold my stare. Others smile while more give me cautious, wary stares, afraid to incur the wrath of Abena by appearing too friendly to her niece but not wanting to be out-and-out disrespectful because, well . . . dying 'n' shit.

"Hey, Auntie." Ah, RIP Erik Killmonger. He was the gift that kept on giving. I pause just in front of the steps leading up to that ridiculous-ass black chair, dais, and mirror. My mother and grandmother didn't need all this bullshit to remind people of their rank—their manner, their carriage, how they fucking ruled did all that, not some weak-ass relics. "You summoned." I dip into a deep, sweeping bow that is so courtly, it belongs in Versailles—and no one with a working brain cell would consider it respectful.

If petty had a face, that pretty-faced bitch would be moi.

"Eshe," Abena grits out. As she rises, I note her ringed fingers gripping the arms of her chair so tight, her light brown knuckles are damn near white. My smirk widens until I'm showing all thirty-two teeth. "Yes, I called you here. Two days ago."

I shrug, lifting my hands and pulling off my gloves. In my peripheral vision, I catch my Seven taking silent posts on either side of me. Abena doesn't miss them either, her full lips thinning and shoulders stiffening. But short of ordering them out of the room, there's nothing she can do about it. And if she demands they leave, then she would have to send everyone else out, too. The throne room is full of Mwuaji kapteni, not just mine.

Not my fault mine would air this muthafucka out and play hopscotch in the blood before the rest of them could even reach for their weapons.

"Sorry," I say, my tone all *mmm, not sorry*. "But I had a little unexpected, uh, business come up that I had to handle before I could come here. You know how it is."

I look her dead in the eye as I stuff my gloves in my jacket pocket. Because she gets *exactly* what I mean.

Her brow wrinkles, her mouth turning down at the corners. Oh, and I thought *I* was a brilliant actress. This ho might be Angela Bassett.

"And what business could possibly be more important than an audience with your queen? Because that's what I am, Eshe. I'm your aunt second and your oba *first*. And when I call you"—she leans forward, pinning me with a dark, glittering glare—"I don't care if God Himself has a burning fucking bush in your face, you tell Him to hold that goddamn thought and get here to see what your oba needs from you. Do we understand each other?"

Wheeew, shit.

I want to kill her.

I *need* to kill her.

Three point four seconds. That's all it would take for me to run up those black steps, snatch my karambit from its sheath, and slit her throat from ear to ear. No gun. No gun for her. I want to bathe in her blood. Want it coating my hands, my arms, staining my nail beds. I want to smell it, fucking taste it as it splatters my mouth and eyes.

I'm a monster. I've accepted that—I did long ago.

But for her, I'm willing to become something worse. Something so soulless, even monsters hide from it.

"Easy, Eshe. Easy," Kenya murmurs low enough that only I hear.

Her honeyed Southern drawl doesn't completely tame the bloodlust howling in my mind, but it does tug a leash, and the crimson film in front of my eyes slowly lightens to a pink. It's the gleam of satisfaction in Abena's dark eyes that douses the rest of the murderous rage that nearly consumed me and would have had me commit suicide by queen's guard. Because that's what it would've been. Make no mistake. I would've gotten Abena. But even with my Seven, I would die. There would be no saving me.

That's the law of the Mwuaji.

Assassination of a ruling queen means death.

Some days, though, I'm willing to accept that punishment. As long as it means taking Abena with me.

But then I remember my mother's wish and will for me.

You're going to be a gotdamn force to be reckoned with and a better oba than me and your grandmother.

Then, it doesn't matter what I want . . . doesn't matter that deep down, I don't feel worthy of oba, don't feel worthy of fucking breathing, much less following in my mother's footsteps . . . I have to keep fighting to give Aisha Diallo her dream, make sure her desire comes to pass.

"Do we understand each other, Eshe?" Abena snaps.

"Sure thing, Auntie," I practically purr.

"Good." She falls back in her gawdy chair, crossing her long leather-clad legs. "Now, like I asked the first time, what business was more important than attending your oba?"

"Auntie, you're not going to believe this, but"—I pause for effect because yeah, my ass is a whole drama queen in these streets—"I was attacked."

"What's new about that, Eshe? It's not like you have a shortage of enemies out here gunning for you." She smirks, and the room fills with murmurs of agreement and laughter.

Was that shit supposed to hurt my feelings?

"Now, now, Auntie. No need for flattery." I grin, and Sienna *badly* covers a snicker. "But I'm dead serious—no pun intended. Somebody must've put a hit out on me, because the Huntsman himself came after me."

I ignore the ripple of shock, various versions of "the fuck?" and rumblings that move through the throne room. I don't give a damn about none of that as I stare her right in her eyes, without blinking. Letting her see that I know the truth. Letting her see that by *somebody*, I mean her ass.

Letting her see that she just shot the first volley in a war that I have every intention of winning.

To her credit, nothing in those strong Diallo features betrays her thoughts. No, she waves my words off with a flick of her long fingers and a low chuckle that I'm certain tricks everyone watching into believing she's unbothered.

But they don't know her like I do.

They haven't studied every mannerism, every habit as if their lives depended on it—because mine does.

I have.

And just like when she stood over my mother's body nine years ago, her eyes betray her. The lashes lower slightly, but those dark eyes momentarily shift away from me, and I follow their direction.

Of course.

Her Mirror, who's never far from her side, glances at her. And for so quick a second that most would miss it, their gazes meet, communicate. I'm not most. And I can only imagine what that silent communication held.

"Do you really expect me to believe the Huntsman came for you? If that shit actually happened, you wouldn't be here to tell the story. That man doesn't miss. And as good as you believe yourself to be, you're not *that* damn good." She laughs again, and as expected, everyone joins her like the good lackeys they are. "Try again, Eshe."

"Now, normally, I would agree with you. Not about me not being that damn good, because"—I roll my eyes, scoffing—"c'mon, stop it. Yeah, I am. But I *would* usually agree with you about the Huntsman not missing his target. Yet there's a first time for everything. 'Cause here I am. Alive 'n' breathing 'n' shit. Still . . ." I scratch my temple, balling my face up as if in deep thought. "There's one thing I can't figure out for the life of me. I mean, I'll be the first to admit I can be a little . . . difficult. But the Huntsman? Like, who did I piss off that bad to put that mu'fucka on my ass?"

I shrug, glancing over at Tera and Nef as if they have the answers to my questions. But Tera shakes her head, and Nef just stares at me. Not that I expected an answer from her anyway. She's not a talker. Most people take her silence and refusal to meet their gaze as shyness. But most people also don't realize she's too busy seeking out vulnerable parts of their bodies in which to stick her favorite blade to speak or look at their faces. Their bad.

Abena heaves a sigh. "I'm bored. And not that I'm calling you a liar, Eshe, but—"

"My bad, Auntie. But no worries. My long story just got shorter. He showed up, tried to kill me, but I got the drop on him first, blah, blah, blah. I won't bore you with the details, but let's just say I didn't get a chance to ask him who put the bounty on my head, because I was too busy killing him. Ding-dong, the Huntsman is dead. Huh." I tap my bottom lip. "I think I like the sound of that. No wonder that shit is so catchy."

A deafening silence fills the throne room. The only sound is the wind from outside the building and the tree branches lightly scratching against the windows. There's not even the faintest sound of breath to break the consuming quiet. I don't turn around to take in the reactions of the others in the room.

No, my sole focus and rapt attention is centered on Abena. With a sick and perverse glee, I study every minute flicker of emotion she battles to conceal. Battles and fails.

Fury.

Shock.

And fine traces of fear.

Fury, because the Huntsman failed and I'm standing here when I shouldn't be.

Shock, because I'm announcing a bald-faced-ass lie that I killed the most feared assassin in our world, and she's aware of it but can't contradict me, because then she would be outing herself.

And fear, because she knows I'm as unpredictable and unstable as they come, and that scares the fuck out of her.

I smile, and damn if she doesn't flinch.

"You killed the Huntsman?" She lets out a loud crack of laughter. Shaking her head, Abena leans forward, her long fingers curled around the arms of her chair like claws. "You expect all of us to believe that you accomplished what no one before you has ever been able to? There's no way in hell—"

Her voice breaks off as I drag down the zipper of my jacket and reach inside, then pull out a balaclava and hold it up for her and everyone else in the room to see.

So what if after Malachi left my house last night, I broke into his house, entered the code I've seen him use countless times on the safe in his closet, and borrowed one of his signature balaclavas? Abena doesn't know that, and neither does anyone else here. As I hold up the black leather face covering with the pointed top that resembles the head of a crowned eagle, there can be no doubt that it belongs to the Huntsman.

And if I have the Huntsman's hood, then not only is my story about encountering the Huntsman true, then most likely so is my claim about killing him.

This time, the noise in the throne room is as thunderous as the silence that came before it. Shouts, curses, and even laughter punctuate the air. The words *bad bitch*, *just like her mother*, and *not to be fucked with* circulate among the kapteni and the soldiers. From the anger that steadily darkens Abena's eyes and stiffens her body, I can tell she hears each and every one.

This is exactly what she hoped to avoid by sending the Huntsman after me. What she intended to stamp out before the roots could take further seed and grow vines.

Admiration for me.

Loyalty for me.

Desire for me.

And yet, her actions have given me the opportunity to sow those very seeds of discontent into her own ground.

Without breaking her gaze, I approach the dais and climb the steps.

"Here you go, Abena." I offer her the balaclava with an almost-soft smile. "For you."

To those watching, it appears like a gift from a devoted subject. When in truth, it's checkmate.

She has no choice but to take it. Either that, or look like a sulky, petulant child in front of everyone in the room.

Or the bitter, jealous monarch that she is.

"I want you to keep that," I say, backing down the steps, my hand pressed to my heart. "It's a token and reminder that you'll never have to worry about the bogeyman coming after you."

No one but her and Ekon can see my smirk.

Oh, if looks could kill, I would be—shiiid. Who am I kidding? Abena couldn't take me if Grandma went back in time and fucked T'Challa. Now, her Mirror . . .

Other than me and my Seven, he's the only other real predator in the room. The kapteni, soldiers . . . they're dangerous, absolutely. Hell, all Mwuaji are. It's why we aren't to be fucked with, not just because we run weapons and drugs. We defend ours—territory, product, reputation, family—with a viciousness that has instilled fear in the hearts of many mu'fuckas in these streets.

But still, they aren't on the same level as *us*.

I don't include Abena in our category.

She's only dangerous because her stupidity and greed know no bounds.

What makes her truly lethal is the soulless and unfailingly faithful killer she has at her side.

When I was fourteen, he showed up at the obodo, a damn-near-emaciated sixteen-year-old with haunting blue eyes who didn't speak for months. But he followed Abena around, never leaving her side. Ma told me Abena found him in a brothel, dirty, starved, and bleeding from being used in whatever way the clients wanted to get their shit off—beatings or fucking. The madam there made the mistake of thinking Abena fell into the category of desiring that kind of perversion. My aunt is many things, but a pedophile ain't one of them. She tortured the fuck out of everyone there, then had the house torched to the ground.

To my knowledge, there isn't a sexual relationship between Abena and Ekon. No, the bond connecting them goes much deeper than fucking. He would slit his own throat for her just after tearing out the heart of anyone who came for her.

Present company included.

That kind of devotion and the utter emptiness in his startlingly bright gaze makes him the second most dangerous person in the room.

I wink at him.

And he stares at me, unblinking.

I have no doubt he knows Abena sent the Huntsman after me. There's no secret she has that he isn't aware of. No order she's issued that he hasn't carried out. No body she's laid out that he didn't put there in the first place.

"Well." I clap once. "This has been fun." Not. "But I gotta get out of here. Fight night, y'know. Attempted murder and murder always get my blood pumping. I hope to see you there, Auntie."

With a mock salute, I pivot sharply on my heel, but my name halts me.

"Eshe." Abena waits until I turn back around to face her, and though fury still darkens her eyes, a smile curves the dark red slash of her mouth. "Aren't you forgetting something?"

I tilt my head, waiting. Nah. I didn't forget shit. But obviously she thinks I did.

"You didn't bow before your oba before you left. Bow, Niece."

Hatred chokes me as we stare at each other, and just as she doesn't hide the triumph gleaming in her eyes, I'm sure I telegraph the rage seething in mine.

I'd rather disembowel myself with a rusty spork than bow to this bitch, but to disobey a direct order would be outright disrespect at best, treason at worst. And the twitch at the corner of her mouth relays that she's enjoying this. Enjoying knowing that it's killing me a little to genuflect to a woman I despise.

But I don't have a choice.

Not for now.

But even if it'll mean both of our blood coats that fuckery of a chair, she'll pay.

For this.

For my mother.

For everything.

Grasping a hold of that thought, I bow so fucking deep at the waist, the cast of fucking *Bridgerton* could take notes.

And moments later, when I straighten and meet Abena's gaze, neither one of us is smiling.

This time, when I turn around and stride out of the throne room, she doesn't stop me. No one does. As I clear the doors, my kapteni follow, joining me in the foyer. We all remain silent as the soldiers at the front doors pull them open, and we exit the compound.

"That shit had to hurt," Maura says, stating the obvious in her airy, cheery voice that belongs to a gotdamn Disney princess, not a murderer.

Penn backhands Maura across her chest, and the freckle-faced, petite redhead winces.

"Well, fuck. Ouch."

Sighing, Penn pulls a pair of gloves from her back pocket. "What next, Eshe?"

"Let's meet."

That's all I need to say as I jerk on my own gloves and stalk toward my bike. Up until now, we've been moving slowly, chipping away at the foundation of Abena's empire. But the moment she sent the Huntsman after me, *slow* got drop-kicked out the window. Fuck slow. We're moving full force ahead with our plan to get that bitch off the throne. I don't even need to close my eyes to see my mother's deep crimson blood staining that sidewalk like an oil spill. And that blood still cries out for justice, for revenge. Those needs follow me into my sleep. Only more spilled blood will appease them. Abena's blood.

And I'm just the person to do it.

I'm the *only* person to do it.

Minutes later, the eight of us roll down the isolated obodo road, three of us on motorcycles and the rest in cars. As I pull up to the gate, that reflexive instant of panic flares within me as it's done since I was sixteen. I'm waiting on the day when those big iron sentinels won't open, trapping me on this compound.

I don't know what I fear most.

Being trapped or dying.

But today isn't that day, and as they slowly ease open, I release a low, heavy breath and hit the throttle, taking off as if demons unleashed from the pits of hell are on my rear wheel.

"I can't believe that bitch. She's got to fucking go." Nef's flat statement rings in the thick silence of my living room, and from the grim faces on the other six women gathered, they all agree with the sentiment.

I know I sure the fuck do.

I just played the recording that Laura gave me for my Seven, and their reactions match mine. Disgust. Fury. Betrayal.

Just when you thought Abena couldn't sink any lower, that bitch hit hell.

Kenya raises her hand as if she's in a classroom waiting to be called on. "So, we taking that ho out, right?"

"Is Lion-O the hottest ThunderCat?" I shoot back.

Kenya scrunches her face. "Nah. That's Panthro with that big-dick energy."

I blink. "Get out."

"Okay, okay." Tera holds up a hand toward me, palm out. "We have an assassination to plan. Focus."

I mug Kenya. "I don't even know who you are right now." Tearing my gaze away from her, I roll my shoulders. "A'ight. I'm ready."

For the next hour, we lay out a strategy for tomorrow night.

It's short notice, but we're all professionals here. Highly motivated professionals.

"Good." Tera lifts a shot of Patrón to her lips, taking a sip. "Now that's settled, but we still have the match to get straight. The lineup's good. We got Dane Graves versus Black Knell as the main event."

"That's gon' be a beautiful fight." Tyeesha nods her approval, tipping her Sam Adams beer to her mouth. "Both have undefeated records, and their fighting styles are a damn-near-perfect match. The downside? At the end of it, we're going to be down one good-ass fighter," she observes with the calm and clinical reason that's earned her the nickname Doc. Well, reason and the beautiful precision that she uses while performing torture.

She's not wrong though.

I run Elysian, the underground fight club, that's just one of my rackets in the family. It's an equal-opportunity space. People of all socioeconomic and geographical statuses rub shoulders in the waterfront warehouse. Just as anyone, whether born with a silver spoon in their mouth or pushed out of their mother's pussy in a crack house, can get their ass in the ring and fight. All that matters is money and skill. Because those are the only two things that will keep you alive and winning in Elysian.

Especially since our fights are to the death.

Only one person walks out of that ring. The other is carried out.

"Yeah, but the bets have been rolling in since this morning when we sent out the message with the lineup. We're already looking at three million, and it's just three o'clock. By the time we open the doors, we most likely will have hit the ten-million mark," I say, twirling my own glass of Patrón, staring down into the gold depths. "Boston is full of Dane Graveses and Black Knells."

Cold as fuck? Yeah, but still true.

"Abena just sent word that she's not attending." Sienna glances up from her iPad, her hazel scrutiny landing on me. Setting the device next to her on the wide arm of the recliner, she leans forward, propping her elbows on her thick thighs. "So what's the plan from here?"

"And while we're discussing that, bitch, where in the *hell* did you get that mask? It looked authentic, and I know you didn't really kill the fucking Huntsman," Kenya tacks on.

"I got my ways." I shrug, taking a sip. "And yup, it's real as fuck."

"Okay, okay, keep your secrets. Just know, I have my own ways of finding them out." Kenya narrows her eyes, jabbing a finger at me, then back at herself before pounding a fist into her open palm.

"You better tell her." Penn points in Kenya's direction, nodding.

Lightly snorting, I set my tumbler down on the glass end table, next to the necklace Tera stripped from her neck as soon as she stepped in my house. All of them did, as if they couldn't wait to shed the stink of Abena off them. I get that shit. I study each face of my Seven before pushing up from the couch and stalking across the living room until I reach the tall, nearly floor-to-ceiling window on the far wall.

The view of the surprisingly domestic and pretty street with its towering trees, softly lit windows, and kids' bikes left in driveways looks innocuous enough. But buying a house on this particular street in this particular neighborhood was the point. Any onlooker can't tell that this cookie-cutter home is heavily wired and armed with a damn-near-impenetrable security system that Nef had installed.

Well, impenetrable except for a certain Huntsman.

"Here's what I want to know," Maura says. "Yeah, Tera let you know that Abena had sent the Huntsman after you. But you didn't know *when*. So how did you figure out when he was pulling up so you could get the drop on him?"

"Y'all never fail to clown me about that tracker I put on his car, but thanks to my forethought, I was able to get the drop on him first," I say, still staring out at the rapidly turning gold and red leaves that have started falling on my front lawn.

"Forethought." Maura snickers. "That's what we're calling it now."

I don't share the details of chaining him to the bed or having his dick in my mouth. They know of my two-year . . . fascination with him, but they don't know how deep it runs. They see it as some crush to tease me about, not as my obsession. But hell, how can I explain something to them that is sometimes hard for me to understand? How do I describe this need I have for this man that defies logic or common decency? I have no boundaries when it comes to him, and all I can say is that from the moment I saw him for the first time, my soul—as dirty and damned as it is—called out to him. No, cried out. Maybe like recognized like. Feral recognized feral. Sinner recognized sinner.

I don't fucking know.

He's mine.

He's mine like no one else has ever been. Not even my mother.

She belonged to the family as well as me. I had to share her, her time. The oba was everyone's equally.

But Malachi? He belongs only to me.

Even if he doesn't accept it.

Fortunately, that's not a prerequisite.

For some reason, I've held back on sharing that with my girls, though it makes no sense. Not when I tell these women everything.

Well, almost everything.

Without my overt permission, I rub my thumb over the smooth flesh where my right pinkie used to be.

"Who knew stalking could save a life?" Kenya snickers.

"I did." I shrug and turn around to face them. "But there's something I didn't tell you. I kind of let you assume that the Huntsman slipped away from me. The truth is . . . I had him . . .

I mean really had him. My gun aimed at his forehead. All I had to do was pull the trigger." I pause, and instead of the leaves skipping in the wind, I see Malachi—not the Huntsman—and those mercurial gray-blue eyes glaring up at me, unblinking . . . accepting his death as I pointed my Glock at his forehead. "But I didn't."

"Say what now?" Tera barks, dropping her feet from the coffee table in front of her to the floor and straightening. "Run that shit back by me. You had him? You had the fucking Huntsman dead to rights—the key word here being '*dead*'—but you didn't kill him?" She shakes her head so hard, her brown bangs swish across her dark brown skin. "Nope. I said that shit aloud and it still doesn't make sense. Now I know you have this crush on him and shit, but the mu'fucka did come there to *murder yo' ass*. You're damn right I believed he escaped or maybe even you two got into it but he still got away. But not ever did it cross my fucking mind that you *let him go*. Because that would mean you deliberately allowed *the deadliest assassin in our world* to live so he could return and have another shot at *murdering you*. Explain that shit to me. Please."

Even though Tera spoke, all of them watch me with varying degrees of disbelief. Even Nef, who usually doesn't display any emotion at all.

Thrusting my fingers through my hair, I grip the curls and tug, letting the pinpricks of pain flaring across my scalp center me, help me focus my thoughts. Folding my arms across my chest, I lean back against the wall and meet each of their gazes.

"I don't know," I answer honestly. When Tera scoffs, throwing back the rest of her Patrón, I shove down my own burst of anger. "Shit, I'm telling the truth. I don't know. Maybe I thought by sparing him, I would make him owe me, and I'd have a favor from the Huntsman." *Lie.* Not shooting him in the face was so much more complicated than that. So much more . . . primal and *raw* than that. "But that came back to bite me in the ass when he showed up at my house and we fucked up my den fighting. Now he just wants to kill me and Abena. Because that stupid bitch thought it was a great idea to try and murder him for failing to complete the hit."

I still have to shake my head at the gotdamn *audacity* of that shit. If the move weren't so blatantly suicidal, I might applaud her pluck.

"Hol' up, hol' up." Maura stands, waving both hands in front of her face. "Let me get this straight. After you give this mu'fucka a Get Outta Hell Free card, instead of being grateful, he really *did* come back around and try to kill you? I mean, I know that's the assassin's creed or some shit, but yo, that's ungrateful as fuck. And that's *after* Abena does a double cross and comes for his head? I hope he didn't give that ho her money back," she grumbles.

"Yep, that about covers it."

I'm glad she agrees with me that Malachi is being pretty unreasonable and ungrateful, too.

Tuh. Men.

"So how did you really get his balaclava?" Doc asks. "Come on and spill it. No more of that 'have your ways' bullshit."

I grin. "A little B and E. Since Abena broke into his place earlier, I doubted he would return to it. So I figured it was safe to get in there, borrow one of his hoods, and use it to shore up my story about killing him."

"I'm still confused as fuck why you didn't actually kill him. Especially since that means you now have to worry about two targets on your back," Nef quietly says. "But I also have to say, taking that balaclava was genius. She might know he's not dead, but she can't contradict you without saying how she knows. And now word's spreading through not just the Mwuaji but other families about how you took down the Huntsman, making you a living legend. Abena fucked herself."

Yeah, she did. In more ways than one.

If Abena believes I didn't get the mental brutality she tried to inflict when she sent Malachi after me . . . She took my kidnapping, one of the most traumatizing and triggering events of my life, and attempted to send me spiraling back there before having my life taken.

Earlier, I said she wasn't one of the most dangerous people in the room.

I revise my opinion.

Because that capacity for sadism shouldn't be underestimated.

That she would seek to do that to me when it was her fucking incompetence and carelessness that allowed me to be kidnapped in the first place nine years ago . . . Ma had entrusted Abena with my detail, as the family's security had fallen under my aunt's responsibilities at the time. Ordinarily, I wouldn't have needed more than one or two guards, but since I was on my way to a concert, Ma ordered more security. But Abena forgot to arrange it. And I, being an impatient teenager concerned only with shaking my ass in front of one of my favorite artists, left, giving my guards no choice but to follow me. And I was taken as soon as I hit Boston city limits.

For two weeks, I was starved, beaten, tortured while my mother hunted my captors down. Even as traumatized as I was after my rescue, I didn't miss the coldness between Ma and Abena. A part of me always wondered if one of the reasons Abena had my mother murdered was fear of Ma striking against her first because she blamed her sister's neglect for my kidnapping.

In the end, the why doesn't matter.

The only thing that does is my mother's death and her blood that coats Abena's hands.

"You do know your aunt's going to come for you again, right? She'll have to be sneakier about it since two attempts on your life so close together will be suspect as hell. But she's not going to stop," Penn points out.

"Penn's right." Tera picks up her glass again and squints at me. "Listen, we've been moving in the shadows for the last two years, slowly and quietly bringing more people to our side, forming alliances. And shit, truth be told, Abena has been doing most of the heavy lifting for us. People are tired of her digging too deep in their pockets, taking a higher percentage of their shit. She's getting richer just sitting on her royal ass while everyone under her is doing all the actual work, taking all the risk. But, shit, we could still argue that's what you do for family. But what you don't do is fuck family over. Promote those who kiss your ass, curry your favor, while stealing and doing dirty those who are earners, those who prove their loyalty. Those who would lay down—and have laid down—their lives for blood before belief. Those who get sent up, never turn, and when they come back out, don't receive recognition for their sacrifice, much less a fucking penny for them or their families."

Tera surges to her feet, her glass still clutched in her hand. She stalks across the floor toward the built-in bar, and with stiff, jerky movements unlike her usual fluid, menacing grace, she splashes more alcohol into the tumbler. We silently watch her, not needing to peek into her head or those bottomless black eyes to comprehend she's thinking about her own family.

Park Washington went away for first-degree murder when Tera was seventeen. He'd been one of the most feared and prolific enforcers for the family, and Tera's father, whom she loved with all the worship saved for superheroes and Prince. This was a hit Park hadn't committed, and the cops knew they didn't have shit on him, but since Park wouldn't turn, they sent him away for the murder anyway.

All he asked was that Abena take care of his wife and kids. Of course, she assured him she would . . . and that promise lasted as long as it took for the gavel to land, pronouncing him guilty. He'd been sentenced to life without parole, and all the income that should've been going to Tera's mother and family laced Abena's pockets. In her words, there were no free rides. That's when Tera jumped off the porch, following in her father's footsteps. We'd been best friends long before then, but to provide for her family, she came to work for me. As her best friend, I know Tera once had dreams that didn't include . . . this. She's fucking good at it. One of the best. But her father wanted more. Hadn't wanted blood on his baby girl's hands. At the time of her father's trial, she held an early acceptance letter to Yale, where she intended to major in history education.

History education.

Abena had a lot of shit to answer for.

Family was the core of who we were. It made us more than an organization or a gang. It was *everything*. And Abena was fracturing us from the inside out.

"She's going to pay, Tera," I murmur, studying her stiff shoulders. "Her attempt on me speeds up the timeline and places us in a better position. Abena is smart, but she's also sloppy, arrogant. She's gotten comfortable and believes she's above the law of her own family. No one is. Doc, where are we with Richter and Moorehead?" I ask, mentioning the two kapteni with territories in Buffalo, New York, and Niagara Falls.

"They sent word while you were at the cottage. Off the strength of your mother, they're with us."

I nod, not tripping.

The two OGs have been around, ruling their areas, since Ma's time. Backing me out of respect for her name and memory is one of the highest forms of regard they could give me. Though I've been pulling my weight for the Mwuaji, making my mark, once I'm oba, it will be up to me to prove they've made the right choice in indulging in something as dangerous and risky as treason.

I'll live up to that faith.

Theirs and the same faith my mother placed in me.

"Bisa and Taraji are also in," Tera says, turning around, setting her glass down on the bar behind her. Her body loses some of her tension, and I bet it's due to the slightly fanatical gleam in her dark eyes. "Both of them came up under Dad, and they don't give a fuck about 'forgive and forget' when it comes to him. And Dad told me to tell you he got you."

I nod again, but under my folded arms, my fingers fist so tight, my nails bite into the tender skin of my palms. Having the support of Bisa and Taraji is big as fuck. Their influence reaches not just among the ranks of our soldiers but to other families as well, since they control the harbor and anything that comes through it—guns, drugs, art, animals. Anything but people. We don't do that fuck shit. So yeah, having them at my back? It's major.

But Park Washington? Knowing he's "got me"? Even from jail that mu'fucka got mad pull in the streets. And when Abena betrayed him and, worse, abandoned his family and gave his li'l girl no choice but to become a killer like him instead of ending up a Yale graduate in somebody's classroom, she earned herself an enemy nobody in their right mind would want.

Abena stoked the embers of her own downfall nine years ago when she killed her sister, my mother.

But she's fanned them, flame by flame, by fucking over her own people year after year.

And now those chickens are coming home to roost in the form of a rebellion, and I'm leading the fucking charge.

"For now, we make her think we're moving like normal," I instruct them, shoving off the wall and returning across the room to the couch. Sinking down to the cushion, I pick up my drink again and toss the rest of the Patrón back. "So for now, we handle business like usual. Abena can suspect anything she wants, but she won't get any evidence from us. Treat that bitch like fucking Queen Romanda 'n' shit. In the meantime, Nef"—I dip my chin in her direction—"I need you to send out encrypted, completely secure messages to Bisa, Taraji, Moorehead, and Richter to see when's a good time for all of us to meet. Let them know D-Day has been moved up and I want to strike in the next three weeks. So, the sooner we can meet, the better."

She's already moving toward the door before I finish speaking, her head bent over her phone.

"Tera, can you contact Park and find out who else he has in mind about reaching out to? I'm not stepping on his toes or getting in the way of it. I trust him completely and am willing to let him do his thing. I'd just like to know who he's thinking of."

"Gotchu."

"Kenya, Maura, I need you to return to the obodo and follow up on the list of names all of you compiled from earlier. Just feel them out, see if they're receptive to you. Also track the temperature there. Monitor any of the chatter. Abena knows you're mine, and her Mirror wouldn't dare let anything slip, but those sheep she keeps around her aren't as careful. And of all of us, people tend to like you two the most."

"It's the freckles and the accent." Kenya points to Maura first and then jabs a finger toward her chest.

"And the pussy, girl. Stop playing." Penn snorts, flicking a hand.

"Did she just call my pussy 'friendly'?" Kenya gasps, splaying her fingers wide over her abundant chest, that Southern drawl on full display. The offense would've been almost believable if she didn't ruin it by breaking out in a wide grin and giggle, kicking her feet. "Listen, I can't help it if the mens likes them some tits and ass. At least I send them out happy."

Her li'l psycho ass is like a fucking praying mantis, killing men after she fucks them. Hey, who am I to judge? We all have our issues.

"Penn and Doc," I say, raising my voice before Penn can issue her comeback, "you'll keep up appearances at Elysian. I don't put it past Abena or any of her minions to do pop-ups outside of fight nights. At this stage, we can't afford for anything to go wrong. And, Sienna." I refresh my glass. "There's a shipment arriving at the port in three nights' time." I grin. "Abena's accepting guns from the Donatos, and they've paid her ten million to get them here safe, through customs, and delivered. For something to happen to those guns . . . like, say, ending up at the bottom of the river? Well, it wouldn't be a good day for my auntie."

"Say less." Sienna tilts her head. "And what're you gonna be up to while we're carrying out our assignments?"

I grin.

"Why, hunting a huntsman, of course."

"This bitch crazy," Kenya mutters.

I glare at her, jabbing a finger in her direction. "Don't think compliments are going to make me forget your earlier blasphemy. We beefing over that Panthro shit."

About an hour later, they've all left, and I survey my living room. For the most part, my girls cleaned up after themselves. But the couple of napkins and empty glasses have my ass itching. If I don't clean up now, I'll probably dream about the shit. Sometimes being a neat freak can be a killjoy.

Sighing, I set about straightening up. A half hour later, the dishes are washed, furniture returned to their proper places, curtains draped correctly, and carpet vacuumed. I grab a damp dish towel and head to the coffee table. Sinking down on the couch, I notice Tera's necklace. The gold and diamonds in the apple-shaped pendant wink under the recessed lights in the ceiling. Wonder if she's realized yet that she left it behind. Her ass is going to be in a sling if Abena finds out since they were ordered to never remove them.

As if the thing will grow fangs and spit venom at me, I carefully pick it up. It's a beautiful piece, I can't deny that. Abena might be a soulless barracuda, but she got taste. Still, generosity isn't one of her virtues. If anything, she's much quicker to take from her own rather than spread the wealth. As a matter of fact, I can't remember a time where she ever spent the kind of money these necklaces must've cost on anyone except herself. The shit was suspect as fuck.

I frown.

Nah, something in the milk ain't clean. That muthafucka stank as fuck.

Studying the jewelry with newer eyes, I slowly run my fingers along the chain, searching for . . . I don't know. Not finding any irregularities there, I turn my focus to the pendant. I give it the same treatment. Nothing on the front. Flipping it over, I begin my search over again. Nothing. It could be exactly what it's supposed to be—a harmless yet expensive token of appreciation.

But the niggling sense of foreboding won't let up. It's an itch on the back of my neck. And I've never ignored my version of a Spidey sense.

Taking another look, I trace the front and back once more. Noth—

"Hold up," I murmur. "Hold up, hold up."

Retracing the seam along the bottom of the piece, I smile.

Yeah, right there. I didn't imagine it.

Lifting the gold-and-diamond apple up to the light, I see the slightly protruding bump. My smile widens into a grin. I jerk up my pant leg and remove the dagger there. Within seconds, I maneuver the tip under the bump and pry it out. As soon as the piece is free, a small blinking object falls out, tumbling to my lap.

I set the necklace down on the coffee table and carefully pick up the minuscule thing that looks like the red pill from *The Matrix*.

A tracker.

Abena embedded a tracker in the necklaces.

That sneaky bitch.

Do all the necklaces have them? Or just the ones given to the Seven?

I'd bet Mirror's left nut only my crew has 'em. How long had Penn said they had them? A few days?

Shit.

I close my eyes, picturing Tera when we met the informant. Had she been wearing the pendant at the time? Squeezing my eyes tighter, I picture her. Try to remember when we returned to our bikes, and she unzipped her jacket.

No. I release a pent-up breath. She hadn't been wearing it. But shit. None of them knew their movements were being tracked. They will soon though.

Fucking Abena. I have to give it to her; that shit was crafty. This, paired with the assassination attempt, solidifies that Abena suspects how the tide is starting to change. She's gunning for me, and maybe she's figured out I've been coming for her all along. This move though . . . This one I can turn around and use to my advantage.

And I plan on doing just that.

CHAPTER SEVEN

Eshe

The brackish scent of Massachusetts Bay weighs heavy on the night air. The waters of the port gleam under the moonlight like onyx. The distant din of traffic can't drown out the gentle lap of the waves.

Blah. Blah. Blah.

I'm ready to hear the whisper of my Remington M24 and the muffled thud as the bullet meets its target.

I'm ready to hear screams.

It's been a slow few days.

I survey the area, taking note of a large shipping crate that a couple of workers moved to the end of the dock about ten minutes earlier. They're oblivious to the danger that lies in wait above them. Since yesterday and the meeting at my house, we've mapped out the area and are intimately familiar with it. I let my Seven in on the truth about their necklaces, and now we're using them to our advantage. If Abena decides to check their locations, she'll find my girls at Elysian and riding around downtown Boston. In reality, Nef, Doc, Kenya, and Sienna and I are stretched out on top of other containers, our rifles at the ready. Tera, Penn, and Maura take point on the ground. We're spread out, but I can still feel, fucking taste, the excitement and anticipation in the air. Not only are we snatching bitch-ass traffickers' souls and saving women and children from certain hell, but we're gathering proof that Abena is involved in committing one of the family's cardinal sins.

We have a plan in place to take out Abena. But if all goes well this evening, that timeline will be pushed up.

And it'll be the end of a nine-year sentence.

"A'ight, y'all. A black Hummer is pulling up now," Kenya's low voice announces through my earpiece. "Look alive, sweet peas."

I suppress a snicker.

"We have four targets—I mean, men—heading toward the pier," Kenya says. "Not Mwuaji. Doc, they're headed in your direction."

"Got 'em," Tyeesha says, voice calm, steady.

As the men walk into view, I press my eye to the scope, getting the one on the far right in my crosshairs.

"Still no sign of Abena?" I murmur.

"No. It's all clear over this way," Kenya says.

"It's five after eleven." I frown. "Abena should've been here."

I raise my head, reasons why she hasn't arrived yet flying through my mind. This is her meet. She should've been here before her clients. Something—

"Abort mission," I hiss, and start breaking down my rifle with practiced, quick motions. "Get out of here. Now."

Radio silence meets my order. No one questions it. The fact I know where each of my Seven is situated is the only reason I catch glimpses of their hurried movements. I pack my M24 and scurry down the side of the container. As soon as my feet hit the pavement, I take off toward our meeting point, sticking to the shadows.

I run flat out for half a mile, and only when the black Ranger comes into view do I slow down. Grabbing the driver's door, I fling it open and throw myself behind the wheel. After reaching under the seat, I snatch the keys and jam them in the ignition. Only seconds pass before the passenger and rear doors are jerked open, and Nef, Sienna, and Maura jump inside. I don't even wait until their doors close before I slam on the gas and haul ass out of there, trusting the rest of my Seven have made it to their ride and aren't far behind me.

"The fuck happened back there?" Nef asks as I turn onto Drydock Ave.

"Call Tera," I rasp out. "Make sure they got out of there safe and then put her on speaker."

Moments later, Tera's voice echoes in the Rover's interior.

"Yeah," she says. "We're good here. Not far behind you. What happened? Why did you call it?"

"We weren't alone out there," I let them all know. Falling quiet, I clench my teeth, jaw throbbing. "I saw movement right under where Doc was posted up. Whoever it was hadn't been facing the water where the meet was supposed to go down. That tells me they weren't there for that. Everything in me is saying they were there for us. They knew we would be there and were waiting for us to make a move so they could take us out."

"How many?" Nef asks, voice flat. Deadly.

"I only saw the one, but that just means the rest of that team was well hidden. And there had to be a team. One person couldn't eliminate all of us."

Silence permeates the inside of the Rover, and not a peep comes from over the phone. Someone had to betray us. Not one of my Seven. I trust them with my life, and their loyalty to me is unquestionable and unwavering. So who?

The other person in this equation is Laura, but hell, she's the one who put us on. Still . . . Something about her hadn't stopped gnawing at me. A familiarity. A sense of . . . unease about the whole situation. But damn, she had the recording. And her story was credible. About her niece, her family . . .

Family.

"Holy shit," I snap.

"What?" Nef and Tera demand at the same time.

"That Laura chick. She was wearing a wedding band and ring."

"Yeah. And?" Penn presses.

"Abena was wearing the same ring yesterday. Minus the band." I chuckle but ain't shit funny. "She played us. She *fucking* played us." I slap my hand against the steering wheel, ignoring the sting in my palm. Laughing again, I shake my head, instantly realizing why "Laura" struck me as familiar. I was related to her. "I gotta give it to the bitch. She's good. The getup, the story. She deserves an Academy fucking Award."

"Are you sure?" Tera asks.

"Yeah, one hundred percent sure."

"You know what that means, don't you?" Sienna asks. "Abena got to Dakari. He helped her set us up. *Fuck!*" I glance in the rearview mirror in time to see her pound the side of her fist against the window. "How long? How long has he been in her pocket and potentially feeding her information about us?"

Quiet once again descends between us.

"I don't know." I tighten my grip on the steering wheel until my fingers start to tingle. "But I'ma find out."

I approach Elysian, the warehouse where we host the underground fights. At least that's what we use it for on those particular nights. Right now, at one o'clock in the afternoon, we got different business to be about.

The steel door slams shut behind me, the sound echoing in the vast space. In just a few hours, this place will be filled with people screaming and shouting, eager to be entertained by blood, gore, and death. I mean, who am I kidding? It is a good time. But at this moment, the ring is empty, the concrete floors are bare of chairs.

Well . . .

There's one chair.

And Dakari is tied to it.

Like a bloody, fucked-up Christmas gift.

And I loooves me some Christmas.

"Hey, Dakari." I clasp my hands behind my back and smile at him. "So glad you could make it."

"Yeah, he was a little hesitant at first. But after I convinced him that we really, really needed to see him, he came along." Penn claps a hand on Dakari's shoulder. "Ain't that right, Dakari?"

He doesn't answer, but I don't miss the small, muted whimper.

"Aw." I poke out my bottom lip. "Penn, I think our boy here is a little uncomfortable. Are you, D?" He remains quiet, but his hazel eyes swim with horror. Mmm. I could orgasm off all that delicious fear. "I'd hate for you to be experiencing any kind of discomfort. Ooh." I wince. "You got a little blood"—I circle my finger in front of his battered, bruised face—"well, everywhere."

"Eshe, please. I—" he croaks.

But I place my finger flat against his busted and swollen lips.

"Shhh. Don't spoil the moment." I reach behind me and grab my gun, then tap it against my thigh.

"Eshe, I swear—"

I swing, smashing my Glock into his mouth. The chair—and Dakari—fly backward. His head bounces off the concrete, and I wince. That's going to be one helluva headache.

Well, y'know, if he would be alive in the next five minutes.

Which, spoiler alert, he will not.

"I said shut the fuck up. Damn!" I glare at him. "Why muthafuckas gotta be so hardheaded?"

Spreading my arms wide, I glance around and am met with a chorus of "I don't know," and "muthafuckas just don't learn," and "just no home training." Shaking my head, I wait for Nef to pick Dakari up. Blood oozes from his already-fucked-up mouth and drips onto his chin and ripped, dirty T-shirt.

"Now, before I was interrupted . . ." I crouch in front of him and, tipping my head back, meet his eyes. Correction, eye. One of 'em is swollen shut. "It hurts me to see you here like this, D. Not more than it hurts you, but gotta say, the betrayal cuts deep." I splay my fingers wide over my chest. His busted lips part, and I narrow my eyes on him. "If you open your bitch-ass mouth to lie to me, I'm going to hit you in it again. But this time with a bullet."

He wisely decides to not speak. A shame.

"Good choice." I praise him, patting his knee. "Now, what information did you pass on to Abena? How much does she know about us?" When he doesn't immediately start talking, I chuckle and pat him again. "My bad, bruh. You can speak."

"I—I didn't tell her anything," he says, garbled voice thick with unshed tears. "I don't know that much to tell her other than you recruiting me to be a pair of eyes and ears in the obodo. And I didn't say anything about that. I swear, I didn't betray you."

"Mmm, that's debatable." I seesaw my hand back and forth. "Then why you? How did you end up arranging the meeting for Abena? Did she just pick you out all eenie-meenie-miney-moe and shit?"

He starts to shake his head, but his face spasms in pain, stopping the motion. "No. Abena didn't explain why she approached me other than to say I'm not as careful as I thought." He coughs, and more blood stains his mouth and chin.

Probably some internal damage there.

"So what did she promise you?" Tera asks, coming closer until the tips of her boots nudge the chair leg.

"Good question," I cosign. "What did Abena promise that was so good, you sold us out?"

"I didn—"

I raise my gun and point it at his chest. "Lie again with your Benedict Arnold ass. You didn't know if I was walking into an ambush or would walk out of there alive. So miss me with that 'I didn't, blah, blah, blah' bullshit. Just answer the question."

He bows his head, and his chest heaves as if he's choking back a sob. He better hold that shit in. There's no crying in torture.

"Abena threatened to have my mom and li'l sister killed." He lifts his head, and his hazel eyes glisten with unshed tears. "They're all I got, man. I'm responsible for them. I couldn't let her . . ." He chokes up again and sucks in a shuddering breath. "You gotta understand that."

I slowly rise to my feet, staring down at him. Anger kindles in my chest, and it's a spark away from flashing into a full-on forest fire.

"I don't have to understand shit, D. Only a bitch-made muthafucka would betray those he's supposed to be loyal to. All you had to do was come to me, to one of us, and tell us what Abena was holding over your head. You're family. Your mom and sister—

they're family. Do you really think I would've let you or them suffer? Why would you want me for your oba if that's what you believed of me? Nah. I don't understand shit." I take a step back from him. "See you in the upper room, ho."

Before he can blink, I lift my arm again and fire a bullet between his eyes. The smell of smoke, sulfur, blood, and shit saturate the air.

"Gotdamn, I hate that part." Sienna wrinkles her nose. "Death ain't dignified, sis."

"Whose turn is it to clean up?" Kenya asks, propping her fists on her rounded hips. "Not mine."

"I did it last time." Penn holds up her hands, palms out.

"And I did it the time before," I throw in.

"That doesn't count," Tera snaps. "Only one way for this to be fair. Paper, scissors, rock. C'mon, bitches."

With a groan, we huddle up in a circle, fists out.

"One, two, three." We draw our arms back and throw our hands forward.

Seven rounds later, Doc tosses her head back on her shoulders.

"Fuuuuck."

Cackling, we leave her to it. I push open the door, then step outside and squint against the early-afternoon sun. I inhale a deep breath, one that doesn't stink of death. Or betrayal. That last one hurts my nose more.

"Where you headed now?" Nef asks me, pulling her car keys from the front pocket of her black jeans.

"Home." Actually, I plan on heading over to Malachi's loft and doing a little B and E. It's been a minute since I rolled around in his sheets. God, that man smells like soap, pain, and bad decisions. Just *intoxicating*.

Nef nods and heads toward her car. "I'm about to go to the crib and go through the camera footage of the obodo from the past couple of days. See if there's anything of importance that we need—*shit!*"

She dives for the ground at the gunshot. A bullet strikes the gravel, kicking up pebbles and dust. On reflex, I drop and scurry for the back of Sienna's GTO just as another bullet pings off the rear panel. She's going to be pissed about that.

"The fuck?" Fierce anger at whoever would have balls enough to come for me and mine burns through me. I grab my gun and, sliding the safety off, peek above the trunk and then fire off several rounds in the direction of the shots. They're coming from the vicinity of the thick trees off the left of the property. "Call out!" I glance to my right and glimpse Nef, face a stone-cold mask, shooting her SIG toward our would-be assassin. Crimson stains her white shirt on the upper arm. "Call out, dammit!"

This time, a chorus of their names ring out. Relief floods me even as I continue pulling the trigger. All of them are safe. I don't know how I could handle losing one more person . . .

The gunfire from the trees stops, and the resulting silence is tense, thick. Cautiously, I shift from behind the GTO, still not certain it's entirely safe.

"Nef," I call to her, "you good?"

She nods, lowering her weapon and glancing down at her arm. "Yeah. It's just a graze. I'm good."

"Eshe!" Tera yells at me.

"Yeah?"

"Who the fuck did you piss off now?"

Isn't that a good question?

CHAPTER EIGHT

The Huntsman

I swear to fuck, if I had a soul, that shit would be itching.

People call me a psychopath, but only those with real personality disorders could enjoy this kind of shit.

Not the violence. Not the blood. Nah, the two men currently pounding the hell out of each other in the elevated ring, sending flecks of blood splattering on those gathered closest to the podium, have the adrenaline in my veins singing.

It's the number of bodies packed into this warehouse. Who the fuck actually enjoys being around this many people? That's *got* to be a sign of a psychopath.

Though my gotdamn skin feels like it's about to crawl away from my body, the plus side is it's easier for me disappear in this crowd. Even with my height and size. But my job is being a shadow, to move unseen and unheard. Before, I believed it was something my mentor, Derrick Trudell, had taught me. I don't belong to Creed, but Derrick does—or he did. You didn't get chances to make errors with that organization. You failed, you died. It's how they maintained a reputation for excellence and a roster of only the best assassins.

But I've never learned to play well with others.

I had an opportunity. After Derrick found me on the streets of New Haven, by rights, he could've killed me. After all, I'd mistakenly witnessed him take out a federal judge with a predilection for young boys. Instead, he took a thirteen-year-old me under his wing, fed me, taught me how to hone and diversify the skills I'd acquired way too early. How to make money at it. At sixteen, I was as good as him. At eighteen, I surpassed him and was invited to join Creed but declined.

And at twenty-six, I lost the only person I'd been able to call friend since losing my family.

All these years, I thought he'd given me this talent for murder, this gift of violence.

Now? Now, thanks to fucking Eshe Diallo, I can't dig it out of my mind that maybe I was born with some twisted, perverse genetic code for it.

Since Eshe's revelation about my father—about my family, their death, and Abena's hand in it—a couple of days ago, I haven't had a chance to deal with it.

Nah. I've refused to deal with it.

For thirty-three years, I've held one belief. One sacred belief about my life. My family has been on this glistening, clean, incorruptible pedestal that can't be stained by who I am. Mordechai Bowden, construction worker, and Sharon, kindergarten teacher. Normal, loving parents who, through no fault of their own, created a monster.

But if what Eshe said is true, I'm not just a monster but the spawn of one.

Rage boils in my gut, rushing for my chest and head, and clenching my jaw, I deliberately shove the emotion behind a steel door and lock it. I'm good at that. Compartmentalizing or just burying shit so deep, it ceases to exist.

It's what I did to Malachi Bowden.

Until Eshe called him forward.

Another reason to despise her.

Eshe saunters through a closed door just under the glassed-in "box" that holds a luxury suite. It's as if just the thought of her name invoked her like fucking Candyman, except my hate's so great, I didn't even need to call her name five times, just once. My gaze skates over Penn Dawson and Tyeesha Vega standing on either side of her before it latches back on Eshe. Homes in on the perfect thrust of her breasts, barely covered in a cropped, black long-sleeved sweater that shows off a stomach with enough rounded flesh for a person to sink their teeth into and bite. The tight black leather that embraces the wide flare of hips created for a man to hold as he beats that wet pussy up from the back, watching the hypnotic rippling of her ass and the creaming on his dick. On the same leather wrapping around thick thighs and strong calves. She's this gorgeous, threatening Amazon who doesn't need those knee-high laced boots to appear powerful. She exudes strength, might. They seep from her pores like an animal's pheromones, and even from this distance and over the teeming crowd, I can scent her.

Cedarwood.

Earthen musk.

Violence. Like the electric sizzle in the air just after lightning strikes.

Sex.

I hate that I can identify it.

Hate her for embedding it in my nose, my head, my skin so that erasing it—erasing her—is next to impossible.

A flicker of movement out of the corner of my eye snags my attention, and I lift my hands to my hood, tugging on it and hiding more of my face. Grim gratitude sparks in my chest, reminding me why I'm in this pit in the first place.

This. A familiar song hums inside me. As I glide forward, slipping through the patrons whose focus is fixed on the ring, the whispered melody steadily grows until its sweet aria fills my head, my veins.

The tall, muscled figure clothed in a hoodie similar to mine, a puffy coat, and jeans doesn't notice me as I slide up behind him. His first mistake? Staring too long in Eshe's direction. Too obvious. Second mistake? Using a flashy-ass Desert Eagle. The fuck?

Third mistake?

Coming for her.

I didn't think it would take long for Abena put out another

contract on her niece. But damn. The bitch moved fast. This amateur will surely be the first of several gunning for her.

Eshe is mine to kill, and no one's going to watch the life leak from those hazel eyes but me.

In one motion, I throw an arm around his shoulders, and with my other hand, I snatch my deadlock dagger from the sheath at my waist and shove the blade between his third and fourth ribs, tearing through his lung and puncturing the heart. I twist the dagger, ripping through vessels and tissue, destroying the organ beyond repair. To anyone looking, we probably appear like one friend helping his drunk-off-his-ass boy stay on his feet.

Easing his deadweight against my body, I carry him out of the main room and down the dark hallway leading to the bathrooms. I quickly move to the storage closet at the far end and shove him in. I use his sweatshirt to wipe off the blood on my knife. Shit. Not like he minds. Straightening, I slide the dagger back in the sheath and exit the closet, scanning the shadows, ensuring no one's giving me any attention before I return to the main part of the warehouse. He should stay hidden until they clear this place out in the morning. And by then, I'll be long gone.

Turning around, I thread back through the screaming, adrenaline-pumped throng of people, and for a moment, I allow their bloodlust to fuel my own. That kill right there . . . it wasn't enough. Barely scratched the surface of the itch, the fucking hunger that gnaws at me. It's been three days since I popped those two soldiers at my house, and that barely satisfied the need that never fully slept. Even now the sibilant crackle in my blood slowly evaporates, but the residue lingers, demanding another fix, another hit.

As if of its own volition, my gaze darts back to that railed-in platform.

"Fuck."

It's empty.

Quickening my stride and using my width and strength, I shove through the mass, scanning the bodies for Eshe. *Shit*. For someone who is a fucking princess of the underworld, she moves reckless as fuck—

"Goddamn, bruh. Watch where the fuck you're goin'. These shoes cost more than your fucking life . . ."

I jerk my head toward the tall man with short, perfectly styled hair, his slender frame clothed in an expensive, tailored pin-striped suit. The one his parents will be burying him in.

Maybe he reads his death in my eyes because he recoils, the color leaching from his skin.

"Listen, I—I didn't . . . I mean, I'm sor—"

"The fuck outta here," I growl.

He whips around, bumping into several people before disappearing from my sight.

"Damn, that's impressive. I can't be a hundred percent certain, but I think ol' boy just pissed on himself. And all from a look." Fingers dance down my spine, and I stiffen, both repelled and . . . and . . . *Fuck*.

"Don't," I grind out as Eshe comes to stand in front of me, her bright eyes too seeing, too assessing.

I don't have a memory of fearing much. Not since Miriam died. It's like seeing her doll-like, crumpled body on that stained floor tore all emotion out of me, including the capacity to be afraid of anything.

But staring down into this woman's gaze, I have the unprecedented need to glance away.

To . . . run.

She tsk-tsks, those same thin, elegant fingers that inflicted such sweet agony on my body hovering over my chest—directly above my pierced nipple. "Don't what?"

She shifts closer to me, her earthy scent wrapping its steely grip around my neck, tightening until I can barely breathe. I'm not here for this. Yet, with just the barest brush of that handful of firm titties against my chest, of those lush thighs against mine, my focus, my fucking purpose, stutters, goes staticky and offline.

Suddenly, I'm not in the middle of a warehouse full of death and violence but hurled into a realm out of time and space, where only she and I exist. Where only her spiked, razor-sharp knowledge and my desperation exist.

"Don't what, Huntsman?" she repeats, tipping her head back. Those disobedient fingers move under my hoodie, and the threat of their touch warms my skin, but they don't press against my flesh. I'm caught somewhere between thankful and ravenous, and I clench my teeth, locking down the rumble of sound that would reflect that confusion. "Don't run my fingers over this beautiful skin again? Don't think about how it felt to watch it split open under my knife?"

She surges to the balls of her feet, dragging her nose up the middle of my chest to the base of my throat, sniffing me like a beast just before it goes for the kill—or the fuck.

My dick jerks against the zipper of my jeans, pressing hard as if trying to get at her. Electric pulses race from my balls up my spine to sizzle in the back of my neck before tracking a return trip down to my throbbing length. It takes every scrap of self-control I possess not to thrust a hand through that mass of dark auburn curls, shove her to the ground, and make her mouth do something about my hard-as-fuck cock.

"Don't get under this same skin?" she continues in that low, almost-contemplative voice that probes too deep, seeks too far. A voice that vibrates through my clothes to my skin beneath like the touch I'm denying both of us. "Don't see what you try to hide from me like I'm everyone else?"

Slowly, she sinks back to her feet and tips her head to the side. I expect that dick tease of a mouth to curl into her usual smirk or taunting grin. But her lips are curved into a dark snarl. A light that's damn maniacal gleams in those gold-and-green eyes.

"You made the mistake of coming for me, Malachi Bowden," she whispers, but I hear her warning with crystal clear clarity. "And now those consequences are your bad. I warned you about who you are to me, and you chose to follow me anyway, so now here we are. Two years. Two fucking years," she hisses, and I frown at the cryptic words and the narrow-eyed fury twisting her face. But like a switch, in the next moment, her expression clears, and it's smooth as glass. Almost . . . pleasant. "Malachi. The Huntsman. The man. The bogeyman. You're both mine. And I'll cut the throat of anyone who even looks like they're thinking of fucking you." A sigh escapes her, and she slowly shakes her head before rolling upward again and pressing an oddly tender kiss to the underside of my jaw. "You should've stayed away."

Malachi. The Huntsman . . . You're both mine.

You should've stayed away.

Rage. That's what should be pouring through me like fire-licked gasoline. Not a fierce need. Not a roaring hunger that screams so loud, she should be reeling back and staring at me in horror, in fear.

Not a yearning so soft, so fragile, it trembles against my sternum with butter-soft wings.

A faint metallic flavor hits my tongue. Blood. I've bitten my tongue. The cost of holding back the howl of pain, the snarl of lust, the whimper of need that has nothing to do with an aching dick. My lungs seize, and when they stutter to working order again, she's gone, melted into the thick masses surrounding us once more. The vacuum we disappeared into for those few precious seconds dissolved, and we're once again among the living, the real world where she's my prey, a moving target with my sight dead set in the middle of her chest.

I give my head a hard shake.

What in the fuck just happened?

Fury at Eshe, at my damn self, swirls through me like a Category 5 storm. Fuck stealth. I plow through the bodies in front of me, following in her wake.

Fuck Eshe Diallo. My fingers flex, stretch, curl again. Feeling the frantic flutter of her pulse under my hands as I imagine slowly tightening my grip on the slender column of her throat.

She played the wrong muthafucka—

The blast erupts through the warehouse like a rampaging dragon, heat and a great clap of sound rolling through the space. I fly, but my fall is cushioned by the crush of bodies beneath me. For a moment, I lie there, the screams and cries assaulting my ears.

"No."

The word rips from my chest, lost in the chaos around me. After launching to my feet, I jump over the prone bodies littering the floor, dodge people not laid out by the bomb, knocking more out of the way.

Where the fuck is she?

Shit.

Fuck. *Gotdamn.*

Blood, the meaty scent of burning flesh, and black, cloying smoke choke the air. Jerking the collar of my hoodie over my nose and mouth, I ignore the ringing in my head, the aches and throbbing of my battered frame.

She was in the path of the blast. But she can't be. No. Fuck no. She can't be . . . There.

A knee-high boot. A leather-encased thigh.

The dogpile of bloody, soot-stained, motionless bodies covers the rest of the petite frame, but I'd recognize it anywhere.

The blood in my veins ices over, and I stop several feet away, an unmoving statue in a roiling sea of madness.

Somebody's going to die.

Painfully. Slowly.

Badly.

And I'm going to enjoy every fucking second of it.

I stare at the steady rise and fall of her chest.

It's been seventeen hours, and Eshe still hasn't woken up.

Maybe I should slap the shit out of her, I contemplate, biting into my slice of cheese, mushroom, and onion pizza. It'd hurt, but all this sleep can't be healthy either. She should've been awake by now.

I snort, shaking my head as I swallow, then take another huge bite. Stretching one arm across the top of the chair I'm straddling, I tip forward, balancing on the back legs. By all rights, I should've left Eshe in the rubble of Elysian. It would've made more sense than bringing her ass to one of my safe houses. Especially since, thanks to her and her fucking aunt, I can't go back to my main home. Logic screams that leaving her in that underground club would've solved one of my problems.

I'm quickly realizing logic and Eshe Diallo don't occupy the same space when it comes to me.

Because what fucking sense does it make to dig her out from under that pile of bodies, carry her out of what was left of that warehouse, bring her here, and personally tend to her wounds, only to turn around and kill her?

Yeah, I should've left her ass there.

Malachi. The Huntsman . . . You're both mine.

Glaring at her, I toss the crust toward the grease-stained box and rise from the chair, the legs hitting the floor.

Slapping her sounds like a better and better idea.

I take a step toward the pullout couch but abruptly draw up short and pivot, stalking across the buckled and scarred hardwood floor toward the seedy studio apartment's tiny kitchen. I yank open the door of the refrigerator that was probably popular about two decades ago and pull out a bottle of water. Grabbing a towel off the top of the fridge, I drop it on the floor and shove it against the bottom to catch the water leaking out. With more force than necessary, I unscrew the cap and tip the bottle up to my mouth. I down half the contents before retracing my steps across the room. Only when my ass hits the seat of the chair do I notice the bright brown-and-green gaze on me.

Nah, that's not right.

I *feel* it on me first.

The tiny hairs on my arms stand at attention, quiver as if a breeze ghosted across my skin. Only, every instinct I possess relays it's not the air from the ancient window AC unit causing the reaction. The insubstantial yet tangible touch is too primal. Too *her*.

I've known Eshe Diallo a handful of days—and I use *known* very loosely since my dick in her mouth doesn't really count—and yet I recognize her touch to the very marrow of my bones.

To my nonexistent soul.

She doesn't move, and neither do I. We engage in a visual standoff for several silent moments. But I'm the master at being quiet; she can't compete.

"Well, I'm not dead, though I feel like fucking deep-fried death." She closes her eyes, a faint wince playing over her strained but beautiful features seconds before she fixes her stare back on me. "What happened?"

Not surprised she doesn't remember, I say, "An explosion. From what I could tell, it probably came from under the ring, since it and the area surrounding it got the worst of the blast."

"How bad?" she asks, voice flat, face blank.

I shrug a shoulder. "I didn't stick around to assess the damage, and with the smoke, people, and debris, I couldn't really tell at the time. But the shit didn't look good."

She nods, the thick fringe of her lashes hiding her eyes from me. Part of me wants to march over to the bed, grip her scratched chin, and demand she look at me. Insist she let me see those eyes so I can decipher what's going on in that sharp mind.

But I remain with my ass rooted to the chair. It would be a colossal mistake to voluntarily touch this woman. Shit, in my head, I've committed this cardinal sin so many different times, in so many different positions, Satan is looking at his watch, waiting on me like, *Ticktock, bitch. Ticktock.*

"I need to get in touch with my girls. Where's my phone?"

"Fuck I look like? Your errand boy? It's probably under a pile of cement blocks and shit. You lucky I got your ass outta there."

"Dammit." She chews on her bottom lip for a moment, and I

stare. Hard. I want that juicy, lush flesh in my mouth. "I have to check on my Seven. See if they're okay."

The worry and frustration in her voice shouldn't do anything to me. But the fact she's just woken up after being caught in the blast of a bomb and her first thought is for her people? Yeah, as much as I don't want to admit it, that does something to me.

"I have burners. I'll get you one."

"Thanks." She narrows her gaze. "Why did you?"

"Why did I what?" I ask, lost at the sudden switch in topic.

"Why did you get my ass out of there?"

I stare at her, unblinking. No way in hell I'm answering that.

Mainly, because I still don't know the answer to the question. Even if I did, I wouldn't give her what she wants. Because something tells me I wouldn't like the truth.

"You haven't asked where you're at," I say instead.

"Don't need to. Your Dorchester place."

Shock ripples through me, and it takes every bit of self-control I possess not to allow my expression or body betray it. But Jesus Christ. How does she . . . ?

The shock hardens into a dark block of ice that settles in the middle of my chest. The cold seeps into my veins, my blood.

"How do you know that, Eshe?" I ask, the emotion as empty as my conscience.

A smile ghosts across her full mouth, and I zero in on the wound bisecting the corner of her bottom lip. She either doesn't know how close she is to death or doesn't give a fuck.

Since she is who she is, I'm going with the latter.

"I already told you, Huntsman. Two years."

"I don't know what the fuck that means."

"There isn't much I don't know about you."

Why that sends a fissure of fear down my spine as if she issued a threat, I can't grasp. Don't want to. I just know it makes me mean.

Meaner.

"I'm going to enjoy killing you, Eshe. Other people, it's just a job. But you? I'm going to take my time with it. Find out the spots that make you scream out and make sure I play there the longest with my knife. By the time I finish, you're going to pray for death, and there won't no mercy coming. Not from God, and for damn sure not from me."

She blinks. Blinks again.

"I think I just came," she whispers.

I surge to my feet, disgust soaring its way through me on crimson-edged wings, and it carries me across the one-room, bottom-floor apartment and out the door into the tiny foyer. Disgust not at her. That would be too easy, too simple.

Nah, it's all directed at myself.

Because I had to get the fuck up out of there like a goddamn coward before I crawled on that bed, tore the covers back from her lushly curved body, thrust my hand between those thick thighs, and found out for myself if she really had nutted all over my sheets.

After scrubbing my hands over my short sandy curls, I interlock my fingers behind my head, tipping it back to stare at the water-stained ceiling. I can't even lie. There's a part of me that wants to charge out the front door onto the cracked and broken lot that the empty, blue multilevel house sits on. Inhale the air that smells of car exhaust, fried meat someone's cooking for dinner, and the faintest whiff of weed. Shit, I'm desperate for anything that doesn't carry the scent of cedarwood, musk, and earth as rich and brown as the beautiful tone of her smooth skin.

But I don't trust her. Even battered, bruised, and with alarms set around my nailed-shut windows, I don't trust Eshe not to escape. So I'm fucking trapped. As trapped as she is.

Aren't we two fucking peas in a pod?

Releasing a low growl, I drop my arms, turn on my booted heels, and return to the apartment. Eshe's no longer lying down but sitting with her back propped up against the back of the pullout couch. As if she's been waiting on me to reenter, her gaze finds me as soon as the door opens and, like a fishing rod, reels me in, tugging me across the room until I'm back in the chair I abandoned.

Without removing my gaze from her, I reach over, grab the nearly empty pizza box, and toss it onto the bed. She's the first to break our standoff when she dips her head to the contents and greedily scoops up one of the three slices left. When she moans, her lashes fluttering down as she chews, my entire body tightens until it threatens to snap in half with the slightest nudge. My dick bricks up, volunteering as fucking tribute to be that volatile nudge.

Locking down the vicious curse clawing its way up outta my chest, I insert immediate distance between me and her by returning to the kitchen for a bottle of water. By the time I approach the bed once more, she's wolfed down one slice and is already biting into the next. I lob that at her, too, and she catches it one-handed without pausing a beat in eating.

"I like what you're doing with the place," she says around a mouthful of pizza.

I survey the room as if I don't know every nail, splinter, and water stain in the apartment. Still, I see it through her eyes. The boards nailed over the bulletproof windows. The peeling wallpaper. The brown water stains dotting the ceiling. Yeah, it's a pit. And it serves its purpose.

"How long have I been out?" she asks.

"Seventeen hours."

"Damn." Her eyebrows wing up. "You cleaned me up and dressed my wounds."

I don't answer since she's stating the obvious.

"And put me in your T-shirt." Dropping the water to the bedcover, she pinches the shirt and lifts it to her nose, inhaling noisily. "Mmm. Smells just like you, too. Like murder, mayhem, and sex. All my favorites."

She's trying to get a rise out of you. Don't give in. Don't give in, muthafucka.

"Pizza. I'm not surprised we're here eating this. It's your favorite, after all. Doesn't matter the topping." She tips the slice to the side, studying it like it's an unknown species instead of an

Italian dish. More surprise undulates through me, but I must do a shit job of concealing it because she shakes her head as if she's a teacher and I'm her disappointing student. "How many times I have to tell you there isn't much I don't know about you?"

She shifts against the back of the couch as if seeking a more comfortable position. Since I don't sleep more than four hours in a stretch, I don't have any additional pillows to offer her.

Goddammit. This ain't the Holiday Inn, and I ain't hospitality services.

Ignoring the discomfort flashing across her face and the equally fleeting need to ease it, I lean against the wall, crossing my arms over my chest.

"All right. Given name, Malachi James Bowden. Thirty-three years old. Birthday May nineteenth. Shoutout to the Tauruses. One sister: Miriam Tanai Bowden. Died at the age of four. First kill at ten, the foster father who murdered your sister. Second kill, two months later. Mike Flannery, the pimp in Worcester who beat and tried to rape you."

I don't move, but shock pins me to the wall all the same like a dissected frog splayed wide with all its organs and guts on morbid display.

"Hired assassin Derrick Trudell took you under his wing at thirteen, and you started killing for money. You don't need me to tell you the reputation you've earned since then." She tilts her head, and that feeling of being studied, examined, increases. But I remain still under her scrutiny, refusing to give anything away. Anything more, that is. "You like to read; your home library is really impressive." A small smile tugs at the corner of her mouth, and just how the fuck she knows that is worrisome. Oh right. I have video of her breaking into my shit and walking around like my place was hers. Don't need to be Sherlock Holmes to figure out it wasn't the first time she'd been there. "You don't watch a lot of TV, but when you do, your go-tos are the old black-and-white classics. Bette Davis, Barbara Stanwyck, Edward G. Robinson. Your favorite snack is apples. Your favorite drink is Glenlivet

18—not to be a snob, but that's shockingly highbrow. I would've pegged you for a Corona man, myself."

Shut up. Shut the fuck up.

The guttural words reverberate off my skull like a desperate mantra, growing in volume until it fills my head like a deafening storm.

But underneath the growled winds . . . I swallow hard. A part of me I hadn't even been aware existed until this woman chained me to her bed and took her knife to my skin, brought my body to life with her mouth, shudders with each detail she drops. That part craves each point. It's been so long since I've been seen. Since someone knew me. Saw, knew Malachi, not the Huntsman.

Not since Miriam.

And until this moment, I didn't understand that the hungry, gnawing emptiness inside me was . . .

Loneliness.

"Apples were . . ." I rasp, the words slipping out of me of their own volition. Horror sizzles inside me, and despite being a whole-ass grown man of thirty-three, embarrassment scorches my face. And yet, I can't stop the rest of the words from escaping. "Apples were my sister's favorite food. I hate them but eat them for her."

"I missed that detail somehow," she murmurs, as if talking to herself, her gaze dropping to the untouched bottle of water. After a moment, that startling sharp focus shifts back to me. "Tell me something: Is that why children are off-limits? And why people who order those hits have been known to disappear? Oh, you're a killer, same as me. And you make no apologies about it. But you have a code of honor that's all your own. And fuck anyone who doesn't get it. But I do. I have a theory. I think it's your way of honoring your sister. Of protecting her from the monster you weren't—"

I shove away from the wall and stalk to the window, fists hanging by my sides. Tension rides me harder than a whore with a forty-dollar trick. My first inclination? Hurt her. It's what I'd do to anyone else who dared speak to me like that. They wouldn't be able to talk without a throat. And God knows I want to put my hands around hers. But only to squeeze tight while I beat that pussy up like it offended me.

I drag a hand down my face.

The desire to find out how she knows all this seethes inside me. But that would require asking her questions, and I . . . can't. I can't open myself up more to her than I already have. Exposing more of my underbelly will drive me closer to insanity, and no one wants that. This world won't be able to handle that.

Shit.

Eshe has me betraying myself, the very values and codes that have kept me alive for the last twenty-three years.

It was a mistake bringing her here.

I knew it when I tossed those bodies off her.

I knew it when I carried her out of that tomb of a warehouse.

I knew it when I brought her here, washed her, and bandaged her wounds.

Time to bring this back to business. I need to keep her alive long enough so I can kill her.

Turning back to her, I, of course, find her gaze on me. Whenever I'm in her vicinity, Eshe's always studying me as if I'm this specimen that either amuses or fascinates her. Like a toy she delights in playing with before she tears it apart limb by limb.

I resist reaching down and adjusting my dick in my black joggers.

"You realize that bomb was meant for you, right? Not a message for your aunt or the Mwua—"

"Abena."

I frown. "What? Isn't that what I said?"

"No, you called her my aunt. Don't refer to that bitch that way. She ceased being family the day she had my mother gunned down in the street like a dog."

I nod. Okay, yeah. I get that.

"You were the target of that bomb." When she doesn't speak again, I cross the room and pick up the chair, turn it around, and drop into it. Leaning forward, I prop my elbows on my thighs, linking my fingers together between my spread legs. "Seems I'm not the only person after you anymore. I took out another assassin tonight who was there for you. Another contract has been put out on your life. And I have no doubt Abena is behind it."

"Not that I'm questioning your reasoning or your information, but why do you say that?"

"Because of the reward. Three million—two less than she paid me. But the promise that whoever kills you can take your place as olori sweetens the deal. The power and earnings that brings in more than makes up for that two million."

Fury floods her features, and I catch myself edging closer as her eyes crystallize into golden shards.

"That's not how we work. She can't hold up a family position—a fucking hereditary or earned position—like a bargaining chip for personal and political gain."

"She know that? Because my source isn't wrong."

My source might be a teenager, but Jamari is one of the most brilliant hackers I've ever encountered. This shit here is child's play, and he wouldn't give me bogus information.

"There would be a fucking rebellion. I can't imagine any true Mwuaji accepting an outsider—someone outside our family—in the position of olori. She's not even promoting a soldier but a fucking mercenary who's not blood? What in the actual fuck?"

Her chest rises and falls under my T-shirt, the only sign of her rage. Any other person would be ranting, maybe throwing the nearest object, pacing the room. But her fury's so frigid, the lick of it's giving me frostbite.

I didn't think she could possibly get sexier, but she did. She *is*.

The murder, the *hate* in her eyes . . . it calls to every damaged, broken thing in me. And not to heal. Not to comfort.

To mate.

To join her jagged pieces with mine.

Her harsh chuckle echoes in the room.

"I don't know why I'm surprised, but fuck if I'm not. Blood

before belief. That bald-headed bitch had her own sister killed for power and sent you after me, so why am I shocked that she would sell out our traditions, our beliefs, our family?" She shakes her head on another of those rough laughs, her gaze going hooded. "This you? I'll admit, it would be the most elaborate assassination attempt I've ever heard of. Blow a spot up, then save me to get my guard lowered just enough to kill me. Have I judged you wrong all this time and missed an unseen ambitious streak?"

"You're upset, so I'ma let that slide. But anyone else would have my bullet decorating the back of their head for that insult." I straighten, leaning against the back of the chair.

She defiantly stares at me for several long moments before dipping her chin. Her form of acknowledging my words and an apology.

"I'm a killer, not a king," I tack on for no reason whatsoever. I don't owe her an explanation.

"I believe you."

I shouldn't give a fuck that her acceptance matters. But it does.

"That shit last night wasn't me, but if you do pray to a god or goddess, you might want to start getting some time in with him or her. Because one of the people who picked up the contract—and the one responsible for the bomb—was Poison."

"Poison?" Eshe balls up her face. "Huh."

"What the fuck does 'huh' mean?"

She frowns, her gaze going unfocused for a few moments. With a small shake of her head, she looks at me. "Earlier today, someone took shots at me and my Seven. I assumed it might've been a Mwuaji soldier sent by Abena. But now . . . Who is this Poison, and why haven't I heard of him before?"

"Not a him. Her. And because she doesn't care to be known. She doesn't give a fuck about reputation or any of that shit. Which should give you a clue of exactly how dangerous she is. She's been around for about ten years, and no one knows exactly what she looks like because if people call me a shadow, she's a goddamn ghost. And just as good as me. Maybe better and more dangerous, because you're right—I don't take out kids. Her? She's not restrained by that kind of code. It's only about completing the mission. That's it, that's all. She won't give a fuck about the position of olori, and yes, she gets paid, but neither money nor power drive her. I called her a ghost? Nah. Let me correct myself. If they call me the bogeyman, then she's the Terminator. Focused. Unstoppable. That's who's on your ass now."

"Is that supposed to scare me?" She tips her head to the side, and if I'm not mistaken, there's genuine curiosity in her voice.

I snort, irritated. "Now isn't the time to play whose clit is bigger, Eshe."

"I would invite you to find out, but that would mean you'd have to compare. Then I'd have to add another body to my count. And I've killed enough people who thought they could get away with touching what's mine." She smiles, but her tone is as flat as her eyes. "But I'll do it again. And again."

Her words take a minute to sink in, and my eyebrows arrow down over my nose. "What're you—"

She pops up a hand. "I'on want to talk about them hos who fucked around and found out. Unless there's something you need to tell me." Her brilliant eyes narrow on me, heat flickering in them. "Like you doubled back and couldn't find them . . ."

She seems to be waiting on me to supply her with an answer— or an apology . . .

"What the hell is going on right now?" I'm so fucking confused.

Her expression clears, and she leans back against the couch, picking up the forgotten and undoubtedly cold slice of pizza. The way her teeth chomp down on the crust is faintly threatening, and my dick jumps in both horror and interest.

Shit.

Even my mans is confused as fuck.

"Nothing," she finally says around a mouthful of food.

Yeah, okay. I've never been in a relationship, but even I know what *nothing* means. It means a fuck ton of *something*.

Swallowing the bite of pizza, Eshe grabs the bottle of water and twists the cap off. Without removing her gaze from mine, she drinks deeply. "As I was saying, I'm a firm believer in staying ready so you don't have to get ready. I've dealt with Abena Diallo all my life. One of my eyes hasn't had a good night's sleep in nine years because it's always open. So nah, Huntsman, I don't need you to tell me to be vigilant. And as far as fear? I don't know her." She demolishes the rest of the slice, then tosses the crust into the box. "You're wrong."

I stare at her, loosely linking my fingers together on my stomach, and silently wait on her to explain, because those are two words I don't hear often, especially not paired together. And if I do, I guaran-fucking-tee the person doesn't repeat them. Ever. At least not on this plane.

"This Poison—you believe she's more dangerous than you or me because she doesn't have shit to lose and no principles holding her back. That's not a strength; that's a weakness. Me? I'll go to war for mine. I'll fight dirty. Lie. Cheat. Go to the lowest, filthiest pit in hell, fuck the devil, and then gut him while he's still shaking from a nut with my pussy on his breath. That's how I'm coming behind mine. There's nothing I won't do, no line I won't cross, no rule I won't break to protect those I love. Because without them, I have nothing. The only person more fucked up than one with nothing to lose is the person who has everything to lose—and knows what it's like to have nothing. They'll do anything not to go there, to feel that again."

I don't move a muscle, but inside? Inside, my heart pounds against my rib cage with huge meaty fists as if it's trying to punch holes through to get to her. For a second, I don't recognize the sensation crackling like a live current. It shortens the breath in my lungs, sensitizes my skin until even the slightest caress—like the brush of my shirt or the stale air in the room—feels too much, damn near painful.

That ferocity. That passion. That brutality.

Like a caveman with his first sight of fire, I desire to creep closer on all fours, craving its heat, its beauty. But fear it. Fear the pain of its touch. The intensity of its power that I have no hope of controlling.

So, when that fire throws back the covers and crawls across the mattress, my voluminous T-shirt riding up silken thick thighs, flashing a teasing glimpse of bare plump folds, I don't move away. Don't move closer. I'm trapped by my own wants, my own uncertainties, my own inadequacies.

She perches on the edge of the bed like a beautiful exotic bird—no, that's too easy, too easy. An eagle. Gorgeous, yet cunning, deadly. Ready to strike. And right now, I'm in her sights, her prey.

And fuck if I don't want to be run down to the ground by her, feel those nails curl and dig into my flesh, draw blood while she fucking feasts.

"You know what I do want to feel again, Huntsman?" she murmurs, shifting to her knees. Her handful of breasts sway free under the gray cotton, momentarily distracting me. That and the shadow of her beaded dark brown nipples. I swallow, my mouth watering for a taste. Just one.

Briefly closing my eyes, I shift my attention back to her face.

If she noticed where my focus was fixed, she doesn't call me out on it or seem pissed off. Judging by the gleam in her hazel eyes, it might please her.

"I asked you a question. Do you know what I want to feel again?" She scoots back a bit, falling to her ass, bringing her knees up.

I wouldn't answer even if I could.

And let's be clear. I can't.

My shirt falls to her hips, hiding not one goddamn thing.

Her legs cradle the prettiest pussy I've ever seen. Bare. The same shade of mahogany as the rest of her body on the outside with a delicate pink on the inner lips. Already, she's glistening, as if just my eyes get her wet. With those shapely legs propped up, I'm blessed with an unrestricted view of her ass's full lower curves.

Though I make sure to always keep the apartment's temperature at a cool 62 degrees, I swear the furnace just clicked on in this bitch. Because I'm sweating. It's like a blacksmith's bellows took up residence in my chest, and each rise and fall emits enormous blasts of heat and fire.

It requires a strength I didn't know I possessed not to grab my dick and deliver a punishing stroke and squeeze. But shit, with that utterly perfect pussy framed by her thighs like a fucking Van Gogh painting, cum might decorate the backside of my joggers with just one pump of my fist.

Eshe eases onto her elbows, slowly letting her legs fall to the sides, and fuuuck. A growl rolls up from my gut to my chest and rumbles in my throat. She cocks her head, staring at me.

"You, Huntsman," she says. "I want to feel you again. And I'm not above keeping count. You owe me an orgasm. What were your exact words? Hol' up because I want to make sure I quote you correctly." She taps a fingertip against her cut lower lip. "Riiight. 'Lick it.'"

Yeah, I did issue that order, didn't I?

And she followed it, though it hadn't been with submissiveness. Nothing about the encounter in that freakishly fairy-tale cottage was about submission. It was a fight for dominance all the way until she wiped my seed from her mouth and pulled a gun on me.

Now, here she lies with her legs sprawled wide, demanding the same from me. Ordering I concede to her what she never once gave me. Not even with my dick lodged in the back of her throat.

"No?" That smirk rides her mouth. "That's cool. I'll start without you."

Lowering her back to the mattress, she slides one hand up and over her T-shirt-covered body, cupping her tit, squeezing it. She arches into her caress, loosing a low, sensual moan. The other hand winds a path down her torso, traveling farther until it slips between her thighs and covers her pussy. Another groan dances on the air, only this one is deeper, sexier, drenched with lust.

Abena could send a whole army of Mwuaji soldiers through that front door right now, and I still wouldn't be able to tear my gaze away from those nimble, elegant fingers tunneling through those swollen, soaked folds.

Holy shit.

Holy fucking shit.

Eshe's body twists, slowly undulating on the bed to a silent, hedonistic tune only she can hear but that has me caught up in its intoxicating melody. I'm a willing prisoner, cuffed to this chair as surely as she had me chained to her bed days ago. Now, though, the shackles are hunger, obsession. Invisible but just as strong.

Stronger. Because it's my own need that keeps me here.

I lick my dry lips as she plays in her pussy, teasing her clit with firm, tight circles. More moisture leaks from her, running down her slit to the crack of her ass. Oh shit, I want to kneel before her, drink it all up. Fucking lift my sheets to my mouth and suck them dry of every drop of her juices.

A shudder rocks her, and she gasps, her legs going so wide, her knees almost press to the mattress. My teeth clench, choking down the roar barreling up from my goddamn soul. The wild rocking and jerking of her hips can only mean one thing—she's nearing orgasm. She's reaching for that nut, and it's without me.

I'm a fucking hypocrite, a head case.

I won't allow myself to touch her. But I don't want her to release without me.

This woman is bent on driving me goddamn crazy.

Her grunt punches the air as she drags four fingers through her pussy, spreading the lips wide and thrusting three of them inside her.

"Oh fuck," she whines. Her breathing is labored as she lifts her hand. Her lashes flutter, and her bright eyes meet mine in a collision of gazes that pilfers whatever air I have left in my lungs. My chest damn near caves from the impact, and I battle the sensation of hanging on to my sanity like a gutter fighter. "If you don't want it"—she pants—"I do."

She sticks all four fingers into her mouth, her lips closing around them. On a long, low groan, she sucks them clean. Her tongue flicks against each digit, slipping around each knuckle and supping on every fingertip. She leaves nothing behind but clean brown flesh when she pops her hand free.

But it's that smile. It's that fucking smug, slightly unnerving, and wholly beautiful smile that snaps the last of my threadbare restraints.

Before she can lower her hand back to her soaked flesh, I'm on my knees at the edge of the bed, my palms are flattened against the inside of her thighs, and my face is buried in her pussy.

"Oh *God*. Shit." Her cry echoes throughout the room, and her body stiffens beneath me as if struck by a bolt of pure electricity. "Malachi!" she screams, her fingers digging into my head, nails scraping my scalp as she shoves my face deeper into her soaking-wet flesh.

But fuck that. It's not like I'm trying to go anywhere. Not even Jesus himself could come down and rapture my ass away now that her fresh yet musky flavor is coating my tongue. Now that her silken sex is rubbing against my lips. Now that I'm satiating the hunger she started. Fuck her. *She* started this.

Now I'ma finish it.

I latch onto her clit, graze my teeth over it, then not-so-gently bite. Another scream pierces my hearing, and she quakes beneath me. What feels like a flood of cream messes up my lips, beard, skin.

More, more, always more.

I'm nowhere near done with her yet.

This greed is nowhere near satisfied.

"Again, goddammit. Give it to me again," she growls. Grasping my head, she lifts it until I meet her gleaming, lust-filled gaze. "Don't stop until I let you up, got it?"

Yeah, I got it.

Bowing my head, I lap at all that juice. It's mine, after all. I hauled that nut out of her. It belongs to me. Slipping my hands under her ass, I tilt her up, dragging my tongue from her clit, over the entrance to her pussy, and down to her asshole. I ignore the little sound she emits and the tensing of her muscles.

Like I said, it belongs to me.

I flutter the tip of my tongue over that tight little hole, licking and then sucking, only drawing back when she releases a broken gasp. But by no means am I done. Nah. I need to feel her. All of her. I thrust two fingers into the hole protected by her folds, burying them high and deep.

"Goddamn." I grunt, pulling them free until only my fingertips remain, teasing the entrance before driving them forward again. "Why this pussy so wet, olori?" Thrust again. "Huh? You gon' drown me in this shit."

Her nails claw at and scratch my scalp, my jaws, my shoulders. Growls rumble out of her, and they're so sexy, I vow to myself right here and now that I'll feel them roll down my dick as they climb up her throat.

"Fuck me, Malachi," she snarls. "Fuck me with that mean-ass mouth."

Her body shudders, her hips twisting in a violent rhythm. The walls of her pussy clench so hard, they almost shove me out, but with my own snarl, I lower my head, suck her clit into my mouth, and shove harder against her, reaching higher inside this too-tight, slick sex. I seek out that smooth, firm patch and press my fingertips against it, rubbing, rubbing, not giving her any mercy.

"Jesus." She pants, heels digging into the bed. "Malachi . . ."

"This is what you wanted," I remind her, clamping an arm around her hips, holding her in place. "C'mon and get this nut like the bad bitch you are. 'Cause ain't shit good about you."

I massage her G-spot, never letting up. Her curses burn my ears, spurring me on, fueling me. I attack that little engorged bundle of nerves cresting her sex, licking, sucking, biting. And when her choked scream rends the room seconds before her walls collapse around my fingers, I lift my head, a fierce, brutal satisfaction barreling through me as a stream of clear fluid squirts up from her pussy, spraying my mouth and chin, coating my beard and the front of my shirt.

Lowering my head, I lap at it like sipping from a hose on a hot summer day. When the stream slows to a trickle and then stops, I still sip at her hole, chasing every drop. With a soft whine, she pushes my head away.

"What the *fuck* was that?" Eshe rasps, easing her legs closed and curling them toward her chest.

I stand, looming over her still-shaking body, a damn-near-primitive pride expanding inside me, filling me at the wild, raw, vulnerable look in her eyes. I'm two seconds away from pounding my fists against my chest like a caveman.

Gripping the bottom of my T-shirt, I whip it over my head and swipe it over my chest, neck, and face. I'll need to take a shower—we both will—but at this moment, I want to rub her essence into my skin. Mark myself with it.

"I licked it," I say, tossing the ruined shirt to the floor, edging closer to the bed.

She shakes her head, her curls a glorious tangle on the bedcover. "The hell?" she whispers. "This muthafucka don't talk and then suddenly he fucking bilingual in coochie and ass."

The urge to chuckle surges in me. It wars with the need to pounce on her.

Shit.

She has several assassins on her ass, and one of them is the deadliest in the world. And possibly on my ass too since I didn't complete the contract with Abena. Eshe's aunt wants her dead and, probably even at this moment, is plotting her next move to eradicate her niece from this earth. I still want blood from both of them.

All this should be at the forefront of my mind, because the shit is real.

But she's awakened something in me.

I've had sex before. Plenty of it when the urge strikes. But I've never craved it, and it's never felt like *this*. Like I'm going to claw my way out of tissue and bone if I don't have more. If she doesn't have more of me. Fucking has never felt . . . necessary.

Not until now.

And that fucking terrifies me.

Someone becoming necessary is a weakness. Someone becoming necessary is handing my enemies a way to maim me.

To destroy me.

Miriam was the last person who gave me a reason to breathe, to exist. And when she died, I almost did, too. Allowing Eshe to creep into my skin, my bones to be my reason . . .

No. Never.

My soul fucking rebels at the thought.

Yet . . . yet that knowledge, that deep-rooted fear doesn't stop me from edging closer to her.

Her eyes flare wide, excitement lighting them up, as I lift a knee to the mattress—

My phone rings.

I pause, unmoving. I really contemplate saying *fuck that phone* and continuing with exploring the limits this woman pushes. Discovering who I become when I'm face down in her.

It stops ringing.

Then starts again seconds later.

Shit.

That's my personal phone, and very few people have the phone number. Even fewer would be calling me. After shoving off the bed, I stride over to the small couch tucked in the corner under the window.

Snatching up my jacket, I remove the cell from the pocket and glance down at the screen.

Jamari.

Flicking Eshe a glance, I press my thumb to the ANSWER button and raise the phone to my ear.

"Yeah."

"H, I've been trying to reach you," Jamari says, and the urgency in his voice clears the last of the lust seething in my blood.

"What's going on?"

Eshe sits up, turning around in the bed and facing me. Her jeweled gaze fixes on me, alert, sharp.

"Is Eshe Diallo with you?" I don't answer, and he huffs out an annoyed breath. I don't know why he bothered to ask.

Yeah, I might use him to get info for me, but that's because he's going to do it anyway. I've tried to get Jamari to leave me alone, to go back to being a regular sixteen-year-old who doesn't associate with a killer. Nothing's worked so far.

I made the mistake of snapping the neck of a home invader I spotted climbing through a bedroom window. The house had been Jamari's, and the woman I'd prevented from being raped and probably murdered was his mother. Since Jamari had been in the room, I'd also saved him from witnessing that shit and being scarred for life. Shit, saved him from becoming me. Since that night two years ago, I haven't been able to get rid of Jamari. And at some point, I stopped trying. Still, I'm not dragging him any more into my world than he already insists on being.

"A'ight, fine." The clacking of keys fills our connection for a moment. "For argument's sake, let's just say she is with you. Then she should know Penn Dawson was admitted to Mass General. She was one of the injured at that warehouse explosion."

Fuck. One of Eshe's Seven, and one of the women I spotted her with last night. I don't need Eshe to tell me how she feels about Penn Dawson. She comes under the umbrella of the people Eshe mentioned earlier—the people she would go to war over.

"You got any more details?" I ask.

"She came in with several injuries, but the worst of them are a punctured lung, ruptured spleen, and broken arm. She's out of surgery now, but they have her in a medically induced coma because she also suffered some swelling of the brain, and they're waiting for that to go down. They have her in the ICU for now."

"Shit." I pinch the bridge of my nose. "Okay, good looking out. Just her? No one else?"

"No. I searched, and none of the other Seven have been admitted for treatment."

"Good shit. Thanks."

Ending the call, I round the end of the bed and head toward the small chest of drawers near the door. I open a couple of them, removing a sweatshirt, another T-shirt, and a pair of joggers similar to the ones I'm wearing. I turn around and toss the bundle onto the mattress.

"What's going on?" She slides off the bed, peeling my shirt up and off her, completely unashamed of her nudity. There's no way in hell I can't look at her petite, wickedly curved frame covered in all that smooth, beautiful brown skin. No way my gaze doesn't trace over the very flesh I just feasted on like a starved man. "What was that call about?"

I want to turn away, get my shit together, because all that naked, perfect *her* is distracting as hell. Especially with her taste still lingering on my tongue, my lips. But stellar pussy or not, I'm not fool enough to turn my back on Eshe.

"You need to get dressed so we can go. Penn Dawson is at Mass General."

She freezes, her hand hovering over the sweatshirt. Her eyes . . . shit, her eyes glass over, and before I can stop myself, I move toward her. Why? I don't know. Something—*everything*—in me needs to erase that glaze from her eyes. Permanently eradicate the cause of it from this earth. But as quick as that haunted look took over her gaze, she snaps out of it, and I draw to a halt. Because I was about to make a complete ass of myself over something that has nothing to do with me. Something that isn't my business.

Someone who isn't my business.

Goddamn.

I said before that Eshe Diallo is dangerous.

And every time I've been in her company, in her fucking presence, she's proven it.

"Tell me everything you know," she coldly demands, quickly dressing. My clothes dwarf her, and yet she still manages to appear intimidating.

While I run down the info Jamari gave me, I pull on my boots, a hoodie, and my jacket. I hand her the only footwear available—the boots she wore last night. Again, the knee-high boots should look ridiculous with the enormous sweatshirt and joggers, but she remains regal and proud. No wonder Abena wants her dead. No one laying eyes on Eshe would mistake her for anything other than what she is—a queen.

Unlike when I broke it to her that one of her Seven is in the hospital, she maintains her stoic demeanor as I detail Penn's condition. She occasionally nods, gathering up the empty pizza box and water bottle and carrying the refuse to the kitchen to toss them in the garbage. I frown, a little perplexed, a hell of a lot captivated as she straightens the covers on the pullout, sets the two pillows right, and arranges my chair with its back aligned against the wall as she passes it. She just cleaned my shithole of an apartment.

"I'm guessing your source is reliable," she says, waiting for me by the door, that sharp gaze watching as I strap on my guns and knives.

"Yeah." I cock my head. "We gon' talk about that?"

"What?"

"That." I tip my chin in the direction of the room. "You playing Molly the Maid in my shit."

"Oh." Pause. "No. Did they have any word on the others?"

Narrowing my eyes, I debate whether to push the issue. That wasn't normal.

A memory from when I was a kid shimmers and solidifies in my mind before I'm fast enough to prevent it. My mother, her beautiful, shoulder-length dark curls pulled up in a big puff on top of her head, poking her head inside my bedroom to make sure I picked up my room of all the toys and books I'd played with before coming to the dinner table. Shit. It's been damn near decades—two to be exact—since I thought of that. Since I *allowed* myself to think of that. I blink, giving my head a small shake, and the memory dissipates like smoke, leaving me a little unsettled by its appearance. I lift a hand, rubbing my knuckles over my chest and the aching soreness beneath it.

"Huntsman?"

My head snaps up. Huntsman. She's back to that after calling me *Malachi* when I had my mouth on her pussy. An ugly part of me wants to remind her of that. A bitchy part. But then I remember that Malachi doesn't exist. Eshe is the only person who can't seem to remember that.

"The others?" she presses.

"They're good. At least the hospital has no records of them being admitted for treatment."

Again, she nods and reaches for the doorknob.

"Hold up." I walk over to the old, scratched dresser and grab a black blindfold off the top. "I need—"

"Nah, we're not gonna need that." She waves a hand, pulling the door open with the other. "I could give you the longitude and latitude of this address. Blindfolding me is just overkill."

She exits, leaving me to stare after her.

"Goddammit," I growl, striding across the room and out the apartment. "This way." I grip her upper arm and turn her toward the rear of the house. "I know you're upset, but you gotta move fucking smarter. Do you not remember anything I told you? There's a damn Terminator on your ass. And walking out in the middle of the street like you're fucking bulletproof is one way to prove you're not."

"Look, they could empty all of Mount Doom, and I'm still headed to that hospital. Nothing is going to keep me from checking on Penn. I need to put my eyes on her myself. That's the only way I'll feel that she's safe. That she's not . . ."

She trails off, and I glance over my shoulder, but Eshe stares straight ahead, her expression a clean slate that I can't decipher.

The urge to stop—to pin her to the wall behind her by the throat and demand her thoughts, her feelings, her pain so I can't just share but fucking *gorge* on her like a deranged incubus—snaps and snarls at me. But I resist. Somehow, I resist and keep walking toward the door that should lead to another lower-level apartment but instead is an annex to an underground tunnel that leads to a garage nearly a block over.

Call me paranoid, but being this careful and vigilant has kept me alive this long. Having Eshe beside me has my shit itching. Not even Jamari has seen the inside of these walls, much less joined me here.

But now Eshe has.

I don't want to dwell on what that means.

I jerk my chin toward the black Ford GT with the illegally tinted windows. In seconds, we're seated and rolling out of the garage onto the busy Dorchester Street. She doesn't say much during the twenty-minute ride to Mass General. She's so . . . still. No fidgeting. No talking. Hell, I can't even catch the soft sound of her breathing.

Not for the first time, I want to pry and discover what she's thinking. Without rival, Eshe is the most fascinating creature I've ever encountered, and for the past few days, I've found myself obsessing over her. Wondering what lies under the layers.

Am I safer not knowing?

My fingers tighten on the steering wheel, and I shift slightly away from her, placing more of a mental distance between us than a physical.

The sooner I get her to the hospital and out of my car, the better.

Though, even with a car renowned for its speed, the last twenty minutes seem like twenty hours before I illegally park in front of the Charles/MGH stop. With her fingers wrapped around the handle, Eshe glances over at me.

"Thank you, Malachi," she murmurs. "For everything."

At the sound of *that* name, I glare at her, but she unflinchingly meets my gaze. And what I see there has the snarled admonishment extinguishing on my tongue.

Me popping up at both that cottage and her house to kill her didn't faze her in the least.

Finding out her aunt put a hit on her didn't scare her.

Discovering one of the most mysterious and successful assassins out there tried to kill her didn't even cause her to flinch.

But this—this hospital, her friend inside—has fear fucking swimming in those eyes.

"Eshe . . ."

Before I can say anything else, she slips out of the car, firmly shutting the door behind her. My scrutiny follows her as she crosses the street, steps on the sidewalk, and enters the front entrance of the hospital. When those doors close behind her, I pull off, headed back toward the other side of town.

Except I don't make it far before I'm whipping my Ford GT into an open parking spot a block over from the hospital.

"Fuck," I growl, stepping out and locking the door.

This might be the dumbest thing I've done in recent history. No, taking the job to kill Eshe Diallo was the dumbest, but this—following after her—is definitely a runner-up. Everyone except for Eshe and Abena believes I'm dead. It's the best cover I could ask for to move unseen. And look at me risking that shit. And for what?

Yeah, I still don't have an answer.

Pulling my hoodie up over my head, I stick to the early-evening shadows and hurry back to the hospital, then slip in through a side entrance, avoiding security and cameras. Mass General is a huge hospital, but it's also very busy, and no one pays attention to me as I make my way to the intensive care unit.

The fuck am I doing?

My fists clench in the front pocket of my sweatshirt. The only answer I got is Eshe is my kill, no one else's. But the answer, the justification for me stalking her down in this hospital, needing to lay eyes on her, sounds false in my head, tastes like a lie on my tongue.

The only thing that feels faintly truthful is she's mine until she's not.

I round the corner, nearing the bank of elevators and the main nurses' station just as Eshe steps forward from a group of women of various shapes, sizes, and ethnicities. They all bear the same menacing edge. They fan out around her like a protective living wall; the six women must be the rest of her Seven.

A tall, older white man with dark hair and a petite woman with golden-brown hair and burnished-brown skin emerge from a room directly across from the nurses' desk. Deep lines etch both their faces, and they stop in front of Eshe. Though she's obviously younger, they dip their heads in deference, and Eshe clasps their hands before embracing first the woman and then the man. They must be Penn Dawson's parents.

I can't hear their conversation from my position behind the wall, but Eshe appears to be comforting them before she eases past them to enter the hospital room. Two of the women—Tera Washington and Nef Grant—take up position on either side of the door, while the other four stand with Penn's parents.

Eshe's safe. No one's getting in that room. Not with her personal guard here.

I can turn around and go about my business. I *should* turn around and go about my business. Which is hunting Abena and ridding her of that worthless thing she calls a life. Eshe is on my list, but her aunt rides the top of it. I dragged her out of that warehouse and delivered her back to her people. So yeah, I can go.

And yet, I remain standing here, hidden in plain sight, for several more minutes before finally leaving as silently as I arrived.

CHAPTER NINE

Eshe

She's okay. Penn's going to be okay. She's not like Ma. She's coming back to me and will be as good as new.

I keep repeating this mantra in my head, trying to get it to sink in. A punctured lung, ruptured spleen, broken arm. The doctors are saying the swelling on her brain should go down soon. In the grand scheme of things, her injuries could've been much worse. She's going to make a full recovery. But that logic doesn't unravel or erase the filthy, snarled knot of guilt and dread in my gut. So far, no luck. But I'm not giving up. Because once I stop chanting it, I'm afraid I'll charge out of this loft and wage a war on the streets of Boston, flooding the gutters with blood in revenge . . .

I drag myself back from the edge. Steady myself from spiraling down a dark, crimson-drenched hole that I may not climb back out of until this murderous rage inside me is satisfied.

"Abena's going to fucking pay for this," Maura hisses, her usual smile missing, and the killer that lurks behind her pleasant expression is on full display.

"This wasn't Abena," I say, not removing my gaze from Penn. "Well, not directly."

God, with her hazel eyes closed, her light brown skin mottled with bruises, and her long dark brown hair flat and tangled around her round face, she looks so . . . small. Defenseless.

Nah, fuck that.

Never defenseless.

Not as long as she has us here surrounding her.

"What do you mean this wasn't Abena?" Tera demands. "Who else would come after us? Come after you?"

I glance up, not having realized that she and Nef entered the hospital room and closed the door behind them. The seven of us gather around Penn's bed like a guard. Like a human shield between her and whoever is stupid enough to come after her.

"I said not directly. Since the Huntsman didn't get the job done, she put out another hit on me. Tonight was the work of another assassin by the name of Poison. And I think the same person tried to take us out at the warehouse."

"How do you know all this?" Nef's dark brows arrow down over her equally dark eyes. She must really be worried about Penn in order to show that emotion on her face.

"The Huntsman."

Quiet swells and thickens in the room as they all stare at me in varying degrees of disbelief.

Kenya tilts her head, confusion balling her face up. "Uh, one more time?"

I sigh. "The Huntsman. He pulled me out after the bomb went off and . . ."

"And?" Kenya and Maura damn near yell together.

"And he took me to a safe house and got me together. And fed me pizza."

And gave me the best fucking orgasm I had in my life, but this ain't the time or place to go into that.

"The fuck?" Sienna looks me up and down. "You sure we ain't talking to your ghost right now? That's two times you've come into contact with the fucking bogeyman and lived to tell the tale. That makes you either the luckiest mu'fucka walking or the aforementioned apparition."

"Three times, but that's neither here nor there."

I wave off their assorted versions of "the hell" and "bitch, what'd you just say?" and "you's a lie."

"Anyway, the point is this assassin, who's apparently some badass bitch who's even deadlier than the Huntsman, is on my ass, and, by association, yours, too. This"—I brush my hand down Penn's arm, careful of the IV needle, and gently cradle her hand—"is what she's capable of. What we now have to look out for on top of whatever else bullshit Abena has planned or intends to send our way."

"And after Sienna sent that Donato shipment deep diving, the bullshit's about to come hard and fast. Abena's a cunt, not an idiot. She's going to know who's behind that even if she doesn't have proof," Doc says.

"And that's all that matters. She can't accuse me if she doesn't have proof." I jerk my chin at Sienna. "She doesn't, right?"

Sienna mugs me, offended. "Seriously? As far as they know, while in the middle of transporting that container, the barge mysteriously caught fire. Probably an engine problem. Anyway, the whole thing ended up sinking, taking everything with it. Damn shame. But, hey, that's what insurance is for."

A cold, fierce satisfaction burns through me. Abena's going to have a hell of a time explaining why millions of dollars' worth of guns belonging to the mob now reside at the bottom of the Charles River.

"Poison, Venom, whatever the fuck his name is—" Tera growls.

"Her," I correct.

"Huh?"

"Poison is a she."

Surprise flickers across her face, but then it's almost instantly replaced by a hard fury.

"Well, good for her equal-opportunity ass. Either way, she might've set the bomb, but it's Abena who's pulling the strings, still getting others to do her fucking wet work. Penn is in this fucking bed because of *her*. We already got our plans set in motion. Bisa, Taraji, Moorehead, and Richter said they can meet as soon as Wednesday of next week. That's a week from now. With their influence, manpower, and weapons, that's damn near the numbers Abena has backing her."

I nod, anticipation a fire in my veins.

"Are they all willing to meet in one location?"

"Yeah."

"Good. Set it up for Wednesday at nine P.M. in Buffalo. If all of us roll out to the meet, it'll look suspect as hell. So, Tera, Nef, and Doc, you'll go with me. Kenya, Maura, and Sienna, you'll stay here and watch over Penn and keep our presence seen here in Boston to cover our absence."

They murmur their agreement, the same feral eagerness that courses through me filling their faces.

"In the meantime, we keep the pressure on Abena. Hell is going to be coming her way from the Donatos. And a buy is scheduled for Thursday night from the plug. Coke and pills. Unlike that bullshit meet at the docks, I know this one is legit." That's another thing that will change. How the fuck are the Mwuaji the biggest family in our region and yet we're depending on someone else for our product? *We* should be the fucking plug, and buyers should be coming to *us*. "Sienna, Nef, and Maura? Take a team of soldiers that are loyal to us and make sure that buy doesn't go down. But don't kill Abena's people. Just the suppliers. And if the Mwuajis there don't take the drugs, you go in after they leave and take it. Either way, shit gon' be tight for Abena."

I smile at the thought.

"While she's distracted with the shitstorm on her left hand, she'll be blind to what's happening on her right," Tera murmurs.

My smile widens. "Exactly." After a moment, it bleeds away. "While Penn is here, we take shifts watching over her. I'll take the first one." I slightly tighten my grip on her motionless hand, silently willing her to squeeze back, move a finger, any-fucking-thing.

But she remains so still. So quiet.

The door to the room opens, and we all turn, expecting the doctor or nurse. But that's not who enters. Rage pumps through my veins like a virus, infecting my blood, every organ, every cell. In this moment, I'm created of fury.

"I came as soon as I heard," Abena says, gliding farther into the room with Penn's parents behind her. "I was so sorry to hear about our Penn's injuries."

Syrup practically drips from her words, her tone, but her eyes? Her eyes tell the true story. They gleam with an almost-gloating satisfaction. Maybe no one else sees it, but I catch the insincerity, the smugness underneath that saccharine voice.

I want to reach out and touch the bitch. With my knife.

It takes everything in me to remain next to Penn and not leap across this bed and bury my dagger into Abena's throat.

"Thank you for coming by to check on our daughter," Brian, Penn's father, says. Grace, her mother, stands next to him. She lowers her dark gaze, but not before I glimpse the hatred there. She knows what's up. She sees right through this snake shit Abena's on. "My wife and I appreciate it."

"Of course." She clasps Grace's hands in hers. "And rest assured I have my people on finding out who's behind the explosion. They won't get away with hurting one of mine."

Hers?

This ho.

I don't need to look around to see the other women's reactions. I can practically *feel* the disgust and hate radiating off them. It's damn near palpable and throbbing like a telltale heart.

"Thank you," Brian murmurs, while Grace slides her hands free. If Abena notices Penn's mother rubbing her palm against her pant leg, she doesn't show it.

"Niece." Abena turns to me, and the corner of her mouth quirks. "You must be worried. I know what Penn means to you."

"I know you know. We're just glad you weren't there. Would've hated to see you . . . hurt," I say, voice flat. Now it's crystal clear to me why she decided not to come to Elysian. "Brian, Grace, I'm going to give you time with Penn. It's a little too crowded in here. I'll be right outside."

I head toward the door and pause to kiss Grace's cheek and

hug Brian, then exit the room. Sienna, Doc, and Tera follow me, leaving Nef, Kenya, and Maura inside. Ain't no way in hell we're leaving Abena in that room with Penn unprotected.

We're quiet, standing outside the door, the noise of a busy hospital creating its own soundtrack for our pain, our grief, our rage. Only several feet away from us stands Mirror and a couple of other soldiers. His bright blue eyes steadily meet mine, and I don't look away. If his spooky-looking ass is feeling froggy, I'll be more than willing to jump.

About ten minutes later, the door opens, and Abena emerges with Brian. As if she telepathically sent him a message, Mirror approaches us, a golden apple in his hand. Abena takes it and extends it to Brian.

"Please take this as a token of my esteem and love for your family. If you need me, please don't hesitate to reach out and let me know."

Brian accepts the solid-gold token and nods. "Thank you. We appreciate this and you stopping by."

Smiling, she pats his hand, then turns and strides down the hall. But not before giving me a small devious smile.

I want her fucking blood in my mouth.

"Fake bitch," Brian mutters.

Though there's nothing funny about our current situation, I still chuckle to hear reserved, sophisticated Brian Dawson call Abena out of her name. Or, in other words, speak truth.

He squeezes my shoulder and returns to Penn's room. I wait until the door closes before turning to Sienna.

"Follow her. See where she's going, if she makes any stops, who she's with. Hit me up with reports."

"Got it."

As Sienna walks in the direction Abena disappeared, Tera says, "I've never wanted to body someone as much as I do her. She comes up here to rub in our faces that she can touch us. That she *did* touch one of us. I'm trying to be patient, but I want to be the one to watch her life bleed from her eyes."

"You're not the only one," I softly say, still staring at the bank of elevators as if I can see them closing in front of Abena. "She's going to pay though. Believe that shit."

Forty minutes later, I glance down at my phone. It's been damn near an hour, and no word from Sienna. Not a call or text. Unease creeps into my stomach. I lower my cell, but several minutes later, that niggling feeling hasn't left.

"Fuck it." I scroll to my Favorites list and dial Sienna's phone.

It rings once, twice, three times. Just before it goes to voicemail, an unfamiliar voice greets me.

"Who the fuck is this?" I bark, my worry barreling into anger.

"This is Vanessa Laurel, a nurse in the ER here at Mass General. A Sienna Browder was admitted. Are you a relative?"

"Yes, her sister. I'm on my way down there now."

"Okay, I'll—"

I hang up on her and am already moving for the door.

"Eshe." Tera calls my name, following me out of Penn's room. "What's wrong? What's going on?"

"Sienna is down in the ER. A nurse answered her phone. I'm headed there."

"Not without me."

We rush to the other side of the hospital, and within minutes we reach the ER. A petite, dark-skinned nurse stands by the admission desk, and we approach her.

"Are you Vanessa?" I demand.

"Yes, I am. I'm sorry you had to find out about your sister this way."

I wave her words off with a flick of my fingers. "You're good. What happened to Sienna?"

"Apparently, someone found her in the hospital's parking deck suffering from a gunshot wound to the shoulder. She's in surgery right now. I can take you up to the surgical waiting room, and as soon as the surgery is done, the doctor will come out and talk to you."

"Is she . . . ?" I pause, swallow hard. "What are the . . . ?"

The nurse looks at me with sympathy, and I want to cringe away from it.

"The wound missed anything important, but she had a lot of blood loss. Dr. Kregg is one of our best surgeons, so she's in good hands." She lifts a clear plastic bag that I didn't notice her holding. "Here's your sister's effects. I didn't want to leave them in the ER since we don't have a room for her yet."

I accept the bag from her.

"Thank you," Tera murmurs.

"No problem. I'll be right back to take you up to the waiting room."

She pivots and heads for the doors that lead back to the ER.

"Eshe."

I tear my gaze away from those doors and glance at Tera.

"Look." She dips her chin, gesturing toward my hand.

I lift the clear, plastic bag, and I don't need her to say anything else. Sitting on top of Sienna's clothes is a golden apple.

A muffled yet deafening noise roars in my head. It grows louder and louder the longer I stare at that fucking apple.

I take it for what it is.

A sign.

A warning.

She got to Sienna. And at any time, she can get to my other Seven.

The guilt, thick as tar and just as filthy, returns to coat my mouth, chest. I briefly close my eyes, then open them, meeting Tera's dark, enraged gaze.

"No more waiting. We're bringing the war to that bitch's front step."

I sit with my back pressed against the wall of the shadowed loft, tucked into the corner as if hiding there can also hide me from my racing thoughts or prevent my cracked, warped mind from venturing to a street on a different dark night, leaving me unable to claw my way back from the past.

No, gotdammit, no. There's nothing good that lies down that path. I have to stay grounded in the here, the now. Penn doesn't have anything to do with Ma, and neither does Sienna. They're not the same.

She's okay. Penn's going to be okay. Sienna's going to be okay. They're not like Ma. Penn and Sienna are coming back to me and will be as good as new.

Regardless that Penn still hadn't moved, hadn't woken up by the time Tyeesha arrived to take over the next shift at the hospital . . . Regardless that Sienna lies in another hospital room, recovering from a GSW. They're still going to. Be. Okay.

I cling to that even though the assurance is as thin and delicate as a spider's web. The fact is my friends, my *sisters* are in that hospital because they chose to follow me. Because of me. I almost lost two of the few people I allowed close to me since Ma died, and the thought is suffocating. The guilt is a noose around my neck. Sitting there, watching Penn's round, bruised face, looking so small . . . listening to the machines beep and hiss as they worked to monitor her breathing and heart rate . . . hearing her parents' hushed voices and soft cries . . . Studying Sienna, her shoulder bandaged, and her face spasming with pain even in her sleep . . .

I can't avoid the knowledge that this is on me. If not for me, they and all the rest of the Seven would be safe from this Poison, from Abena. This is my war, and I dragged them into it.

Who else will be sacrificed for my revenge? My ambition?

A sound from the rear of the loft reaches my ears, but I don't glance in that direction. Don't need to. Even when the light tread of footsteps pauses and a shadow disturbs the thin strip of moonlight peeking through the wooden blinds pulled over the floor-to-ceiling windows, I still don't move.

Why would I?

I mean, I'm in *his* domain, after all.

"You're determined to either fuck with me or die. Which is it?"

Now I shift my attention from the far wall and meet the barrel of a Glock 26 and Malachi's narrowed blue eyes. My lips part, but after a moment, I close them. What can I say? Because admitting that I feel safest with the hired assassin determined to take my life doesn't sound particularly smart. Or sane. It sounds way too fucking pathetic.

What's even more pathetic? The relief and lust that flood my body. Good thing my ass is planted on the floor. Both have me equally weak at just the sight of him. At just the whiff of his leather, storm-struck, and gun oil scent, that taut knot slowly loosens in my chest, and I suck in a breath. But at the same time, a corresponding twist tightens low in my belly in a sweet, dark, heated pain.

That's what he is to me. For me.

Confusion and clarity. Pleasure and agony. Vice and purity.

My Achilles' heel.

"Fuck," he mutters, disgust lacing his voice. Tucking his weapon away behind him, he stretches his arm toward me, and I don't hesitate to wrap my smaller hand around his much larger one.

He tugs me to my feet, the corner of his mouth curling as his gaze flicks down to the corner where I was sitting, tucked between his couch and the wall.

"The fuck you doing here, Eshe?" he demands, dropping my hand as if he can't stand touching me. If he wiped his palm on his joggers, I wouldn't have been surprised. Wouldn't have stopped me from going upside his head for the blatant disrespect and hurting my feelings, but nah, I still wouldn't have been surprised. "Do I even need to bother asking how you know about this place, too?"

I release a heavy sigh. "Dead horse. Let that muthafucka lie down, damn." I drop down on his couch and cross my legs up under me. How many times I got to tell this man he's mine? Is it my fault he doesn't believe me? Or won't accept it? Not that he needs to accept the shit for it to be true. "For such a brilliant man, you're acting as dense as a bag of Remy straight bundles."

He looks at me with that spooky, dead-eye stare. "I have no idea what that shit means, but I'm going to assume you just called me stupid. And if that's the case, let me remind you, you broke into my shit like you're homeless."

I ball up my face. "You're so insensitive. The correct term is 'unhoused.'"

"My bad, then. You in my shit like you unhoused as fuck. Why're you here?"

I pause, my heart suddenly beating a thick, nervous tattoo in the base of my throat. My pulse races like the cops are in pursuit of it. Slicking my tongue over my bottom lip, I momentarily squeeze my eyes closed. When I reopen them, Malachi's gaze jumps from my mouth to my eyes.

"The truth?" I rasp.

"Sure. Why not?" His blank, stoic face doesn't reflect the sarcasm dripping from his tone.

"I—I . . ." *I need you to alleviate my guilt. To tell me I'm not at fault even though I am.* Instead, I lick my lips again. "I . . . I'm hungry. You got anything in there to cook?"

I bounce off the couch and stride across the open living space for the kitchen. Yes, I'm obsessed with him, and I may have even stalked him for the last two years, but I have *some* pride, dammit.

The spacious loft is as different from that tiny, run-down studio apartment in Dorchester as Glenlivet 18 is from Wild Irish Rose. While cockroaches would've called Maids.com into that bitch, this place is . . . lovely. Big, lush plants with colorful flowers so vibrant they could be fake fill the space that isn't occupied by furniture. Like his other place, tall bookshelves cover one wall, overstuffed with books. A case of swords, daggers, and axes is mounted on another wall. Blinds cover the floor-to-ceiling windows, but the view of moonlight glistening on the dark waters of Boston Harbor is breathtaking.

This place is just one of the several he owns around the city—hell, the state. And I'm aware of almost all of them. Like I've repeatedly told him. It's been two years of . . . being *absorbed* with him. So there isn't much I'm not aware of when it comes to the Huntsman.

"You mean you don't know?" he asks.

"Frozen pizzas, stir-fry, some vegetables, and a couple of Salisbury steak dinners. Not much in the fridge, though, besides some water and eggs. That orange juice is beyond its expiration date." I shrug. Why ask questions he already knows the answer to? Ignoring his silence that somehow manages to scream, *Bitch!* I pull open the lower cabinet next to the stove and remove a large pan. I set it on top of an eye, then move to the freezer and remove the bag of stir-fry. Something simple that's fast and requires little thought to prepare. I can handle that. In seconds, I have a little bit of olive oil sizzling on low, the bag torn open and the contents poured into the pan.

Without looking over my shoulder at him, I wave toward the pantry. "I know you have some minute rice in—"

Long, hard fingers wrap around my upper arm in an unyielding grip that sears my skin through layers of cotton. Malachi turns me around and, with hands curled around the edge of the counter on either side of my hips, traps me between the gray marble and his big body.

That heat seething inside me flares hot and bright, leaping into flames that a purely primal, wild part of me jumps and dances around to in a primitive beat. Gotdamn, I want to climb and claw at him, leave his golden skin in bloody ribbons even as I sip and lick at that life-giving fluid. Suck at the wounds I inflicted, tend to the wounds that he'll wear like badges of honor. As marks of my ownership.

My breath damn near evaporates in my lungs, my heart stuttering, but the pulse in my pussy takes up the charge, thudding so fast, I choke back a whimper of pleasure-pain.

"You're a sick li'l bitch, aren't you?" he snaps.

Eyes I didn't even realize had closed jerk open, and I meet his glittering gaze.

I chuckle. "Sick bitch? Okay, I'll be that. But what does that make you, then?" I slowly slide a hand between us, granting him an opportunity to stop me. He doesn't though, and I dip my hand lower and lower still until I cup his dick through his joggers. And I moan at all that flesh in my hand. Again. Instantly, my mouth waters, and my jaws ache with the memory of all this cock stretching me. I need this distraction. No, that would be relegating him to something insignificant, ephemeral. I need *him*. "This"—I squeeze him hard enough to make my fingers ache and his eyes flare brighter . . . brighter—"must make you a sick fuck, too."

Giving him a good, long stroke, I tip my head back and smile, feeling mean. Feeling savage with the need to draw blood and make him just as vulnerable as I am.

Shame swirls inside me; I'm not a good person. I never claimed to be.

And if tonight has proven anything, it's that the people I care about most are more than likely to end up collateral damage.

They're okay. Penn and Sienna are going to be okay. They're not like Ma. They're coming back to me and will be as good as new.

A smile curves my mouth, and the sharp edge of it tastes cruel.

"Everyone's so terrified of you, they speak your name in whispers. The bogeyman's bogeyman. The Huntsman." I keep pumping his dick, even while I try to lacerate him with my words, dent that impenetrable shield so he's as raw as I am. I'm attacking him on two fronts—sexual and emotional—and so far, neither is working. His body remains as rigid as a statue, his face as cold as a Boston winter. "It's not just your size or the fact you move like a ghost. Or the way you can stand so still, it's almost unnatural. More than all that, it's your eyes. That startling, clear blue where a person can see their soul reflected back at them—if they have one. A person peers into that empty, crystalline stare and glimpses a thousand screaming souls. Even now I'm wondering if you hear them," I whisper. "Can you keep a secret?"

Of course, he doesn't answer. Well, that's not true. His eyes, blazing with heat, clearly tell me to go fuck myself.

I switch hands, still gripping his dick, and lift the other to cup his chin. I fully expect him to jerk his head away from me or order me not to touch him as he's done in the past. Tendrils of shock undulate through me when he doesn't evade me. When my thumb grazes the lush curve of his bottom lip, he slightly stiffens but doesn't move.

And in that second, this . . . punishment and self-flagellation for him takes a sudden turn. Like when I had him chained to my bed in the cottage, this isn't about pain but something else. Something so multilayered, murky, and complicated, I don't have the words for it, but this is no longer my version of self-harm. It's a plea for him to . . . Jesus. Help me. Free me.

Give me something to make me scream, release this hurt.

Release me.

"A secret," I repeat. "Can you keep it?"

He still doesn't reply, but it's answer enough.

"Other people might be haunted by the lives they take, but I'm not one of those people. When I sleep, the only face that haunts me is my mother's. The faces of the other dead? They don't torment my dreams. And when I look into your eyes, I see the same thing. That's why I think they're so beautiful. A beautiful nightmare."

Silence falls between us, but it seems like my words ricochet off the walls of the kitchen, growing louder and faster with each pass.

His jaw clenches, unclenches. Clenches. Unclenches. He repeatedly swallows as if he's battling back words or perhaps something stronger. That impassive expression remains unreadable, and to anyone else, that's what he would be—unreadable. But I'm a scholar in everything Huntsman. And a Ph.D. in Malachi Bowden.

He's fighting me. Waging war against my words, against whatever they're stirring inside of him. From the hard, pulsing dick in my hand to the ticcing of his jaw under my palm, he can't hide from me.

"You're a pawn, a toy."

That garners an outward physical reaction he's unable to control.

His chin jerks back toward his neck, and I curse myself for not tempering the bald statement. Yes, I'm usually blunt, but this time, I could've softened the blow. No one likes to hear they were played.

He steps back from me, lowering a hand and firmly knocking my hand away from his dick. One step. Two. Three. Until he's leaning against the huge island.

"I'm no one's plaything, olori."

Olori.

Last time he called me that, he growled it between my legs.

I can't help it; my gaze drops below his waist to where his cock shoves against his pants in an angry salute. My palm burns as if the mammoth curved length is branded into the skin. With effort, I raise my scrutiny, and while his dick might be bricked up, his face and eyes appear unaffected, frigid. This isn't Malachi I'm talking to. Not the man who dove face-first into my pussy, then turned it out like a sprinkler system. This is the calculated, in-control Huntsman.

"No, you're not. At least not knowingly," I agree, crossing my arms over my chest. "I keep telling you there isn't much I don't know about you, and you still don't seem to get why. I have knowledge of details about your past, your favorite foods, your favorite movies and books, that no one else does. I keep popping up in your safe houses. Even when we fought, didn't you wonder how I anticipated some of your moves? Yeah, I'm damn good, but I still had an edge. How do you think I know all that?"

He studies me, those gray-blue eyes moving over my face as if searching for answers that he hasn't allowed himself to analyze too deeply until this moment, when I won't let him avoid it any longer. And I catch the exact second that the truth strikes him.

His mouth twists, while his eyebrows arrow down in a fierce scowl.

"You fucking stalking me, Eshe?"

I smile and shrug. "I call it 'research' or even 'reconnaissance,' but okay, since you didn't know I was following you or put cameras in your shit, I suppose technically it could be labeled 'stalking.'"

It's fanciful thinking to believe a blast of fire emanates from him, but hand to the Man, billows of heat roll off him and damn near singe my clothes from my body. Anyone else would be terrified at the fury and pain—mine—blazing in his eyes. But not me.

Oh noooo, not me.

I push off the counter and shift forward, eager to be burned by those flames, by that rage. Shiiid, I want to be consumed by it until nothing's left but ashes. And then, if that muthafucka don't pick up those ashes and rub me all over his naked body, I'ma know somethin'.

"I can't even put the blame on you; it's really mine. Somewhere, I must've played my hand, slipped and forgotten how closely I was being watched. There are times I forget how much of a cunning and dangerous cunt Abena really is, and that got me caught up." I frown. "Of course, I'd heard rumors about you like everyone else, but two years ago on February twenty-second, you came to Elysian. No one else seemed to notice you, but I did. It was how you moved—so a part of the darkness that even I questioned if you existed. But you did, and that night, I followed you when you left. And I saw you track a man, watched you kill him. Watched your face as you did it."

I squeeze my thighs together as my clit thumps and liquid arousal spills from my pussy onto the sweatpants he loaned me.

"What did you see?" he asks, his gaze flicking down.

I don't need to bow my head to glimpse my nipples that are undoubtedly pushing against my sweatshirt.

"Euphoria. Satisfaction. You like what you do. Nah." I shake my head. "You *love* what you do."

"I might nut when I snap your neck, olori," he whispers.

I shiver. Full-body shiver.

I anticipate glimpsing disgust in his gaze, but like I told him—accused him of—earlier, we're both sick fucks.

"Like I said, I'm to blame for you being used. If you have enough resources, money, and motivation, any information is available. And Abena has plenty of all that. I don't know exactly how or when she found out—maybe she had me followed, or I was just careless and didn't cover my tracks. None of it matters now. I should've caught it when there were one too many slick comments with your name dropped in when she'd never mentioned you before. Yeah, she knew."

I smirk, but the anger that always accompanies thoughts of Abena kindles in my chest, and I run my thumb over the skin replacing my amputated pinkie. When his scrutiny skims down, I drop my arms, forcing my hands to relax at my sides.

"When I found you in the woods, I was surprised, but then again, I wasn't. I hadn't expected Abena to make a move on me so soon. But I underestimated her; she sent you of all people after me. She knew what she was doing; she couldn't have found a more brilliant method of punishment. Either I die knowing it's at the hands of the man I developed a . . . preoccupation over. Or I kill that same man and have to live with the pain, grief, and guilt of knowing I took his life. Whichever outcome, she wins."

"*Liar.*"

The word isn't a roar, isn't a crash of sound. It's more of a low, rumbled hiss, and yet it still echoes in the kitchen like a clap of thunder. I blink, taken aback for a second by the power, the intensity of it.

When that big body moves with the quickness of a man half his size and weight, I'm not prepared for it. He lunges for me in a burst of speed and strength that's fueled by the rage glowing in his bright eyes, that curls the corner of his mouth into a fierce snarl.

Does he feel like a feral beast? Has that pure fury stripped away some of his humanity? I hope so. Civility is so overrated.

Adrenaline rushes through me, and I bring my knee up and

kick him hard in the thigh. The impact sings up my own leg. He stumbles a little but keeps coming for me, his open palm flying for my chest. At the last second, I dodge it, but the heel catches me in the shoulder, sending me spinning in a half circle. Pain radiates bright and hot from my hip as it knocks into the stove.

Snatching up the pan, I hurl the hot stir-fry at him. He ducks the food and hot oil but isn't fast enough to miss the back of the pot when I slam it into his temple. Blood trickles from his hairline, and he staggers for only a second before he's hot on my heels again.

Excitement is a lethal melody in my veins, and I dart around the island, grabbing the expandable baton he has taped underneath. Snapping it open, I break it into two pieces and grip the handles, edging back toward the living room.

Malachi stalks me like the beast I compared him to, his nose flaring, his eyes hooded and tracking my every move. He grips the bottom of his hoodie and jerks it over his head, tossing it to the side, and my pussy spasms so hard, the shit feels like a contraction. The light-gray T-shirt clings to his wide shoulders and chest, and never have I wanted to beat the ass of a shirt before. But gotdamn, there's a first time for everything.

For several long moments, we study each other, waiting to see who's going to make the first move. The ferocity that marked the beginning of the fight has passed.

That was rage.

This is foreplay.

Malachi charges me, but at the last second, he feints left, blocks my swing with one arm, and wraps the other around my waist. But using a hook kick, I sweep his feet out from under him, and he hits the ground, taking me with him. We both roll, but in opposite directions, facing each other in low crouches. I still clutch the batons in my fists, and without removing my gaze from him, I toss both of them across the room.

Electricity arcs through me, from the soles of my feet, up my spine, over my scalp, and right back down. My breath whistles in and out of my lungs, and it's a deafening rush of air in my head.

Malachi waits, as still as a statue. And stares at me.

But disgust doesn't brighten his eyes like diamonds. Anger doesn't burn there.

Fascination does. And fucking glee. The same glee I glimpsed on his face the first night I saw him. The night I saw him take a man's life.

I called him twisted. And he is. Just like me.

And that makes him irresistible.

I slowly crawl toward him, and those lovely eyes flare before the dense fringe of lashes lowers, partially hiding his gaze from me. He sits back on his knees, but I keep coming to him. Keep crawling until I'm directly in front of him. Only then do I rise to my knees, too.

"You want to kill me," I murmur, gently grabbing his hand and placing it around my neck. "Hurt me. Try it."

His fingers immediately grip me.

And squeeze.

I softly gasp, arch into his hand, press deeper into that delicious hold. I don't know what he glimpses on my face, but I feel absolutely fucking euphoric. The air I breathe is in his hands because I allow it, and that knowledge has me so wet, my thighs are damn near sliding against each other.

"You're not even trying, Malachi," I taunt, lifting my hand and covering his. "Come on and make me believe that you want my blood staining that black, beautiful soul."

His grip tightens, and for a second, I can almost read his want—no, his *need*—to silence me. And crushing my throat under his fingers would accomplish that. Why? Or rather what? What did I say? Which of my words are goading him to that precipice?

"Shut the fuck up. You don't know what you're talking about." He snatches his hand away from my neck as if my skin singes his palm and fingers.

That snarl ricochets against my skull, joining the replay of all the words I've said. I can't parse it. Not when one thing stands out too clear, drowning everything else out: the disgust threading his voice. But something whispers that it isn't directed toward me. No. That's all projected toward him.

I tilt my head, and though a latent sense of self-preservation urges me to back away from him, telling me that he has the power to hurt me like no other being on this rock, I remain where I am. Crowding him. Forcing him to look at me. Making him be near me. See me.

And staring into those bottomless blue eyes? It's like peering into the abyss and having my soul reflected back at me. I want to cringe and cower from it. But another part of me—the part of me that craves to own all his secrets, his desires, to be his obsession—can't look away.

Is it possible to hate as passionately as I want? Because I do.

He makes me weak by *being* my weakness.

And *that* part of me almost hates him.

"I don't know what I'm talking about?" I repeat. "You called me a liar, and although we've established that is definitely one of my vices, I still take exception to that. So which part? About Abena using you as a pawn to get to me? I agree she's not very imaginative, but—"

"I don't give a fuck about her."

"Then what, Malachi?" I murmur.

"Last time I'm going to tell you: Stop calling me that name," he warns me through clenched teeth.

"It's your name though," I point out, still softly.

Tension is a tangible, nearly visible entity in this room. It fairly streams off his big body in waves. My nature—at least with him—is to poke. But instinct coaches me to hold off. To wait. To give him time. To hold out my hand to him as if he were a wary, wounded, yet still very dangerous predator, then allow him to come to me.

"It's not my name," he finally says, and the words sound as if they traveled through miles of gravel to reach me. "Not anymore. Malachi died years ago."

Died with his foster father on that dirty linoleum floor. He doesn't include that, but I hear it as loud and clear as if he did.

"Fine." I pause. *"Huntsman."*

But because he committed the equivalent of licking my hand and I'm that *give an inch, they'll take the city block* mu'fucka, I edge closer. And closer still until my nose bumps his, until my breath mingles with his.

"Why don't I know what I'm talking about?" I press, unwilling to let it go. I can't. At this point, it's almost physically impossible. "You set me straight on it not being about Abena. So it's not about her sending you to track me down. Definitely not about me tracking you. So, what is it? What is it?" I hum, eyes narrowed, studying his beautiful impassive face.

Then a thought flashes in my head an instant before disbelief and anger catch fire behind my rib cage. My hand shoots out, gripping his jaw in a firm hold that gives him no choice but to look at me.

"The fuck? Is this about my calling you beautiful?" My fingers press deeper into his skin, molding to bone. I won't be surprised if I leave bruises behind shaped like the ridges and whorls of my prints.

I snatch my hand away, but before I can scoot back and place much-needed space between us, his hand shoots out and cuffs my wrist.

"This is about you following me and thinking you know me." He jerks me closer until his breath brushes my lips in an almost kiss. "You got some obscure-ass facts from a fucking family tree that don't mean shit. It just makes you a stalker with a research fetish. What the fuck do you, of all people, know about beauty? About a soul? You're up here trying to pry into my brain when you can't even be truthful about your own shit."

For the first time ever with him, a sliver of fear wiggles its way into my heart, and I want to pull away, afraid of what is about to come out of his mouth.

As if he anticipates my move, he raises a hand and cups the nape of my neck, holding me in place. I could fight him, slam the heel of my palm into his sternum, and use that action to roll and grab the batons. But I'm trapped not just by his grip on my neck but by his words, the cold yet wild look in his eyes, the cruel yet vulnerable slant to his mouth.

In this instant, he's a boxer coming out of his corner, swinging wildly so he doesn't go down for the count.

"You're questioning me, but you still haven't answered why you're here. Why aren't you at the hospital with the people you're supposed to love and protect? The people who need you. Instead, you're here, hiding."

"Shut up," I whisper, now my turn to order him to stop talking.

For the first time, well . . . ever, he smiles.

And it's cruel.

It's beautiful.

"Oh yeah, you're hiding, olori. And running scared. Someone coming for you? You don't give a fuck about that. But coming after your—"

I surge forward, crushing my mouth to his.

CHAPTER TEN

Malachi

Shock sweeps through me, and I can't move.

Her soft, supple mouth presses to mine.

Jesus. I . . . I've never . . .

Her tongue sweeps along the seam of my lips, and though mine remain closed, I swear I can taste her. Taste that sweet and earthy musk.

It's that tease of flavor and the blood pumping hot through my veins, filling my cock so fast, so hard, I'm momentarily light-headed that causes me to inhale sharply. Causes me to release a moan so rough, it emerges from the deepest, darkest parts of me.

Causes me to permit her what no other person has ever had from me.

I don't close my eyes; I can't. It's too late for that. Too late for me. And though I've lived thirty-three years and have seen more than most people should, this is something brand-new. And I don't want to miss a second of it. The press of her mouth to mine? It shudders through me like an earthquake, reconstructing my very foundation.

Eshe pulls back, studies me for a long moment; then whatever she sees has her eyes flaring brighter. With only the rushed, jagged rasp of our breath punctuating the room, she leans forward once more and takes my mouth again.

Takes.

Claims.

Fucks.

This mouth is hers, and I open under the thrust of her tongue, surrendering to the hungry demand in it. Surrendering to the ravenous greed snarling and snapping inside me.

Yeah, I'm not ashamed to admit this is my first kiss, but I'm a quick study. I don't need a tutorial in how to meet her lick for lick, suck for suck. Desire is the best teacher. My grip tightens on the back of her neck, holding her firmly in place as I mimic the glide of her tongue against mine, follow every twist and flick over the roof of my mouth. And soon it's me who's pushing inside her mouth, chasing her moans with my tongue, sinking my teeth into the damn-near-indecent curve of her bottom lip.

I can't get enough.

Not of her taste. Of the texture. Of the little catches of breath and needy groans.

I. Can't. Fucking. Get. Enough.

The fingers of my other hand lift to tunnel through her thick, dark amber curls, fist them, and drag her head back so I can fuck that mouth harder, faster.

One hit. That's all I needed, and now she's an addiction, a craving in my veins.

"Fuck," I grunt. Lifting my other hand to her head and tangling my fingers in the red-and-brown curls, I tip her head back and press my forehead to hers, closing my eyes so I'm not staring at that pretty, damp temptation of a mouth. "There's something else you don't know about me."

"Doubtful. Go ahead though." She rubs the pad of her thumb over my bottom lip, then slides it between hers, slightly moaning, her lashes fluttering. "What is it?"

"I've never kissed a person on the mouth. You were my first. You *are* my first," I say, a low, gravelly admission.

She blinks, her bright gaze roaming my face as if searching for a sign that I'm joking as she slowly leans back. "No. That's not true. You just snatched my soul through my pussy earlier tonight. And I've *seen* the people you've fucked—"

"I never said I haven't fucked. I said 'kissed.'"

What seems like . . . horror spasms across her expression. A chilly, bony fist seizes my heart and squeezes. The fuck? What the hell was that about? Did the thought of being—

"God, Malachi, I'm sorry." Her pained, fervent voice snatches me out of the angry, humiliated spiral I was edging toward. "I didn't know."

The apology is so out of left field, I can't reply or stir when she cups my jaw.

"I shouldn't have taken that from you without your permission. So much has been taken from you—you should've been free to offer that to me or whoever you chose to be your first. If I'd known, I wouldn't have—"

I quiet her with another kiss.

As fast and brutal as our first was, this one . . . this one is a seeking, almost-tender thing that asks questions as much as it demands everything. The languid roll and lick of my tongue is an incongruent dichotomy to the rock-hard length of my dick.

I would've never believed myself capable of gentle. Of tender. And shit, I'm not. This is Eshe.

Sliding one of my hands to the front of her throat, I circle it, relish the quick throb of her pulse. From one instant to the next, the kiss shifts into a hotter, wetter mating. A wilder one. I tighten my grip, hoping against hope that I leave bruises. That I'll look down and find this lovely, smooth skin bearing my personal brand. The thought has me growing harder, and I squeeze her neck. She arches into my hand and moans, encouraging me, goading me.

Goddamn, she's going to be the end of me.

And I'm going to let her be. I'm going to let her be my destruction and enjoy every fucking second of it.

As soon as the thought passes through my head, I wrench my mouth away from hers, shooting to my feet, bringing her with me. In one motion, I haul her over my shoulder and stalk from the living room toward the stairs and the bedroom above.

The one thing on my mind? The *only* thing?

Getting my hands on that beautiful, powerful, wholly deadly body. Getting inside that body.

Once I gain the landing, I toss her onto the king-sized bed with the plain black sheets and immediately follow her down. Slapping my palms on either side of her head, I crowd her, crouched over her smaller curvy frame, mimicking the same position she treated me to days earlier. And though our roles are reversed this time, the same lust, the same feral heat bends and kinks inside me, grinding all reasons why I shouldn't do this—touch her, put my mouth all over her, fuck her—to dust.

Everything in me roars with the need for this, for her.

The only question left is where to put my first bite.

My gaze zeroes in on her mouth. That disrespectful, corrupt, beautiful mouth.

It's been my downfall and my revelation. And I want more. More of those full lips. More of that bold tongue. More of those teasing, dangerous teeth.

More of the strange . . . buzz that both whips me into a frenzy and feeds something deep inside me that I wasn't even aware was starving.

I duck my head, distracting my own dangerous thoughts by setting the edge of my teeth to the graceful column of her throat. Even now, my fingers curl into the mattress, eager and itching to circle her neck again, feel her pulse flutter and race against my skin, thrill in that sign of her potent, gorgeous life force under my hand. Under my control. That power is only sweeter with the knowledge that this unstoppable force of nature wrapped in smooth brown skin and thick, luscious curves has submitted her power to me. That surrender is more intoxicating than any kill.

With a hum that rumbles in my chest like a rusty engine, I follow up that scrape with the flat of my tongue. Cedarwood and hints of jasmine hit my taste buds with the strength and power of a sledgehammer.

"Are you going to fight me, li'l queen? Are you going to run?"

I ask against her skin, rolling my tongue over her rapidly beating pulse.

Her breathy chuckle brushes my ear. "I never run; you should know that by now, Huntsman. But fight you? Oh yeah. If you want, we can get all good and bloody before we fuck." She bows beneath me, rocking her hips upward. "I know you'd like that," she softly taunts.

I rake my teeth down the side of her throat again, but this time I'm not so gentle. Her moan drenches the air with pleasure and unashamed lust. She twists harder beneath me, spreading her legs and planting her feet on the mattress. With a move that's too sharp, too powerful for me to control, she flips, and suddenly I'm under her.

Before I can buck or try to unseat her, regain control, she strokes that hot little pussy over my cock, branding me. My back bows at the searing pleasure, and I clap a restraining hand to her waist and slide the other around her neck. What's becoming my favorite resting place.

She slaps my hand away and replaces mine with hers at my throat. My pulse thunders in my ears, growing louder and louder as her grip tightens. Her hazel eyes gleam with excitement, with the same need pumping through me. I press my head back into the pillow, arching into her hand, pleading for—demanding—a firmer, tighter touch from her.

Did I think she was submitting to me?

Did I believe I wanted that?

No, I may have wanted her submission, but right now I need the woman above me, grinding over my dick with a sadistic gleam in her eyes.

"Rub that pretty cunt all over my dick like you got an itch to scratch," I say, digging my fingertips into her skin. Hard enough so anyone who looks here will know that the feared olori of the Mwuaji let me get close enough to mark her.

"You've become a regular fucking Chatty Cathy." *Goddamn*,

that mouth. Twin needs claw at me. Give her something to fill that insolent mouth—my tongue . . . my cock. And the warring desire wants her to keep talking, continue teasing me. Only she would dare. Only she gets this pass from me. "I really do have the power of the p."

She smirks, and I surge upward, crushing my mouth to hers. It's a hard, almost-punishing thrust of tongues, raking of teeth. When I tear my mouth away, her breath breaks on my lips in heated, fast puffs, and her gaze is bright, fucking glittering.

"Shut up," I growl. *Keep talking.* The contradictory command echoes in my head.

That wicked, taunting smile revisits her lips as she shimmies off me and strips out of my too-big clothes. I've learned several things about Eshe in the last few days. One of them? Modesty is theory, not practice. She doesn't try to conceal her breasts or shaved pussy from me. No, she stalks across the room to my bathroom, comfortable in her skin. When she reappears, she climbs onto the bed and crawls up my body again. Her small, firm, and absolutely perfect breasts are on full display, and my mouth waters to get around those large dark brown tips.

Earlier this evening, I feasted on that juicy flesh between her thighs but neglected to get a taste of those gorgeous tits. Not this time. I'm not going to make that mistake again.

"You're going to be my gift to myself before I—" She bites her lip, cutting off the rest of that sentence. That admission. "C'mere."

"Before you what, Eshe?" I ask, dread pooling in my chest, temporarily eclipsing the lust. My gaze roams her face, searching for . . . something.

She shakes her head and slips her hand behind my neck, pulling me forward until I'm sitting up.

"Atonement," she murmurs. Before I can question that further, demand an explanation, she palms the back of my head and brings me close until I'm face-to-face with those beautiful breasts. I inhale the scent of her skin, and shit, she's not playing fair. I sink beneath the undertow of desire and deliver a sharp nip to her neck and her collarbone. Then I make my way to the tits that have been tormenting me since I woke up to her straddling me in that cottage. I've watched them, free and jiggling, and my palms and fingers itch to plump them, mold them, pinch the berry tips.

I surrender to that fantasy.

On a low growl, I suck a nipple into my mouth, drawing hard. Goddamn, it's better than in my imagination. Her high, tight cry cracks on the air seconds before she drags her nails over my scalp and holds on to my head. The tiny flares of pain from her nails only egg me on, and I curl my tongue around the beaded tip, tormenting it with alternate long, hungry licks and fast stabs. I shape the other tit, squeezing and pinching the nipple.

Eshe writhes against my mouth and hands, those nails digging into me, one clutching me close and the other gripping my shoulder. Her hips roll and slide to the rhythm I'm setting, and she's caught on so quickly, so expertly, I reward her with a graze of my teeth over her swollen nipple.

Another cry rips from her, and I lunge upward, taking her mouth, wrapping my tongue around that muted scream. When I return to her breasts, switching the first for the neglected one, her soft but ragged pants punctuate the air. Only once the second nipple is rigid and a dark, angry brown do I bend her back and trail my lips down her torso to her slightly rounded belly and the shallow bowl of her navel.

"Wait." She plucks at the back of my T-shirt. "Off. Take this off."

For a moment, I go still. Another first. I've never had sex completely naked. A swift lowering or raising of clothes has been all that's needed in the past. She's the first woman I will be skin to skin with, and . . . Yeah, a whisper of fear shimmers in my chest. I've had her pussy in my mouth, and my dick's been down her throat, but this—this will be different. This will be more than a stripping away of clothes. I'm once more giving her something I've never offered another person.

And a part of me is terrified of what Eshe will do with that.

"Hey." She grips my chin, tips my head up. "Huntsman. Where'd you go?"

"Don't call me that. Not here." The demand slips free of me before I can rescind it.

She stills, peers up at me, and shit, I wouldn't blame her if she shoved me off her, telling me and all six of my confused-ass personalities to get it together.

Instead, she cocks her head and strokes my jaw, continuing to silently study me. "Mala—"

I violently shake my head.

"No."

I can't. I just . . . can't.

Not when I'm more physically bare with another person than I've ever been. She can't ask me to be emotionally exposed, too. She might be ready for that—she's also had two years of following me to prepare. I've had literal days to try and become accustomed to the explosion that is Eshe Diallo.

Shaking my head again, I gently shove her off me and jackknife off the bed, strip my clothes and boots off, and dive back onto the bed. Though her hot, soaked pussy leaves a wet path on my thigh as I stroke my bigger naked body over her curvier one, I don't give in to that siren call. Not just yet.

A low, grated groan rumbles out of me as my chest rubs over her belly, over her soft breasts and diamond-hard nipples. I clench my teeth against the agonized pleasure slamming into me like lightning bolts as my piercings make contact with her beaded tips. Eshe lifts her arms, wraps them around my head, and for a moment that's too long and entirely too brief, I bury my face in the crook of her neck.

This . . .

Touch. Skin to skin. Limbs tangled.

It's too much—too raw, too intimate, too exposing.

And, goddamn me to hell, it's not enough.

Inhaling sharply, I ease out of her embrace and sit back on my heels. Her gaze drops to my dick, and it's nearly a physical caress. I fist myself, hissing at the hot jolt of electricity that sizzles up my spine and races back down to tingle in my balls. Slowly, I pump my flesh, twisting my wrist when my hand glides over the swollen and weeping tip. Her tongue peeks out, swiping a path over her bottom lip, and fuck if I don't feel that small lick at the base of my dick. Immediately, I'm snatched back to the night when she swallowed me down, right over that nimble tongue and into her tight-as-fuck throat. The growl that rolls out of me is impossible to contain. And I don't even try.

"You're looking like you want another taste, little queen," I grind out.

"And if I did, you'd give it to me, wouldn't you?" she says. 'Cause it's not a question.

As if her mind is drifting back to when she sucked me dry, her gaze flits over my chest, abdomen, and thigh. Landing on the places she cut me. It's impossible, but those spots tingle, burn. Especially the ones on my dick. I want that again with her. Soon. But right now . . .

"I just had you all over my face and down my throat," I murmur, staring at her puffy pussy lips and the small clit peeking out from the top of them. She fucking shines, she's so drenched. Even as I watch, more moisture leaks out, and this time, it's me who drags my tongue across my lips. "It's only been hours." I dip a finger between her folds, getting it all good and sticky with her. Then I slide it between my lips and suck that delicious wet off my skin. I can't hold my eyes open when her distinctive flavor hits my tongue. Sweet and tangy with a musk that's all her. "Doesn't matter. Might as well be fucking days."

She doesn't reply, doesn't utter a word. Just spreads her thighs wider.

And I dive into her.

Holy fuck. Holy *fuck*.

That hint of her doesn't compare to being face-first in her pussy. I'm drowning in that delectable musk, gorging on it. I open my mouth wide, trying to take her whole sex in my mouth, like a glutton trying to gorge on a feast instead of taking a piece at a time. There's no slowing me down; there's no patience. Not with my tongue spearing between her pussy lips, gathering all that cream. Not with her pretty little clit fluttering with every lick and suck. Not with the small, tight entrance clenching and releasing, clenching and releasing. She is a buffet, and I'm the starving man who just pulled up to the table.

Eshe's thighs squeeze my head in a vise grip. Her hands clutch my head once more, and fuck, she's not a passive rider. Like the warrior she is, she fights me for her pleasure, riding my mouth with sinuous and then sharp, jerky thrusts. My lips and chin are fucking covered in her, and part of me wants to rub the essence of her into my skin so she claims me as much as I claim her.

Claim her.

My mind balks, recoiling as if just faced with a vengeful spirit. I've never desired to claim someone, brand them. Not before her.

And it terrifies me.

The last time I cared—I loved—she was brutally taken from me to a place that I couldn't follow. Different situation, but the terror is the same. It's real.

I slap her thigh, and her eyes narrow on me.

"Turn over. Ass in the air," I order.

She rises on her elbows, eyes narrowed. Slowly, she eases backward and then prowls toward me.

"Nah, Malachi, this ain't that. You turn over." Her tone is soft, but there's steel underneath, and I'm reacting to that note before my mind even acknowledges it.

Without breaking our visual contact, I drop to my back, and she gifts me with a smile that's both beautiful and sinister. Both set my blood pumping, my dick throbbing.

She climbs on top of me, not stopping until she's clutching the headboard and her pussy hovers over my face. I inhale, palm her thick thighs, and push my face into her cunt, dragging Eshe's unique perfume into my lungs. It centers me, forces the panic to retreat, and once more I'm lost in her. I lightly bite one puffy lip and slowly sink two fingers inside her. Slick, smooth muscles clamp down on them, and more of her juice trickles down my hand. I lap at the trail, catching every bit of her. I'm of the *waste not, want not* school of thought, and I'm not wasting one goddamn thing about her.

A long, low moan escapes her, and she rocks against my mouth, spreads her legs wider. Reaching a hand down, she clutches my head harder to her. I get the hint. As I take up an almost-punishing pace in her pussy, pulling free and slamming my fingers inside, twisting my wrist and corkscrewing between those quivering walls, I latch onto her clit. My knuckles pound against her folds, and goddamn, that pussy sucks at me so tightly, so greedily, my fingers might very well be bruised black and blue.

A steady stream of cries falls from her as she bucks and grinds those gorgeous hips. I savor the slap of my fingers against the inside of her thighs and her soaked flesh. With a hungry growl, I suck harder on her clit, flicking it with firm licks. Thrusting my way high up into her, I curl my fingertips, stroking that smooth pad that draws a full-body shudder from her, as well as my name on the tail end of a scream.

Her cunt clamps down on me, and in the next moment, she showers me in cum. *Fuuuuck*. It runs down my fingers, my knuckles, my hand, dripping onto my chin and neck. How the fuck am I supposed to have normal sex again? Return to other people after this sight? After her goddamn bathing me? And I haven't even had my dick inside her yet.

Her chest heaves, and finally, her body relaxes, though shivers continue to run through her. I lap at the residue of her cum, cleaning her thighs of all evidence of her orgasm. I'm so fucking hard, need to be in her so damn bad, I'm in physical pain. I want that—that rain shower of cum—on my cock.

As if the same thought claims her mind, she shifts backward until her pussy slides over my dick. The groan that escapes me is pained, greedy. Sweat dots her chest and throat, and unable to resist the lure of it, I swipe my hand over her slickened skin and lick the perspiration from my palm.

She mimics me, gliding her hand up the middle of my chest, up my throat, until she's squeezing my jaw. Lowering over me, she whispers against my mouth.

"You gonna put that dick in me, Malachi?"

It's an invitation. A challenge. And I'm more than ready to answer both.

"Eshe." I call her name even though her lust-bright eyes are fixed on me. Her breath ghosts over my lips, and my stomach cramps for another taste of her even though I just had my fill. "I've never fucked without a condom, little queen," I murmur, and it shouldn't be possible, but her eyes gleam brighter with a fierce light.

One that says she likes what she just heard. What did she say before? She claimed me as hers. And though she doesn't speak, her snarled *mine* echoes in my head. I've never brought anyone to my places before. Hotel rooms, alleys, bathrooms—but never where I lay my head, so there's no reason to have condoms stashed here. And I don't have one on me. But even if I did . . .

Call me a stupid muthafucka, but I don't want nothing separating her pussy from me. I'm already wearing her on my skin, and I want all of her. No barriers. At least not physically.

Her hand shoots out, circles my throat again as I did to her earlier. And her grip isn't loose. It's firm, threatening, constricting my air, and I can feel every pump of blood through my veins.

"Know who you're fucking," she softly warns, her overbright gaze roaming my face. After several seconds, she slides that hand to the nape of my neck. "Get inside me. Now."

Anticipation surges, and a hot band loops around my lower back, pulling tight. Gliding my dick through her saturated folds, I get good and wet. My cockhead nudges her clit, and she bares her teeth at me, hissing.

Fuck.

Reaching behind my neck, I grasp her wrist and bring her

hand to my mouth—her hand with the missing pinkie finger. Her eyes flare, and she tries to jerk her arm back, but my hold on her hand tightens.

I lower my head and brush my lips over the smooth patch of skin . . .

And drive inside her.

Her lips part on a silent scream, her head tipping back. I grind my teeth against the back draft of ecstasy that blasts through me.

Holy shit.

This pussy is fucking fire.

I still, all my muscles locking. I'm dying inside her.

Or being born again.

She's so goddamn tight. So wet. So blistering hot.

I try to ask her if she's good, tell her how fucking amazing she feels. But the clasp her pussy has on my cock is the same one lassoing my throat, my voice. I can't speak. Can't move. Can't do anything but fucking *feel*.

And if I thought her silken, muscled clasp on my fingers was pure pleasure, wrapped around my dick, it's euphoric. Her sex quivers around me, and it's like tiny kisses over my flesh, sending electrical spasms down my legs, to the soles of my feet, and then back up.

"This pussy," I grind out. "Goddamn."

Releasing her hand, I study her face for any hint of discomfort. I spy lust in her hazel eyes, in the skin pulled taut over her cheekbones, in the parting of her swollen lips. But no distress. No pain.

Thank. Fuck.

I inhale a breath and wait . . . wait for her to move. To take me. Fuck me.

She spreads a hand around the base of my throat and flattens another on my chest. Eyes not leaving mine, she rises up, easing off my dick, and it practically screams in protest. Yeah, this pussy is that perfect, that . . . comforting. When only my cockhead remains inside her, I restrain myself from impatiently thrusting upward, stretching her, branding her. I want to mold her, break her in so only my dick will satisfy her. Only with me will she feel whole, complete.

And maybe I'm fucking projecting.

Eshe sinks her teeth into her bottom lip and drops down my length, plunging me back inside her, and my mind and body damn near shatter with the exquisite pleasure. With her eyes at half-mast, she rides me, taking me over and over. Just like I wanted, like I needed. It requires every bit of restraint not to take over, to sublimate my urge to ram into her until I'm spinning into orgasm. But more than an orgasm, I need her to take me there. I hunger for her lead, her control, because in her hands, I've never felt . . . safer.

I shake my head, hard, as if I can physically dislodge that thought. That ridiculous, dangerous thought. Grunting, I focus on my Eshe, on that silken grasp of her pussy, on the flex of her thighs, the slight tremble of her stomach, the fierce pleasure hardening her face. I lower my gaze to where we connect, fascinated, fucking enraptured by the sight of my flesh shuttling in and out of her . . . Watching her flesh welcoming me . . . seeing my length covered in the wetness I'm eliciting from her body . . . it shoves me toward the edge, and I'm grabbing onto the shreds of my control, my sanity.

Eshe falls forward, her hands slapping against my shoulders, staring down at me. Her mouth works, and seconds later, a flash of silver appears on her lips. A razor. That's what she went to the bathroom for.

My body clenches with anticipation, with hunger. I know what's coming, and fuck, I crave it.

She bends her head over my chest, and it heaves up and down with my heavy breaths. The edge of the razor touches my skin but doesn't pierce it. And she doesn't move to cut me.

I know what she wants. And with my body strung as tight as a bow, my fucking bones damn near crying out for that dark sting, that bite, I surrender.

"Do it," I snap. When she still doesn't move, I growl. "Give it to me. Please."

A low hum rumbles out of her, and in the next second, that sweet, hot pain sings through me. She cut me just under my collarbone. And before I can suck in a breath, she slices me again, right under the first.

I can't contain my groan, don't even try. She's ripped me bare and shredded my pride. Fuck pride. I want more.

"More. More, goddammit."

With another of those hums, she swipes the razor over my nipple, reopening the wound from days ago. Pleasure-pain so hot, so bright, it nearly consumes me, tears through me, and I arch into it. I clench my teeth to imprison the hoarse cry scrambling up my throat. She's slicing me and steadily fucking me, gloving me in that slick, searing heat. It's enough to break me, send me careening into insanity. And I'd welcome it.

Eshe plucks the razor from her lips and covers the seeping cut, sucking on it, rolling her tongue over it.

"Fuck." I grab her hips and, unable to stop myself, slam up into her.

Her chuckle vibrates against my chest, and she lifts her head, mouth stained with my blood. Leaning forward, she kisses me, sharing my very essence with me, and I lick every drop from her lips and tongue. This is primal, maybe even sacrilegious.

And I fucking love it.

She straightens, then falls forward, curling her fingers around the wooden headboard and bowing her smaller frame over mine. With a feral snarl, she rides me, bruising our bodies as they crash together.

The room fills with the sounds of our wet skin smacking, the softer but equally erotic suction of her sex releasing and accepting me. Of her moans and my grunts. Our bodies are in combat, and neither of us is retreating. We're both racing, battling, straining . . .

I reach up, tweak a large, distended nipple, then stroke lower, not stopping until I sweep a firm, tight circle around her clit. One. Two. Three swipes. Then I pinch it.

"Oh fuck." Eshe screams, throwing her head back. The tendons in her neck stand out in sharp relief; her thighs tremble around my hips.

And she breaks.

Her pussy clamps down on my dick, rippling, milking. I stare at her face, taking in the mask of lust twisting it, reveling in that pleasure that seems edged in pain. It's the same sensation that barrels through me. Her sex is so tight, my cock is no doubt marked and branded. And yet, I still fuck through those grasping muscles, burying myself inside her until I can't hold out. Not anymore.

On a low roar, I nut, and it seems endless. Stream after stream of cum shoots in this pussy. We rock and grind against each other, giving and taking every measure of our release. Finally, we slow, moving in an almost-gentle glide instead of the furious pounding of flesh to flesh.

On a sigh, she tumbles to the mattress, sprawling beside me, and silence permeates the room. But it's not awkward, not heavy with tension. For once, a . . . peace settles over me, and while a frisson of fear whispers through me, the contentment, the . . . wholeness overwhelms it. Overwhelms me. A lethargy seeps into my muscles, weighing them down, and my body slowly sinks into the mattress.

I should get up, go shower, treat my cuts, dress, then go downstairs and clean up the kitchen. Make sure the loft is secure. Do anything but sleep in this bed beside her. I don't do sleepovers. Have never trusted anyone enough to be that vulnerable and close my eyes around them.

Yet I don't move.

My mind spins with chaotic thoughts, slamming against my skull again and again. I just experienced the biggest, most soul-stripping orgasm of my life. I should be tired, wiped out. And my body is just that. But not my brain. I have too many questions about this woman who exposes a side of me I'm not sure I like. I for damn sure know I'm comfortable with it. The vulnerable side. The scared side. One question though . . . One question screams louder than the others.

"Why?"

A beat of silence. Then: "Why what?"

"Why have you been following me? Been watching me? Why *me*?"

"Simplest answer? I don't have an answer. At least not one that makes sense. Remember in *Twilight* when that weird-ass wolf inappropriately imprinted on that baby with the equally weird-ass name?"

Yeah, I don't know what the fuck she's talking about. "No."

"You didn't miss much. But what I'm saying is the first time I saw you, you imprinted on me. You crawled inside me like poison, changing me, infecting me . . . killing a part of me. I wasn't the same person after that. I *breathed* for another glimpse of you. And it became an all-consuming need, hunger. You call it 'stalking'; I call it 'necessary.' I couldn't stay away. I can't now, even though it would no doubt be healthier for us both if I did. But I don't give a fuck about none of that. Not boundaries, not health, not being appropriate. I can't lie. Sometimes I hate you for how you've become a compulsion for me. Sometimes I wish I had never laid eyes on you. But the truth is from February twenty-second to now, I'd crash out behind you. I have."

My heart pounds so hard, it bruises my sternum. Something that tastes too close to fear swarms in my chest, coats my tongue. I feel . . . claimed by her in this moment. And it terrifies me that I like it. That I crave more of it.

"Why did you stay in the shadows? Never approach me?"

She gives a soft chuckle. But there's no humor in it.

"Sometimes the known is safer, kinder than the unknown. I haven't been scared often or of much in my life. But you? Even discovering all the details about you down to your favorite food, I still didn't *know* you. If I kept my distance, you couldn't hurt me. Reject me. You could still be mine."

She shifts, rolls over on her side, and when I turn my head, she meets my gaze, her stacked hands tucked under her cheek.

"I haven't seen a lot of beauty in my life." Eshe's voice is hoarse in the thick silence. Probably from the screaming as she came hard and long. It might make me an asshole, but I don't give a fuck—pride coasts through me that I'm the cause of that abused throat. "Death. Street wars. Betrayal. Hate. Blood. Violence is our norm, and suffering is our currency. It's literally what we bank on for survival. It's what I was born into, and what soul I have thrives on it. I'm not ashamed to admit that. It's who I am. But it's not all of me. I am my mother's daughter. I'm the Mwuaji olori. I'm a sister, a friend. It's why I can recognize beauty when I see it. Because they humanize me. They remind me darkness only makes the weakest light shine brighter. That without pain, joy is empty and a cardboard caricature."

She reaches out, swipes a finger through the trickle of blood at my collarbone, and lazily paints my skin with it.

"You're more than the Huntsman. More than the underworld's bogeyman. You're a son, a brother. You're Malachi Bowden." I shake my head, hard, but she holds up a hand, halting my damn-near-frantic movement. After I still, she splays her bloodstained fingers wide on my chest, directly over my heart. "Yes, you are. No bomb, bullet, or sick-ass fuck can take that from you. Do you want to know why I called you a beautiful nightmare?" Her fingertip traces my piercing, brushes the cut directly above it. "Because not all nightmares are scary. Some are revelations, some are protectors or warders, and others are messengers. You're all three. Terrifying, deadly, but still so gotdamn beautiful."

She pokes a fingernail into the newly opened wound, and a sliver of delicious, burning pain slashes through me. Her gaze dips to it. Propping herself up on an elbow, she leans over me, drags her tongue over the cut, her low sound of pleasure vibrating over and through me. Her lips close around my nipple and piercing, teeth catching on the metal and tugging, not so gently.

Another punch of dull pain reverberates through me, and my hips grind into the dick-hardening sensation.

Eshe wastes no time crawling back on top of me, grinding her pussy over my length, coating it in her juices before sliding down over it. She sucks me deep like a hot, tight mouth, and our groans drench the room. My hands fly to her wide hips, pinning them in a hard, inflexible grip as I fuck her from the bottom. Her nails dig into my shoulders, her head tipping back her on shoulders.

Eshe.

She's my beautiful nightmare.

And right now, digging so deep inside her I can't find my way out, I don't want to wake up.

CHAPTER ELEVEN

Eshe

Holy shit, being this lazy should be criminal.

Even hidden several feet away in the dark shadows of the woods surrounding the obodo, I still have a clear view of the stark-white marble of the compound and the startling lack of security around the rear of it. Lowering my monocular, I shake my head. Yeah, we're in the fucking suburbs, and the buildings are located on acres of private property encased by barbwire fences, but *I* made it through. And not by the gotdamn front gate either—riding my motorcycle down the access road that runs parallel to the property, hiking it in the two miles from there, then climbing the fence in the dead zone where the security cameras don't reach. And shit, here we are.

Nah, I stand corrected. This kind of laziness should be punishable by death.

Oh right. I smile grimly, tugging the face covering of the hooded black ski mask and storing the monocular in a pocket on the outside of my thigh. It'll be a lot of death by the time I'm through. Gotta find those silver linings.

I should feel bad about literally bringing war to the steps of the Mwuaji community's heart. Or what is supposed to be the heart of it. There are innocents here. Soldiers and staff who are just doing their jobs. But then there are those here who are fully culpable in the chaos and destruction that Abena has forced on this family. They've cosigned it with either their active participation or their silence and inaction. Now them? I'm not going to feel bad about laying waste to them at all.

I'm minutes from committing the highest form of treason—assassination. And anyone who gets in between me and my target is just collateral damage.

And though a part of me is already mourning the loss of life—the loss of the little pieces of the soul I have left—I'm good on that.

Flipping the release on my holster, I start to hum "Ready or Not" by the Fugees. But the tiny hairs on the back of my neck lift, and in one motion, I whirl around, dropping to my knee, and grabbing my dagger from the sheath on my thigh—

"If you want to die, there are easier ways to go about it. Me, for instance. I'm more than willing to get the job done."

"Son of a bitch." Jerking my face covering up to my forehead, I glare at Malachi. Yeah, that's right. No more Huntsman. That man's dick has rearranged my insides. We *go together*, go together. I don't give a fuck if he won't let me say his name aloud. His mama named him Malachi; I'ma call him Malachi. "What the hell are you doing here?"

He arches an eyebrow, the only inflection in his expression.

"I should be asking you that, *olori*." I don't miss the stress he places on my title. "What the fuck are you up to?"

He crosses his powerful arms across his wide chest, and gotdamn, I'm trying to focus on anarchy. Coming in here with those guns popping against his black camo shirt is just wrong.

I wave a hand and turn back around, fixing my attention back on the obodo.

Why aren't you at the hospital with the people you're supposed to love and protect? The people who need you. Instead, you're here, hiding. And running scared. Someone coming for you? You don't give a fuck about that. But coming after your . . .

I blink, Malachi's words, the same words that drove me from his bed in the middle of the night, rebounding in my head. He'd been right. An assassin's sights set on me? I'm good with that. But Penn almost dying and then Sienna being shot and left for dead in a dirty parking deck? And the rest of my Seven—my sisters—possibly getting hurt or worse because of me and my decisions? No. I can't have that.

Abena started this when she had my mother killed.

It's up to me to finish it.

"Why ask questions you know the answers to?"

"Shit." He grips my arm and turns me back around to look at him, mugging me. "This is stupid as fuck. You're letting your emotions write a check your ass can't cash. You have to stand down."

"I ain't gotta do nothing but stay Black and die. And Michael Jackson and Jesus showed even those two are optional." I curl my lip. "Besides, the only reason you don't want me running up in there is because it'll fuck up your plans to murder me. Am I right?"

"Yeah."

"Well, damn." I jam my fists on my hips. "My pussy's still curving to your dick and you're out here talking 'bout murdering me. I'm just telling you right now: You want back in this good shit"—I point down between my legs—"you're going to have to come with flowers, candy, or some new throwing knives. Something. I mean, serious groveling."

"Sorry, olori. I don't get off on crawling, and my dick doesn't rule me. You and me? We still got business at the end of the day. And you got me fucked up if you think I'm just gonna stand by and let you roll up in there half-cocked because your conscience is playing goddamn footsie with your trigger finger."

I grind my teeth together, and when I speak, I'm faintly surprised a cloud of molar dust doesn't escape. "You can't *let* me do shit. Me bouncing on your dick doesn't make you my man or keeper. Now you can get out of my way, or I can put you out of my way. Those are the only choices I'm giving you. That's me being nice since you got me all relaxed with orgasms. Consider yourself hashtag blessed."

I don't wait for him to release me but jerk free of his hold.

Stepping back, I give him one last hard look. He meets mine with one of his own, those gray-blue eyes promising all sorts of retribution for my loose mouth. Under other circumstances, I would goad him to get just a little of what his gaze telegraphs, but I don't have the time right now.

I got a date with Abena.

And I don't wanna be late.

Tugging down my face mask again, I begin my half-mile trek through the woods toward the obodo. In ten minutes, I reach the edge, hunkered down in the shadows.

"Un-fucking-believable," I mutter, narrowing my eyes. Other than the huge spotlights focused on the rear of the compound, there are no guards in sight. Not a soldier, not a guard, no infrared beams, nothing.

Either Abena's negligent as hell or arrogant. Or both. Since she's greedy as a muthafucka, I'm going with both.

Careless or egotistical she may be, but I still need to be careful if I'm going to infiltrate without being made. Scanning the yard, I note the only patch of shadows cast by the arsenal "shed," and I dart in that direction. Only when I'm under its overhang do I straighten to my full height.

The side door to the main building stands only feet away. A fire escape climbs the side, but it only reaches the second floor, not the third, where Abena's apartment lies. Another set of stairs leads to the basement level and security office, a huge training area, gym, and medical center. The door to the main level it's going to be.

Swiftly crossing the dimly lit area, I pick the lock, and seconds later, it clicks. I silently scoff, twist the knob, and push the door open. In Ma's time, there would've been alarms set on every door and window, and no one would've been able to breach the property, much less the house. How far we've devolved as a family is pathetic.

Rolling my lips, I bite the top one and quietly step inside. Silence greets me. As it should. Contrary to Malachi's assumption,

I'm not moving completely random. Though Abena is a chaos agent, she's also a creature of habit. Doesn't matter if she's been partying, fucking, or sleeping like a baby, she has a cup of peppermint tea at 2:30 every morning. That's my in. My opportunity to get to her.

I pause in the mudroom, listening for noise—voices, footsteps. Not hearing anything, I still reach into the same side pocket with my monocular and pull out a stick with a small circular mirror on it. I slowly hold it out and peek into the glass. No one appears in the reflection. Satisfied, I return it to my thigh. Carefully stepping out, I—

A big, unyielding hand clamps down on my shoulder, yanking me back behind the wall and into the dark shadows of the mudroom. My heart leaps for the base of my throat, and I send my elbow flying back into a rock-hard wall of abs. A familiar sensual scent infiltrates my nose a second later, and I pivot, meeting bright eyes through the rectangular hole in the dark ski mask.

"I don't have time for this," I snap lowly.

"I don't either, but here we are. No plan. Your overemotional ass about to go off half-cocked so we can get killed. Or worse."

I frown. "What's worse than getting killed?" Well, aside from being kidnapped and trapped.

Like I said, all that's visible are his eyes, but they're giving, *Bitch, I wish we had time for show-and-tell*.

Before I can reply, he slides around me and disappears into the corridor.

"Shit," I mutter, then quickly, lightly charge after him.

I know this place better than every feature on my face—nah, every feature on Malachi's face. I've crawled, walked, scaled, run every inch since I was a baby. Just because I moved out once I hit eighteen and Abena couldn't hold me here any longer doesn't erase my memory. Or the love for it etched into my heart. My grandmother, my mother—our mothers before them—all lived and ruled here. This obodo is our history. And now history is about to repeat itself with me assassinating a ruling oba.

An almost-eerie calm settles over me as I follow Malachi up the curving staircase to the second level. We pause at the top, scan the floor, then continue on to the third floor. A part of me wants to balk at letting him take the lead. Especially when this is my mission, my aunt, my burden. But there's also no one I'd trust more to head into war beside other than my Seven.

Then there's the fact that, given he still wants to kill me—so he says—the smart thing to do would keep him in front of me rather than in back of me.

As Malachi's foot hovers above the second-to-last step, I tap his shoulder. He halts and glances back at me. I shake my head and point down at the step. As long as I can remember, that step squeaked. It would possibly alert someone to our presence.

He nods, getting my message, and climbs over the step. I repeat the motion, and seconds later, he reaches the third landing with me right behind him. Malachi flattens his back to the wall and peeks around the corner. Without looking back at me, he holds up two fingers, relaying there are two soldiers standing guard.

After easing his hand to the sheath at his thighs, he removes one, then two knives. He pauses. Then, in a motion so fast that it's damn near supernatural, he moves out and hurls them down the hall. I'm right behind him, running. And before the bodies can hit the ground, I catch one and he hooks the other. Carefully, we lay them down on either side of the door. Just as Malachi bends down and removes his weapons from the soldiers' throats, the door at the end of the hall that leads to the kitchen opens, and a guy holding a tray and tea set steps out.

Shock flashes over his face. In the few seconds between him digesting that we're standing in front of him and dropping the tray to go for the gun at his hip, I'm at his throat, my SIG jammed under his chin.

"Don't even think about it. I'll kill you and help your mama pick out the picture for the programs and the T-shirts. You get me?" He nods, his dark eyes narrowed, the tea set on the tray not betraying one rattle. Admiration for him trickles through me. Even with a gun trained on him, he's not cowering. "You're going to take that tea in to Abena like you usually do. Don't go in there trying to be cute. I'm telling you now—if I even feel like you're attempting to throw ol' girl a lifeline, I'm blowing your shit back. Understood?"

He nods again, his attention flicking over my shoulder. That tea set still doesn't rattle in his grip, but I don't miss the flash of fear in his eyes. Can he tell who's standing behind me? Malachi isn't wearing his signature balaclava, but those eyes might be a giveaway.

I mentally shrug.

Won't matter after tonight.

"Go." I shift to the side and move in behind him, SIG pressed to his spine.

Malachi's presence is a large protective wall at my back. I intended on carrying this out on my own. But in this moment, I'm . . . not mad that he's here with me.

The server knocks on the door, and seconds later, Abena calls out.

"Come in, Marshall."

Marshall glances over his shoulder at me, and I dip my head. His jaw flexes, and he releases a sigh as he twists the knob and opens the door. He doesn't falter as he strides into the room, his gait easy, natural. Malachi and I hang back, letting him shield us until Marshall has made it halfway into the room. Abena, sitting up in her bed, her attention focused on the tablet on her lap rather than the man holding her tea, doesn't notice when we slip in and close the door behind us.

"Evening, Abena," I murmur.

Her head shoots up, her wide dark eyes slamming into mine. Shock loosens her lovely features, her lips slackening even as her body stiffens against the mountains of pillows at her back.

"What the fuck is this?" she rasps, her gaze swinging from me to Marshall, then back to me. I guess she hasn't noticed Malachi yet. But then again, that's his special talent.

I move forward, partially hiding Marshall behind me and keeping her attention centered on me and not the kid who did nothing but be in the wrong, shitty place at the wrong, shitty time. Still . . . I relieve him of his gun and toss it across the room.

"I believe they call it 'chickens coming home to roost,'" I say. Abena dives for her bedside table and the alarm button that's located right under the drawer, but I bury a bullet in the pillow not even an inch from her fingertips. The silencer compresses the blast of the gun, but she still flinches, cradling her hand as if I shot it instead of the bundle of down. "Aht, aht. We don't need to involve any more people."

"I always knew you were a traitorous bitch, *Eshe*," Abena sneers. "I hope you didn't really believe that little mask would hide who you are." She laughs. "God, I should've smothered you in your sleep years ago and saved myself the trouble."

"Don't flatter yourself, Auntie." I roll my face covering up and offer her a feral smile. "I want you to know who's taking your worthless, ain't-shit life. And let's be clear: You couldn't kill me in *your* sleep, much less mine. That's not what you do, how you're built. You'd much rather have someone else do your dirty work. Guess you figured it worked with the mother, why not have a go again with the daughter, right?"

Rage gathers inside me like a tropical storm, gaining power and speed, threatening to tear everything down in its path. I'm set on destruction—Abena's. And if I go down as a result, well, fuck it.

"Your mother, your mother. Aisha, Aisha. I'm so fucking sick and tired of hearing you whine about my goddamn sister. She was a cunt just like my mother. Just like you. And the best thing they ever did for this family was lie down and die like the bitches they were," Abena snarls, hate twisting her features into a hard, ugly mask.

"You disrespectful piece of shit."

She laughs, tipping her head back, and I can just imagine my knife going across her throat, splaying it open, and her blood coating me.

"No, *Niece*. That's 'you disrespectful piece of shit, *oba*.' Your queen. A position you will never know. You will never sit on that throne. You will never be your precious Aisha." She smiles, and if mine was feral, hers is savage. "You're welcome."

You're welcome.

Yourewelcomeyourewelcomeyourewelcome.

A scream swirls in the pit of my stomach, and it surges upward, throwing blows against my ribs and heart, clawing at my throat. It howls in my brain, buzzing, buzzing. My vision goes red—

"Kill her. And let's go."

The cold, rational voice in my ear shoves the haze back a fraction so it's a film, and the furious winds in my ears ease to quiet noise. Fury continues to have me in its grip, but I'm no longer a berserker on the edge of mass annihilation.

"You." Accusation drips from Abena's voice as she throws the covers back and swings her legs over the side of the bed. "You're supposed to be dead."

"Do it," Malachi urges.

As if I need the encouragement.

"Do this, Eshe, and the full weight of this family will be on your—" Abena snaps.

"Shut the fuck up," I growl, charging over to the bed and pistol-whipping her across the cheekbone.

Fierce satisfaction burns through me like the Olympic fucking torch when her skin breaks open and crimson blood sprays across my lips. I lick them. Behind me there's a commotion, but I trust Malachi to handle it. Nothing's going to stop me from this now that I'm so close, I can literally taste it. I press the SIG to Abena's forehead and pull on the trigger . . .

"Eshe! Move!"

A gun blast nearly deafens me, and a pained grunt reaches my ear just before a solid body slams into mine. I roll, staring up into a bright blue pair of eyes—but not Malachi's.

Ekon's.

In a whir of motion, he vaults off me and grabs Abena from the bed. I jump to my feet, right behind him, but the closed door to her bedroom shudders, shouts coming from the other side.

"Fuck!" In the time I glance from her door, Ekon, with Abena cradled in his arms, disappears into one of the obodo's many hidden passages. Some I know of and some I don't. Helplessness and rage consume me as the wall beside the tall armoire slides shut. "Where did he come from?"

I spin around, scouring Abena's bedroom, and Malachi, his fist wrapped around Marshall's arm, points toward an open door on the other side of the room.

"What is that?" Malachi asks Marshall, who wipes blood from a gash on his forehead.

"An adjacent bedroom." He pauses. "The Mirror just started using it."

Malachi's head turns to me. "You didn't know that?"

Embarrassment rushes to my face because I hear the accusation in his tone. That Abena's in the wind and we're trapped here because I went in emotional without all the facts.

"Obviously not." I look at Marshall. "Is there a way out of here? Another exit besides the hall?"

When he doesn't immediately reply, Malachi lowers his arm toward his leg and the knife sheath there. Marshall shakes his head, holding up a hand.

"You don't need to do all that shit, Huntsman. Yeah, I know who you are," he says, his voice strong. He glances at me with a sigh. "I had to try and protect her. She's my queen, and the title deserves my loyalty even if the person doesn't." The bedroom door makes an ominous crack, and the shouting gets louder. They're close to breaking down the reinforced door. We don't have much time. And from Marshall's rushed tone, I assume he guesses it, too. "There's a hidden exit in the Mirror's room. The third brick to the right in the second row above the mantel. It's false. Push it in, and it'll open a door in the wall next to the fireplace. Once you get inside, there's another brick right next to the opening, smooth and larger than the others. Press it and it'll close the wall back. Now hit me."

Neither I nor Malachi needs an explanation about the why of his last request. Malachi draws his arm back and punches him so hard, Marshall crumples to the floor, knocked out.

"Shit." I try to go to him. Try to kneel and see if the kid is still alive, but Malachi grips my arm, preventing me.

"He's fine. He'll wake up with one hell of a headache, but he'll live. Let's go. We don't have a lot of time before they come through that door. And we still don't know where Abena and her fuck boy are."

As much as I hate to admit it, he's right. I got us into this shit, and I can't further risk our lives. Guilt swims inside me, threatening to drown me from the inside out. We bolt across the room, locking the adjoining door and hopefully granting us precious few moments.

"Over here." I race ahead of Malachi to the fireplace, reciting Marshall's directions. I locate and push the brick just like he said, and I hold my breath. "Damn." I expected it, but God, relief streams through me like a swollen spring flood when the section of the wall seamlessly, noiselessly parts. "Malachi."

I wave for him, and he nods, but pauses to shove a huge dresser in front of the door to slow down the onslaught from the other room. And good thing, too, because a loud crash and rush of thunderous feet shake the floor just as he finishes. My heart pounds against my chest wall like Thor's hammer, and with each strike, two thoughts ricochet against my skull: *If he dies, it's your fault. You will never be your precious Aisha.*

"Eshe, close the wall," Malachi barks. He doesn't wait, reaching past me and slamming his hand against the brick. Then he jerks my mask down, covering my face. "Let's go. You have to lead since you're more familiar with this building than I am. So, whatever's going on in your head, get over that shit until later. We need to get out of here."

I nod, though I only pack down the weight of my guilt, my shame, and my self-directed disgust. They're already seeping into my blood, bones, and tissue like waste, and there's no rooting them out. But he's right. It's my responsibility to get us out.

The one thing I didn't think to bring was a flashlight, but as we quickly move, dim lights built along the walls blink to life, illuminating the way. Silently, I send up a prayer to my ancestors because I know damn good and well Abena's ass didn't implement this shit. Though I've never been in this passageway, it's going down, and we're in the east wing. Which means we're closer to the side of the compound that butts up against the Charles River.

And the side that's farthest away from the woods and my bike. Goddamn.

"I'm not exactly sure where we're going to end up at, but I think we won't be far from the river. We'll need to make a run or swim for it."

He doesn't answer, and I ignore the plummeting of my stomach and keep moving. At least fifteen minutes later, we arrive at a door, secured from the inside with a steel bar.

I reach for the bar, and he sets his hand over mine, stopping me. "Ready?"

Not needing him to elaborate, I nod. Ready for whatever we might face on the other side. Ready to fight our way out. Ready to die.

"Yeah." I raise the bar and slowly push the door open just wide enough to slip out side by side into the darkness.

My hands go for my SIG and my Glock, and I grasp—no, desperately sink into—the calm and peace of having the weapons in my palms. It takes a few seconds, but my eyes adjust to the shadows, and I recognize where we stand.

"The road and the river are on the other side of the yard and the fence," I murmur, pointing my Glock toward the barbwire fence about five hundred yards away. Five hundred well-lit, heavily guarded yards.

"Aye." I tilt my head back and meet Malachi's bright gaze. "See you on the other side."

Despite the guilt still churning in my chest and gut, I grin and run for the first body and gun pointed toward me. Ducking, I wrap my arm around the back of his neck and yank down, pulling him off-balance and shooting the soldier behind him at the same time. Jerking my arm back, I let him up and pop him in the temple, then move on to the next person.

I shoot, punch, kick, and slash my way across the yard. Never pausing, never stopping. And they keep coming. I can't allow myself to look across or behind me for Malachi, because one second, one mistake, could mean my life. And I trust the Huntsman to make it out of this alive.

He has to.

Because that's one death I don't think I could bear.

A soldier rushes toward me, his dagger glinting in the moonlight, and I pull the trigger on my Glock. Nothing.

"Fuck," I mutter.

Thinking fast, I hurl it at him, and the butt smashes into his forehead, and his feet fly out from under him. I run, bending down long enough to slash his throat, and then leap, hitting the fence. I scramble up, and bullets ping the wire next to me, but I keep going, not slowing down.

A huge body climbs next to me, and for a moment, I think it's a soldier, but the ski mask, wide shoulders, and flash of blue as he glances at me clue me in to his identity.

Thank God.

As if his height and weight mean nothing, Malachi clambers up the twelve-foot fence like an acrobat, before flipping over the top and scaling down the other side. When he hits the ground, I quickly but carefully swing my first leg over the top. Mwuaji soldiers are closing in on me, and my lead shrinks with each passing second. Gritting my teeth, I lift my other leg and climb down . . .

Or I try.

And try.

Fuck.

Fuckfuckfuck.

My hoodie is caught on the wire, so tangled that I can't even slip out of it.

I look down, my lips parted to call out to Malachi for help.

But there's only empty shadows at the bottom of the fence.

He left me.

CHAPTER TWELVE

Malachi

I stare at Eshe from the dense shadows surrounding the perimeter of the obodo's fence. She should give up. The Mwuaji soldiers are damn near on top of her, her hands must be cut up from grabbing onto the razor wire, and from my vantage point, her top is good and tangled. The only way it's coming off is with a good layer of skin and tissue.

And yet she continues to struggle and fight.

That's the shit that got her in the situation she's in now.

The shit that damn near got both of us killed.

Didn't nobody tell your big pussy-whipped ass to go after her.

Facts.

Can't argue with myself when I'm right. I should've kept my ass in my bed and let her go on this suicide mission by herself. Ill planned. Running off emotion. Those two elements right there are guaranteed failure. And after warning her of that, even then I should've said fuck it. I'm in the business of killing, not getting killed. And still, I followed.

She's dangerous. For me. For herself.

If I'm fucking smart, I'll see this shit as a sign—a goddamn omen like them fucking wise men and their star—to get the fuck on. Abena now knows I'm alive when, before tonight, I had some kind of anonymity since Eshe spread the rumor that she killed me. That's done.

I don't owe Eshe shit, and she's brought me nothing but trouble.

I turn, wade deeper into the shadows.

Shit.

Racing back across the couple of hundred yards, I pull my Glocks and jam fresh ammunition in them. Double fisting them, I fire on the Mwuaji soldiers climbing too close to Eshe, picking them off like fish in a barrel. Their cries pierce the night, and they fall to the ground, colliding with others or hanging from the fence, limbs twisted and snagged in the razor.

Sliding one of the guns into the holster at my back, I continue shooting even as I haul ass and vault onto the fence directly beneath Eshe. Making quick work of scaling it, I hurriedly holster my second gun and pull out my knife, then slice away the back of the hoodie. She falls out of the shirt, and I catch her in my one arm, stabilizing her body until she hooks her fingers and feet into the wire.

I glance down, and *fuck*—more soldiers charge toward us. So many. And I don't have either of my weapons in my hands. I'm fu—

The crack of gunfire ricochets in the night air seconds before a bullet plows into a soldier reaching for Eshe. An instant later, another bullet sends another one wheeling back and off the fence. Then another. And another.

Someone is picking off the Mwuaji soldiers one by one. I don't question it. Not right now. There'll be time for that later. At this moment, we just need to get the fuck outta here.

"Here." I hold my Glock out to her, and when her gaze meets mine, a ripple of *something* courses through me. It's something I don't have the time or inclination to dissect. "Take it."

She curls her fingers around the grip and takes aim, firing as she clambers down. Our boots hit the ground at the same time, and we waste no time in booking it in the direction of the river road. Even when the bullets cease slamming into the grass at our heels, we still run. And don't stop until the lights of the compound are far in the distance.

Before we fully disappear into the night, I look over my shoulder and up toward the compound roof, the direction from where the bullets came. A shadow, darker than the rest, shifts from the others. The form is tall, thick. Feminine.

I can't see her face—have never seen her face—but I know with a certainty that the figure is Poison.

Why would she essentially save our lives? Shit, I don't know. Maybe because if the Mwuaji kill us before Poison, she doesn't get paid. And the Creed will look at our deaths as a failure. Then they will come for her.

So yeah, I don't know the reason behind her actions, but being from the same world, I can guess. And fuck it. I'm thankful no matter how mercenary.

"No, this way," I say, veering to the right when she would've continued straight.

We've been going for at least twenty minutes without stopping, and Eshe has kept up with me, not falling behind or complaining. I can't even lie, I'm impressed.

"The road back to Boston is this way." She jabs a finger over her shoulder.

"Yeah, and every Mwuaji soldier is going to be watching that road and the area on either side of it. I've arranged another mode of transportation. This way," I repeat, then take off, leaving her to follow me. Or not. It's up to her.

Several seconds pass, and then her footsteps pound on the ground behind me. She trusts me. It's the only reason why she would place her safety in my hands without further follow-up questions or proof. Yeah, I got her down off that fence, but part of me still wants to snatch her up and shake her for being so foolish as to believe me. *Me*, of all people.

But the other part . . .

The other part yearns to wrap a hand around the back of her neck and yank her to me, tip her head back, and claim her mouth again.

I do neither.

We push through trees and underbrush, and the loamy smell of the Charles River permeates the air. Soon, we crouch down on the bank and wait. Minutes later, a thin white light flickers once, twice, three times in quick succession.

"That's our signal and ride."

Reaching back, I grab her hand and, still bent down, race as quietly and quickly as possible toward the light. A darker shadow bobs on the water several feet away, and I approach it, tugging Eshe behind me.

"H," the obscure figure in the canoe softly calls, and raises a hand. He throws his hood back, and Jamari grins at me. "I thought I was going to have to come look for you."

"Stop calling me that stupid name. And no, you didn't. You were going to keep your ass in the boat like I told you."

I let Eshe climb into the canoe first and move to the middle. Then, with a low grunt, I shove the small boat off the bank, wade into the water a little, and follow them into it. The vessel rocks for several moments before settling. Jamari releases an exaggerated sigh, and shaking my head, I yank off my ski mask, pick up an oar, and begin paddling. He does the same.

The half-moon is high and bright in the sky, and we avoid the part of the river illuminated by its pearly glow. Soon, we've adopted a smooth rhythm, and we're skimming across the river. It's quiet, the only sound the muted dip of our oars hitting the water. We're not far enough away for me to completely let my guard down, to relax, but for the first time since entering that hidden passageway, we don't have people with guns on our asses.

I focus on the steady, almost . . . hypnotic movement. Focus on it and studying the graceful line of Eshe's back, the tangled mass of curls. At some point, I gave her my shirt to cover her half-naked torso, since I'd only left her in a sports bra up on that fence. And though my shirt swamps her in the overly large material, it can't hide the slump of her shoulders, the slight bow of her head.

I've never witnessed defeat on Eshe. Not even when I walked into my loft earlier tonight. But right now? I may not have seen her wear it, but I recognize it.

My fingers tighten around the oar.

Stay right where you are, muthafuckas. Don't you move. Don't trace the line of her spine. Don't caress the nape of her neck. Don't you fucking dare stroke those curls.

I briefly close my eyes and inhale a deep breath. When I open them, I meet Jamari's wide gaze. I give him a flat, baleful stare, and he smiles, then shifts his attention over my shoulder. A few seconds later, I catch the flaring of his eyes, and he looks at me again.

Silently groaning, I grind out, "Don't do it."

For the first time, Eshe seems to stir, and she straightens, glancing at Jamari, then over her shoulder at me, faintly frowning.

Jamari cocks his head. "Now, H . . ."

"No, you—"

Jamari clears his throat, settling the oar across his lap. "Don't you leave him, Samwise Gamgee. And I don't mean to."

Eshe emits a sound that's somewhere between a gasp and a laugh. Half turning, she faces me, her full, pretty lips forming an O. I stare at them, imagining my dick spreading that small circle wider and wider before I give myself a hard mental shake.

"Did he just . . . ?" Eshe waves a hand toward Jamari.

I scowl in reply.

"What?" Jamari chuckles, dipping his oar back in the water. "You weren't thinking it?"

"No."

Eshe peeks back toward the shore we just left. "I mean . . . it is kinda giving *Lord of the Rings*."

I groan. "Don't encourage him."

Quiet falls between us.

Then a snicker.

Shit. I pinch the bridge of my nose.

"I heard it as soon as I said it. Fuckers," I mutter, just as they laugh uncontrollably.

Warmth bubbles up in my chest, and maybe it's the night, the rush of the near-death experience, or the release of stress, but I loose a low, soft chuckle. The shit's so foreign, so weird, it feels like rusty nails scraping over my throat. Sounds like it, too. And yet, it feels . . . good.

Eshe's and Jamari's laughter abruptly cuts off, and they both gape at me.

"The fuck?" Jamari whispers.

"What's happening right now?" Eshe frowns, looking two seconds away from setting the back of her hand over my forehead as if checking for a temperature like an old-school mama.

"Fuck both of you."

More cackling, and then we row across the Charles River to safety.

"Bunking down in the same place twice? Isn't that breaking some unspoken rule of yours?" Eshe asks, as I punch in the code to the rear entrance to the warehouse on the waterfront.

Leaning forward, I wait for the retinal scan to finish and then push the door open.

"Only your stalking ass knows about my other properties," I remind her. "And there were just two people who knew the location of my main place. Abena found it because she paid someone off for the information."

We reach the second level, and I repeat the same process on the reinforced steel door, then enter the loft.

"I'm going to assume that person has been efficiently and painfully unalived."

I don't reply. Because what's understood doesn't need to be explained.

"Who was it? No offense, but you're not just antisocial and extremely mistrustful of the human race as a whole but paranoid as fuck. Who did you allow to have the info of where you laid your head?" she presses, striding across the living room, her usually graceful, confident stride almost disjointed, jittery.

Frowning, I study her as she crosses her arms over her chest and restlessly paces from one side of the room to the other.

"Derrick."

Her head pops up at my answer, confusion wrinkling her brow. *Join the club.* I don't know why I'm telling her any of this. Shit. I don't know why I'm talking, period.

"Derrick," she repeats. "But he's been dead for seven years."

"Yeah, he has been." A splinter of old, dusty pain pulses beneath my skin. Funny how I haven't thought of him in years—haven't allowed myself to—and now he's been on my mind a few times in as many days. "He was the one person I trusted for years. Not since . . ."

I duck my head and start for the kitchen. It's going on seven o'clock in the morning now, and the only sleep I've had was those couple of hours after Eshe and I fucked. I need coffee, a shower, then to crash for at least two more before getting up and hunting down Abena to finish the job we fucked up.

"Before he died, he spent a lot of time at my place. We were damn near roommates because he didn't have family. Never risked getting seriously involved with someone or having kids because that only gave his enemies easy targets."

I fall silent, what Eshe relayed about my own family jumping to my mind. God, I wish my own father had been as fucking thoughtful as Derrick. Not being born would've been a blessing compared to being abandoned and watching my sister die in front of my eyes. Shaking my head as if that can eject my thoughts, I round the island and open the cabinet door over the stove. I pull down the box of coffee pods and pop one in the machine.

Just as I grab a cup from the cabinet above me, Eshe pads into the room behind me, nabs the broom and dustpan from the closet—I don't even bother asking how she knew of it—and starts cleaning up the mess we left last night.

"I'm guessing Derrick told someone he was staying with you," she murmurs into the silence several moments later.

I nod as the fragrant, strong scent of freshly brewing coffee permeates the air.

"Yeah, his Creed handler and a man he considered his best

friend. Also the man who took him out when Derrick failed to complete a hit."

Gutting Noah Lacombe had been a long time coming. I don't give a fuck that it hadn't been personal for him when he'd blown the back of Derrick's head off. Just a Tuesday. The only thing that had saved his life seven years ago was knowing Derrick believed the same thing. But betraying me to Abena? That greenlit my hatred that had never fully disappeared. And when I sliced that tongue from his mouth before putting a bullet between his eyes, I made sure the shit was for old and new.

"I can see you over there just reminiscing." She snorts, sweeping the last of the soggy vegetables up into the dustpan before dumping them into the garbage can. "I hope you made him hurt." Switching out the broom and dustpan for the mop and bucket, she glances over at me. "Who's the other person who knew about the location of your place?"

"Jamari."

"Yeah, he didn't betray you," she says with an abrupt chuckle.

I stare at her as she takes the bucket over to the sink and fills it with hot water and dish detergent. *I* know that, but how does she?

"Why do you say that? You was in his company for a few hours. Not enough time to make that kind of determination."

She looks up at me from where she's crouched under the sink, a bottle of bleach in her hand. "And it took all of ten minutes of those hours to know how much that boy looks up to you and worships you. I think he'd throw himself in that river he rowed a whole-ass canoe across before betraying you. When you're around snakes long enough, recognizing purity of soul isn't hard to do. It shines like a beacon, and you have two reactions: Dirty it or protect it."

"Yeah?" I remember my cup of coffee and pick it up. "Which side do you fall on?"

She straightens and looks me dead in the eye, shrugging a shoulder. "Depends. But Jamari? He's a fucking national treasure. Protect it."

I snort, handing her the cup. Surprise flashes in her hazel eyes before she hesitantly accepts it. Not caring to see the gratitude in those pretty eyes, I turn around for another cup and pod.

"That national treasure is one of the best hackers on the dark web and at this very moment is either being hunted or recruited by the FBI. At sixteen."

"All I heard is he's as brilliant as he is sweet. With very discerning taste in movies."

"Jesus."

I pop the lid down on the coffee maker and focus on that while she laughs and mops the floor.

"How did he know to be waiting for us on the river?" she asks, wiping the mop back and forth, and it's almost as if she's lost in a trance. And I'm damn near caught up in it, only the hiss and pop of the brewing coffee yanking me out.

"I didn't know what I was going into, so on my way to the compound, I contacted him and told him to be on standby. Woods surround three sides, and the river borders the other. Escaping by land would've been expected, and that's probably where they're searching even now. The odds of them thinking we went to the river were slimmer."

"You just have canoes on hand?" She side-eyes me.

"You don't?"

"Can't say I've ever needed one. But then again, I'm not a paid assassin." She tilts her head, studying me when I shrug. "You don't feel bad involving him in your shit? I had a body count at sixteen. I can just look at Jamari and tell he doesn't know what it is to look in someone's eyes and see the life leave them. Not everyone belongs in our world."

I turn around, taking my time and deliberately picking up the cup of coffee. The seconds afford me time to get my annoyance at the insult she delivered under control.

"You claim to have spent two years stalking me—"

"Studying you."

"—and yet you still ask me some shit like that." I lift my cup, sipping the brew. She doesn't flinch, just steadily meets my hard stare. "You're the one who ran my shit down. So yeah, I don't do hits on kids, and I also don't willfully involve them in my business. But, contrary to what you think, you don't know Jamari. Yeah, he's brilliant and loyal, but he's also stubborn as fuck. And no matter how many times I tell him to leave me alone, he won't. It's that same loyalty that won't let him forget he ever met me. So it's either I take him under my wing and monitor his activities or let him go off on his own and get killed. That's what tonight was about. Feel me?"

She nods, her thoughtful scrutiny leaving me feeling splayed wide open, exposed. I'm seconds from telling her to find something safe to do when she resumes mopping. Once she finishes with the floor and empties the bucket in the bathroom—again, not asking how she knew its location in the loft—she returns to the kitchen and scrubs the pan.

"You don't have to do all that," I say, sipping my coffee with a scowl. "I don't need a maid."

"I don't mind. I . . . need it, actually."

"Nah." I set my coffee cup down, and when she glances at it, I shift, blocking her view, and reach over, twisting the faucet off. "What you need—what we both need—is a shower and sleep."

Irritation immediately flashes over her face, tightening her beautiful and tired features.

"I thought we covered you trying to tell me what I can and can't do. Refresher course." Her soapy hands ball into fists. "You can't."

I crowd closer to her, bumping her chest with my own. Bowing my head over hers, I get up in her face until our noses bump. Of course, Eshe doesn't back down. No, she pushes closer because that's what this is about. For her, anyway.

"You wanna fight, olori? Work out what has you practically climbing these damn walls? 'Cause you've been acting like you strung out since we got here. Now I'm tired. I've been through a fucking gauntlet of shit tonight, and the last thing I'm going to do at God o'clock in the morning is indulge you and the guilt or whatever the hell is eating yo' ass up. You got two choices. Either I can give you a hit of this dick to calm your li'l ass down, or you can get in that fucking shower and take your ass to sleep so we can figure out our next step with Abena. What's it gonna be, olori?"

Her narrowed gaze roams my face, and for a long moment, I return that stare, waiting for her to pop off. With Eshe, there's no telling. No one could ever call her predictable. But as the seconds tick by and I don't back down, the tension gradually eases from her body, and her lashes lower, a long, low breath shuddering from between her parted lips.

"Shower," she murmurs.

"All right."

There's no gloating in my voice as I raise my hand and cuff the back of her neck. Squeezing the sides lightly, I tilt her head back, and the sadness—no, the desolation—etched there is a gut punch.

This woman with the eyes of a raptor, face of a warrior angel, body of a sinner, and soul of a monster chained me to her bed, forced me to share it, then broke me with savage pleasure. And now she's doing the same, but she's tearing me apart with the need to destroy the source of her pain, her grief.

I didn't ask for this, for damn sure don't want it.

I'm not that beautiful soul she once called me, and I never aimed to be. But in this moment, and for the first time since I stood between my Miriam and her murderer, I want to be. God help me—the same God who forsook me on that same night when both my and my sister's blood stained that ratty-ass trailer's floor—I want to be.

Shock ripples through me at the unwanted revelation, a quake that rocks so deep, I involuntarily take a step back and away from Eshe, but with my hand still gripping her neck, I bring her with me. And if that isn't a sign, a fucking omen, I don't know what is.

Jesus Christ.

She stalked me.

Repulsion creeps through me, leaving a slick, oily grime behind. Not because I'm disgusted by her twisted actions. No, my revulsion is self-directed. Because I'm not repulsed. I'm hard.

What kind of sick fuck does that make me?

Hers. It makes you her sick fuck.

My mind whispers the claim before I can shut it down, and the electrifying shock of it is enough for me to release her. I pinch my forehead, rubbing it, and looking everywhere but down at her upturned face.

"Huntsman," she says, and I drop my arm, a bolt of something I don't recognize charging through me at the sound of that name on her lips.

That's a lie. Yeah, I do. I recognize it.

Revulsion.

"Malachi," I growl.

She doesn't betray a noticeable reaction, but I can practically see that big-ass brain of hers working behind those pretty eyes. "I thought you didn't want me to call you by that name."

I didn't; shit, I don't. And I'd snatch the throat out of anyone else who uttered it so they wouldn't make that fucking mistake again. I don't want to be reminded of the innocent boy I was— the person I abandoned to become the monster I am. But somewhere in the past few days, I've started to crave that name from her. Hunger for how she looks at me when she says it. Like she sees the man as well as the assassin.

Like she can't get enough of both.

That has my head reeling, my heart speeding so fast, I grip the counter to steady myself.

"Malachi," I repeat, not offering a further explanation. I don't have one.

But as she peers into my eyes, for the first time since she made the outlandish claim, I believe—I believe Eshe knows me.

"Malachi," she murmurs, dipping her head in acknowledgment. Because she's her, I halfway expect to see some kind of smirk, some kind of *I told you so*. Instead, looks toward the stairs and the bedroom. "Shower?"

"Yeah, shower."

CHAPTER THIRTEEN

Eshe

I stare down at the burner phone Malachi loaned me since mine is still buried under a pile of rubble somewhere at Elysian. Sighing, I sink down on top of the toilet lid in Malachi's cavernous and surprisingly spotless bathroom. One thing I've learned about Malachi—he's clean, organized. I assume it has more to do with a forensic mindset than a *cleanliness next to godliness* one, but I appreciate it, nonetheless. Just one more thing that has me itching to do *unclean* things to him.

It's easier to focus on my ever-present lust for him than what I have to do next.

Closing my eyes, I punch in the private number I know by heart, as it hasn't changed in fifteen years.

"Yeah?" Tera answers, suspicion lacing her voice.

"It's me," I say.

"Eshe? What number are you calling from?" I can picture the frown that's no doubt darkening her face.

"A burner. Listen, Tera." I pause, swallowing past a throat gone tighter and tighter, a glass fist of guilt and shame gripping me. "I fucked up tonight."

She goes quiet. "What happened, and what do you need me to do?"

No panic, no anger. No judgment. When I deserve so much judgment.

"I . . . I infiltrated the obodo tonight and went after Abena. I tried to take her out."

I wait for the explosion—shit, bad choice of words—from Tera, and I don't have long to wait.

"Gotdammit, Eshe," she hisses. "What the hell were you thinking? Going in there without a plan? Without *us*? Anything could've happened. Anything. You could've been captured. Killed. Shit." Her breath blasted in my ear. "We had a timeline. A fucking plan. Hell, we just discussed it. Why would you put your damn life on the line for some crazy-ass shit like that?"

"I know, I know." There's nothing else I can say but that. I fucked up. Bad. "Seeing Penn and then Sienna in that hospital hurt. Seeing Penn's parents' faces—the fear and pain there—that was all on me. And I couldn't take it. I had to do something about it."

"Nah, Eshe, that night was on the person who set that bomb, and it's on Abena, not you. Same with Sienna being shot."

"But she was after me. Everyone was hurt because Abena is after me."

A beat of silence pulses over our connection so loud, it echoes in my head.

"Eshe, where are you? I'm on my way to come—"

"No." I shake my head even though she can't see the gesture. "I'm fine. I'm with . . . the Huntsman," I admit on a murmur.

A long, loud beat of silence pulses in my ear.

"The Huntsman? What do you mean the Huntsman? Jesus be common sense the size of a gnat's ass, Eshe, *please* tell me you didn't just say what I think you just said?" When I remain silent, she huffs out a string of inventive and long profanity. "The fuuuuuuck. Are you crazy? Why? Just tell me why? Is he the one who convinced you to go on that stupid-ass mission? It sounds like something he'd do," she mutters.

"No, Tera, it doesn't, and he didn't," I snap, inexplicably irritated by her attack of Malachi. Well, *attack* is a strong word, but I don't like her denigrating him. Inhaling a breath, I hold it, then slowly exhale, pinching the bridge of my nose. "And yes, I am with him. Going after Abena? That was all me. As a matter of fact, he tried to stop me, and when I wouldn't listen, he had my back. Then later, when it all went to shit, he saved my life. He returned for me when he could've left me."

I still don't know why he did it. He was outta there, off scot-free. But he came back.

For me.

Tilting my head, I stare at the open doorway and the shadowed, empty bedroom beyond. Just when I believe I have that man nailed down, he does something selfless like rescue me or tells me to call him by the name he hates and had expressly forbidden me to even utter aloud.

Shaking my head, I refocus on Tera.

"Well, I'm thankful he didn't let you take your stubborn, emotional ass into the obodo alone. But as grateful as I might be, he's the Huntsman, Eshe. And that alone is good enough reason not to trust him. The only thing we know for sure about him is he's a killer. No, two things for sure. He's vowed to kill you and Abena. Tonight was delayed, not denied." She huffs out a breath, and I don't need to be in front of her to imagine the clench of her jaw or dip of her eyebrows over her nose. Of my Seven, Tera is the closest to me simply because she could be considered my second-in-command. Therefore, she has more freedom to speak to me than the others do. "You're drawn to him. Fascinated by him. You have been for a while, that's no secret. And I kind of get the appeal. But don't let your pussy get you caught up. How do we know he isn't working with this Poison woman—"

"Tera." I softly but firmly cut her off, and she immediately goes quiet. "Do you trust me?"

"Yes," Tera says without hesitation.

"Then trust my judgment when it comes to the Huntsman. He's not in league with Poison. He doesn't need her help in coming for me, and he's had plenty of opportunities before now to finish what she started if they were partners." Like when I was unconscious for hours on his pullout couch. Only more proof that his vow to kill me is a little suspect. "Yeah, he . . . interests me.

Probably more than is healthy. But I'm not dickmatized, Tera. Far from it. If anything, I see him too clearly. And this isn't about him. It's about me. About my actions and the danger they've now put you and the others in."

"No." There's a thud like a fist or another body part connecting with an object. "I know what you're about to say and fuck no. So don't bother," she grits out.

"I will bother and I will say it," I murmur. "When she can't get to me, Abena will come after the next-best thing. She'll go after the ones under my protection, the ones I care about, to draw me out. And after what happened tonight, all the gloves will be off. I humiliated her. I exposed a weakness in her armor by infiltrating the obodo and getting so close to her. She's coming for blood, and if she can't get mine, she'll settle for yours to make an example of you to others who would dare to sympathize with me. You know that, Tera."

"I'm not leaving you," she states firmly, stubbornly.

"Yes, you are. And that's not a suggestion, that's an order from your olori." It's not often when I have to pull rank on the women who aren't just my kapteni but my sisters. But we haven't faced times like these either. "I need you to get in touch with Nef, Kenya, Doc, and Maura and let them know what's up. Tell them it's code white." It's our signal that the shit has hit the fan and we need to separate and go to ground. It's a DEFCON 1 situation. "I'll call Penn's parents and tell them to get her moved to one of my safe houses, where I'll have a full medical staff waiting on her. Same with Sienna."

"Eshe . . ."

"Got it, Tera?"

A long pause that seethes with anger and frustration. I hate that she's angry with me. But I'd hate it more if Abena or Ekon hurt her—or worse—because of me.

I'd turn into a bloodthirsty, vicious creature they'd have to put down . . . but not before I took out half of fucking Boston with me.

And if it were Malachi?

These streets would run red, the gutters overflowing with a sea of crimson.

That's how I'm coming behind mine.

"Got it," Tera finally says. Then: "How can I reach you? On this phone?"

"Probably not." I sink my teeth into my bottom lip, loneliness already creeping inside a chest cavity cracked wide by despair. For a long moment, I let the chasm pour in, allow myself to choke and gasp on that dark sense of isolation. "I'll find you."

Her breath is heavy, deep, as if she's trying to control the air pushing in and out of her lungs—and failing.

"Three days, olori. Three days before we come find you. We're having that meeting next week. And we're finishing this. Together. So: Three. Days," Tera vows, and then she hangs up.

I lower the phone, sightlessly staring at the black casing. A heaviness, like a huge black boot, presses down on my sternum. I grind the knuckles of my free hand between my breasts as if the twisting motion can unlock my chest wall so I can reach inside and snatch this pain away.

My aim in storming the obodo was to protect my sisters from any more harm. And in my recklessness, I placed them in even more danger. I fucked up. And now . . . I know only one way to shield them, to draw fire away from them.

My mother once told me that to be oba meant to walk alone.

I now know what she meant.

Deliberately, I shove past the ache and dial Nef to get Penn's parents' number. Twenty minutes later, I have their promise to move Penn and Sierra out of Mass General and Nef's assurance she can loop the security cameras to conceal their movements. Kenya and Maura are going to guard them until they're underway to the safe houses and then get ghost themselves.

"You finish checking on your people?"

I glance up, meeting his bright blue eyes, then lower to the acres and acres of taut golden skin stretched over wide shoulders, deep chest, and corrugated ladder of abs. And that V just above his hips calls to me, begging for my lips and tongue to map all that delicious territory . . .

Shit, my body might be exhausted and bruised, and my spirit and pride are in tattered pieces, but I'm conscious. And as long as my brain has activity, I'll want this man.

"Yeah." I set the phone on the soft-gray double sink, staring down at it. Grinding the heels of my palms in my eyes, I heave a sigh. "I warned everyone about tonight's . . . events and told them to go underground until further notice. Tera argued but she'll listen, and the others will, too. I . . ." I swallow, dropping my hands to my lap. "I'm more worried about them moving Penn safely and without detection. She and her parents are the most vulnerable right now. Shit."

I shoot to my feet and pace the confines of the bathroom, thrusting my fingers through my hair. Malachi watches my restless, agitated movements, and his silence balances on my shoulders, weighing me down with heavy condemnation.

"Say it," I snap, jerking to a halt in front of him. The self-directed anger is nearly a physical burn, and only pain will extinguish it. Mine. His. Doesn't matter. I need to . . . hurt. "Just say it, gotdammit. You told me so; you were right. If I hadn't run up in there tonight, I wouldn't be here. My family wouldn't be hunted like animals, flushed out in order to trap bigger game—me. You wouldn't have had to put your or Jamari's life on the line to save my ass. I was reckless. Selfish. Just thinking of my revenge. Only thinking of myself. Say it, dammit," I hiss.

He remains quiet, those gray-blue eyes never moving from my face. They probe my eyes, and I don't flinch from the invasive inspection. I want him to see my fury, my pain . . . my shame. I don't deserve to bow my head, to hide. Every insult, every judgment he passes on me, I accept.

"Take a shower," he finally says, and turns to walk away from me.

No.

The scream reverberates in my head, and I reach for him, grab his muscular arm to do—what? I don't know. I'm not thinking. I'm moving on straight primal emotion and instinct. But as soon as my fingers brush his skin, he spins around, and my spine meets the bathroom wall. His large frame looms over me, his hands flattened on either side of my head. His earthy, wild scent mixes with the lemony aroma of whatever cleaner was used on the tiles at my back, and I inhale it with every harsh breath.

"I gave you your choices downstairs, and you made your decision. You want absolution for tonight? Go to your fucking priest or pastor or whoever the fuck will listen to your sins so they can give you penance. That person ain't me. Will never be me." He pushes closer so his chest grazes my breasts. Bends his elbows so his mouth is almost level with mine, and his gaze sears me. "We all make choices, and every one of them—good or bad—has consequences. Being in this fucking life is a choice. Your Seven know who and what they signed up for. When they chose to give you their loyalty, they understood what that entailed, understood who that made them a natural enemy of. They're not naïve or foolish. You over here playing martyr isn't just an insult to them and their allegiance to you, it's fucking hypocritical. Because given the chance, you'd do it over again. The same way. Except you'd just shoot your aunt faster before she could get away."

He cocks his head, his scrutiny putting every damn lie detector to shame. My chest rises and falls on my labored, heavy breaths, even as my heart slams against my chest.

No, I want to scream. *No, shut up. You don't know what you're talking about.*

But he does.

It's like those eyes peered inside me and unlocked the key to the secret thoughts I didn't want to uncover, much less admit to.

I feel ashamed because I have no shame.

I feel guilty because I have no guilt.

Not about placing my Seven in danger. God, no. I'd slit my

own throat before letting someone put a knife to theirs. I'm their olori, and that's more than a title to me. It means I'm their protector, the last defense between them and Abena or whoever would come for them. And I've failed them in that.

My lack of remorse stems from not regretting going after Abena. The stalking her. The hunting her down. Glimpsing the fear in her eyes. It was all intoxicating, heady, and it only fed the thirst for her death at my hands.

"What'd you call me once? A beautiful nightmare? You'd know about that, wouldn't you, *olori*? Watching you, the calm on your face, the fucking delight in your eyes as you crept through those halls, as you attempted to murder your aunt—you're the shit that wakes people up in the middle of the night screaming." He skates his lips over my cheek until his mouth hovers above my ear. "And you loved. Every. Fucking. Second." I close my eyes, trying to block him and his too-accurate truth out. "Nah, Eshe, you came for me. Now you got me." He lowers a hand, grips my chin, and tips my head back. "Open your eyes, goddammit. Good little olori," he mockingly praises with a sensual yet cruel smile when I obey his order. "Now, I gave you the chance to get in the shower. Since you're still dressed and not in the tub, I'm taking that as you've changed your mind and are going with the other option: Get this dick."

With that as my only warning, he reaches down between us and rips my shirt over my head. My pants and underwear follow, and since I toed off my boots and socks in his bedroom before heading into the bathroom, he doesn't have to fool with removing them. Planting a foot in the seat of my panties, he hauls me up, leaving the pool of clothes on the floor. My ass hits the cold sink, but the hot press of his open mouth on my neck has a shudder rocking through me for a completely different reason. He doesn't need to palm my thighs to spread my legs wider. I'm already making room for his waist and hips. Raking my nails down his bare chest, I lean forward and lick the welts I leave behind as if applying salve to each one.

He fists my curls, but instead of dragging my head back, he presses my face harder to his skin, relaying what he wants without words. And I oblige. I set my teeth to his skin, following the path of my nails, pausing over his nipple to bite, catch his barbell piercing, and tug. Suck. With his hand still tangled in my hair, he guides me to his neglected nipple, and I deliver the same treatment to it. Nipping. Licking. Sucking.

I scoot forward on the sink, and his dick shoves against my abdomen. Touching him, having my mouth on him, has me aching and so damn drenched, I'm leaking and wetting up my pussy lips and inner thighs. Only he can assuage this erotic pain. Only he can put out this fire threatening to incinerate me from the inside out. But I don't want it put out. I want it enflamed, stirred, blown on until I'm consumed to the point of ashes.

Jerking my head back, I slap my hands to the counter, wrap my legs around his waist, and lift my ass off the cool marble to grind my pussy over his dick. Pleasure blasts through me, and I whimper. Again. I do another dirty grind, rubbing my whole sex, from my clit to damn near my perineum, over him, and I shudder and grunt. I glance down, and damn—there's something about the sight of my wet saturating the front of his pants that has a proud, territorial surge swelling inside me.

"You like that, huh? Like seeing the mess you're making?" Malachi tugs my head back, and his mouth covers mine, his tongue plunging between my lips in a nasty, wild kiss that has my hips twisting, bucking. I swear, for someone who had their first kiss less than a day ago, he's a Mensa-level genius at it. Fuck, the way he eats at my lips, draws on my tongue—I almost believe he can't get enough of kissing. Can't get enough of kissing me. He's become the teacher, and when he pulls that lascivious mouth free, I try to follow, desperate for another lesson . . . or admonishment. "You've made that mess, olori. Now you got to get down there and clean it up."

Anticipation spikes in my veins, heightening the lust to nearly unbearable levels. It's only been a week since I had that monster dick of his in my mouth, down my throat, but it might as well have been a year. And I'm starving for him.

He cups my hips and lifts me off the sink before setting me on the floor. One of his hands returns to my hair, and while he exerts pressure, silently ordering me to my knees, he reaches behind me and grabs a towel, then tosses it to the floor. His tearing open the front of his pants, freeing his dick, and slapping the flared, damp head against my bottom lip should contradict the chivalrous action of softening the brunt of the hard floor on my knees. But it doesn't. They complement each other. One has me digging my short nails into his muscular ass, and the other has me parting my lips wide and welcoming him deep inside me. Pain and pleasure. Aggression and submission. Two sides of the same questionable yet irresistible coin.

Malachi's eyes gleam with a fierce inner light, a mask of pure, harsh lust stamped on his brutally beautiful features. Humming, I hollow my cheeks, sucking harder. While most men prefer their head without teeth, this is Malachi. He wants that hint of pain. Craves it. And I need to give him everything. Setting the edge of my teeth on his dick, I graze his flesh as I ease off him. His loud hiss and the tightening of his grip on my hair has excitement racing through me, and my thighs tighten, intensifying the throbbing in my pussy.

With a hungry moan, I bob my head up and down, swallowing him over and over, taking him farther and farther each time. He tastes so fucking *good*. Like fresh, wild, windswept rain and earthen musk.

There's so fucking much of him. Fisting the bottom half of his steely length with both hands, I twist and pump, my lips bumping my fingers. Spit runs down my chin, his flesh, my stroking hands. If I made a mess before, now I'm sloppy. He doesn't seem to care. No, if that curl of his mouth and the almost-incandescent light in his eyes are anything to go by, he *loves* it. And when I back off him, dip my head, and suck one ball and then the other into my mouth, letting my tongue tease that sensitive strip of flesh right behind them, by the sound of the loud, rumbling growl in his chest and the tautening of his powerful thighs, he might propose to my ass.

"Fuck." He releases my hair only to slide his fingers into the curls at my temples and pull the strands back, baring my face for his hot gaze. "You a nasty li'l bitch, aren't you?"

My answer is to suck on his cockhead, free it with a soft pop, and then spit saliva and cum on his dick. As I swallow him back down, he releases a sound that might be a rusty, serrated chuckle or a hoarse swear. Maybe both.

"Goddamn. Yeah, you are. Give me more of that shit."

Holding my head steady, he thrusts his hips back and forth, fucking my face with no mercy, seemingly with all his power. And dropping my hands to his hips again, I take it. My eyes water, my nose runs, and I don't care. Just as long as he continues to pummel my throat with that gorgeous, thick cock.

Lifting my head, I suck in a breath and fist him again, coating my fingers in *us*. Meeting his gaze, I lick my lips, savoring the potent, decadent flavor of his precum. His eyes narrow as he traces my lips with a fingertip, then pinches my damp chin and tugs my mouth open. Wider. I don't wait for him to press his dick back into me; I lean forward, parting my lips, and greedily take him in.

As he glides over my tongue, I slide a wet finger behind his balls, over that smooth path of skin between them and his ass. I stroke it, and when Malachi stiffens, I keep gently touching him, waiting on him to tell me to stop—or not. When his hold on my head tightens and he resumes fucking my mouth, I have my answer. I explore further until I find a softer spot and give it a firmer caress.

"Goddamn. Eshe," he growls. His flesh throbs in my mouth, swells bigger, nearly filling my mouth beyond capacity.

Humming, I don't let up, not even when his thighs lock and the pull on my hair edges toward pain. His thrusts speed up, and I'm damn near choking on the dick. Low, gravelly rumbles steadily pour from him, and I want more. I want him to break for me.

I press against that soft spot one more time, then thrust that wet finger into his ass, unerringly finding his prostate. On another hum, I rub and massage the fleshy area.

"Fuck!" he roars, his head thrown back on his shoulders.

His big body shakes, and seconds later, cum blasts the back of my throat. I gulp it down, not missing one drop. Not that I have a choice. His grip on me doesn't ease, pinning me in place. Not that I'm going anywhere. I'm right where I want to be—on my knees, mouth open, throat penetrated, belly full of his seed.

Slipping my finger free of his ass, I lick the last of his cum from his still-hard dick. Before I can stand, he wrenches me to my feet, rips my sports bra over my head, and hikes me into his arms. I cling to him, wrapped around him like a wet shirt, ankles locked at the small of his back. In three long strides, we're in the shower, and with a rough twist of the knobs, he makes hot water rain down on us. Still in his black pants, Malachi presses me to the far wall, his broad back taking most of the pounding of the water.

I'm captivated by the feral gleam in his eyes as it mirrors the scream in my blood, in my head. My nails claw at his shoulders, and I almost don't recognize the ragged, uncontrolled sounds emerging from my throat. I'm arching and twisting against his huge body, against his stunningly hard dick. God, he just came minutes earlier, and now he's as heavy, as full as if he'd never poured down my throat.

"Malachi, fuck me," I demand. Beg. I'm past the point of caring about pride. Just as long as that dick gets inside me.

"Say it again." He cups my ass, spreading the cheeks until there's a pinch across the hole there. I whimper at the dark, delicious pain. "Say it again," he growls against my lips.

I don't need to ask what part of that he needs me to reiterate. He might not accept or believe it, but I've known for two years: He's mine. I know him. And I know what he needs.

"Malachi." I cup his face with one hand and circle his neck with the other. "Malachi. Fuck me so hard, I feel you in my chest."

Burying his face in the crook of my neck, he thrusts inside.

My breath propels from my lungs, lost in the steam rising around us in the glass shower walls. A scream lodges in my throat as I bow against him, my breasts pressing to his chest. On reflex, my fingers tighten around his throat, and my nails dig into his cheek. Pleasure, exquisite pleasure, races through me in electrical currents, and I'm captive to it. I blink against the shower water as it pelts my upturned face.

"The fuck." He withdraws, triggering a cascade of shivers inside me. I groan as the length and width of him stretches and brands my pussy even as he pulls free. "Why're you so fucking wet, little queen? Goddamn."

On a tortured groan, he slams back inside me. The tile rubs against my shoulder blades, his thrusts carrying me up and down the wall. With another hard stroke, he tears another scream from me—and an orgasm. Just like that. It barrels through me, and I'm helpless, swept up in its power.

"Shit. It's like that?" He fucks me through the release, and as soon as I stop trembling, he takes me to the shower floor, flipping me to all fours. The tile is unforgiving on my palms and knees. Steam rises around us like a cloak, and I can barely see the bottom of the sliding door. It's like being enshrouded in our own private world of heat, water, and sex.

Covering my smaller body with his, chest pressed to my spine, Malachi sinks his teeth into my shoulder and buries his dick back inside my still-spasming pussy. "Baby, the way you take me. The way you fucking. Take. All of. Me."

His voice, so rough, so hoarse, it coasts over my skin, another sensory caress on top of all the others. Water pools around my splayed fingers and knees. The musky scent of sex mates with the sharper smells of pine soap. The blunt pain of the bite combined with the power of his possession as he tunnels back and forth, back and forth, hitting my spot over and over, has me writhing on the dick, both running from it and throwing my ass back into his every thrust.

Even my body is going crazy in lust.

"C'mere." He curls a hand around the front of my neck and straightens, pulling me up with him so my back hits his chest. Cupping my chin, he turns my head toward him, and he claims my mouth, kissing me like a dying man. "You can't take this good pussy from me, Eshe. Not ever. Promise me." He crushes his lips to mine, draws hard on the bottom one. "Promise me, goddammit," he demands in that same serrated, desperate voice as he pounds me.

"I promise, Malachi." Yanking free of his hold, I fall back on my hands and glance over my shoulder at him. "Fuck your good pussy."

His big hand cuffs the nape of my neck, and with an animalistic roar, he beats my sex up. I again throw it back on him, meeting every stroke, every thrust, and when that hard palm comes across my ass with a sharp slap just as his dick hits that place high inside me, I seize again. My pussy locks down on his cock, and I go rigid, coming all over him with a scream.

"Fuck. Goddamn, fuck," he growls.

Both of his hands grab my hips, and he rides me with short, powerful lunges through my milking walls. Then, with a low, muted roar, he orgasms, the hot bursts of cum coating my sex. He falls over me, chest plastered to my back, his breath harsh and heavy in my ear. I close my eyes, savoring the smell of him, the sound of him, the feel of him.

He's mine.

Malachi Bowden is mine.

And I have to let him go.

CHAPTER FOURTEEN

Malachi

I step out of the bathroom, rubbing a towel over my head, but my attention focuses on the petite, too-still woman sitting on the far edge of my bed. I drop the damp towel in the hamper, move to the dresser, and remove a clean pair of sweatpants, but my actions are blind, muscle memory motions.

Images of the last hour assault me like one of the rifles I have locked up behind my closet wall. Eshe damn near sucking the skin off my dick and snatching my goddamn soul with her finger in my ass. Me taking her down to the shower floor and fucking her like a wild, ravenous thing. Me demanding she tell me that her pussy belonged to me.

Me nutting so hard and so long inside her, I almost blacked out.

I definitely lost a part of myself back there.

No, I *surrendered* a part of myself back there. And though she was under me and I covered her, she possessed all the power. She possessed me.

Looking at Eshe Diallo, she appears to be a small, thick, gorgeous woman with hips and ass for days. The average person wouldn't perceive that her sick body is as dangerous as a loaded weapon. That she's a chameleon, calculating and brilliant.

And none of those details is why my gut is in a vise grip.

Why that too-tight, pained sensation veers so close to fear.

Why I can't stop staring.

As if feeling my gaze on her, Eshe slightly turns, peering at me. And it's a good thing I still have a hand braced against the dresser, because damn, just that small glance is enough to nearly fell me like it's an axe taken to a tree.

Jesus.

She's the carnality of Gomer wrapped in the purity of Madonna. The perfect contradiction.

The perfect menace.

A stealthy, quiet voice inside my head whispers that I should put her out now, immediately, before she causes any more damage, inflicts any more harm. But I shut the thought down. Not because it's cowardly. Nah. If I believed for a second that tossing her li'l ass outta here would rectify the problem, I'd forgo the door and head for the fucking window.

But it's much too late for that shit.

Not since that night decades ago have I been so consumed with emotion. Eaten alive with it to the point that my brain buzzes, is awash in it. Then, it was pure rage and grief. Now? It's every-fucking-thing. Fury. Lust. Pain. Exhilaration. Confusion. Hunger. She's turned me into a fucking Disneyland of emotion, and I both detest and crave her for it. I so desperately need it to be hate. Because if it's not, I might end up throwing her through that window anyway. Better that than suffer the pain of getting attached again and losing another person . . .

"Downstairs," I say into the thick, tense silence, pushing off the dresser. "What did you mean by you needed to clean the pan?"

A faint smirk ghosts across her lips as she turns more fully toward me, crossing her legs under her. "All that"—she jerks her head in the direction of the bathroom—"and *that's* the first thing you come up with? Me cleaning the pan?"

I shrug. It isn't. That comment has been nagging me since she made it. Yeah, digging in her perfect pussy became priority number one for me, but the way she worded it, the particular inflection in her tone, hunkered down in the back of my head like a squatter.

She dips her head, staring down at her hands, specifically the one without the pinkie finger. She flips that hand over, touches it, a gesture I've noticed her do several times before. I can tell she's self-conscious about the injury, but there's no need. Not with me. I'm not fetishizing her or the wound, but it makes my dick hard. The idea of her suffering doesn't get me hot; the knowledge that the pain didn't break her but only carved into the badass woman who stands before me does.

"I can still see the blood," she murmurs, caressing the spot of her absent finger. "Still smell it, too. It's funny how I can tell you the exact shade of the red, the dirty metallic scent of it, but the pain of my finger actually being cut off? That's not as clear to me over the years."

She lifts her head, and I'm reeled in by that gaze like she's a big-game fisherman. And I'm helpless on the hook. I cross the room and stop next to the bed, my fists thrust into the pockets of my sweatpants.

"I sat in that chair, shivering, in pain, terrified, and to not pass out, all I could think about was cleaning up the floor. In my sixteen-year-old, delirious-with-hunger-and-agony mind, if I did away with the mess, then the kidnapping and the hell I was going through would go away, too. All I had to do was clean it up."

She falls silent, as if she's trapped back in the past. A past that still seems to trigger her. Meanwhile, the word *kidnapping* ricochets through me like a bullet striking bone. Ice-cold shock slides down my spine and spills over my skin.

"You were kidnapped?"

Cocking her head, she blinks and studies me. "Yeah. You didn't know that?"

"Before my time." Yet the rage rippling through me belies the nine years that have passed since the event. It roars in my veins, my head, demanding blood. "What happened?"

"Me being young and impatient and a mistake in communication with my security created an opportunity for a gang to kidnap and hold me for ransom. At some point they must've rethought who they were demanding money from and making an enemy of, because two weeks after I was snatched, they released me without getting the ransom. But the damage had been done."

"Did they ever catch them?"

She shakes her head. "No," she says, and huffs out a dry, short chuckle. "Not for a lack of trying. When my mother died, she was in the middle of going scorched earth locating them. No one was safe. Including Abena."

My chin jerks back toward my neck. "What the hell did Abena have to do with it?"

"She was in charge of all security at the time, including arranging my detail. It was her fuckup that's partly to blame for me being taken. Or at least that's what my mother believed."

"Is that why she had Aisha murdered?"

"Only Abena can answer that," Eshe says, cold steel in her voice. "But to answer your original question, I came away from that . . . event without a finger but with a new hang-up. I need shit to be in its place. Neat. Hell, it's saying something about that dick that I left all that food on the floor last night before fucking you." She smiles, and the strained tint to it has me fighting to keep my feet rooted right there beside the bed and not round the end of it. Not scoop her up off the mattress and lower her on my cock so I can fuck those shadows from her eyes and from that fake smile. "Right now, I'm battling the urge to go in that bathroom and make sure the shower is wiped down, the sink is spotless, and the floor is free of our DNA and water. Oh, and that you put the toilet seat down."

I give a low snort and lift one knee onto the bed, then the other. I crawl across the wide expanse until I crouch behind her and bury my face into the space between her neck and shoulder—a space that seems created for me. I breathe her in, that earthen scent mixed with the fresh smell of my soap, and even now, after having her, after nutting in her mouth and pussy, I find arousal winds through me in a hot, sinuous slide.

Her hand rubs over my head, back and forth, back and forth. Maybe she can't help but touch me like I can't stay away from her. This is like some Deeper Magic, like in Narnia. Except instead of that power being etched into a Stone Table, she's carved some spell, some curse into my skin, bone . . . soul.

I've been alone for so long, it feels somehow wrong to allow this . . . intimacy. But there's this tiny deprived part of me that longs for this. Though I've never experienced it, that same part recognizes it and hungers for it.

"We're all fucked up in our own way and out here doing the best we can to cope. To make it in this goddamn zoo we call a world," I say, words muffled by her throat.

"What's your coping mechanism?"

I pause, my heartbeat a thunderous echo in my head, against her back. "You already know."

She softly chuckles, but it's not amused. More self-deprecating. "Your books. Movies. Apples. They're your comfort and connection."

I lift my head and stare at the window covered by the blackout curtains. How does she . . . ? Shit, you'd think I would've stopped asking that pointless question days ago. But her damn uncanny *insight* into me when I've made a career of being invisible is at the very least uncomfortable, at the most dangerous.

No one knows me . . . I made sure no one could possibly know my identity, my secrets. I buried that shit so deep, an archeological dig would come up with only dirt and stones. And now, in this moment, I'm grateful to be sitting behind her in the dark. It doesn't erase this crawling, vulnerable sensation of being so terribly exposed, but Eshe can't see my weakness.

And thank fuck, neither can I.

"Why didn't you kill me?" To my own ears, my voice sounds as if it's traveled over miles and miles of unpaved, pockmarked road, and there's nothing I can do about it.

Nothing I can do about the desperation, the need I can't hide.

Eshe turns, twisting her body fully toward me, so even the shadows are no longer my barrier. I've never had an issue copping the flat, blank mask that camouflages my thoughts and nonexistent emotions. It's the face of the assassin that has become more than a persona for me over the years. It's who I am. But looking into her jeweled eyes . . .

There's desolation.

Longing.

Need.

Grief.

Everything that claws at my chest, attempting to gnaw its way free. A glimpse into her eyes is like staring into my own damned soul, and it's as liberating as it is terrifying.

Her long, elegant fingers lift and feather over my jaw, trail down my throat, and sweep to the back of my neck. A warmth blooms inside me, and for a second, I lean back into her touch, sink into her strength.

"Who says I won't?" she murmurs, her gentle grip a direct contrast to her deadly question.

She could. If she thinks I didn't notice the Glock tucked under the pillow, she takes me for a half-assed assassin. And *that*, I am not. Shit, mine is hidden under the edge of the mattress.

But could I pull that trigger on her?

I want to say yes. *Fuck*, I want to say yes.

But wanting and doing . . . The waters have become so muddied between us, and for the first time, my job isn't so black-and-white.

"Don't play with me, Eshe," I warn on a low growl, and she shivers, her lashes fluttering closed. I silently and savagely curse. The least she could do is fucking pretend that I don't affect her so profoundly. She should guard herself more securely around me. "Answer the question," I snap, irrationally angry with her. "Why didn't you kill me?"

"I've already told you *countless times*, but you don't want to hear the truth." She tightens her grip on my neck, squeezing hard before sliding her hand to my cheek and cupping it in a caress that's too gentle, too . . . tender. It's ten times more threatening than a knife to my jugular vein. "You refuse to believe me, so is there any point in repeating it?"

"You've never answered that question directly. So do it. I'm listening. No riddles. No double-talk, Eshe. Just speak plain and honest."

She cocks her head, studies me closely for several moments that seem to stretch into hours. Her thumb rubs over my bottom lip, back and forth, back and forth.

"All right. But for the record, I've always made it plain. You're just not in the space to hear me. But here you go, Malachi: I didn't kill you, because you're the Huntsman. And you're Malachi Bowden. And both of them are mine. They both belong to me. I already explained to you what that means. I come hard behind mine. I will fuck this whole world up and leave nothing behind but bones, because there's nothing I won't do, no sin I won't commit to protect those I love. Nothing is off-limits, including bringing down a queen who threatens their lives. Get me now? Is that plainspoken enough?"

I jerk my head back, and if I could crawl off the bed and away from her until I crouched in the far corner, I would. But I settle for flinching as if my skin touched hot lava. And I recoil. I, Malachi Bowden, the Huntsman, fucking *flinch*.

Because in the blink of an eye, with words that are as deadly as any loaded gun, Eshe Diallo became the bogeyman. And she terrifies the fuck out of me.

Her expression doesn't change, but resignation whispers through her eyes. "Malachi . . ." she murmurs.

"The fuck," I interrupt on a snarl, shifting back on the mattress and placing the smallest amount of space between us. I need it though. I need some space so I can fucking *breathe*.

No sin I won't commit to protect those I love. Nothing is off-limits, including bringing down a queen who threatens their lives.

No sin I won't commit to protect those I love.

My chest seizes, and shit, it's like I'm having a goddamn heart attack. Only, I know it's not that. Panic bands around my ribs, squeezing harder and tighter. Gold and black spots blink in front of my eyes, and her words echo over and over in my ears under the dull roar howling there. I vault from the bed, and as soon as my feet hit the floor, I begin pacing the length of the bedroom, making sure to steer clear of Eshe. Yeah, I'm fully aware I'm like a bleeding, wounded animal protecting itself while growling and snapping at anyone who dares come near it.

In a very real way, I'm fighting for my life, and she's the threat. And her claims of protection, of devotion, of . . . love are the very imminent threats.

I violently shake my head, my jaw flexing.

"You asked me—" she begins.

"No." I slash a hand through the air, throwing a narrowed look at her. "You're lying. You can't love me." The words grind out of me, so low, so guttural, I almost can't understand them myself. "That's not possible."

"Why?" Her tone is even, damn near conversational, and for some reason, that just pisses me off more. She's tearing me to pieces, and she's so fucking calm about the wreckage. "Why isn't it possible? Because you don't want love? Or . . ." She cocks her head. "Because you don't think you're worthy of it?"

I don't answer.

"Why wouldn't you be worthy, Malachi?" she asks again. "Because you have blood on your hands? On your soul? Because you hand out death like other people give out advice? Because . . ." Her voice lowers, and dropping on all fours, she crawls to the edge of the bed and then kneels, scrutinizing me with that bright gaze. "Because you like it?" she asks in that throaty, hypnotizing voice. I stare at her, stuck, pinned to the floor like a butterfly fixed to a corkboard. "Because that makes you a monster? Even monsters need love. Maybe we need it—deserve it—more."

I can't move because, against my will, she has my attention. My fingers tingle with the urge to touch her, to graze the stubborn edge of her jaw, brush the lush curve of her mouth. Trace the stark line of her cheekbone. I want to imprint her skin, her thick, curvy body, with my hands, my mouth, my dick.

It's that desperate *want* that has me remaining in place when everything in me screams to abandon this room, this apartment. To run.

To leave before she does it first.

"Why?" I grind out.

"Why do we deserve it more?" Apparently taking my silence for affirmation, she continues, sitting her ass on her heels. "People like you and me . . . We've known more darkness than light. Seen more violence than peace. Experienced more death than life. Have even been a part of dealing in that death. That darkness, that death? It can crawl inside you, take up residence, and leave a stain that's impossible to erase. And if we're not careful, that stain can grow and swallow us whole. But love, for people like us—monsters like us—is the difference between losing our soul and keeping our humanity. Everyone deserves it. But who do you think *needs* it more? Someone who's only been protected, cared for, adored, sheltered? Or someone who's only ever seen the worst this world has to offer, been handled by it? We do. We need it more. Unpopular opinion, but I believe love was an invention just for us."

By the time she finishes speaking, my breathing is harsher, more labored. Tremors ripple through my body, as if it's being subjected to electrical shock after shock.

I don't know who moves first—her or me.

Before she can climb off the bed, I'm on her. Climbing on top of her. Covering her. Quickly discovering this is my favorite place in the world to be. I crush my mouth to hers, parting her lips with mine. The kiss is wild, furious, nasty. And then, like the quiet after a destructive storm, it turns tender, softer.

A humiliating whimper lodges in my throat.

The warning screams inside my head, rebounding off the walls. But it's much too late for that. My control has taken a direct frontal assault, and it doesn't exist anymore. And I drive my fist into the mattress beside her head. Once. Twice. Three times. Eshe doesn't flinch, doesn't try to evade the blows only inches from her face. She just stares up at me, lips swollen from our kiss, her eyes bright, fathomless pools.

"I don't want your love."

"I didn't ask for your permission. You don't get a say in this."

I shove off her and stalk to my dresser. After snatching a drawer open, I grab a T-shirt and pull it on, then head to the closet.

"Get dressed," I throw over my shoulder.

When silence greets my order, I glance at her, and she slowly swings her legs over the edge of the bed, but she doesn't stand.

"You want to give me an idea what for? Midday snack? A little recreational reconnaissance? Or maybe some loungewear for a *Young and the Restless* binge? I hear Nikki's lost her memory again and Victor's . . . Victoring."

"You think this is a joke?" I snarl, grabbing my boots and slowly straightening and turning around. Goddamn. Her social cues couldn't be that fucking off.

"No, Malachi." She stands with a shrug. "Just asking a question so I know how to proceed."

"How to proceed," I repeat on a growl, dropping the boots to the floor with a thud as I advance on her. "Nah, you tell me, Eshe. You're the one eventually leaving, right? Like I didn't understand that 'atonement' shit," I sneer. "Talking 'bout how you love me when you about to get ghost as soon as you what? Get some sleep? Get another nut?" I shoot her a disgusted glare as I fall to the bed and snatch open the bedside drawer. I grab a pair of socks and pull them on and then pick up a boot again. "Get dressed," I order without looking at her.

My heart lodges in my throat, and I can barely breathe past the blockage. She can keep that fucking love. Like I said, I didn't ask for it. I don't want any parts of it. Every person in my life who has every loved or cared for me abandoned me, left me—died on me. Not one exception.

My parents.

Miriam.

Derrick.

All dead. All left me behind to survive in the world on my own. Every last one of them claimed to love me.

Fuck love.

Love isn't some saving grace or lofty aspiration. It's a virus, a threat more dangerous than any weapon of mass destruction. People have killed in the name of it, and empires have fallen for its sake. And here she stands, throwing that word at my feet like I'm supposed to . . . what? Be thankful? Embrace it? Want it?

No. Hell no.

If I allowed it, she would be my fucking kill shot.

And I have no intentions of allowing that.

I need her to get the fuck out before she leaves me.

Get the fuck out before I beg her to stay.

Her scent of cedarwood and musk reaches me before she does, but I keep my gaze trained on the task of getting my boots on. Looking at her clothed in just my T-shirt with all that beautiful brown skin and her thick, gorgeous thighs on display might dent my resolve. And right now, I can't afford to be shaken. I'm fighting for my survival, and it's every man for themselves.

As it's always been.

"Malachi . . ."

"Since your bike is still where you left it, use one of mine or borrow a car. I have trackers on all my shit, so I'll know where to pick it up." I finish tying my boots, stand, and stride back to the dresser and grab a long-sleeved shirt. "That should also give you some padded time with Poison. She'll be looking for your vehicles, not mine, unless Abena has already passed on the information that I was with you in the compound. In case she has, you need to have your head on a swivel while you get to wherever you're going. And make sure your people know that, too. Don't trust anyone they don't personally know, because no one has seen Poison's face and can identify her."

"I'm leaving to protect you."

I briefly pause midmotion, eyes closing and jaw clenching. My hands fist the shirt so tight, I'm faintly surprised the material doesn't rip. But after a moment, I jerk the shirt down over my head. Not bothering to reply, I sharply pivot on my heel and stalk for my closet. Shoving aside clothes, I press my palm to a spot on the back wall, and a second later, the panel flickers green. The wall slides open, and I step inside a room that holds an arsenal of weapons.

The door closes behind me, and I scan the walls mounted with various guns, knives, and throwing stars. I quickly grab two duffel bags and store Glocks, SIGs, an AXSR rifle, daggers, and ammo in both bags. Exiting, I move back into my bedroom and find a fully dressed Eshe standing next to the bed. I toss the duffel bags on the bed.

"One is for you."

I need away from her, but no way am I letting her go out there unarmed other than what she had from her "raid" on the Mwuaji compound. I don't trust her now that she made that bullshit declaration of love, but the thought of her not being on this side of the veil? A shiver treads down my spine, and I curl and flex my fingers.

"Take it," I order, pointing to the bag.

"Malachi, look at me." She doesn't wait for me to comply but moves into my space and grips my chin, forcing it down so I meet her gold-and-green gaze. The knowledge that if I didn't want her touch, I could easily remove it—and her—swishes in my stomach like sour swill. That means . . . that means I still haven't fully learned my lesson and am a fucking stupid-ass glutton for punishment. "Thanks to me, whatever anonymity or neutrality you enjoyed is gone. Once Abena saw you in her bedroom with me, you became as much her enemy as I am. And not because you failed a job. It's personal. All this"—she shakes her head—"it's on me. So it's on me to protect you in the only way I know how. And that's to put as much distance between us as possible so you're not collateral damage in this war between me and her. I don't know what else to do."

I listen; I hear her. But all I can see is me and Miriam riding in the backseat of my mother's car as she glances at us over and over again in the rearview window, tears glistening in her brown eyes. Can see me and Miriam sitting outside the CPS worker's office as the first of several worthless-ass foster parents walk up to us with smiles that don't come anywhere near their cold eyes.

Can only see Miriam's limp, broken, impossibly still body as the paramedics carry her out on a stretcher. Leaving me alone. Without anyone to protect, to love. Without anyone to love me.

With those images moving like a morbid carousel through my head, Eshe's voice might as well be Charlie Brown's muthafuckin' teacher in my ear.

I step back, giving her no choice but to drop her hand from my face.

I don't need her explanation. I don't need anything from her but one thing—to get the fuck out. This time, I'm the one walking away. Leaving. If this is some *get her before she gets me* shit, well, so be the fuck it. I'm not giving another muthafucka the chance to do that to me.

Especially not in the name of *love*.

Fuck that and fuck them.

"You can take that bag and pick which bike or car you're going to take. I'm pretty sure you know where they are."

That beautiful gaze roams my face, and it's damn near tactile. I force myself to remain stationary and not recoil from it.

Or lean into it.

Finally, she nods. "Okay, Malachi. Okay."

The quiet resignation in her tone has my throat squeezing closed, the constriction an almost-primitive instinct against doing something irreversible. Like begging her to stay. Like handing her something capable of slicing into me deeper than that dagger she wielded the first night we met ever could.

By sheer force of will, I remain quiet.

And a moment later, Eshe turns and leaves the room, disappearing from my sight. And minutes after that, the silent alarm on my bedroom wall signals that she's exited the loft.

Relief should flood through me. If nothing else, a grim satisfaction should take up residence inside my chest. But there's nothing. And I do mean *nothing*.

Just emptiness.

Closing my eyes, I inhale a deep breath. But instantly, I recognize that for the mistake it is when my lungs capture her distinct scent. Even when she's not here, she's here.

I gotta get outta here. Now. And I don't know when I'll return. Not for a minute. Not until the residue of her has dissipated and no longer coats this place like dust.

But first . . .

I sit down at my desk and fire up my computer. For the next two hours, I do a deep dive, trying to find anything I can on Poison. Which, by the time I power the laptop down and stretch, isn't much. She's like the fucking ghost I called her. Eshe is a force to be reckoned with, but against this phantom assassin? She might not live out the next twenty-four hours. Eshe Diallo may not be mine, but I'm not going to throw her to the wolves either.

While Poison's focus is on killing Eshe, mine will be on taking her out.

Yeah, she covered our asses back there at the obodo. But she's still a threat. And one that needs to go.

I stand and make my way over to the bed. Grabbing the duffel bag, I stride out of the room and jog down the steps. I don't let my gaze sweep the first floor, because in a matter of twenty-four hours, this place has become a shrine to her, and I can't look any one place and not be reminded of her.

Head down, I pause to set the alarm system and then exit the loft out of a different door than we entered hours earlier. The one Eshe took. It leads down another set of stairs and to an underground garage with a fleet of motorcycles and cars. Immediately upon entering, I note the Camaro ZL1 is gone. I nab the keys to the Dodge Challenger SRT Hellcat and, when I reach it, pop its trunk. Just as I settle the bag inside and round the car to climb into the driver's side, my cell vibrates in my pocket. My stomach bottoms out. *It's not Eshe, asshole. She doesn't even have your number.* Not that *that* little hindrance would stop her.

Shit. She shouldn't be calling me anyway. We have nothing to talk about.

Reaching into my pocket, I remove the phone and Jamari's number fills the screen. It isn't disappointment that swirls and fills that hole in my gut. It fucking *isn't*.

I swipe my thumb across the screen and hold the phone to my ear. "Yeah?"

"H," Jamari says, and the panicked, worried note in his voice makes him sound like the sixteen-year-old he is. "Check your messages."

He doesn't need to clarify which messages. It can mean only one thing. I go to my dark web server that Jamari created for my Huntsman communications. Thanks to him, even by dark web standards, the shit is unhackable. Anyone who tries—and a couple of people have tried—finds themselves on the receiving of a nasty-ass Trojan virus that corrupts and destroys years and years of information on their systems.

He and I are the only two people with access to it, so, in order for someone to send a message to me, they must be a return client with the code to reach out. A heavy, ugly sense of foreboding steals over me, and my movements are almost clumsy as I tap the speaker button and navigate to the server on my phone.

"You there, H?"

"Yeah," I say. In seconds, I pull up the email account and immediately recognize the name on the most recent message.

Fuck. That ominous feeling grows, spreading like black ice across my chest.

"Look at the attachment," Jamari instructs, voice thickening as if he's about to cry. "Oh shit, H. I can't . . . I didn't mean to see . . ."

He breaks off, and I swear, my hand trembles a little as I press the clapboard icon.

The dark, grainy image fills the phone's screen, and everything in me freezes. Sweat breaks out over my suddenly hot skin, and I lock my knees to remain upright. Inside my head, a loud howl joins the screams from the phone.

Eshe.

Bound to a chair.

Face bruised.

Blood pooling on the floor.

Her screams echoing in the room.

A half circle of people, faces hooded, surrounding her. One kneeling in the blood, a stained knife raised in front of them.

Bile blazes an acidic path from my stomach to my throat, and I swallow convulsively, battling back the vomit.

It's her worst nightmare. Abena has thrown Eshe back into the torture she suffered as a child.

Rage and smothering fear and an incomprehensible grief dogpile on top of me, and I slap my hand onto the car, steadying myself.

No. No. Fucking *no*.

Whimpers punctuate the air, and dimly I realize it's me. Those wounded animal sounds originate from me.

"H." Jamari's voice penetrates the spiral I'm tumbling down, and fuck, I forgot he was on the phone. "Are you okay?"

"Yeah," I rasp, sounding anything but *okay*. "Is this real, Jamari? Not photoshopped or computer generated?"

"No." A beat of silence. "From what I can tell, it's authentic. It's her. There's more."

"Another video?"

"Yes, but not of Eshe. It's from Abena Diallo. It came in a separate email."

I quickly back out of the current message and find the one Jamari mentioned. The fury swirling inside me is fucking biblical.

And as I tap on the email and then the video, I delicately inhale and quiet the roar in my head so I can hear the audio.

Abena's smiling face appears on the cell's screen, and my fingers squeeze the phone so tight, the casing gives a warning *crack*. Dragging in another breath, I carefully loosen my grip and press Play.

"Hello again, Huntsman. It's rare I can greet someone who resurrects from the dead, but here we are." She smirks into the camera, but her brown eyes glitter with malice.

Bruising mottles her left cheekbone, and stitches hold her skin together. Eshe really fucked her up.

Good.

"By now, you've seen the video of your little . . ." She huffs out a humorless chuckle. "I don't know exactly what she is to you. Partner in crime? Friendly pussy? Although I think we can both agree there's nothing friendly about my niece." This time her laughter is more genuine and a hell of a lot crueler. "Whatever she is to you, Eshe is fucked. When she dared to come for me in my own house, she signed her death warrant. No one, and I mean no one, does that and gets to walk away. Including you, Huntsman."

That eerie smile on her face fades, and she blankly stares into the camera. Which is somehow more unsettling than the smile.

"You should've stayed dead. You had an out, and you should've taken it. But since you want to play Captain Save a Ho, Huntsman, here's your chance to do it again. Eshe forfeited her life when she tried to kill her queen. But the choice of how she dies is now in your hands. I can send her to you piece by piece. Not a problem since I've already started." The corner of her mouth quirked. "Or you can show up at the address I've emailed you and trade yourself for her. And she can take her chances as osu and be shunned and hunted by the family she betrayed. Your decision, Huntsman. Ticktock. The clock is ticking, and I'm not a patient woman. You have until five to get here before I take the decision from you. And just to remind you, my choice includes parts of your girlfriend being mailed out in gift boxes."

The video ends, and I stare at the thumbnail of Abena's face for a long moment until Jamari breaks the silence.

"What're you going to do, H?" he asks, that tremble still in his voice.

I tap the phone screen, glancing at the time—3:34 P.M. That doesn't leave me much time. The address in the email is the compound.

"Jamari, call the burner I have ending in thirty-five forty-three."

"Bet. Hold on."

The seconds I wait pass like hours before he returns on the line. I'm damn near climbing the walls of the fucking garage by then.

"No answer. Try it again?"

"Yeah."

He tries it three times, and all three produce the same result. Eshe doesn't answer. Fuck.

I pinch the bridge of my nose.

"Thanks, Jamari. I need to go."

"What're you going to do? What do you need me to do?" He shoots the questions at me with rapid-fire quickness.

"I don't need you to do anything," I say, replying only to his last query.

The first one . . . What's understood doesn't need to be explained. There's only one thing I can do. With Eshe not answering the phone, I have to assume she's still trapped. I don't have time or room to play the faith game. Not when her life is possibly on the line. That's a risk I'm just not willing to take.

Christ. What are they doing to her right now? Those screams play in my ears like a ghost's rattling chains and haunting shrieks.

A world without Eshe in it . . .

The bile sloshes in my gut again.

I can't . . .

My chest seizes, and my mouth goes desert dry. Pressing a fist to my sternum, I rub the aching spot.

No. The choices Abena gave me are shitty and shittier. But Eshe stands a better chance of survival as an osu, an outcast, on the run with at least her Seven at her back than tied to that chair and slowly carved to pieces. And this world needs Eshe Diallo in it more than it does the Huntsman.

When it comes down to it, the choice isn't one at all.

"I have to go, Jamari. But I lied. There's one thing you can do for me. Earlier, Eshe took the Camaro. Track the car to its last location and find it. Then see if you can get in touch with one of her Seven. Eshe's going to need them when she's released."

"Fuck, H. You're going to—"

"Jamari, get that done for me. I'll hit you up later."

I won't. The most obvious outcome includes me not walking away from this. But with Jamari sounding like he's barely holding it together, I can't voice that truth.

Ironic.

Just hours ago, I drove Eshe out of my house because I refused to risk getting attached to another person only for them to eventually leave me. Again.

And now here I am, doing the same thing to Jamari, someone who, against all my best efforts, I've come to care for.

Yeah, irony is a bald-headed bitch.

"Are you—" He coughs. "Are you coming back?"

This time, he sounds younger, so much more vulnerable than his sixteen years. I pull the driver's door open and slide into the seat. I close myself inside, and his low, muffled sniffles that it seems like he's trying to hide are amplified in the quiet.

"Probably not. You know what to do if that's the case, right?"

"I don't want—"

"Jamari." I catch his shuddering breath, and I close my eyes, his pain echoing inside me. This is why I don't let anyone get close. Why I shouldn't have allowed *him* close. "You know what to do, right?" I press.

"Yeah. Yeah, I gotchu."

"Good. I have to go." I lower the cell, but the frantic sound of my name stops me, and I return it to my ear. "You need something?"

"No," he says. "I mean, yeah." Then a pause. "I—I love you."

And the call ends.

Staring out my windshield at the garage wall, I slowly lower the phone. His low, hurried declaration reverberates in my head over and over, and part of me wants to dig it out at the roots and salt it. But another part—the part that grieves not just dying but dying alone—embraces those words from the boy who stubbornly became my friend. Embraces and holds on to those words so I won't pass onto whatever exists beyond this world by myself.

I glance down at the phone, note the time.

And with the image from the video of Eshe flickering across my mind, I start the car and pull out of the garage, steering my car toward Needham.

Toward death.

Toward Eshe.

Thirty-five minutes later, I turn onto an access road and pull up to a structure that looks like a large shed. If not for the armed guards who had to open the gate and allow me in about a half mile back, I'd mistake the small building for being abandoned.

As soon as I shift the gear into park and step out of the car, the entrance to the building opens, and four men and three women, heavily armed, file out. I keep walking toward them until someone yells, "Stop, dammit. Don't move."

The *thing* inside me snaps and roars at the order, at the need to rip that gun from his hands and beat him with it until he can't speak or move. That hunger surges so strong, my body tenses, and I stare at his throat, visualizing my first blow.

But then the image of Eshe inside that shed flickers in my head. A phantom echo of her scream assaults my ears.

I stop.

"Search him." Abena emerges from the shed, and despite the early-evening shadows, huge dark shades cover her eyes.

They're not large enough to conceal the bruises on her skin or all the stitching along her cheek. Nice try though. Two of her soldiers approach me and pat me down. I don't miss the slight tremble of their hands and their apparent aversion to touching me. When they finish and step back, I lift my pant leg, and ignoring the yells and shouts to "stop" and "hold," I remove the trench knife and hold it out to the guy who searched that leg.

"Here. You missed this."

Rage and real fear gleams in his dark eyes as he takes the knife, and yeah, he should be afraid. Abena will most likely slit his throat with that weapon for the oversight. And usually, I'm above the petty shit, but that muthafucka is assisting in holding Eshe hostage, so it's fuck him for the short amount of time he has left on this earth.

Which isn't that long.

As the female soldier slaps zip ties on my wrists, the other five crowd around me, herding me toward the shed. Behind me, the suppressed, sharp sound of a gunshot disrupts the evening air. On my left, a tall, slender woman with dark red hair stiffens, and I catch her low, shaky inhale. The man Abena killed—he was more than a Mwuaji soldier to her. That was obvious. He meant something. Something personal.

Did Abena miss that? Or does she just not give a fuck?

What would Eshe have done in that same situation? Would she have been a more merciful leader? Deserving or not, the Mwuaji should have the chance to discover the answer to that for themselves. If not for Abena's jealousy- and greed-fueled actions, they would know.

They lead me into the interior of the building, and quickly, my eyes acclimate to the dim lighting. It's spartan. A table set off to the side, a bench pushed against the back wall, and a chair set in the middle of the room.

A chair.

No Eshe.

"Where is she?" I growl, fury and panic rolling through me, nearly fucking swamping me. I pack it down and focus on Abena, who strolls in front of the chair and sinks down onto it, crossing her legs. "Where the fuck is Eshe?"

"Oh wow, Huntsman." She smiles and props her elbow on her thigh, leaning forward. "If I didn't know any better, I'd think you had feelings for my niece. Please don't tell me the infamous Huntsman has fallen for Eshe Diallo? Makes sense though. Why else would you be here, ready to trade your life for hers?" Her smile widens. "Oh God, I hope so. That would make what's coming even more delicious."

She stands, the smile dropping from her lips and leaving a cold, blank mask.

"Put him down."

A side door opens, and two more soldiers roll in a gurney. My muscles tense, but I still don't see Eshe, don't know where Abena is stashing her. And until I lay eyes on her, I can't afford to fight. So I allow them to strap me to the gurney, and as the cuffs tighten across my chest and arms, I can't help but compare this to the last time I was chained to a bed. Can't help but compare the woman who gave me the darkest, sweetest pleasure with the edge of her knife to the bitch who stands over me now, wielding a dagger and staring down at me with lust shining in her dark eyes.

Can't help but think how that time catapulted us here to this moment.

We're full circle.

"What was that shit you talked when I offered to fuck you before?" She draws the blade of the knife over the edge of my jaw, down my neck, then slides the tip just under my skin at the base of my throat. "'Try it,' I believe your words were," she purrs, gloating.

The bite of pain is negligible, doesn't even warrant a flinch.

But my stomach roils, and bile churns, searing my chest and throat. Because this feels *wrong*. Dirty.

"While I was waiting on you to get here, I passed the time imagining all the ways I could 'try it.' Too bad sloppy seconds aren't my thing, but damn, you make me almost reconsider."

She leans over me, presses an open-mouthed kiss to my throat, and it requires every bit of control in me not to strain away from her touch that burns my skin like acid.

I'm going to kill her.

I don't know how. But even if I have to pull a Jesus Christ, I'm ripping this bitch's throat out and spitting in that hole.

"The only thing that would make this better is if Eshe were here to witness this." She grips my chin and jerks my face toward her. "Too bad she's not, Huntsman. Too bad she's *never been here*. That video? A little clip of my niece's kidnapping from years ago. Who knew it would come in handy? Glad I kept it."

A sheet of ice slicks through my veins, and for a moment, my lungs cease pumping. I yank my gaze from the ceiling to glimpse the triumphant glint in hers, and the rage starts to eat away at the shock.

She's never been here.

Abena didn't have Eshe? The fucking cunt tricked me. And for the first time, blinded by emotion, I fell into the goddamn trap.

Yet, under the anger . . . relief threads through me like silver filaments.

Eshe's okay. She's not hurt, hasn't been tortured like an animal. If my being here means she avoided that fate, then I'd still do it again.

I smile.

And I turn my head back toward the ceiling. But not before I catch the bewildered shock that slackens Abena's face.

"Oh no, muthafucka. You're going to give me what I want. Where the fuck is Eshe? You two left the obodo together, so don't try to tell me you don't know. Give her to me, and I'll make your death quick," she snaps.

When she doesn't get shit out of me, she emits a low, vicious snarl and jams her knife into the meaty portion of my arm. Red-hot pain flashes through me, but experience informs me the injury isn't life-threatening. I grind my teeth, not releasing a sound.

Or an answer.

That enrages Abena more.

"Where, Huntsman?" she demands, this time plunging the knife through my opposite arm, the same place.

And she gets the same result. Nothing from me. She's wasting her fucking time. I was raised on fucking pain like a baby reared on their mother's breast milk.

The bitch played her card. And lost.

Over and over, she slices my body, drenching me in blood, cocooning me in agony.

By the time she drops the knife to the silver table, she's splattered in crimson and sweat, and I'm weakened from blood loss but still silent. In the half hour she's worked me over, I've inhaled the searing ache, the sharp, blinding pain. Consumed it until I'm almost high like an addict. I teeter on a needle's edge, caught between scorching pleasure and agonizing pain, my body strung tight like a bow.

But I remain silent.

"I can do this all night, and there are plenty of places on your body to run through." Abena leans over me, slicing my shirt down the middle and baring my chest. "I'm not going to kill you, because you're too fucking valuable alive. But I can make you pray for death."

I dip my head, meet Abena's manic gaze. "Fuck. God."

Her face darkens, and for a moment, I think she might break that vow not to kill me.

"You want Eshe so bad, you can be just like that bitch, then," she sneers, picking up the knife once more.

With a sharp, brutal swing, she hacks off my finger—the same finger Eshe's kidnappers took. The blowback of pain crushes my spine to the gurney, and I damn near bite off my tongue, trapping the roar that barrels out of my throat. Abena grabs a blowtorch and aims it on a metal disc. Once it glows red, she jams the disc onto the stump where my finger used to be, and my body shakes as I almost pass out from the agony. Black claws at my vision, gnawing at my consciousness, and I scrape and fight to stay alert.

My chest heaves up and down, my breath deep rasps in my ears.

"You're so ready to die for my niece," Abena goads. The smell of my burned flesh taints the air, as does my hate. "Let's see if she's willing to do the same." Without looking away from me, she raises and waves a hand, beckoning someone forward. In seconds, one of the soldiers from outside appears at her side. "Go ahead." Abena impatiently dips her head toward me, and he lifts a phone, focusing it on me and scanning my entire bloodied body.

The bitch is gonna be pissed when she finds out that shit is useless. Eshe's cell is under a pile of rock and cement. No way that video is getting through to her.

Sucks for Abena.

After several moments, he hands the phone over to her. She watches the recording, and satisfaction blooms over her face. Her gaze returns to me over the cell.

"What's the saying? A picture's worth a thousand words? Looks like I don't need you to answer my questions after all, Huntsman. Once I send this to my niece, we'll both find out if you mean anything to her, won't we? If you're lucky, you'll get to see your precious Eshe again before I slice you open from one end to the other in front of her. You might say 'fuck God,' but she's going to meet him screaming your name."

CHAPTER FIFTEEN

Eshe

I close the door of the apartment behind me and wait to hear the locks engage. Only then do I shift away from it, scanning the hall for any movement. But the entrances to the other two homes on the third floor of the building remain closed, and a perusal of the floor doesn't betray any shadows beneath the doors.

Striding for the end of the corridor, I continue to visually sweep the area until I bypass the elevator, twist the knob on the exit, and step into the stairwell. It was probably foolish to visit Penn. Selfish even. But I had to lay eyes on her, had to make sure she was safe. And she is. Thank God. At least I can wipe that sin from the slate. Or at the very least cross a line through it. The doctor with her promises a full recovery and the relief at that news removes some of the pressure from my chest. I can breathe just a tiny bit easier.

Now, hopefully, Malachi's car still affords me an extra layer of protection from the assassin on my ass long enough for me to visit Sienna at her safe house and then make it to Ma's cottage. If this Poison is as good as Malachi claims, then I can't avoid her forever. But this will grant me some time to form a solid plan before the three-day deadline Tera instituted.

Tera.
Penn.
Sienna.
The rest of my Seven.

Malachi.

Drawing Poison to the cottage means she will be away from my people. The people I love. My fingers clench around the railing, and I briefly pause on the steps before forcing myself to continue. *Malachi.* God, I want to be angry. I want to scream, yell, throw the tantrum to end all tantrums just to release this . . . pain. The pain of rejection, of loss, of grief.

I don't close my eyes, and I haven't since leaving his loft. When I did, I too-vividly saw the cold rage in his face, the bright steel in his eyes. Heard the contempt in his voice. Felt the heated disdain that rolled off his golden skin.

The first person I've said *I love you* to since my mother . . . The first person I've ever fallen in love with . . . And he wants nothing to do with me or the damaged heart I have to offer. For the first time, I wonder if there's something defective in me. Something so abnormal that stalking a man and claiming him as mine seems acceptable. Something so flawed that it renders me unlovable and broken beyond repair.

Is that what Malachi sees when he looks at me? I'm good enough to fuck but not to love?

Pain, bright and sharp as a dagger's blade, stabs me in the chest, and I halt again, nearly stumbling on the step as I suck in a shallow breath that tastes of orange and turpentine.

I open eyes that I didn't realize had closed and stare at the freshly painted mint walls. How pathetic does it make me that I'd still run for him? Still pin that red-and-white bullseye on my back for him?

Fucking very.

Forcing my feet to move, I descend the rest of the stairs and don't stop until I push through the bottom door into the apartment building's spotless lobby. As soon as the door closes behind me, I pull out the burner phone Malachi gave me and turn off the Do Not Disturb. Glancing down at the screen, I notice three missed calls. I frown, not recognizing the number. Before I can decipher who it could be, it rings again. And it's the same number. Who the fuck is this? It's not from one of my Seven. And they are the only ones who would call the cell . . .

Maybe it's Malachi.

The thought, with its hopeful tone, jumps in my head before I can quash it. But I slide my thumb across the screen with a bated breath anyway.

"Hello?"

"Eshe?"

"Who's this?" I demand, jerking to a halt in the middle of the vestibule and frowning down at the black-and-white diamond pattern on the floor.

"Jamari. Remember me?"

My eyebrows lift but not my confusion. And a band tightens around my rib cage, shortening the breath in my lungs.

"Yeah, Jamari. I remember. Why're you calling? What's wrong?" I ask, moving again and pushing through the building's entrance. I jog down the front steps, aggravation flaring like a struck match at the sight of some asshole wearing a backpack leaning on the rear of the Camaro. "The fuck?" I murmur. "Hey, muthafucka—"

Jamari straightens and turns to face me, lowering his arm. I follow suit, briefly glancing down to end the call since I'm staring at the person on the line.

"Hi, Eshe . . ."

"Jamari." I slide the burner into the back pocket of my pants and ease my gun out of its holster. "How did you find me?"

His eyes widen, and he pops up his hands even though I haven't pulled my Glock completely free yet. "Hey, wait, wait. The Camaro. Before he left, Malachi told me he loaned you the Camaro. He wanted me to track it down and bring it back. But you're not supposed to be with it."

Unease skates down my spine, tingles at the base. Leaving my Glock at my back, I take a step toward him.

"What do you mean, 'before he left'? And why wouldn't I be

with the car? Where else would I be? Or better yet, where do you think I'm supposed to be?"

He slides his hands in the front pockets of the bomber jacket and glances around. Maybe he senses the same disquiet I do.

"Get in the car." I unlock it with the key fob, and we both slide in. As soon as his door closes, I turn to him. "A'ight. Talk."

"A few hours ago, H received a video of you." His brown gaze roams over my face as if searching for . . . something. "You were being tortured. There was blood. So much blood. And your screams." He swallows, and the look in his eyes . . . "Abena gave him an address and ultimatum: Show up and exchange himself for you, or she would cut you in pieces. I saw the video myself. But now, up close . . ."

"I've been here since I left Malachi's loft earlier today. Abena hasn't—" The fuck? Tortured? Screams? My pulse starts to race, and without my permission, I stroke the too-smooth skin flap where my pinkie once was. "Jamari, I need you to think carefully, okay? What was I wearing? Or what did you see in the room? Anything you can remember."

"I don't need to remember. I can just show you."

He pulls out his phone, and in moments, I'm staring at footage of sixteen-year-old me strapped to an all-too-familiar chair, in a room that I still see in my nightmares. When that video ends, he plays the one of Abena with the instructions she left for Malachi.

"That fucking bitch," I whisper.

"I don't get it," Jamari says as I pass him back the phone. "Why would she go through all that trouble to get him? He didn't have anything to give her."

"*He* is what she wanted. If she has him, she has me."

"Fuck," Jamari breathes. "She's using him as bait to trap you."

"Yeah." I chuckle, sightlessly staring at the apartment building through the windshield. "If it worked once, why not try it again?" I shake my head. "Only, it's been hours since she's had him. Why hasn't she . . . ? *Shit.*" Dread and fear twist my stomach, which cramps so hard, I almost double over. "Jamari, my phone was lost in the explosion at Elysian. Is there any way you can access the phone company's records and get my texts or phone calls?"

"Hell yeah." He zips open his backpack and pulls out a laptop. After I give him my info, he has my records pulled up in an alarmingly short amount of time.

"Holy shit." I gape at him. "You're like a Black Penelope Garcia."

He smirks. "Nah, ma. Don't get shit twisted. She a white Jamari Scott."

Turning the laptop toward me, he taps on the most recent message at the top of the column. All amusement flees his face when he clicks on the attachment included in the text. His low, pained whimper mirrors the one I trap before it escapes me.

Other than that sound, silence fills the car as we watch the short, shadowed, but startlingly clear video of a bloody, injured Malachi. My attention zeroes in on one wound in particular. She cut off his finger. That evil muthafucka cut off his finger. The scream that surges up from the depths of my soul—from the soul of that tortured sixteen-year-old girl—gathers in my chest and explodes. Only years of discipline imprison the enraged, anguished howl, but it ricochets in my head, temporarily deafening me.

I failed. I failed *him*.

The sole reason for me walking away from Malachi was to protect him, and yet . . . the very thing I sacrificed to avoid happening occurred. Abena got her hands on the one person who has the power to bring me to my knees.

"Eshe?" Jamari's soft, hesitant touch on my shoulder snaps me from my plunge into madness and rage. "Eshe. Did you see the rest of Abena's text?"

"No," I say, my voice a hoarse rasp. "What does it say?"

"That you have until tomorrow night to come to the obodo, kneel before her, and confess to treason in front of the family. If not, she'll kill H."

I wrap a hand around the steering wheel, squeeze until the leather creaks a complaint. "Okay." I nod, then glance at Jamari, my heart lodged at the base of my throat. I swallow, but cotton fills my mouth. "Thanks for your help."

"Yeah, no problem. What now?" he asks, shutting his laptop down and returning it to his backpack as I start the car.

"Now you tell me where to drop you off."

He shifts in his seat, leaning against the passenger window, gaping at me. "What? No, no way. I'm not going anywhere but with you."

I shake my head. "Nah, Jamari. That's not happening. I'm not heading to the fucking mall. I'm walking into an ambush. I couldn't protect you. Shit, taking you with me would be a guarantee of your death."

"I'm not asking you to protect me. H is my friend—no, he's family. I'm not sitting my ass at home while you go into that place. Alone, too? Nope, that's not how this is going down. Either we can go together and work on a plan on how we're going to save H *and* you, or I can find a way in there on my own. But I think our chances of everyone surviving would be higher if we work together." He flinches when I glance at him, but he doesn't back down. "And technically, it's not an ambush because there's no element of surprise and all parties are expecting each other."

"How the Huntsman hasn't drowned you in the nearest puddle speaks a lot about that man's level of self-control," I growl with more frustration than anger. Thrusting a hand through my curls, I steer the car out onto the street and try to reason with a goddamn *teenager* again. "Look, the last thing *H* would want is you in harm's way. Since he's not here to protect you, that shit falls to me, and I—"

"No offense—and I really mean that because I bet you know fifty-seven different ways to kill a person and dispose of the body. Did you know there's a whole dark web chat dedicated just to you? No?" he babbles, and if we weren't discussing his stubbornness in the face of Malachi's, my, and his impending deaths, I'd find it adorable and amusing . . . And that chat flattering. "Anyway, no offense, but there's nothing you can say that's going to change my mind. I'm in this with or without you. He's done too much for me and my moms. Ain't no way his life is on the line and I'm not helping to save it when he's saved mine."

The passion in his voice convinces me there's no point in trying to argue with him. And shit, I got respect for the loyalty he has for Malachi. It only goes to prove what kind of man he is to inspire that kind of devotion. The man I see Malachi as, but he isn't able to. Refuses to see.

"Fine." I shoot him a hard glance. "But you follow my every order. If I tell you to jump, you—"

"Ask how high. Got it."

"Nah, mu'fucka. You get that ass in the air and stay there until I tell you to come down."

"Wow. Okay. I think the laws of gravity might have a say in that, but I get your point."

"Good."

Possible plans of action whirl through my head, and I discard every one of them. If it were just me, I wouldn't give two fucks about the risk, but with Jamari in my care, moving more cautiously is a must. It's not just my conscience I have to wrestle with—especially since that would be a really short match considering I don't have much of a conscience—but he belongs to Malachi. So he's precious cargo. Which means he's now mine, too.

"Where're we going?" he asks, breaking into my thoughts.

"Someplace safe where we can figure out a plan to get our boy back." I don't mention we still have a Terminator on our asses.

"Cool." Pause. Then: "Are you going to call your Seven to meet us wherever 'someplace safe' is?"

I frown. "How do you— Know what? Never mind. No." I shake my head. "It's bad enough you're involved in this suicide mission; I'm not dragging them into it, too. This is my mess, and it's not their responsibility to clean it up."

"Are you serious?"

I slow the Camaro to a stop at a red light and glance at Jamari. "Do I look like I'm kidding?"

He mugs me and turns to the window, giving me the back of his head. Then, a few moments later, after the light changes and I pull off, he coughs.

"Permission to speak without the risk of you blowing my head off?"

I snort. "Yeah, kid."

Though he is causing my trigger finger to itch. He's a mouthy li'l shit.

"I don't doubt you love your girls, but you're being selfish as fuck."

My foot slams on the brake, causing both of us to jerk forward. My seat belt stretches taut across my chest and horns from other cars blast at me, but I don't give a fuck about none of that. My attention is solely fixed on the teen sitting next to me. The teen who's 3.3 seconds from me kicking his disrespectful ass outta the car into moving traffic.

"You care to repeat that?" I calmly ask.

With his eyes wide, the white nearly swallowing the dark brown irises, he shoots a look behind us, but I shake my head.

"They can move the fuck around. I asked you a question. You want to repeat that?"

He swallows. Hard. And nods.

I gradually ease my foot off the brake and move forward because, right now, I'm not in the position to draw attention to myself. But sixteen or not, this kid can get it.

"I said"—he swallows again but pushes on, and I swear, despite me wanting to drop-kick him in his throat, he earns even more begrudging respect from me—"I don't doubt you have mad love for your girls, but you're being selfish by not letting them know what's going on so they can help you."

I chuckle, and out the corner of my eyes, I don't miss him recoil.

"I'm just saying," he blurts, "you would willingly lay down your life for them with no hesitation or questions, but you're not allowing them the opportunity to do the same for you. You're not even giving them the *choice* to do it. And that's what's selfish and a little bit arrogant, if I'm being honest, because you're making it for them like they're not grown women fully capable of deciding whether they want to stand by you or not. And we both know they would. And that's probably why you won't ask. I get it though. It's why H pushed me away in the beginning and refused to let me help him. But he couldn't get rid of me. You have your own crew willing and ready to have your back. Not only will they be pissed if they find out you went into this shitshow without them, but imagine how they'll feel knowing they could've been there for you and weren't. They'll never forgive themselves. Or you. I'm just saying, Eshe. Use them. That's what they're there for, and they want to be."

Shit.

I blow out a breath. "You sure you're sixteen?" I mumble.

He grins. "I'm fucking wise beyond my years. I keep telling H that."

"A'ight, Samwise the Brave. Frodo wouldn't have got far without Sam."

"Yoooo!" Jamari holds a fist up to his smiling mouth. "You get it, too, right? Right?"

I laugh, shaking my head.

An hour and a half and several phone calls later, I turn down the isolated road in the New Hampshire woods. The look of awe on Jamari's face is a little comical and a lot sweet. It's obvious he's an urban kid who hasn't been out of Boston's concrete jungle. I can just imagine how the isolated beauty of the thick, towering trees lining the single-lane street like sleeping giants would appear to him, even in the dark. Especially in the dark.

"Holy shit," he breathes when the cottage comes into view. "It's like a fucking fairy tale."

He's not wrong. It's one of the reasons I love it. Not just its incongruity to this world but to me.

"It was my mother's," I explain to him because . . . Yeah, I don't know why.

"It's cool," he says, sounding years younger than his age. But then he leans forward, chin almost touching the dashboard. "Huh. Do you think one of your Seven beat us here? Because whose car is that?"

I was so focused on the cottage and his reaction to it that I didn't even notice the black Charger parked just in front of the garage. My heart slows and so does my pulse. Everything snaps into crystal clarity, and I decelerate, bringing the car to a stop several yards away from the front door.

"Wait here," I order, grabbing my Glock from the center console and turning off the interior light.

I don't wait to see if he complies but open my door just wide enough to slip out and, crouching, creep toward the strange car. Pressing my back to the rear panel, I sneak a look inside and see that the vehicle is empty. Anger flares to life behind my sternum, and I direct my narrowed glare toward the cottage. I know the fuck not someone didn't break into *my* place. *My mother's* place. The sense of violation, of *wrongness*, scalds me, dirties me.

I hope they enjoyed those fingers they used to get inside, because they won't have them for much longer.

Just as I straighten and head for the back of the cottage, the front door cracks open and a tall, slender figure steps out onto the porch. I halt, lifting my gun . . .

The porch light flicks on.

"Who the fuck are you?"

CHAPTER SIXTEEN

Eshe

I stare at the beautiful Black woman who shouldn't be leaning up against the living room wall in my mother's cottage. A warning trips down my spine, like one predator scenting another.

And that's exactly what she is—a predator. The warm-chestnut skin, tight brown curls, and delicate features don't hide the monster lurking behind those stunning gray-blue eyes. Like recognizes like.

And yet, she's a complete stranger.

An oddly familiar complete stranger.

"It took you long enough to get here," she says with a slight smirk that doesn't reach her bright but empty eyes.

"I repeat, who the fuck are you?"

She tilts her head, curls brushing her shoulder. "Think on it a little, olori. I'm sure it'll come to you."

The front door of the cottage swings open, and Tera, Doc, Nef, Kenya, Maura, and Sienna—pale and arm in a sling—rush in, followed by Jamari. My heart swells with joy in my chest at the sight of Sienna, even as I wonder why the fuck she's here instead of at the safe house. But she's not paying attention to me. None of them are. Their eyes lock on the woman across the room, and like one body, they immediately fan out, weapons drawn and aimed at her.

I return my attention to the assassin, staring at her, hard. "You're Poison."

Her smirk deepens, confirming my answer.

"The fuck? The bitch who's trying to kill you?" Tera snaps. "Well, good. She's made our job a helluva lot easier."

She lifts her gun higher, ready to fire, but I hold up a hand.

"Wait."

Tera scowls at me. "Wait? For what? She blew up our warehouse. Probably the same one who took shots at us. She's the reason Penn is hurt. Unless you're telling me to hol' up to break her shit like she did Penn's, then I don't understand."

"Yeah, I get it, and I'm right there with you. But"—I turn back to Poison—"you tracked me down here for some reason. And since neither one of us is leaking yet, I'm figuring you have something to say first."

The assassin pushes off the wall and strolls closer. And I want to choke-slam her for being so fucking cavalier when Malachi is somewhere being tortured at this moment.

"Look, I know you got this whole secret assassin shit going on, but I'm on a time crunch with the life of someone I care about on the line. So if you don't mind getting a move on?" I ask, twirling my hand.

"I know all about Malachi being held by Abena."

Ice slicks through me and crystallizes into a freezing, numbing rage. How does she have information we just received? *How does she know his name?*

I stalk forward, not stopping until we're damn near nose to nose. I can see the gray striations in her eyes.

"Who. The. Fuck. Are. You?" I grind out. But the longer I glare into her bright, *familiar* eyes, the impossible, crazy, yet all-too-real answer starts to take shape in my head. And yet, as *impossible* as it may seem, I still whisper, "Miriam."

For the first time, emotion flashes in her gaze. An indecipherable emotion, but there just the same.

"I've heard you were smart," she says, and though it sounds condescending, the tone carries a faint hint of praise.

Shock barrels through me, and I lock my knees to keep me upright.

I shake my head, still in denial even though I know it's true.

"How is this . . . ? It can't be . . . You *died*. He told me he watched you die. He fucking grieves you to this day."

Fury fast burns away my shock because it's becoming clearer and clearer that Malachi's baby sister all grown up is standing in front of me, alive and relatively well, except for the whole psychopathic-killer thing. And she let him believe . . .

"You bitch," I breathe, rage lacing my tone. Before I even acknowledge what I'm doing, my SIG is in my hand, and the barrel is pressed to her forehead. She doesn't flinch, doesn't show any reaction at all. "You let him torture himself all these years for not protecting you. He's suffered believing he failed you when you needed him most. And all these years, you've been alive, been here, and never once thought to ease his pain. My soul might be dirty as fuck, but at least I have one."

"You don't know what the fuck you're talking about," she says, voice even as if she's discussing the chance of rain. I want her to be rolling in goddamn remorse. Fucking bathing and stinking of it. And . . . nothing.

"Then enlighten me."

"No."

I chuckle, and Tera and Kenya look at each other. Yeah, they know what that laugh means. I'm two seconds from leaping on top of her, and I won't be hugging the ho.

"I don't owe you shit except a bullet, since that contract is still open. But since Abena fucked with the wrong person—the only family I have left—I now got skin in the game."

"That's a little hypocritical, considering you bombed a place where the only family you have left was at," Doc points out.

Miriam cuts a glance at her. "I didn't know he was there, so it doesn't count."

"Doesn't . . ." I scrub a hand down my face. "Why are you here?"

I can feel the hours, the minutes ticking down, and my skin itches with each passing. I don't have time for this shit.

Malachi doesn't have time for it.

Miriam unzips her leather jacket and reaches inside. The sound of guns cocking punctuates the air, and she holds up a hand and slowly removes the other, holding a thumb drive. "Anyone have a laptop?"

"Right here." Jamari moves to the small table under the window and removes his laptop. He sets it on the table, and Miriam hands him the drive. Moments later, his fingers fly across the keyboard, and then he turns the computer around. "Is this what you need?"

"Yes. Here." Miriam pushes the laptop toward me, and screenshots of several emails fill the monitor. "Read those."

I meet her gaze for several long moments before lowering mine to the screen. At first, I'm not sure what the hell I'm looking at. But then, as if a light switch is flipped and a dark room is suddenly bathed in blinding light, it hits me. Correspondence from nine years ago between Abena and someone named MackeyGhost11. And it's about my kidnapping. The more I read, the more nauseated with fury I become. I'm damn near incoherent.

Abena.

Abena was behind my kidnapping the entire time.

Abena suggested the ransom amount and cutting off my finger to send to my mother.

Abena is the faceless tormentor in my nightmares, and all along she's been smirking in my face. Reigning over my family. Stealing the life my mother should've had. Living free with no repercussions.

"I'm going to be sick."

I dart down the hall for the bathroom, slamming the door open against the wall just in time to vomit in the toilet. I keep purging my stomach until only bile empties out of me and pain streaks through my body.

"Come on, Eshe." A cold washcloth is pressed to the back of

my neck as I sink to the floor. Kenya flushes the toilet and hunkers down in front of me, studying me. "You good? We read the shit and it's fucked up. I'm so sorry. You ready to go back out there?"

I swallow. Nod.

"Good. Let's go." Standing, she extends an arm toward me, and I grab her hand. She tugs me to my feet, clasping my elbow to steady me. "Clean up and then come back out there."

I nod again.

She cups my shoulder and squeezes. After she leaves, I remove the washcloth, wash my mouth out, and splash water on my face. Staring at my reflection in the mirror, I almost don't recognize the woman gazing back at me. I look . . . broken. Beaten down. If Abena were in front of me at this very moment, I might surrender just because I'm so fucking tired.

Tired of secrets.

Tired of failing.

Tired of not being enough.

Tired of . . . being.

Heaving a low, heavy sigh, I grab a hand towel and pat my face dry, then return to the living room. Everyone looks up, not saying anything as I reclaim my seat in front of the computer.

"She's a dead bitch walking, Eshe," Tera says. Promises.

And a sweeping scan of the people gathered around the table shows me they all agree with her vow.

Briefly closing my eyes, I dip my chin in acknowledgment, then refocus on the laptop screen.

"How did you get this? Where?" I ask Miriam.

"Your mother's second-in-command, Zuri."

I blink. "Zuri?" I rasp. "Where did you see her? When . . . ?"

"Your aunt had her hunted down and murdered months after your mother. But before then, she passed along this"—she nods toward the computer—"to a friend in Creed for safekeeping. That person happened to be my mentor. Before she died, she passed it along to me just in case I ever needed . . . leverage."

A wave of grief for Zuri sweeps through me. After all this time, I at least know what happened to her.

"Is this why Abena had my mother killed?" I ask Miriam.

"From what was told to me, yes. Aisha suspected something was off as soon as she realized Abena had failed to arrange the proper security for you. So she started digging. She also kept people on Abena's ass. I think that's why they aborted the kidnapping after a couple of weeks without getting the ransom. Well, that and your mother had the Boston streets looking like an Egyptian plague." She smiles, and damn if it doesn't hold a hint of admiration. "Not long after your return, Aisha received confirmation about Abena. From what I understand, the day she was gunned down, she was supposed to be meeting with an informant."

"You mean Abena had her shot down before she could make that meeting," I say.

"Yeah." Miriam shrugs.

"Do you have the proof?" Nef quietly asks.

"No. I only have what you see there . . ." Miriam looks at me. "But you have the proof."

"The hell are you talking about? If I had proof that Abena was behind my kidnapping, do you think I would've sat on it for all these years?" I huff out an abrupt chuckle. "Fuck you playing at?"

Instead of answering, Miriam strides down the hall, before stopping in front of Ma's bedroom door. We follow her, and when she pushes the door open and walks inside, everyone else files in, but I . . . don't.

I hover in the doorway as a flash flood of memories rushes to greet me. It's been nine years since I've stepped foot into this room. And though it's impossible, I swear, under the dust and stale air, I can still catch Ma's scent of jasmine and vanilla. That, too, is a ghost. This room is full of them.

Inhaling, I force myself to walk forward, remembering why we're here. Who we're here for. Miriam moves across the dirty floor to the cobweb- and grime-covered—yet gorgeous—oval-shaped mirror that was Ma's favorite. It sits above the black marble vanity, its ornate gilded frame a thing of beauty from a long-ago time. When I was a little girl, she'd sit me in her lap while she applied her makeup or fixed her hair and tell me how pretty and strong I was, how I would be a powerful and fair queen one day.

Lifting the furnishing from the wall with a grunt, Miriam lays the mirror on the bed. A dirty cloud puffs up, but I barely pay it any notice. No, all my attention is grabbed by the flash drive taped to the back of it.

"What's on that drive is enough to hand the Mwuaji throne over to you," Miriam says.

"Who put this . . . ?" I can't complete the sentence.

"Zuri did." Miriam removes the flash drive and hands it to me. "From what I was told, your mother wasn't able to get the information from the informant the night she died, but what's on there"—she nods at the drive in my hand—"is more of what she gathered herself. And it's damning. Aisha gave Zuri that as insurance in case she didn't make it back from the meeting. And Zuri came back here and hid it before disappearing."

"All this time, the answers were right here," I murmur, cradling my future in my hand. "Thank you." I glance at Miriam. "But we still got beef forever over how you abandoned your brother."

"Like I said before, you don't know what the fuck you're talking about. Disrespectfully. My story—our story—is just that: ours. You've only been here for the last part and have no idea about the earlier chapters or what went on in between," Miriam snaps, and this time I don't have to question what emotion sizzles in her bright eyes.

Anger.

Pain.

I get what she's saying—I don't know her. I don't know what the last almost two decades have been for her. But I also can't help but hear the pain in Malachi's voice, see it etched in his face when he talked about her.

"I don't know, sis. The loose goat don't know what the tied goat do."

Silence falls over the room, and with a frown, I turn and look at Kenya.

"Okay, I'll volunteer as tribute." Sienna raises her uninjured arm. "Uh, boo. What the fuck you talking 'bout?"

Kenya shrugs. "All I'm saying is you don't know what you'd do unless you were in another person's shoes."

"Why didn't she just say that?" Jamari whispers to Doc.

"I hit kids, li'l boy," Kenya whispers back in that sweet, syrupy voice of hers.

"I don't really care if you understand or not. What I do understand is my brother's life is at stake. And I'm going after Abena with or without you. Might as well be with you since you're down a person." She glances at Sienna. "And a half."

"Okay." I nod. Because, shit, the heffa has a point. We need as much help as we can get, and having a Terminator super-assassin on our side would definitely help even the odds. "Sienna, I'm going to get on your ass later about why you're not still in the safe house. But right now, we need a plan."

"I contacted Richter and Moorehead as soon as you called me earlier," Doc says, leaning against the desk, seemingly uncaring of the years' worth of grime covering it. It seems appropriate and even fitting that we're planning a coup in Ma's bedroom. "Abena already summoned us to the obodo for the . . . show. It seems she's calling everyone to the compound to witness your execution. It'll take them a few hours to gather their people and about seven more to get here, but that should be more than enough time to make the deadline Abena's given you to turn yourself in. They said they'll be ready for whatever you need."

"Same with Bisa and Taraji. They've been waiting years for this day. We all have," Tera adds, a sneer curling her lips.

"They're sending in people ahead of time to stash weapons. But they'll be there with the numbers you need."

"Okay, exactly what's on this?" I hold up the flash drive. "And how is it going to help me bring Abena down?"

Miriam smiles, and I fear no one, but she got me reaching for imaginary rosary beads. "I have ideas."

CHAPTER SEVENTEEN

Malachi

The last time I stood in this throne room, it was to accept the job of hunting down and assassinating Eshe Diallo. Now, just days later, I'm here again, but as the sacrificial lamb for Eshe instead of her killer.

Fate, that bad-bodied cunt, has a fucked-up sense of humor.

Pain hums through me, a constant companion that at times talks louder, its voice more annoying, and at others murmurs to me in a low whisper. Blood cakes my clothes and skin. Last night, Abena had someone come in and do the bare minimum in patching up my wounds. As in throwing butterfly bandages on injuries that clearly require stitches. But she can't have me bleed out before killing me in front of Eshe and everyone else she's gathered for this sick-ass sideshow.

This bitch need to get Iyanla to fix her mu'fuckin' life.

And for me to say that shit, it's saying something.

The air of . . . gaiety in here is disturbing. Like we've transported back to some French court with frivolous nobles and silly jesters and the one reigning supreme is the biggest joke of them all. Abena sits on that ridiculous ebony chair rimmed in silver and diamonds with the crown of blades fashioned on top of it. Is it lost on everyone but me that she had to give herself a crown just like she had to steal it? Because earning one was beyond her. She doesn't have the disposition or heart of a real queen, so she had to kill for the crown, and here she is, prepared to murder again to keep it.

Yeah, a joke.

As if she feels my eyes on her, her head turns in my direction.

She has me propped up against the far wall, a guard on either side of me—soldiers from the night before—while waiting on the festivities to begin. The multitude of eyes on me crawls across my skin like a parade of ants, and I can't say I blame them, given my condition, and that, until I was marched in like a prize fucking pig, they all thought I was dead. Not every day you see a dead man walking.

A smile curves her mouth.

I stare at her, let her glimpse the fury and hate howling like a hungry wolf inside me. Let her see her death.

And I watch that smile bleed from her face.

Yeah. I might die today, but fuck if I'm going alone.

"Show some fucking respect," the soldier on my right snarls, then jabs me in my wounded hand.

A back draft of red fire rolls up my hand, through my arm, and into my chest, stealing my breath. Sweat dots my skin under my replaced shirt, and my gut roils with bile.

But I don't flinch, don't move except to shift my gaze from Abena to him.

His light brown skin reddens, and fear creeps into brown eyes even though he tries not to show it.

Tries and fails.

"Simeon," the one on my other side snaps. "He's chained and not a threat. We're above that shit, and it's not what we do. It's not who the fuck we are," she says, almost to herself. I catch the barest thread of self-disgust in her voice, and I remember her. She's the soldier affected by the killing of her own the night before. Yeah, she might want to tighten up, or she won't last long—like her friend. "Now, we're here to guard the prisoner, nothing else. Keep your hands to yourself and fucking *guard*."

Simeon's jaw clenches, works back and forth like he wants to say some shit, but ultimately, he gives her a sharp nod and mutters, "Yes, ma'am." Then his whole face perks the fuck up as he turns toward the back of the throne room. "Oh shit. She's here. I can't believe she's actually here." He shoots me a look, his dark eyebrows pulling down over his nose. "She came for you."

Though my mask doesn't slip, the same confused wonder that fills his voice winds through me.

Confusion. Awe.

A terrible, deep fear for her.

And a wild, blinding . . . shit. *No.*

Why is she here? What the fuck is she thinking turning herself in for *me*? Not for me. I'm not . . . *Fuck.*

The female soldier grips my forearm, holding me in place, and I didn't even realize I'd moved, shifted forward. I glance down at her, and she gives me the smallest shake of her head. It's nearly unnoticeable.

Then she dips her chin again—it's so slight, it's barely there. But it is, and I turn my attention back to the wide double doors.

And Eshe.

If Abena or anyone in this throne room expected her to be cowed or humbled walking inside here, Eshe disappoints them.

Pride swells inside my chest, and though not twenty-four hours ago, I told her she wasn't mine, this feeling in my soul doesn't give a fuck.

Dressed simply in a long-sleeved black shirt, jeans, and boots with her dark auburn curls brushing her shoulders, she calmly strides inside, shoulders straight, head up. She doesn't glance around, her gaze forward, her gait confident, unfaltering.

And though four armed guards flank her, it's obvious to everyone in this room she's a queen.

The only queen.

And from the fury glittering in Abena's eyes and twisting her mouth in a snarl, she knows it, too.

The mass of people crowded into the room parts like a swollen sea before a prophet waving a staff, and she walks right down the middle, not stopping until she stands before the steps of that gaudy throne and its gaudier owner.

Only then does she look away from Abena, and it's to find me. As if she knew where I stood the entire time, her hazel gaze locks with mine, and the impact of it sends a seismic ripple through me.

Mine.

That's what those jeweled eyes whisper to me. And in this moment, I have my answer about why she's here. Why she's turned herself in to Abena.

Because I'm hers.

The pain in my body ratchets down, drowned out by a buzzing, hot electrical current. When she looks away from me, returning her scrutiny to her aunt, I'm left with the handprint—the soul print—of that stare.

That eerie-looking muthafucka with the snow-white dreads strides into the room from a side entrance and approaches Abena, climbing the throne and bending down to whisper something in her ear. She nods, not removing her stare from Eshe. After a moment, he straightens and descends the steps before taking up a position directly beside her chair.

"You summoned me here, Abena," Eshe announces in a clear, even voice, spreading her arms wide. A smile curves her soft, full mouth. "Here I am."

"That's 'oba' to you. 'Here I am, oba,'" Abena says, leaning back in her high-backed chair, fingers curled around the arms.

She's trying to seem unbothered. But goddamn, Abena's bothered. She obviously expected Eshe to come in here crawling on her hands and knees, humbled and begging for mercy. And it's fucking with her bad that shit's not playing out like that. Especially in front of the congregation she's gathered to worship at her altar.

They stare at one another, and you could hear mice fuck in this shit. The tension prickles my skin, tickling my exposed wounds, making them itch. Then, like a small ripple in a too-still pond, the murmurs begin. Soft, at first, but gradually gaining volume. Eshe doesn't appear disturbed by the noise; she doesn't twitch or so much as glance behind her.

But Abena...

A dark, twisted pleasure bends and kinks inside me. Abena searches the room, breaking that visual standoff with Eshe. And I don't know about anyone else, but in my book, round one goes to Eshe.

As Abena's pissed-off gaze lands back on her niece, I'm thinking it does in her book, too.

"Put her down on her knees," Abena coldly orders. The guards on either side of Eshe hesitate, a wariness creeping across their faces. "I said, put her on. Her. Fucking. Knees."

They move at the snarled order, grabbing Eshe's arms and shoulders. When they can't immediately force her down, one kicks her in the backs of the knees, and that takes her to the floor.

I stiffen, muscles coiled, and I'm ready to spring if they touch her again, cuffed and all. Once more, the female guard grabs me, this time just above the heavy, thick cuff on my wrist. I snatch my arm from her, and the motion must catch Abena's attention because she looks in our direction, and triumph gleams in her eyes, lights up her face.

"Now that you're where you belong, where a *traitor* belongs," Abena purrs, leaning back and tapping her long red nails on the arm of the chair, "we can begin." At the word *traitor*, the whispers stir again, and Abena holds up a hand, silencing them. Her dramatic ass should've been an actress since she seems to thrive on this shit. "I've called your olori Eshe Diallo here today to face the most serious charge against our family: treason. How do you plead, Niece?"

Even on her knees, with the guards' hands clamped on her shoulders, she doesn't cower.

"That depends," Eshe says.

"Oh, this should be good." Abena shakes her head and waves a hand toward me. "When the evidence of your lies stands right there in front of everyone. Did you or did you not declare right here in this throne room that you'd killed the Huntsman?"

"I did."

"So you admit you lied."

Eshe shrugs. "Again, that depends."

The arrogance seeps from Abena's face, and her lips twist into a snarl, her eyes narrowing. Despite the situation, I suppress a snort. It's almost fucking comical, Eshe's ability to drive a person crazy.

"Look around you, Eshe. No one finds you amusing. No one thinks treason is a joking matter. Is betraying your family something you take so lightly?" she sneers.

"No. I just want clarification." Eshe tilts her head. "If you're referring to the time when you sent the Huntsman to kill me but I ended up sparing his life instead of killing him, then yes, I lied. But"—she raises her voice over the rumblings from those gathered—"if you're talking about the time he broke into my house, coming for my ass a second time, well, that's a little more complicated. Because that would've been after you supposedly killed him because he didn't take me out. So I don't see how I could've murdered a dead man in the first place. See my dilemma? So you'll have to be more specific."

Her incendiary statement is like throwing gas on a five-alarm fire. Shouts of disbelief and anger bounce off the marble walls, and Abena shoots to her feet. Her second climbs the steps and positions himself next to her, tension drawing his big, tall body tight. The only person not affected by the outburst of confusion is the chaos agent—Eshe.

"The fuck you just say to me?" Abena hisses, and the room falls silent. Probably because these fools are greedy to catch every word. "Did you just accuse me of—"

"Attempted murder," Eshe snaps, cold fury and disdain dripping from her tone. "Don't be such a fucking snowflake, Abena. Not like that hurts your feelings. Especially when that's the least of your crimes against this family. Murder of my mother, our oba, being your worst." She releases a low, maniacal laugh. "Treason? You first, bitch. I call it revenge. Justice."

"This is too fucking much. Even for you," Abena thunders,

her face twisted with a murderous fury. Huh. For the first time, we have something in common. "You actually believe you can get away with this kind of betrayal? I'm going to kill you, Eshe. And it will be my pleasure to do it personally. I'm going to carve your fucking heart from your chest—"

"Like I told you before, what you're asking for—this won't be cheap."

The gravelly voice booms from the room's internal speaker, startling me. The guards on either side of me flinch, and Abena recoils at the sound, her second moving in to steady her.

The fuck is—

Before the thought can fully form, an image flickers on the blank wall next to that mirror behind Abena's chair.

The visual is shadowed, a little grainy, as if the camera was tucked away. But it's clear enough to show the faces of two people in the room.

Abena and her faithful second-in-command. Both appear younger in the image, her second's dreads not as long, but it's them.

"Do I look like money is an issue? I want it done," Abena says, *pacing out of the frame for a moment, then returning. "Mirror, give it to him."*

He bends down, hands the other person in the room a duffel bag.

"That's half of what you quoted me. You'll get the balance when you do the job. And this time, do the damn job. *If you hadn't fucked up the kidnapping, then I wouldn't even be here right now. I'd have enough money to get the fuck out of here and start my own family."*

"We didn't fuck up shit," the other guy scoffs, taking the bag. "It's not my or my guys' fault your sister's a goddamn beast in these streets. It was either return the kid or lose our fucking lives from either her or the head of my family if he found out about it."

"Well, this'll solve both our problems. Kill Aisha, and as the new oba, I'll make sure the investigation goes nowhere. Got it?"

"Yeah, I got it."

Holy. Shit.

Shock pummels the air out of my lungs. The hell? Did I just

hear what . . . ? Yeah, Eshe believed Abena was behind her mother's death, but this . . . to hear what sounds like the plotting of it?

I glance at Abena, whose face is frozen into a horrified mask. Her hand flies to her open mouth, covering it as her head turns back and forth as if searching for . . . what? An ally? A way to escape?

She's not going to find either in this room that's quickly turning against her.

One swift sweep of the crowd reveals the hate flattening their eyes and darkening their faces. Shit, the rage that's slowly swelling, building, it contains a power and heat of its own, and it's all directed toward her.

"I have to admit, I'm disappointed. Having heard so much about the Huntsman, I expected, I don't know, more excellence and care with your work."

The video switches to a scene I'm intimately familiar with. Abena in my house with ol' boy standing right behind her after that initial hit on Eshe went to hell.

Instinctively, I jerk my gaze toward the back of the throne room, looking for a tall, slender figure with shoulder-length brown locs. There's only one person who has access to the security system and the cameras I have running in my shit twenty-four seven.

Jamari.

Jamari's here somewhere. A maelstrom of emotion piles into my chest at the thought of the teen putting himself in danger for my sake. At the idea of him riding to my rescue.

"You want to explain to me why I received word less than an hour ago that my niece was spotted riding through downtown Boston? I paid you to get a job done. To carve her fucking heart from her chest and give it to me in a box. This shouldn't have been too hard a job for the gotdamn bogeyman of the underworld. She's one woman. You mean to tell me the Huntsman can't kill one fucking woman?" she flatly asks. *"Did you even find her?"*

On-screen me doesn't answer, and Abena chuckles, shaking her head.

"And just think, I was going to offer you this pussy as a congratulations for a job well done." In the video, Abena smiles, and it's as cold and calculating to me now as it was then. "I still might get the dick. But as I fuck your cold, dying body instead. The only good man is a dead one, after all."

"Try it."

Abena hesitates, and her second shifts forward.

"Run me my money back, Huntsman."

"Four days left on the contract, Abena."

"I don't think so. One thing I've learned well in life is if you want a man to do the job right, give it to a woman to handle. So consider that contract dead. And you right along with it. Mirror."

It's like a triggering case of deja vu, watching Abena's second remove a cell phone from his suit pocket and put it to his ear.

"Come here. Now. Same way."

A low swell of murmurs ripple through the throne room as moments later, the two now dead Mwuaji soldiers enter my apartment.

"This is where I leave you, Huntsman. I would say it's been a pleasure, but unfortunately, it hasn't."

She can no longer deny sending me to assassinate Eshe just as she did her sister. She's the star of this fucking double feature.

"Bitch!" Abena roars.

Eshe jackknifes to her feet, the guards around her no longer restraining her. Out of my peripherals, I catch movement in the restless, surging crowd. Tera. Doc. Nef. Kenya. Maura. Sienna. Her Seven, minus Penn. And another woman wearing a black hood and face mask. They melt from the rest of the audience, forming a half circle around their olori. It's a blatant show of solidarity, of loyalty.

Of disrespect to Abena.

Tera passes Eshe a bowie knife.

"I challenge—"

Before Eshe can complete the words, Abena's second bolts

toward her, but I clocked the tightening of his body. And before one of her Seven can intervene, I'm already in motion, charging across the room, bowling through people, knocking them to the floor.

"Mine." A roar born of pure rage barrels up my chest and erupts from my throat. I leap in the air, my body crashing into his, taking us both to the floor with an impact that jars my bones. My vision swims at the agony from my injuries, and pain sizzles through my veins. Bile surges toward the back of my throat, but I fight through, shoving the agony, the nausea, back. My life depends on it.

More, Eshe's life depends on it.

We roll, separate, and jump to our feet, facing off. Shock flickers inside me as my handcuffs loosen on my wrists. At some point one of my own guards must've unlocked them—I'm betting on the woman. Removing them, I toss the chains aside.

From what I've noticed, neither one of us talks much, and we don't waste words now as he unsheathes a knife and charges me. I feint to the side, and my ribs scream in protest, but I continue moving into him, taking him by surprise. Grabbing his wrist, I twist it until the bones give an audible crack and the blade falls from his limp, dangling fingers.

I swipe his feet out from under him. His back hits the floor, and I snatch the knife up, and despite the pain radiating from the stab wounds in my arms, I grit my teeth and drive the dagger through his open mouth, pinning him down. His body jerks, seizes, and then his eyes glaze over.

That was for going after mine.

CHAPTER EIGHTEEN

Eshe

"Like I was saying, I challenge you to a koju, Abena," I state loud and clear in front of a throne room full of Mwuaji members, loyal and disloyal. Faithful and sycophants.

My heart pounds as I stand here on the precipice of the moment I've spent the last nine years planning for, dreaming of. What I could've never imagined was my ears still ringing with the bogeyman Huntsman's yell of *mine* or his defending me against Ekon.

Yeah, that was on absolutely no one's Bingo card.

Part of me wants to look over to the sounds of fighting, to make sure Malachi is coming out on top. But I have to trust that he is. That's his battle—one he willingly took on for me. This one here, with Abena, is mine.

And it's time to finish it.

Abena emits a bitter, harsh crack of laughter and paces back to her "throne." Gripping the back of it, she sneers, whipping a hand down at me.

"You really think you can come for me, Eshe? Challenge me? Take what's mine? I don't give a fuck what video"—she flings an arm toward the wall—"or evidence you believe you have. None of it means shit. I'm oba here. I'm *queen*. And I was right to send that bastard Huntsman after you to root out the snake in my family. *My* family, you traitorous little whore. All these years, I saw your hate for me. Your thoughts and plans to turn my family against me. But, bitch, you will never be me. The truth is you're nothing but a nuisance, nothing more than the shit I accidentally step in on my way out the door. And I'm going to treat you the way I would that shit on my shoe: I'll wipe you off and throw you away. Accept a challenge? You must've inherited that arrogance from your mother, and look where she ended up. Dead, in the gutter."

I chuckle, pushing past the need to shoot that tongue from her mouth for speaking on my mother like that.

Abena's pathetic, desperate. Either that or cracked, because there's no way she can actually believe there's a way out of this. No way she can spin that video on the flash drive given to Zuri by the informant she and my mother found.

"A koju's been issued, and either the reigning oba accepts it or rejects it. And if she rejects it, she's conceding defeat and abdicating the crown. That is Mwuaji law," Tera states from my side.

"I don't need you to quote the law to me," Abena snarls. "My family wrote it. Yours just serves it."

"That's where you're wrong, *Abena*." Tera stalks forward several steps, her lip curled in an ugly sneer as she looks my aunt up and down. "I only serve the rightful Mwuaji oba. And that's not you. But since you know the law so well, you also know you must accept or reject the koju issued by the challenger, who is your niece. The daughter of the woman, our queen, who you had killed." With every word, Tera's voice hardens, becomes darker, lower. "Do you have an answer, traitor?"

Bisa and Taraji step forward. And on my left, Richter and Moorehead follow suit.

"You either accept, Abena," Bisa says in his rumbling, raspy bass that rolls like ominous thunder through the room, "or we kill you ourselves for treason. Which hand do you want to die by?"

"Please say mine, Auntie," I taunt.

"You—you can't—" Her lips part as she stares first at Bisa, then the other kapteni. She surveys the room, but her loyalists are condemning in their silence. None of them move forward to aid her, to defend her. Her gaze, bright and liquid hot with hatred, swings to me. I read her capitulation there, and triumph streams through me as she stalks down off the dais.

This is it.

This is fucking it.

Not once does it occur to me that I'll lose this challenge. Not when I've dreamed of the scent and texture of her blood on my skin for years. Pictured what her death mask will look like as I witness the last flames of life flicker from her eyes.

No.

Losing isn't even a possibility.

In moments, the circle around us widens, and I note the strategic points my Seven and Miriam take up. My eyes clash with Malachi's, and I allow myself to feel that second of relief that he's safe. He nods, and I return the gesture, reading the message there.

Take care of business.

Get my revenge.

In my head, I still hear the faint echo of his *mine*. I tuck that into the corner of his mind, carrying it with me as I turn to face Abena.

She shrugs out of her long, white fur robe, leaving her in a white bodysuit and leather pants. Accepting the dagger Richter passes her, she faces me, her teeth bared in a snarl.

I smile.

"The rules are," Tera announces, "no one from the outside can assist or interfere. And this koju is to the death. No mercy. Do you both understand?"

"Yes."

"Let's get this shit over with," Abena spits.

Rage swirls in me, but instead of flowing crimson and burning hot within me, it's cold, focused.

I noticed every cut, every bruise on Malachi. I noticed his missing finger.

Oh, she about to pay for old and new.

Palming my bowie knife, I deliberately run up on her, not giving Abena the opportunity to advance on me. The glitter of uncertainty in her eyes feeds my soul, and I'm going to be gorging on that shit by the time I'm finished with her.

Abena swings at me. I duck, spinning low. Her blade whistles above my head, and I swipe my knife through her top to slice through the skin just beneath her breast, drawing first blood. She whirls around, and I crouch, waiting, anticipation humming through me like a berserker's battle cry.

Pain saturates her features. Good.

In seconds, rage overtakes the pain, and she comes for me, bending low, knife aiming for my stomach. I grab her wrist and take the cut to my upper arm when she yanks her hand away. Gritting my teeth, I flick my dagger, slicing her across her breast, shoulder, ribs. She stumbles back, crimson seeping into her clothes, looking like a slasher-film victim.

She presses her palms to the seeping wounds. Her chest heaves, and the heavier she breathes, the faster the blood pumps from her body. I see the moment desperation and panic creep into her eyes, and I revel in it. With a growl, she charges toward me, and I meet her halfway. Abena flips the knife into an ice pick grip and swoops her arm in a hooking motion, slicing down toward my chest. At the last second, I brace my wrist against hers just as it sweeps past me and grip her elbow with my free hand. Turning, I slam my bowie knife into her stomach, twist it, then wrench the blade free.

Her scream bounces off the walls as she bends over, palms slapping the floor.

"To the death, Auntie," I whisper.

I raise the knife above my head to deliver the final blow to her spinal cord when a blast hits me in the back, sending me tumbling forward. Pain explodes through me, and through it, I dimly hear a lion's roar of fury and pain. Shaking my head, I push myself to my hands and knees, trying to suck in air, but instead it's like I'm inhaling shards of glass.

I look up, and Malachi is above me, a gun in his hands, aimed toward one of the balconies. Another shot rings out, and dimly I'm aware of a body plummeting to the throne room floor. Shaking my head again, to try and clear it of the fog creeping in from the sides, I crawl toward Abena, who is pushing to her knees.

No. That desperation that I glimpsed in Abena's eyes just moments ago whistles through me, wild and burning hot. I've come so close. No one is going to steal her death from me. Rip my mother's justice from me.

With the last of my strength, I feel for the knife I dropped, grab it, and plunge it into her neck. She gasps, clawing at her throat. Blood bubbles from the wound and her mouth. As she falls back, I tumble on top of her.

"See you in hell."

Her eyes dim, then glaze over. Fierce satisfaction and a brutal joy soar through me. *I did it, Ma. I did it.*

"Eshe." Pain racks my body, and I gasp again. Blood fills my throat, mouth, and I cough, trying to clear them. "Baby, open your eyes. *Look at me.*"

The demand in Malachi's voice, the ache in it, impels me to lift my lashes. Hell, I don't remember closing them.

"Don't you fucking die on me," he orders, his eyebrows drawn down over his nose. His gray-blue eyes are nearly black as he stares down at me, cradling me against his chest. Behind him, I glimpse Tera, Nef, Kenya, and Maura, worry and grief etching their faces. I know it's because of me. This pain . . . it can't be good. He buries his face in my hair. "Don't leave me, Eshe," he rasps directly in my ear. "Don't you . . . Everyone who's ever mattered—who I've ever loved—has left me, I can't lose you, too. I can't, baby. Please don't leave me here without you. I've waited so long . . ."

A shudder quakes through his big body, and I try to lift my arms, to wrap them around him, to promise I'm not going anywhere. But neither my arms nor my tongue seems to be working.

And as I sink into darkness, my ears and soul ring with his tortured, hoarse scream.

CHAPTER NINETEEN

Malachi

The steady beep and hiss of the machines monitoring Eshe's vitals and keeping her alive fill the air in the large, private hospital room. It's been three days since she was rushed into surgery for the devastating gunshot wound to her back. If that rifle shot had been just a centimeter off, it would have penetrated her heart. But it ended up piercing her right side and nicking her lung. Thank God, Doc was able to stabilize the wound before the ambulance got there. And yeah, I said *thank God*. Because in that span of seventy-two hours, God and I have come to an understanding where we're at least on speaking terms again. Especially since the doctors said those minutes and that care had made the difference between Eshe being alive long enough to make it to that OR and ending up with a sheet pulled over her head and a tag on her toe.

Shit.

I can't even think about that option.

Can't . . .

My breath catches in my throat, and I grind the heels of my palms against my burning eyes. I've slept maybe a total of twelve hours in the last three days. And I haven't moved my ass from this chair except to take a piss. None of us have.

Hospital rules mandate only one person should be in here at a time, given the severity of Eshe's injuries. But after the first time the doctors tried telling us that, no one attempted to again. Not one of us has budged: Tera, Nef, Doc, Kenya, Maura, Sienna, me—even Jamari. We're all crowded on the couches, chairs, floors.

They refuse to leave their new oba.

I refuse to leave my new . . . everything.

I grind harder until green sparks flare behind my lids and a low ache makes its presence known, joining the others all over my body. At least I was able to have the cuts inflicted by Abena tended to by one of the residents here. They also cleaned and dressed the amputation of my finger. I've been so consumed with Eshe, I haven't given much thought to that. Now I brush a touch over the bandage, and then my gaze drifts to Eshe's hand and her missing pinkie. Abena could take the entire fucking hand if it means Eshe pulls out of this whole and fully healed.

"I just talked to Penn," Sienna says, standing from the couch and setting her phone on the arm. She lifts her arms, stretching. "She said she's feeling much better and is on her way here to be with us. Her parents aren't happy about it, but she's already pissed about missing out on everything else, so not much they can do." She snorts.

"I'm sure Eshe'll like seeing her when she eventually wakes up." Maura walks to the side of the bed I'm not posted on. She brushes her fingertips over the back of Eshe's hand. "Where's that damn doctor? He hasn't been in here this morning to see her. He said she should be waking up by now," she snaps.

I prop my elbows on my thighs, leaning forward and studying Eshe's face. The dense fringe of her lashes. The tilted slopes of her cheekbones. The plump fullness of her mouth. The thick mass of her curls splayed around her head. The steady rise and fall of her chest. The tube inside her mouth, running down into her chest, helping her breathe.

In some ways, she appears to be just sleeping.

But it's more than that. She's not conscious. She's beyond me. Separated from me.

Away from me.

"I'll go find him." Tera stands from the recliner and heads toward the door. Just as she reaches for the handle, the door swings open, and the hooded woman who joined them in that last battle enters. The face mask is gone, but with her head bent, I can't see her features. This is her first time visiting the room in the days since Eshe's been here, and I surge to my feet, stalking across the room toward her.

"Who the hell are you?" I growl.

For a moment, she doesn't move, doesn't answer me. Just as I'm ready to drag a reply out of her by any means necessary, she lifts her head and tugs her hood off.

My chest tightens, my lungs stuttering.

I can't breathe. I can't fucking breathe.

It's an impossibility as I meet gray-blue eyes identical to mine. As I look into the light brown face of my sister.

Miriam.

I stumble backward, a dull, deafening roar filling my head, roaring in my ears. The floor sways, rises to meet me. My back slams into the wall, the impact jarring.

And none of it penetrates, none of it, because I'm staring at a ghost.

"Miriam," I rasp.

After a brief hesitation, she nods.

I shake my head as if trying to cast off this surreal reality that feels like a dream.

"Miriam," I repeat. "It can't be . . . How . . . ?" I can't complete my sentences. Can't get my words together to form a coherent thought. Not when the baby sister I believed was dead is standing in front of me. Alive. Not covered in blood and bruises.

From the depths of my battered and dirty soul, a hoarse cry barrels up my chest, claws its way into my throat, and escapes me before I can trap it.

In two strides, I'm across the room and wrapping my arms

tight around my little sister. She stiffens against me, and I almost back away, let her go. I, more than anyone, understand space, avoidance of touch. But I can't. I can't let her go.

Because a part of me is terrified that if I do, she will disappear.

After several long moments, her body gradually relaxes, and she lifts her arms, sliding them around my waist. And clinging hard to me.

A shudder ripples through me, and I draw her closer, pressing my cheek to the top of her head. How long we stand there, I don't know. We have an audience in the room, but when I finally lift my head, I look around and am surprised to see it's empty except for Eshe still sleeping in her hospital bed.

"Miriam." I say her name again because, shit, I can. "How are you here? And not just in this room, but *here*? Alive? Where have you been? Last time I saw you . . ."

I can't finish that thought, don't even want the image in my brain.

"Can we sit down? This might take a while."

"Yeah."

We get seated on the couch, and I just stare at her. She's a replica of Sharon Bowden, our mother. And except for the eyes, little remains of the girl I remember.

I take in the hood. The formfitting black jacket and cargo pants. The combat boots. Remember the mask from three days ago.

And it clicks.

"You're Poison."

"And you're the Huntsman."

Silence settles between us, and the heavy knowledge of what we have become echoes in that quiet.

"Tell me everything," I murmur, though part of me is afraid to hear her truth.

She inhales, then slowly releases a low yet audible breath. "I don't remember much about . . . that night. Maybe I blocked most of it out? I just know what the nurses and social worker told me when I woke up in the hospital. I had been badly beaten, with a broken arm, fractured ribs, head trauma, and a brain bleed. They thought I'd been shaken, that's how bad the injuries were. The doctors called me a miracle of science because I recovered with almost no lasting damage."

The familiar rage leaps to life inside me, and I want to dig up our foster father and bludgeon him to death again. The list of injuries she described? They're horrific for a child. Little more than a baby.

"When they took you out of the house, though, I thought you were dead. They said you were gone."

"I coded a couple of times from what I understand. So yeah, I guess I did die. And I was in the hospital for weeks. They wouldn't let me call you or bring you to see me. I cried for you, begged them to get you, but they said seeing you would retraumatize me. By the time I could leave the hospital and they placed me in a new foster home, the social worker said you had run off and they couldn't locate you. It wasn't until years later that I found out you'd run after killing our foster father."

"How did you discover that?"

"'Cause I went to kill him," she says, so simply that if I weren't who I am, the unbothered tone might concern me. But I am who I am. And pride flickers in my chest, not worry.

"How did you become Poison?"

"I was recruited. Creed came looking for me when I was twelve."

"So you know about our father?" I ask.

"Yes." She leans forward, propping her elbows on her knees. "I don't know how they found me, but they did. When they told me about Dad's history, I wanted what they could teach me. I don't know if I woke up in that hospital changed or if this . . . darkness was inherited. Either way, I welcomed being a part of Creed. It gave me structure. Gave me purpose. Revenge. And eventually, it gave me a way back to you."

I clench my jaw at that, swallowing the accusatory words that singe my tongue. But she smiles, cocking her head, those identical blue eyes roaming my face.

"You're wondering why I didn't reach out to you sooner. The short answer is Creed wouldn't allow it. They believe family, relationships, they make you weak. And they constantly used Dad as an example to beat that point home. If I had contacted you, tried to form a relationship with you, it would have put a target on your back. One thing I do remember from that night and ones before it? You fought for me. Protected me. And I had to do the same for you. I owed that to you. So I settled for watching over you from a distance. It's all I could allow myself. Until Abena took you."

I rub a hand over my head, drag it down my face. It's a lot to take in. Not only is my little sister alive but she's one of the most feared assassins the world knows. She's been watching over me like a dark angel, and I never knew it. The shock still clings to me like cobwebs, but I let myself start to believe that this isn't a cruel fever dream. That I won't wake up and find my sister has disappeared.

"I thought I lost you twenty-four years ago," I say, my voice rough, serrated. "I've relived that night over and over again. Sometimes I've dreamed where I saved you, put my body between yours and Frank's, and fought him off until the cops got there. But most times, I fail. Fail you, fail me. Fail Mom and Dad. I'm sorry, baby girl. That's what I've always wanted to tell you if I ever had the chance. I'm sorry I wasn't able to keep Frank away from you. I loved you. You were my baby sister, my last family. You are my last family. I know what you've told me, but that's probably only the sanitized version of what you've been through these last two decades, where you've been, what you've had to do to survive. Probably the same I've had to do, if not worse. And I don't care. I'm glad you did it all, baby girl. I'm glad you did every fucking thing because you're still living and I get to see you again, get to have you in my life again."

She blinks, and there's surprise in her gaze. Surprise and

something more. Uncertainty, maybe. Longing. Fear. I'm well acquainted with it all.

"I don't know what repercussions you're facing from Creed. But I'm warning you right now, I'm willing to go to war with the whole fucking organization to have you back in my life. I want to get to know you again. To find out if your favorite food is still apples. If you still get cranky when you're tired. If you still need the TV on to sleep." I huff out a laugh. "I've missed out on too many years to lose you again."

Miriam glances away from me, and her jaw works, a vein at her temple throbbing.

"Yes, yes, and no. Music now," she whispers. After a moment, she turns back to me. "I can handle Creed. You don't fuck with the person who knows where the bodies are buried."

I reach for her, and she stretches an arm out for me at the same time. We pull each other close and embrace again.

Thankful for us. For who we were, who we've become.

Letting go of what we had, what we lost.

Finally grieving my family.

My sister may not be a ghost, but in this moment, I've exorcised mine.

"That better be your sister you're hugged up on."

My head jerks up at the thin, pained, but audible words coming from the hospital bed.

Surging to my feet, I rush across the room and stare down into the beautiful eyes I've been begging God to open for the last three days.

Those eyes that were the first to see right through me and uncover what I tried so hard to deny and hide in my heart have opened once again.

She licks her lips and swallows.

"Mine, huh?" she whispers.

I go to speak, but nothing emerges. I had all those words for Miriam, but for Eshe, they're lodged in my suddenly too-tight throat, trapped by the thick tangle of emotion there. I manage a nod and lean over her, my fists pushing into the pillow on either side of her head.

"Yeah," I rasp, close my eyes, then press my forehead to hers. "Yeah."

CHAPTER TWENTY

Eshe

"I'm not one to stand on ceremony, so my first official day as oba won't include a big speech. Words aren't really my thing, anyway. I'm more of a 'you can get these hands' kind of person." I grin, and light laughter fills the space that used to be known as the throne room.

It's now known as the family room.

And with so many members of the Mwuaji family crowded into it to welcome me, we finally feel like a true family.

Well, almost.

"Needless to say, I'm going to keep this short. I bet you're looking at what's behind me." I glance over my shoulder at the drape-covered furniture and smile. "Forgive me the theatrics, but I took a page out of King Arthur's book."

I turn and nod at the two staff members, one of them being Marshall, the young man from the night of my and Malachi's botched assassination attempt at the obodo. They peel back the sheet of material, revealing a gleaming ebony round table with twelve high-backed chairs surrounding it.

Twelve. The number of perfection.

"The Mwuaji tradition has been one oba who reigns, and that isn't changing. But I'm also smart enough to know that I'm not all-seeing, all knowing. And a family is strongest when all its members are heard, feel seen, are fed. If I'm eating but you're going hungry, what kind of queen am I? No, if you all prosper, then I prosper. To ensure that happens, to make sure we remain

Mwuaji strong and powerful not just to this world but with one another, I'm forming the Queen's Council."

I climb the three shallow steps of an oval-shaped glass dais that now sits in the place where that blasphemous chair of Abena's once stood. It was the first thing I had removed. That ugly-ass mirror was the second. Then I just had the entire room stripped down. Just a bare room. We're starting anew. No throne occupies this dais. No arrogantly fashioned crown. I'm the only symbol of power it needs.

"Tera, Nef, Maura, Kenya, Tyeesha, Sienna, and Penn, can you come forward?" The seven women, who are standing at the front of the room, step toward me, glancing quickly at one another. Yeah, they weren't expecting this. None of them were. "Tera, you're my oldest friend. If anyone's going to be honest with me even if it hurts, it's you. That's why I'm appointing you as my counselor and the first member of the Queen's Council."

My friend's eyes flare wide, and in typical Tera fashion, she simply nods, not making an emotional display of it. But I note the glisten of moisture in her gaze, the movement of her throat.

"The rest of my Seven," I say to the other women, "you aren't just my most loyal kapteni and my best friends, you're my sisters. I wouldn't be standing here if it weren't for you, your fierce love and loyalty for me. No, it's not Mwuaji tradition to have multiple counselors, yet customs are in place to guide but also, sometimes, to let us know we need to pivot and change. Besides, I wouldn't be off to a very good start as oba if I didn't take advantage of the courage, wisdom, and insight available to me right here with you." I smile. "Welcome to the Queen's Council."

They bow their heads, a couple of them placing their hands over their hearts.

"Thank you, oba." Them calling me by that title as a sign of their love and respect has my throat tightening.

God, it's been a month since I killed Abena, since I woke up in the hospital thankful to just be alive. The recovery from the gunshot wound has been slower than I'd like but not as long as the doctors would. I gave them four weeks; they would've preferred six to eight. But I have work to do. A family to lead. A life to celebrate.

"Bisa, Taraji, Richter, and Moorehead, please come forward." The two men and two women wind their way through the crowd to stand in front of the dais. I place my hand over my heart and meet each of their gazes for several moments, letting them see my gratitude, glimpse the loyalty that they selflessly showed and gave me. "Blood before belief. When I called, you came. Even at high personal cost. You had my back when it would have been easier to turn me away, but instead, you stood behind me, offered me your support, your power, your life. I'll never forget. It is my honor to invite you to the Queen's Council."

They murmur their thanks and bow their heads, then move to the side in front of the table with the others. The room erupts in applause and loud cheering, and I grin, joining in. These people are my backbone. And with them by my side and at my back, this family is going to be the most powerful, the most feared.

I inhale, and the pinch in my chest reminds me of my injury and that I still have some healing to do. But it also reminds me of something else. Or someone else.

My heart.

"I'm almost finished, so no worries." I chuckle. "One more change. Not going to lie. It's a big one. No pun intended," I murmur on a snort. I turn and look behind me to Malachi, who leans against the far wall in the corner, arms crossed. "There's one person here who started out as my would-be assassin, who turned into an ally, and who's now mine," I simply say. "And because he's mine, that makes him ours."

I turn and stretch out my hand toward him. A joy damn near too big, too loud to contain swells inside me as he pushes off the wall and strides toward me. That big body is still beautiful. Still powerful. Still deadly graceful. I wouldn't say I tamed the Huntsman, because who can tame such a wild, brutal creature?

Hell, why would I want to? I can say, though, love soothed him, offered him a safe space. Gave him a family.

Not just any love though.

My love.

As Malachi climbs the dais steps and folds his larger hand around mine, I tip my head back, meeting that beautiful gaze. Those eyes burn even brighter since Miriam's return. And yeah, I owe that ho a punch to the throat for nearly blowing me and my girls up, but for Malachi, I'll gladly welcome her to the family. There's always room for more.

And, of course, he has me. The Seven. And the rest of the Mwuaji.

I slide a hand up his chest, close my hand around the front of his throat, and rise up on my toes. He bends his head and opens his mouth over mine. In front of my family, I kiss him. On a groan, I open wide for him, and he thrusts his tongue between my lips, licking, sucking. I'm sealing who he is to me, to them. But I also just can't get enough of *him*. I never will. And they just better get used to the sight of my tongue in his mouth because it's on sight.

After pressing my lips to him for a last taste, I turn back to my family with a smile.

"You've known him as the Huntsman. Let me introduce you to . . ." I glance at him once more, and when he dips his chin, I slowly exhale and continue. "Let me introduce you to Malachi Bowden, my consort, my partner, my love. My family."

The Seven walk to the front of the dais and, as one, kneel in front of us. Bisa, Taraji, Richter, and Moorehead stride over and kneel directly behind them. Then, like a softly swelling wave, everyone in the room falls to their knees, bowing their heads in a show of respect and fidelity that steals my breath. I tilt my head back, my gaze meeting Malachi's.

With a small smile, he stalks down the dais, never breaking our visual connection, and kneels in front of my Seven, pressing a fist directly over his heart.

I love you, I mouth to him.

He nods. *I love you*, he mouths back.

I close my eyes, and an image of my mother flickers and solidifies in my mind. She smiles at me, pride shining in her hazel eyes.

Remember who you are, Eshe. Remember whose you are. Never forget that.

Her words from our last moments together resonate in my head.

I remember, Ma. I'm Eshe Diallo, daughter of Aisha Diallo. Oba of the Mwuaji.

I'm loved.

Clearing my throat, I blink back the burn of tears.

"Thank you. I promise to be the oba my mother raised me to be. The oba you deserve." I flick my hands at them. "Now get your asses up. Got me up here feeling all emotional, and you know I don't like that shit."

Laughter, theirs and mine, fills the family room.

"A'ight, a'ight. One more bit of business before we get to the party portion of this evening."

I sweep a gaze over the room, the joy inside me darkening to something meaner, harder, but no less gleeful as it lands on a particular group that I ordered given a special place of "honor" at the beginning of this ceremony. They stand in the very middle, covertly surrounded by soldiers I secretly assigned to guard them.

"After my mother was killed, we found ourselves in a . . . precarious time. Some of us kept our heads low, simply surviving under a cruel regime. Others bided our time until the moment came when we could exact change. And then there were some of us who stood by and behind a morally bankrupt queen, capitalizing off her corrupt actions that ripped off, penalized, and even killed her own people. Those didn't just cosign her shit by their silence, they kissed her ass, profited off her greed and their people's loss and pain, and then picked over the corpses like vultures left in her wake. See, there's a difference between being powerless to defy a queen and not giving a fuck about the powerless as long as you're the one to put your boot on the back of their necks, too, while you're robbing their pockets. I know too well what it is to be one and have closely watched some of you be the other. That I can't stand, and you don't deserve to wear the name Mwuaji. Nah. You don't deserve to live."

I wave a hand, and the guards, producing their guns, herd the thirty or so men and women forward to the front of the room. Their shouts and curses bounce off the walls, gaining volume in pitch and intensity when my Seven move in front of the dais, assault guns in their arms.

"I would say the loss of life is saddening, but I hear lying is bad for digestion, and that fire-ass macaroni 'n' cheese is on the menu!" Clapping my hands twice, I point toward the family room doors. "A'ight, people! Let's go eat! You guys, though? Say hi to my auntie for me." With a wink and wiggle of my fingers, I descend the dais steps to where Malachi meets me at the bottom.

"That's some fucking speech," he says.

"Right?" I scrunch up my face. "Too long?"

He snorts, shaking his head as we clear the wide double doors. Just as they close behind us, the blast of gunfire and screams erupt on the other side.

I grin.

"Yeah, smile now. Who's gonna clean all that shit up?" Malachi growls, turning around and hauling me against his body.

With a move that leaves me breathless, he hikes me into his arms. My legs automatically wind around his waist, and my arms wrap around his neck.

Nipping his jaw, I laugh. "So, your love already has limits? Good to know."

"I didn't sign up for cleanup duty."

"What're you doing?" I glance over my shoulder as he heads for the stairs. "The cookout is out back." I point in the direction of the kitchen and the rear of the building. "You're going the wrong way."

"No, I'm not. It's been twelve hours since I've been inside that pussy. Food can wait."

"But macaroni 'n' cheese," I whine.

He pauses in the middle of the staircase and mugs me.

"Mac 'n' cheese or this dick?" When I don't immediately answer, he barks, "Are you serious, Eshe?"

"I'm kidding, damn." I laugh, and scowling, he takes the stairs two at a time until he reaches the second level. I lick a path up the front of his throat and to his ear. "Later, I get mac 'n' cheese on your dick? Love is about compromise after all."

"Shit." He turns, presses me against the wall, and grinds his cock into my belly. "Deal."

Chuckling, I scrape my nails over his scalp, and he crushes his mouth to mine, swallowing my laughter. We kiss like we haven't tasted each other in weeks instead of just hours. Tongues tangling, lips bruising, teeth biting. We're ravenous, and all the revelry down the stairs is forgotten as he opens the nearest door and carries me inside.

He tips his head back, and the lust in his gaze mingles with love, and I swear, I can get drunk as fuck off that alone. Knowing I'm loved with zero constraints is heady. Freeing.

Mine. There will never be a moment this man draws breath where he won't be mine and I won't be his. Fuck it—our breath can stop and nothing will change.

Malachi lowers me, and in seconds, our clothes litter the floor. A shiver runs through me at the sight of that big, golden, scarred body. I'll never not want him. Never not want to fuck him.

"C'mon, oba. Take your dick like a good little queen."

He sinks to the mattress, fisting his dick and stroking it in a hard, almost-brutal pump that has my mouth watering. But, as much as I want him sliding over my tongue and abusing my throat, I need him inside me more.

Climbing on top of him, I straddle his lap. And sink lower and lower on his dick, taking him into my pussy.

"Malachi," I breathe. "Fuuuck."

Gotdamn, he never ceases to fill me, stretch me. I swear, I can feel him in my damn chest, that's how deep he is. How is it that every time feels . . . new? Just as significant and special as the last? I bite my bottom lip, tipping my head back on a low, thirsty moan.

Shit. Why question why?

Malachi cups my nape and forces my head back up to kiss me. His tongue curls around mine, even as he grasps my hips and grinds into my pussy, urging me to fuck him. I thought about maybe taking my time, but yeah, that's not going to happen. Not with his dick branding me and an orgasm looming just from his possession.

"Who do you belong to?" I demand, riding him, fucking him. Tendons stand out against his neck in taut relief, and a muscle pops along his jaw. Blue fire brightens his eyes, and my skin feels burned, singed. "Who do you belong to, Huntsman? Who owns this dick?"

"It's yours, little queen. This dick is yours. And this hot little pussy is mine."

He cups me, spearing his fingers over our connected flesh and rubbing his palm against my clit in tight, ruthless circles.

Oh fuck.

Gaining the balls of my feet, I grip his shoulders and bounce on his length, dragging a jagged groan from him that's the sweetest music to my ears.

Pleasure sizzles in the soles of my feet, racing up my spine before cascading back down to gather in my pussy. Malachi's grip on my hips tightens, and he holds me still as he pounds into me from below. Damn, he's beating up my pussy, hitting my spot over and over, and I'm not going to last. I may not survive it.

"Wet me up, oba. Drown me."

He slips a hand between us again, circling my clit until I break and give him exactly what he begged for. Pleasure so enormous, so sharp that it scares me screams through me, and I part my lips on a soundless cry.

A low rumble rolls in his chest as his hold on me turns bruising, and he chases his own orgasm, plunging into me with short, hard thrusts. When he stiffens and his seed coats my walls, I hold him close until the last shudder leaves his body and the last grunt eases from his throat.

We fall back onto the bed, me sprawled on top of his chest, him clutching me to him. Once our breaths even, he pinches my chin and tips my head back until my gaze meets his.

"You do own my dick, Eshe. But my heart belongs to you, too."

I smile and brush the backs of my fingers along his cheek. "That's fair. Since you've owned mine for a couple of years now."

He snorts, and I grin, rising to press my lips to his. Soon a simple kiss becomes heated, a wet, erotic tangle. Groaning, I push off him and climb off the bed. I grab my clothes and quickly pull them on.

"Where're you going?" he asks, leaning up on an elbow.

"I'm getting my mac 'n' cheese. Fuck what you thought."

The Huntsman's laughter follows me out of the room.

Acknowledgments

Thank You, heavenly Father, for making me like that tree planted by water and causing me to always bear fruit, even in a season of drought. You are my source, and I thank You for never leaving nor forsaking me. I love You.

To Gary, thank you for being my hero and backbone. You believed in me before I did in myself, and that faith has never wavered. Thank you for putting up with short tempers, skipped showers, and looming deadlines. You're my rock. Love you.

To Kenya Goree-Bell, who texted me at 1 A.M. with an idea for Mafia Disney princesses and said I should write it. And then pushed me to do it because she believed I needed to not only step outside the box but blow that bish up. LOL! Kenya, you aren't just one of my best friends but also one of the bravest authors I know, and I thank you for inspiring and encouraging me to be just as fearless.

To Juliette Cross, thank you for always being so generous with your time, insight, and imagination. There has never been a time when I've called on you and you haven't answered. Your kindness and humor have been a balm to my spirit for years now, and I'm so glad I get to call you friend!

Thank you, Monique Patterson, for giving me to the opportunity to write the book of my heart that challenged me and scared the bejeezus out of me. You pushed me during this process, offered me insight, and helped me to grow as a writer and author. And in the end, I not only have a book that I love even more but am also just damn proud of. Thank you for taking a chance on me and this series.

To Mal Frazier, thank you for being amazing! You are encouraging, unfailingly positive, and always kind. Your perception, discernment, humor, and sensitivity helped make this book one I am honored to have in the hands of readers. Thank you for everything that you do!

Thank you, Rachel Brooks, for being the best agent and advocate an author and person could ever want and need. I don't even have the words to express how grateful I am for all you've done for me and all you've meant to me. Honestly, my father couldn't have said it better those years ago. My career is in the hands of God and Rachel. And we follow both.

Finally, thank you to all of my wonderful readers! You have been riding with me from book one to now, and I never take your loyalty and love for granted. I'm so thankful for you! And as long as you continue to read, I'll continue to write! Love you guys!

About the Author

Sean Evans of Sean Evans Photography

USA Today bestselling author Naima Simone loves writing sizzling romances with heart, a touch of humor, and snark. Her books have been featured in *The Washington Post* and *Entertainment Weekly* and are described as balancing "crackling, electric love scenes with exquisitely rendered characters caught in emotional turmoil."

She is wife to Superman—or his non-Kryptonian, less bulletproof equivalent—and mother to the most awesome kids ever. They all live in wonderful, sometimes domestically challenged bliss in the Southern United States.